# THE MAKING OF HENRY

Howard Jacobson is the author of eleven novels and four works of non-fiction. He won the Everyman Wodehouse Award for comic writing in 1999 for *The Mighty Walzer*. His latest novel, *The Finkler Question*, won the 2010 Man Booker Prize.

HOWARD JACOBSON

# The Making of
# Henry

**VINTAGE BOOKS**
London

Published by Vintage 2005

6 8 10 9 7 5

First published in Great Britain in 2004 by Jonathan Cape

Vintage
Random House, 20 Vauxhall Bridge Road,
London SW1V 2SA

www.vintage-books.co.uk

Addresses for companies within The Random House Group Limited
can be found at: www.randomhouse.co.uk/offices.htm

The Random House Group Limited Reg. No. 954009

A CIP catalogue record for this book
is available from the British Library

ISBN 9780099472162

The Random House Group Limited supports The Forest Stewardship
Council (FSC), the leading international forest certification
organisation. All our titles that are printed on Greenpeace approved
FSC certified paper carry the FSC logo. Our paper procurement
policy can be found at www.randomhouse.co.uk/environment

**Mixed Sources**
Product group from well-managed
forests and other controlled sources
www.fsc.org  Cert no. TT-COC-002139
© 1996 Forest Stewardship Council
FSC

Printed and bound in Great Britain by
CPI Bookmarque, Croydon, CR0 4TD

For Jenny . . . speaking of love

Huffy Henry hid the day
— John Berryman, *The Dream Songs*

Honour thy father and thy mother
— Exodus 20:12

# ONE

Henry believes he knows exactly when the ninety-four-year-old woman in the neighbouring apartment dies. He hears her turn off. Until now he has not been able to distinguish her from her appliances – her washing machine, her vacuum cleaner, her radiators, her television. But the moment she gives up the ghost he detects the cessation of a noise of which he was not previously aware. A hum, was it? A whirr? Impossible to say. There is no word for the sound a life makes.

'Ah well,' his cleaning woman muses, once word of the death has seeped out, 'what's one more?'

'Plenty, if you happen to be the one,' Henry says.

She sidles a walled Irish eye towards his, oblivious to an Englishman's partiality for space between two people not connected by marriage.

'There we are, then,' she says with a shrug, and goes on with the dusting. They're all shrugging and dusting round here. Not on edge exactly, but fatalistic. Waiting to be blown apart. Henry isn't thinking like that, though; Henry is just waiting for himself to die. There's a subtle political difference. Never mind poison gas in the Underground, never mind helicopters crop-dusting the city with anthrax, Henry sees what's coming as an entirely personal catastrophe, something between him and his Maker and no one else. That's always been the trouble with Henry – he has never been able to grasp the larger picture.

Rather than remain in his apartment while there is a corpse next door, Henry ventures out. This is not something Henry normally enjoys doing. Nothing to do with anthrax. Out, in Henry's view, is a madhouse. Historians of social lunacy will confirm that this is literally the case, that the mad have been let out of the asylums and allowed to walk the streets. But Henry doesn't mean that. By mad, nerve-strung Henry means revving when you're stationary and driving with your hand on your horn – read that sexually if you like, but Henry has in mind incessant honking – he means text messaging the person standing next to you, or being wired up so that you can speak into thin air, conversing with God is how it looks to Henry, or wearing running shoes when you're not running, or coming up to Henry with a bad face and a dog on a piece of string and asking him for money. Why would Henry give someone with a bad face money? Because of the dog? Because of the string?

But there's out and there's out, and this out, Henry concedes, beats others he's encountered. Still too much revving and honking and similar vehicular hectoring – inevitable, given the triple-parking which is the custom here: people nipping out of their cars to say hello to other people who have nipped out of their cars to say hello, and people boxed in by both sorts having heart attacks on their horns – but it's a superior sort of hectoring, and the sports clothes, especially on the elderly, bespeak a greater gentility too, more cricketing and yachting than footballing – due, presumably, to the proximity of Lord's and the boating lake in Regent's Park. As for the bad-faced men with dogs, they rarely venture this far into the comfort zones of NW8. Neither did Henry much before now. Henry isn't from here. As aren't many of the people he sees in the street or bumps into in the lift, which accounts for much of the appeal the place has for him. It's better to be a stranger among strangers, Henry reckons, no matter how jumpy everyone is, than to be even partially at home among the indigenous.

Prior to NW8, Henry had lived postcodeless and with the semi-permanent headache of the never quite settled anywhere, with one dry foot on the cobblestones of the town and one wet one in the drains and delfs of a moor so dour it was a miracle a single flower could find the will to bloom there, and few did.

Walkers came and marvelled, but walkers are only ever passing through. As for the natives, Henry's explanation to visitors to his rented crofter's cottage was that they looked the way they did – blunt-nosed, crook-backed, mole-blind – as a consequence of never having moved from here since around about the end of the ice age, or whenever it was the great muds came. 'Their heads grew beneath their shoulders as a matter of adaptational imperative,' Henry went on, 'and they've never been able to find a way of prising them out since.' Assuming this to be a complaint about his environment, the less subtle of Henry's visitors wondered what, in that case, he was doing living in a cold-water cottage by a delf. What did he expect, for God's sake? At which Henry opened his eyes wide. He did not like people to talk ill of his heartlands. Ever since he could remember, Henry had woken up to a view fringed like an eyelash by the Pennines. The Pennines were his Mountains of Mourne. He attached lyrical significance to their green and purple. They were his Alps. They extended his conception of the possible. They were all foreignness and promise.

He should have stuck with the view. Down here, Henry is happier – which tells you something, since he isn't happy – or at least he is more at home being not at home. But he hasn't been here long. And wouldn't be here at all if he still had his job, or his youth, or someone to love. And if it weren't for the accident of a luxurious southern apartment – the one that has the dead old lady lying next door – passing into his possession.

The luxurious apartment is another reason why Henry would rather be in than out. Crystal chandelier over his bed, sunken bath, electronic drapes – press the keypad and the lights go on, the bath fills and the curtain closes – Henry has never lived so graciously before. The sound system is so good he cannot locate the speakers, he just gets music wherever he goes. A white bare-breasted mermaid, Saudi Arabian in conception, conceals the lavatory cistern, promising to press herself against him when he sits. She has a plastic plug in each of her nipples, from which, Henry initially deduced, fountains must play, though why you would want fountains playing down the back of your neck when you visit the lavatory, Henry had no idea. In the end he worked out that the plugs were simply to protect the nipples when the seat went up. But he is still feeling his way round the place and hasn't given up finding fountains yet.

How it is that the apartment has passed into his possession Henry can explain, it's the why that's the problem. Because there's a God, that's why, would be Henry's best shot, or at least his second-best shot at an explanation. Unless there's a devil and NW8 is earmarked for destruction. The how is much easier. An envelope popped through the letterbox of his moorland cottage, that's how, just as he was considering his future, its contents a life-tenancy agreement with his name on – he takes it to be a life tenancy anyway, though he can't be trusted to comprehend any piece of writing which isn't what his profession calls 'imaginative' – and a letter from Shapira and Mankowicz, Solicitors, outlining the terms of the gift, to wit an obligation, as per the enclosed lease, to make no noise, to house no pets, to let off no firearms, and otherwise to ask no questions, in return for which he can expect to live unhampered and be told no lies. Henry doesn't think it's a mistake, Henry believes he can discern a bit of logic in it, but just in case he's wrong, just in case someone else's name should be on the lease, another Henry Nagel even more deserving than he is, he means to enjoy his good fortune before it's taken away from him again. Like life itself.

Not that Henry wants much more from the inside than he expects from the out. He doesn't riot in the sunken bath, or go to sleep with the chandeliers ablaze. Mainly he potters about in a kimono (an affectation), makes tea in a samovar (another affectation – but then it's all affectation in the twenty-first century, doing anything that isn't slobbing about in running shoes with writing on them is affectation) and searches for peace in his heart. He likes it that he can see London from any of his windows, Regent's Park, the Zoo, the Mosque, Lord's Cricket Ground, the towers of the City. Better than the hills, all that. It means that life is out there if you want it, which Henry doesn't, but he is grateful for being given the choice. You need life to be out there if you are going to find peace in your heart.

'My husband reckons they'll bomb the City first,' his cleaning lady has observed, leaving it as read that Henry's apartment will be a good place to watch it burn from. Henry even wonders if she's fishing for an invitation to come round with her husband when it happens. But this isn't the peace in your heart Henry is talking about. Henry is thinking about himself. He would just like to feel right, for once, vis-à-vis the rest of the world.

The other thing Henry wishes to stay in and do is take his father to task. Who am I? Who are you? Do you love me? Am I a disappointment to you? Don't you want to know whether you're a disappointment to me? Did you never care? Did you never feel bad? Do you ever feel bad now? About me? About Mum? About yourself?

All that.

Isn't Henry a bit old for this routine? At his age, shouldn't Henry be watching daytime television, or playing canasta with fellow irascibles, or doddering to the park with his grandchildren?

Probably yes. Probably very unhealthy doing what he's doing. The trouble is, Henry has no children to give him grandchildren. And no friends disposed to lend him theirs. Henry has dishonoured his friendships, whether by disparaging his friends' achievements, or by turning away from their society, or by borrowing their wives, and you know what friends are like when you start that.

So he has no one to play canasta with him either.

In fact, 'borrowing their wives' is at once rather too cute and rather too buccaneering a description of what Henry actually did, which was more in the nature of running himself down, looking soulful, and confessing to feelings of long-standing devotion which in truth he hadn't known he'd felt until the moment of expressing them. Out of pity for which, or simply out of curiosity, yes, they on occasions borrowed him. Borrowed him, fucked him, and put him back. But as a man with reason to doubt his own ability to be at the active end of any verb, Henry glamorises the little devilishness of which, in his younger days, he was capable.

Either way, whoever borrowed whom, he still has no one to play canasta with him.

And, come to that, no father. Not living. But he had one once. Everyone who doesn't have a father now must have had a father or heard tell of a father once. You can't manage without the *idea* of a father. The idea of a father, especially the idea of rejecting a father, powers the modern world. And you can't reject what you haven't had.

For his part, Henry is just learning to talk to his.

Nothing fanciful. No 'my father, methinks I see my father', no crossing over, no table rapping. Elbows on the dark green banker's desk which came with the apartment, chin in the chalice he makes for it with his too-tight hands, Henry silently delivers himself of his vexations while his father, dead for a decade, listens. It's because he knows his father is only partially understanding – both in the sense of slow to comprehend and reluctant to sympathise – that Henry values his attention. He doesn't want to be humoured. When they start humouring you it means you are headed for an early grave. Go on arguing and you might just live for ever.

That's Henry's father's job – to see things differently and keep his son alive.

*Always was.* (Henry's father, arguing the toss already.) *Not something I was ever given credit for, but that always was my job. Who else was going to save the boy from drowning?*

Drowning in what, Dad?

*As though you don't know. Drowning in women, drowning in books, drowning in sick notes, drowning in your own terrors . . .*

As for why Henry wants to live for ever when he's got no friends, got no one to love, and thinks life's a madhouse – you might well wonder. But it's in the nature of the machine not to want ever to be turned off. Ask the ninety-four-year-old woman in the apartment next to his. Just don't expect a reply.

She has one mourner. Henry no sooner leaves his apartment than he walks into him in the corridor, standing, as though he's just been sent out of class, with his hat covering his genitals. Showing respect for the dead while the people who do what needs doing to a body do it. He is also, it seems to Henry, surveying the condition of the paintwork.

Henry nods. 'I'm so sorry,' he says. Trips off the tongue now. Someone dead? So sorry. Used to be Henry's father always saying sorry to the bereaved. Now the responsibility has passed to Henry. Good morning, so sorry . . .

The mourner is about Henry's age, of an appearance which once – when older men were in vogue – would have been described as 'dapper'. Fallen dapper. Gingery moustache, bounder's eyebrows, jutting jaw, fag-stained teeth, bloodhound cheek pouches, apoplectic colouring. 'Rotten luck,' he makes Henry want to say.

'Been expecting it some time,' the mourner tells him.

'Sorry, I didn't realise,' Henry says. 'I knew she was elderly but I was under the impression she was hale.'

'Hale enough to go on for another ninety years. But that doesn't stop you expecting, does it?'

'No, I don't suppose it does,' says Henry. Then, because more appears to be expected of him, he adds, 'You the only child?'

'Me? No fear. Just the stepson. My father's folly, that one.'

Henry mishears. 'Filly?'

'Filly, folly, same difference. Could never see a woman, my old dad, without doing something stupid.'

Henry notices that the mourner has a way of letting his words die in his chest, as though everything is a damn cheek but there's nothing to be done about it. Though whether that's integral to the man or just a consequence of his bereavement, or a hurried breakfast, Henry has no idea. 'My condolences anyway,' Henry says, trying to hurry on.

The mourner offers his right hand, leaving the left holding the hat with which he covers his respectful genitals. 'Lachlan,' he says, spitting. 'Lachlan Louis Stevenson.'

Tricky name to get your teeth round, but Henry thinks a man of Lachlan Louis Stevenson's age should be able to speak his own name by now without spitting. But then you'd think Henry himself would have been spat at enough times in a long life not to be obsessed with the particle of food which has just landed on his sleeve. Hard, though, for Henry – always has been – to concentrate on anything a person who has just put food on his sleeve is saying. He stares, mesmerised, at it – the speck, the smut, the atom. Bad manners, but he has no choice. For the very reason that he shouldn't be looking, look is all he can do.

Lachlan Louis Stevenson is telling him something about becoming a neighbour, about his plans to move directly into the old girl's place, once she's been removed. It's his by right, apparently. Always has been.

'I'm sorry, what did you say?'

'Was left to me originally, but you have to wait your turn. Couldn't exactly turf her out.'

'Well, everything comes, as they say,' says Henry, shaking his sleeve.

Lachlan thrusts his tongue into his cheek. 'That's word for word what the old boy told me on his deathbed thirty years ago,' he says, as though it's Henry's fault he's had to wait.

\*   \*   \*

We're all still battling the dead, Henry thinks, closing the doors to the mansion block behind him. He tests, then tests again the security locks, listening for them to click, then pushing at them with his shoulder. The wrong sort of people have been seen in the building recently, going from apartment to apartment, selling duff electricity, syphoning it out of one person's supply and into another's, making veiled threats to the elderly, of whom Henry, on his next birthday, will officially be accounted one. No one admits to letting them in. It's possible they just strolled in, a stride or two behind a bona fide keyholder, too old to notice or too frightened to ask questions. That's how it is with buildings occupied by the aged: you might as well go to sea in a sieve. So Henry is double-checking the security locks, then double-checking his checking, by subjecting them to his weight, not a negligible force these days, for Henry is growing portly. If he does this every time he goes out he will seriously weaken the locks, then the second-hand electricity salesmen will be able to stroll back in again.

What the block needs is a doorman. There's on-site porterage, as you would expect of apartments of this quality, but you have to ring a bell for anyone to answer and by the time anyone does you can have bled to death. A person on guard twenty-four hours a day is what you want. Armed to the teeth, preferably. Henry doesn't know about the arms but he has reason to believe a doorman did patrol here once. What is more, Henry believes he has met him . . .

Henry has a theory that the apartment has come to him courtesy of a wealthy mistress of his father's. The apartment was his father's secret love nest, Henry's theory goes; a long way from home, admittedly, too far to nip around to on a bicycle between meals, but his father was always on the road, often having to travel to conferences and conventions on the black arts, and he could easily have kept a second marriage going concurrently with his first. By easily, Henry does not mean financially – he doubts

9

his father could have afforded to feed the chandelier the bulbs it consumes in a week – but easily in the sense that such a thing would have fallen effortlessly within the compass of his father's tractable nature. Someone lays Henry's father down upon a feather bed, Henry's father does not know how to explain he already has a place to sleep. A manners thing as much as anything else. Henry's father does not like to cause anyone offence. Sorrow of sorrows, Henry's mother is then killed in the front seat of a coach with bad brakes travelling to London (no doubt on a failed mission to find the truth), Henry's father no sooner being apprised of the tragedy than he is off south to retrieve the body (in what state Henry cannot begin to imagine – his father *and* the body) and no sooner seeing it than he suffers a fatal double heart attack – grief and guilt, guilt and grief – leaving the pair more united in death, Henry likes to think, than for a long time they had been in life; holding hands, Henry dares to hope, if hands there are in heaven, and who knows, maybe even canoodling again. Whereupon, for year after year, the distraught mistress maintains the apartment as a shrine until she too dies, lonely and contrite, bequeathing the apartment without presumption of ownership, via Shapira and Mankowicz, to Henry, only child of the man she loved. And of the woman, not to put too fine a point on it, she killed.

What inclines Henry to this theory, as well as to the belief that the mansion block once enjoyed the services of a doorman, is a recollection he has of being accosted at his parents' funeral by a weeping red-faced man in a square black coat, much like a town crier or a bailiff in appearance, who asked Henry if he would be kind enough to step aside with him a moment. Were it not for the weeping, Henry would have taken him to be some sort of underworld enforcement agent. Unlikely that his father had gambling debts or was mixed up in a protection racket, but then everything about his father had been unlikely. The weeping, though, spoke against it. Henry had never heard of people who came to beat money out of you weeping as they did it. The man was not family, however distant, that much Henry knew. He had taken his hat off when he should have kept it on, and he hadn't, as was customary, wished Henry 'long life'.

As a matter of religious protocol, ought Henry even to have accepted the hand held out to him? Was a chief mourner permitted to touch or be touched by another person? Was a man who was burying both his parents permitted to look another living soul in the eye, on that day or indeed on any day thereafter? At home the mirrors were all covered. Was that to cut out vanity or to recommend blindness? There was a propriety in not knowing. It behoved Henry, Henry thought, to blunder. A man shouldn't be in control of himself on the day of his parents' interment. So why not let the weeping bailiff, or whatever he was, force open his hand, place inside something which felt like a bag of bizarre copper currency – Azerbaijani shillings, were they? – and then close Henry's ice-cold fingers over it one by one, like a baby's. 'In all the years I stood there in the wind and rain,' he told Henry, pausing between words to wipe his nose on the sleeve of his coat, 'I was never once treated with anything but courtesy. Remember that when other things are said. Not a single discourtesy, not once. But mine is not the only broken heart that's left behind, Mr Nagel. Not by a long chalk. And if you can find it in yourself to make a home here' – tapping at Henry's obedient fist – 'you would be doing a kindness by the living and the dead. That's the message it is my sad responsibility to bring you. You would be doing a kindness. Feel free. You are loved for who you are the son of, Mr Nagel. Feel free.' With which he bit hard on his lip, lowered his shaven head, and returned in the direction of the fresh mounds of earth under which Henry's mangled parents lay, for all the world as though he meant to hurl himself upon them. What Henry found when he finally remembered to open his hand was a set of keys, but to what property he had no idea. He knew his father had spilled out of the house and rented garages and disused railway arches in which to store his bits and pieces all over Manchester, so he assumed it was just another one of those. As for the unknown man, well, his father collected such people by the dozen: the demented strays of his rapacious philanthropy, fans of a kind, enthusiasts of his work. Only now, in line with his new theory of events, is Henry able to work out that those long-lost and long-forgotten keys must have been to this apartment, shrine to a forbidden love, and that the broken-hearted bearer of them, acting on behalf of the even more broken-hearted mistress – who had the tact, at least, to stay away – must have been its doorman.

Those were the days, Henry thinks – practising thinking like the old man he is soon to be – when self was not the enemy of duty, when a man could be sentimentally attached, without resentment, to his job. Try finding a doorman who will weep over a resident now. Try finding a doorman full stop. Upstairs an old lady has just been turned off, and there is no one to notify the inhabitants of the building – you smell her or you don't – let alone shed a tear for her.

And that is how it will be for me, Henry reminds himself. He knows what's waiting. He will hobble homewards one ordinary madhouse afternoon, he will feel a stabbing in his heart, and he will beshit himself. Not very medically precise, but then Henry never has understood much about his own body. Too delicate. Too squeamish ever to find out. But what's waiting is what's waiting, whether you live in ignorance or you don't. He will beshit himself in a public place. He will come out of himself, his own entrails the waste matter of his life and being. See that mess? That's Henry. And all the delicacy, all the careful watching, all the aloof approximations, will have been for nothing.

Better not to go out. Better to be found, like the old lady, in your bed. But he likes the sensation of coming back home, and he can't have that unless he's been out. He walks for forty minutes, surviving attacks by traffic twice, the first time trying to enter Regent's Park, the second time trying to leave it, then he catches the bus to Marks & Spencer in Oxford Street where he has taken to watching people more senior than himself raiding the café – Café Revive it's called, ha! – making provision for what's left of their lives, pocketing free sachets of sugar, free milk, free serviettes, some brazenly, some furtive as squirrels. How long before he's doing this? He feels the depths of his pockets. Now? Should he start now? Two elderly women at a table next to his are reading UFO magazines. They are identically infirm, each with an arm in a sling, each with purple bruising below the left eye, each with a stick hooked on to the back of her chair. Have they been carted away in a spaceship, both of them? Henry wonders. Have they grown demented trying to get people to believe their stories? He knows how they feel. He too has been sequestered among aliens for most of his adult life. He too has never been believed.

He slips three plastic containers of milk into his pocket as he leaves, then thinks better of it and returns them, in his confusion dropping two on the floor. The women from the spaceship, following him, tread on one and spear the other with their sticks. Was that deliberate? Henry wonders. Is this what they've been programmed to do? To spill humans' milk? He quits the café, flustered, conscious that compunctions cause more trouble than criminality. Something the old know, and is time Henry learned: businesses would rather you stole from them than made a fuss.

He'd dodge his bus fare if he dared, but daren't. Back at his apartment block he pushes at the lock to make sure nobody has tampered with it or left it open for the traffickers in contraband electricity while he's been gone. Then he has to frisk himself to find his key. Lost, is it? No, yes, no. How long, how long now before the beshitting starts?

Going up, he runs into Lachlan coming down. If Henry is not mistaken the old woman's chief mourner is looking more cheerful now than earlier in the day. Though it's warm and dry he is wearing a green knee-length oilskin, the pockets of which are bulging, Henry notices, and he is carrying a small portrait of somebody or other in oils. He holds it up, as though at auction, for Henry to inspect. 'Robert Louis, the old ancestor. Staring out to sea on board the yacht *Casco*, bound for Tahiti, the lucky blighter. What do you think? Looks as though he could do with a square meal, but then none of our family ever enjoyed foreign food much. But otherwise, not bad, eh? Especially the frame. Worth a few, the frame. As you said, everything comes. And she won't be needing him to look at where she's going.'

'Why, where's she going?' Henry asks, inattentively. Tahiti, is it?

An alarmed expression crosses Lachlan's face. 'You know . . . A better place.'

'Oh yes, there,' Henry remembers. 'When's the funeral?'

'Not sure. Crematorium's getting back to me. You don't mind her up there for another day or so?'

'No,' Henry assures him. 'No, not at all.'

'Hardly a nuisance, eh?'

'Certainly not that,' Henry says.

What's one more, when all's said and done? And better to be with the dead inside – remonstrating, remonstrating – than with the living in the madhouse which is out.


Henry Nagel, aged nine, proud to be entrusted with the shopping – saveloys and plaited bread and hot red horseradish which his father likes to spoon into his mouth directly from the jar – forgets to bring home the change.

Forgets? Or fails?

Only threepence, but these distinctions matter.

He can see the threepenny bit, the colour of fool's gold, where it lies on the counter, between the till and the sheets of newspaper used for wrapping vegetables and soap powder. How it got there it would take him what's left of his childhood to explain, but it has to do with awkwardness, his fingers not connecting as they should with Elliot Yoffey's fingers. Elliot the grocer's son, pale and tapered like a candle, a young man, not a boy like Henry, but another casualty of the shame plague which is rife wherever Henry goes. Humiliated to be buying meets humiliated to be serving, with the result that the three-penny bit rolls like a hand grenade into no man's land, where Henry can't quite reach it, and Elliot dare not lean over his side of the crowded counter to push it, and Henry would rather go home without than risk compounding shame with more shame by asking.

Who cares about a threepenny bit anyway, even in 1950s Heaton Park where there are trees but money doesn't grow on them. Not Henry's parents. Threepence? We pish on threepence! They aren't rich, the Nagels in the little sunshine semi from which, if you stand on Henry's bed when the sky lifts, you can see the grey-green fringe of the Pennines – but they are bounteously chari-table and forgiving. Except that today they aren't. Explain that. By what law must the mortified always be mortified a second time? Let some little muscled Philistine, member of the Hitler Youth, nephew of Attila the Hun, come swaggering home three-pence-shy and no one says a word. Threepence? Ha! We pish on your threepence. But because it's heart-stop Henry, the world falls in. Go back, Henry, and explain. Go back and take what's yours.

Which he cannot do.

Go back, Henry, taking the bread and the saveloys and the horseradish with you, show them your bill, tell them how much you gave them, and then ask for your threepence change.

Which he cannot do.

15

He shakes his head. Tears rip his eyes like torn paper.

The door. There's the front door, Henry. Now go. And if you are not able to come back with the threepence, do not bother to come back at all.

As though at nine he has alternative accommodation.

Henry's father, the late Izzi Nagel, sits on the edge of his armchair, never comfortable, never at home – hard to imagine him at home here, of all places – and shakes his head. *You want to know why no one says a word to the nephew of Attila the Hun? Do you? It's because he doesn't come back from the shop without the threepence.*

No, he just burns the shop down.

His father shrugs. In a harsh world you have to do what you have to do.

So you would rather, Henry says, that you'd had a Nazi storm trooper for a son?

His father shifts his bulk and sighs – a poor ghost driven to extremity by an extremist son. *If that's my only choice – a Nazi storm trooper or a crybaby, maybe I'd have preferred the Nazi, yes.* Then immediately takes it back, wiping the slate clean with his sleight of hands. UNCLE IZZI – ILLUSIONIST, FIRE-EATER AND ORIGAMIST, his card says. Herzschmertz Henry still carries one in his wallet. Queer to have had a father who always wanted to be called uncle. Almost as queer as to have had a father who always wanted to be called an illusionist and all the rest of it. Not a very good illusionist, fire-eater or origamist – but then you couldn't expect his card to say that. And he did what he could, Henry concedes, with the hands God gave him.

He opens them now, palms towards himself, holding back the tide of his old exasperation with his son. *For your own good, Henry, we sent you back to Yoffey's. We pished on the threepence, but we couldn't allow the world to pish on you.*

So all this you did for love of me?

*All this we did for love of you. To make you strong.*

And you don't think you might have loved me more – and made me stronger – by leaving me alone?

*Parents can't leave children alone, Henry. You bring a child up, you don't leave it alone.*

You could have been a little more sensitive to the particular child I was.

*You weren't short of sensitivity. You were dying of sensitivity.*

Dying of my mother, you mean.

*Dying of your mother's way, yes.*

Except that you wouldn't let her have her way.

*Ha! You think I was able to stop her? You think you are not your mother's son? Who taught you to shrink from everything? Who taught you not to put a hand out and take what was rightfully yours.*

More difficult than you think, Dad, knowing what's yours and what isn't.

*Never stopped you, Henry, taking what wasn't.*

That I got from you.

*That you got from her, God rest her soul. It's when you don't know what's yours that you start taking other people's.*

I never took, Dad, I borrowed.

*And that makes it better?*

No, that makes it worse.

*Exactly. Thank you. That's what they did to you. They patshkied around with your sense of ownership.*

They?

*They, she. Same difference. She was theirs, you're hers. Take my word for it – she spat you out, Henry.*

And?

*And look at you*, his father refrains from saying.

Henry isn't listening anyway. His father wants it done and dusted. Henry the mother's boy, end of argument. Henry his mother's will on legs. But Henry has not yet decided whose boy he is. Where's the hurry? Maybe when he's seventy or eighty. Maybe when he's ninety-four, like his neighbour, all will become clear and he can expire. But for now he prefers to scratch his head over himself. Keeps him young.

Enough, that all this they did for love of him.

And now they're dead.

And they're not the only ones. He can count them off. Just get him started. Irina, Anastasia, Effie . . .


Nothing changes. Sitting out on the High Street the following afternoon, drawn by the sun – he must have sun, madhouse or no madhouse – Henry flirts with the East European waitress. Henry must have East European waitresses. Ah, the old country, he thinks, though the only old country Henry knows is this one. But Eastern Europe is in his bones – Berlin, Vienna, Budapest, Prague. And so are raddled women with too much rouge on their cheeks and too much gold on their fingers. Henry's downfall, his love of raddled women. In Henry's wild heart – the only part of him that was ever wild – it is always Vienna in the snow and the radiators on and the blinds drawn and the 'Emperor Waltz' playing on a faraway barrel organ and an Austro-Hungarian countess with twisted teeth waiting for him under the blankets. Hence St John's Wood High Street, which is the nearest Henry will ever get to the Austro-Hungarian Empire now.

Nothing changes. How to retrieve the threepenny bit, how to get his change from the East European waitress. 'Here,' he'd said, handing her a five-pound note when she brought him out his Viennese coffee, not waiting for a bill, 'save your feet.' Showing that he'd noticed her feet, dainty like the feet of all East European waitresses, in maid-of-all-work flatties. Henry likes that look. A meteorologist of women, Henry knows what it portends. Red sky at night, shepherd's delight; flatties by day, stilettoes for play. She'd smiled at him as she turned, hooking a stray curl of yellow hair back over her ear. Hair the colour of custard. Her smile an inbred Habsburg smile, the lips pendulous and just a little crooked. Hair the colour of curdled custard, now he comes to look again, and the crooked mouth wary. Like him, she's too old to be doing this. But wariness, too, is a detail Henry likes. The wary, he remembers, bite. Thus has Henry missed out on history, not noticed the twentieth century or its passing – war, famine, communism, capitalism, the birth and death of nations, genocide – so engrossed has he been in women.

Unless, of course, he chose to be engrossed in women *in order* to miss out on history.

*Don't look, Henry* – who told him that? *Try not to see*. Which *one* of them told him that?

She hasn't returned with his change, the European waitress, though he has been out on the street with his coffee, taking up a table in the madhouse and enjoying the sun, for thirty minutes. Forgotten, that's all. Forgotten his three pounds, of which he would have given her one anyway. So who cares? What's three pounds in St John's Wood High Street? Get up, leave, and let her have the three pounds. Let her even think he always *meant* her to have the three pounds, for he has a lordly air, Henry, born of not noticing what's going on around him. But what if this is not lordliness after all, but cowardice? Afraid to ask, afraid to cause a fuss, afraid to be thought small-minded, afraid to look Elliot Yoffey in the face, is his insouciance in the matter of three pounds (minus one for the tip) just absence of ordinary adult competence? Fifty years on, is Henry still allowing the world to pish on him?

Back home, on the edge of his armchair, his father will be waiting. *Go back and ask for the money, Henry. Learn to take what's yours. There's the door. Be a man.*

And what will Henry do then?

Wrong to have said that at nine Henry has no alternative accommodation. He has his grandmother's mock-Tudor gingerbread house, which feels and smells like the country though it is only round the corner, left out of his sunshine semi then up the lane, opposite the entrance to the park, in what is known as Jews Row. Widowed, Henry's mother's mother lives with her three straight-backed widowed sisters. In truth, the oldest, much the oldest – Effie – has never had a husband, Anastasia still has a husband somewhere, and the youngest, much the youngest – Marghanita – never quite brought hers to the point of marriage, but 'widowed' is what they have settled on all round. Girls, they are known as. The Stern Girls. Not to be confused with the Stern Gang, though they are all 'widowed' suspiciously early. Widowed and returned to their maiden names.

They are at home when Henry arrives with his satchel packed. Effie is playing Schumann on a small upright piano, Anastasia is sewing, Marghanita is reading Scott Fitzgerald, and Irina, his grandmother, is staring out of the window, as though waiting for Sir Lancelot. Tirra lirra, Henry should be singing, given how much he adores his grandmother, but he has just been told to get the threepence back or never return home, so he is not in a chivalric mood.

'They've chucked me out,' he tells the Stern Girls.

'Who's chucked you out?' they ask in chorus.

'My mother and my father.'

They know what that means. His father has chucked him out. His mother is one of theirs, therefore she would never chuck Henry out. Husbands you chuck, boy children you don't. But Henry's father has his own way of doing things. Not that they believe his father has chucked Henry out either.

When they have listened to his story they each produce a three-penny bit from their purses. 'Keep three and give one to your father,' his grandmother tells him, pinching his cheek.

Henry shakes his head. He can't do that. Lie? *I cannot tell a lie.* But whether that's because he is made of honesty or because he is afraid he will be found out he doesn't know. He suspects the latter. Henry is thin-skinned – he has heard his mother talk about it as an established medical fact: 'Henry has thin skin, you know, not like his father who has the hide of an elephant' – which means he feels everything even before it's happened, and has no protection against consequences. If he lies about the threepenny bit his lie will show through him, and there is no knowing where it will end except for knowing it will end badly.

'In that case,' his grandmother says, throwing on a fur jacket, 'we will come with you.'

'Don't take me home,' Henry cries. 'I am never going home again.'

But home isn't where they are taking him. All in their furs now, like women from another country, like a family of bears strayed into town, they file out of the house, turn right into the lane, and right again, after a quarter of a mile, on to the main road which they cross, imperious as to traffic – Anastasia halting buses with a wave of her fox's tail – until they get to Yoffey's, where, to Henry's unutterable confusion, they march directly to the counter, a foreign invasion – the bears, the bears are here! – and give the reason for their errand.

'For threepence!' old man Yoffey exclaims. 'A family delegation for threepence!'

'Not threepence, principle,' Irina says.

What Henry loves about his grandmother is that she uses punctuation when she speaks. *Not threepence comma principle full stop.* It is from his grandmother that Henry learns that punctuation can be a weapon. With a comma you can hurt someone. And as a person who is always being hurt himself comma Henry hankers after hurting back full stop.

The other thing Henry loves about his grandmother is how upright and fresh-smelling she is. Most of Henry's friends' grandmothers are as hooped and vinegary as cucumber barrels. Not Irina. She stands tall and breathes a sort of floral dignity the way a dragon breathes fire. All the Stern Girls do. Henry thinks this is why they are called girls still: they have never collapsed into the shape of women. It is also, he knows, a condition of their being from South Manchester. South Manchester is long-stemmed and uses haughty punctuation, North Manchester is tuberous, like a potato, and mispronounces everything – buzz, for example instead of bus, botcher instead of butcher, and grass, to rhyme with mass, instead of gr-ah!-ssss, the stuff of stately garden parties where no two people are the same. Henry's mother is from the South, his father is from the North. Hence the commonly voiced opinion that their marriage will not last. All the Stern Girls took 'husbands' from North Manchester, and look where that's landed them exclamation mark!

Old man Yoffey's own marriage is strong but unconventional. Though he is venerably white and wispy-haired, with small watchful red-yellow eyes like a crow's and little bones which you can see poking through his shirt, old man Yoffey intermittently raises his hand to his wife – a woman half his age and twice his size – and on occasions even brings it down. Adjoining Yoffey's corner shop is a bay-windowed two-storey house with a small front garden, overgrown as to lawn (grass) but with carefully tended borders, pinks to one side, burgundy pansies with amazed expressions to the other; a four-foot wall of white brick encrusted with seashells protects the garden from the curiosity of the outside world, and it is over this that old man Yoffey sometimes throws his wife. Because Yoffey is a devout man whose services to the community extend beyond the provision of saveloys and plaited bread, the finger of suspicion inevitably points at drink. Ceremonially – this is the worst that can be said of him – old man Yoffey downs a thimbleful or two of sweet red Middle Eastern wine. Not much, but for some men a thimbleful is all it takes. A model husband the rest of the time, old man Yoffey turns into a wild animal whenever there is a festival or holy day. Pity poor Mrs Yoffey, then, who goes in fear at the very time everybody else in the neighbourhood is polishing silver and celebrating.

Henry knows what the Stern Girls have to say on the subject of alcohol and he has heard tell of an occasion – or 'incident' as it is anecdotally referred to in the family – when his grandmother was passing just as Mrs Yoffey was coming over the wall. Henry likes to think that the incident consisted of his grandmother throwing Mrs Yoffey back, but apparently all that happened was that she had words with Mr Yoffey, that Mr Yoffey had words with her, and that Mrs Yoffey (in Henry's imagination still on her back) took her husband's side. Following which, Henry's grandmother delivered herself of the opinion that the Yoffeys were a disgrace to everybody but each other, whom they richly deserved. And walked on.

That there is no love lost, then, between the grocer and the Stern Girls, Henry can easily understand. But he is still not prepared for the violence of old man Yoffey's reaction to their peaceful deputation.

'So for threepenceworth of principle,' he exclaims, every one of his white wisps of hair on end now, as though he is halfway through being electrocuted, 'you invade my shop.'

'Hardly *invade*,' Anastasia replies.

No one in North Manchester repeats what another person has said like that, allowing it to hang in the air, to echo for ever with its own absurdity. And it goes without saying that no one in North Manchester employs the word 'hardly'. Even Henry feels the condescension.

'Then what would you call it?' old man Yoffey wants to know. 'A social visit? Have you come to see my wife perhaps? Are you here for tea and *hamentash*?'

Henry has tasted *hamentash* and doesn't like it much. But he has been told in Bible class that it has symbolic significance. A *hamentash* is a three-sided pastry, resembling the hat which the arch-villain Haman, chief adviser to King Ahasuerus, and a proto-type Nazi in his own right, wore in the Book of Esther. Those who eat it, Henry grasps, are laughing at their enemies. So does old man Yoffey mean to imply that the Stern Girls have come to laugh at him, or is it Henry who is as bad as Haman?

He is shaking from head to foot whatever he thinks, old man Yoffey, the stiff detached collar he customarily wears becoming separated from its gold stud, and he is gathering up, Henry notices, all the threepenny bits in his wooden till, preparatory, Henry wouldn't be at all surprised, to throwing them at the Stern Girls. That would be a good end to all this, would it not, his grandmother or one of her sisters being blinded by the very threepenny bit Henry did not have the courage to claim as his.

Could he stop this now? Could he appeal to Elliot who has neither moved nor looked up the whole time from the block of cheese he has been garotting with a piece of wire ever since Henry and his reinforcements entered the shop? 'Elliot, I need hardly tell you why I'm here. My change, remember? You dropped it on the counter. I was too diffident to explain I couldn't reach it and you were too engaged to notice. Sorry to put you to this bother.' Would that be so difficult? With someone's eyesight at risk, was that beyond him?

Henry never finds out what is or is not beyond him. Rather than throw coins at women, which he knows he should not do, no feast day being in the offing and no wine, therefore, having passed his lips, old man Yoffey closes his shop. 'Get out, get out,' he screams, 'all of you. And as for you' – pointing at Henry – 'you're banned for life.'

If he were to get up and go into the patisserie and coffee shop on St John's Wood High Street and ask the East European waitress for his change, would he be banned for life? Henry wonders. And would it matter anyway, there being a lot less life left now for him to be banned for?

Morbid again? If only he were. Or if only he were consistently one thing or the other. The problem with ageing, as Henry sees it today – warmed by the sun and fired by the European waitress – is that you don't. At least not where you should – in the soul. At sixty minus a few months Henry doesn't feel a jot less verdant in the soul than he did at sixteen. True, he didn't feel all that verdant at sixteen, but that's not his point. His point is that he's not prepared. Yes, yes, he will beshit himself blah blah, but that's just the body talking. Henry is not prepared *metaphysically* for what's coming. In some part of himself Henry still thinks that something might just happen, a miraculous advance in medical science or a supernatural intervention, which will make Henry an exception to the grinding determinism of mortality. 'Here,' Aubrey Goldman, his foul-breathed doctor for the last forty years, will whisper, slipping Henry powder in a plain brown paper bag. 'Swallow with malt whisky and enjoy, but don't tell anyone where you got it.' Failing which, God Himself, showing up in the nick of time, parting clouds like opera curtains, crying 'Hold! – enough of all this senseless killing', and pointing at Henry, much as old man Yoffey did – 'You, yes, you!' – will ban him from death for life.

Totally absurd, given that after its failure to resuscitate either his father or his mother, Henry doesn't have any faith in medicine, especially as practised by Aubrey Goldman, who omitted to warn his mother of the dangers of sitting in the front seat of a bus, and his father of the risks of taking mistresses; doesn't hold with happy endings; and in God doesn't believe at all. But exemption is his only theological answer to extinction. No life afterwards for Henry otherwise, no scholarship to a heavenly university, no transmigration of himself into the universe, no celestial essence of Henry insinuating itself into matter. It's exemption or it's nothing.

In order that he should enjoy what? More of the same? If anyone is going to be exempted, shouldn't it be the joyous, the kind-hearted, the exuberantly fleshly even? To those who have loved life shall more life be given. By which law Henry ought to have been dead and buried forty years ago.

This, of course, is where the waitress comes in. Not only is she hanging on to Henry's change, she holds in the palm of her hand Henry's right to an eternal life. For his interest in her is proof that he is a deserving case. One of the exuberantly fleshly.

Sitting in a hospital waiting room once, in the days when he had loved ones to worry about and wait for, Henry filled out a questionnaire in a women's magazine. Did he in a general way love wisely or too well – that, if not in so many words, was the test. When he met someone who attracted him did he A) think about her a bit (it was think about 'him' actually, but Henry could transcribe); B) think about her most of the time; or C) think about her ceaselessly to the detriment of everything else in his life. Furthermore, when he met someone who attracted him did he A) worry about whether she was suitable; B) move carefully initially, checking up on her and taking other people's advice about her suitability; or C) throw all caution to the wind and to hell with whether she was suitable or not.

C – Henry answered C to every question, making him, when he came to check his score, an incorrigible romantic, great fun to be with, but not, as yet, a sound marital bet. He was also, he was warned, in danger of being hurt, getting pregnant and contracting HIV.

Does loving your grandmother erotically make you an incorrigible romantic? One of the exuberantly fleshly? No opinions as to that in *Teenage Harlot*. Henry knows the answer, anyway. You cannot love your grandmother erotically. Nature makes provision against such things. Age difference, for example. And a slap from your grandmother. But when a man loves his grandmother in a younger version of herself – in her baby sister say, in the body of Marghanita to be precise – where's the harm? There is, as far as Henry is aware, no canon fixed specifically against loving your great-aunt erotically.

Back from Yoffey's, the Stern Girls make him tea and give him biscuits and ask him what he is going to do now. Though Henry has declared he will never again return to his home, having in effect been expelled from it – the first of two expulsions in one dramatic day – his grandmother and her sisters explain it is not such a good idea for him to go missing, or for them to provide him with asylum until they have informed his parents. 'Otherwise it would be kidnap, Henry,' Marghanita explains.

'Then kidnap me,' Henry pleads.

One by one they take him to their bosom. 'If only,' Effie says. 'Don't think it hasn't occurred to us,' says Anastasia. 'One day, one day,' Marghanita promises him. 'We don't need to,' his grandmother says, pressing the flats of her cool hands to his temples. 'You already belong to us. You are our hope.' But it is she who rings his parents.

Henry overhears the telephone conversation and knows his father, seconded by his mother, is putting obstacles in the way of Henry's changing his address. There's his tea. The Girls will make it for him. There's school in the morning. Henry has his satchel. There's the small disciplinary matter of the threepence change: Henry has been told what Henry must do. Yes, but Henry has tried asking for it, honestly he's tried, the Stern Girls can vouch for that. And? And? Henry can detect his grandmother trying to find a way of turning what has happened to Henry's advantage. But what has happened is what happened. Henry has been banned from the shop which stocks Henry's father's favourite horseradish.

'Banned?'

'Banned.'

'For how long?'

'I think the term was life, Izzi. But you know how these people use language – life doesn't always mean life for them.'

Silence at the other end of the phone. At last, though he is nowhere near the phone himself, Henry hears his father saying 'Okey-dokey', and the receiver going down.

'Trouble,' Irina says.

'We could lock the doors,' Henry suggests.

But it isn't trouble here his grandmother is afraid of. It's trouble at the Yoffeys'. The Stern Girls have all taken 'husbands' from North Manchester and know what rough resolution an okey-dokey portends. An unwillingness to be okey-dokeyed is why none of them have husbands from North Manchester any longer.

They also know the fierce loyalty of which their uncouth in-law is capable. Banishing your own son from his own house in order to make a man of him is one thing. Having someone else banishing your son from a grocery shop for life is another. Outraged in his affections, Izzi Nagel is off to war, codeword 'Okey-dokey'.

'If we open the windows,' Marghanita says, 'I bet we will be able to hear what happens.'

Henry looks alarmed. The sound of broken glass and breaking bones – is that what his failure to pick up the threepenny bit is going to lead to next? Old man Yoffey dead on his sacks of potatoes, Elliot Yoffey struck dumb, that's to say even dumber than usual, Mrs Yoffey a widow, and Henry's dad on death row? Seeing his trepidation, Marghanita, laughing, puts her hands on Henry's ears. Warm on his neck her laughter. If he turns round will Marghanita bury his eyes in her chest? Henry turns, and yes, Marghanita will.

Warm in his eyes, her chest.

As for the Yoffeys, that's soon settled. Leave things to the men, the men will sort them. Threepence? We're going to fight – two grown men, two pillars of our community – over threepence?! From behind the storeroom curtains Mrs Yoffey watches her husband pour a couple of small glasses of sweet red Middle Eastern wine. Here's to you, Mr Nagel – call me Izzi. And to you Mr Yoffey – call me Leo. Thirty minutes and a phone call later Leo and Izzi are getting Henry and Elliot to shake hands. This is the first time that Henry realises Elliot is not just mute with him but mute with everybody. Mute by nature, mute in the medical sense, just as Henry is thin-skinned. Henry's father, Uncle Izzi the illusionist, makes a threepenny piece appear from behind Elliot's neck and magics it into Henry's pocket. Henry who has seen this done a hundred times forces a weak smile; Elliot, for whom every instance of everything is the first, breaks into an idiot grin. Later that evening, while Henry is being tucked into bed by the Stern Girls – 'All right, you can have him for one night,' concedes Henry's father, flushed with syrupy red wine and that consciousness of success which only a conciliator can know, 'but don't spoil him' – Rivka Yoffey is being thrown over her garden wall.

Henry is twenty and very drunk on syrupy red wine himself when it occurs to him to put his arms around Marghanita and kiss her mouth. How old is Marghanita? Fifty? Fifty-five? Sixty? You can't tell when you're twenty. But what Henry can calculate is that when she's a hundred, Henry will be sixty himself, give or take. Too far gone to worry, in other words. Not that he's thinking of proposing marriage to her anyway. All Henry wants is to kiss her mouth and feel her breasts.

They are at a family wedding in the deep South of Manchester, which is Henry's excuse. South Manchester has always made him light-headed. Perhaps because between bombs and spiders he was born there. It is a warm night, the air silky, the trees still steaming after a summerload of rain. It was Marghanita who suggested they walk on the lawn, offering Henry her shoes to carry because the heels are high and she does not want to sink into the soft earth. He takes her elbow just the same, to be on the safe side. And is surprised by how not old it is.

'So your studies are going well?' she asks.

How long has Henry been waiting for this night? Sometimes it seems to him that he studies only to impress women, that he cannot at the last tell the difference between literature and lovemaking. Certainly when he finishes reading a long novel or an epic poem, Henry believes he should be rewarded with female favours. No act of the critical intelligence is over and done with for Henry until it has been completed in sex. What is it that stops him skipping tedious chapters but a sort of erotic conscientiousness, eking out the hours, paying for his pleasures in advance, remembering his manners? Careful reading as considerate foreplay. Things would be in their right conjunction for Henry tonight, therefore, whoever the barefoot woman quizzing him on his studies. But Marghanita is special to him and already entwined around his idea of himself as a boy of letters. Of all the Stern Girls, Marghanita was the reader. His mother, too, but his mother's influence was direct, not misty like Marghanita's. And besides, boys are not supposed to fall in love with their mothers. Henry's heart might be extravagant and score Cs but it is not indecent.

It was Marghanita who persuaded Henry to specialise, if he could, in American literature. 'Nothing happens here,' she told him on the eve of his going off to university, 'nothing big. All we do here is shelter. The grand themes are all American now.'

He remembers thinking there must have been some sadness in her, for her to have said that. And she had a face that easily expressed sadness; rather heavy features, like her sisters, with a broad nose and fleshy lips, but her cheekbones were finer cut than theirs, and her eyes more nervous in their movements and with more moisture in them. Marghanita is the White Russian of the family, he used to think. Of course, by comparison with his father's relatives, or with just about anybody else living in North Manchester come to that – the hordes, the Mongols, the Bolsheviks – the Stern Girls are all White Russians. Aloof, they wrap their furs around their pale skins and sniff the cherries in their distant orchard. But Marghanita is whiter even than her sisters. She's the disinherited one.

So he feels he owes it to her, no less than to himself, not to be another of her disappointments. Maybe he can go further and actually make it all right for her again, help her to repossess the world. He is already doing that for his mother, carrying her colours into battle. So why not Marghanita's colours as well? Henry, knight of the thin skin, redeeming the lost dreams of older women.

'Studies are going OK, thanks largely to you,' he says, steering her further from the lights of the party, unless she's steering him. 'I must say that when I see those other poor buggers sweating over *Beowulf* and Sir Philip Sidney I'm not half glad I took your advice.'

'The Americans aren't disappointing you?'

'Not at all. Though I don't think I'm ever going to be a Melville and Hawthorne fan.'

'Who's your favourite writer these days, then?'

'You make it sound as though I am always changing him.'

'Or her . . .'

'Or her. But it isn't a her at present.'

'Ah, it's someone very "he", is it? Let me guess. Hemingway?'

'No, Hemingway is a bit too outdoors for my liking. And his sentences are too short. I'm more of a Henry James man.'

He can hear, through her elbow, that Marghanita doesn't know her way well through Henry James. '*The Turn of the Screw*,' she says.

'Yes,' says Henry, not telling her that at his university *The Turn of the Screw* is considered to be very un-Jamesian James, 'and *Washington Square* and *What Maisie Knew* and *The Awkward Age*.'

'What's *The Awkward Age* about?'

'Young girls, on the face of it. But in fact, the sacred terror. The irresistibility of some people, even when you know they aren't suitable.'

'The irresistibility of unsuitable persons to young girls?'

Henry stops them by a fountain. A decorative swan is curled around itself, stretching its neck, as though fearful of the jet of water. From a distance he had hoped it was Leda and the swan – that monstrous coupling – but it is only a swan. The hall looks a long way away, its lights appearing to tremble in the hot damp of the night.

'Their irresistibility to anyone,' he says. 'I'm not all that interested in the young girls.'

He has been carrying her shoes, diamantés on brocade, wedding shoes, light, witty, the heels precarious, not as high as Henry likes, not stilts, but concise and pointed, sharp as daggers. It is somehow wonderful to be carrying a grown woman's shoes. But to face her and hold her as he wants he must put them down. He tries the ledge of the fountain.

'Not there,' she says, 'they'll fall in.'

'If they do I'll dive after them.'

'You're one of us,' she laughs. 'I bet you can't swim.'

'I'll take my chance.'

His mouth is on hers. Will the lips taste old? he wonders. Will they be cracked? Will they close tight, forbidding him, or will they have too much give in them, will they yield with old person's gratitude? No one tells you; no one prepares you for this.

A miracle, but her lips are not different from the lips of young women studying American literature at his university. Neither softer nor harder. But she isn't kissing him back. Simply letting him kiss her. He puts his hands up to her breasts, in that case, and for a moment or two she lets him do that as well, almost as though it is part of his education that he should know what a sixty-year-old woman's breasts feel like. And here is another miracle: they too are as unbearably round, as unimaginably firm – as undespairing and as ungrateful – as any woman's a third her age.

Cool, like green apples they are. Granny Smith's? Yes, exactly those, but forget the granny.

She isn't forlorn in body, Henry exults – suddenly it's a family matter for him again – therefore she cannot be forlorn in mind! He could cry now, except that she might not understand what he is crying for. How to tell her that he is crying for the cool apple-green resilence of her flesh?

But that is all of it he is going to be allowed to touch. 'Not such a good idea,' she says, pushing him gently away. *Not such a good idea, Henry, being kidnapped by your great-aunts.*

'The sacred terror?'

She laughs, touching her face, checking that her mouth is where it should be. 'No,' she says. 'You.'


Not such a good idea, Dad.

Nearly Marghanita's age himself now, though nothing like so apple green and undespairing, Henry upbraids his late father. Not such a good idea, setting up this cosy keypad love nest with your mistress, enjoying a second life before you had finished with your first.

*Don't know what you're talking about, Henry, but are you in any position to pass judgement?*

I'm your son. A son passes judgement. Besides which, you are hardly in any better position to pass judgement on me – you always said you wanted me to enjoy myself.

*I did. So why didn't you?*

I enjoyed myself in my own way, Dad.

*No you didn't. You never enjoyed yourself, not even when you were shtupping your best friends' wives. 'No pleasure without pain,' you used to tell me, 'and for the moment I'm concentrating on the pain part – it's called existentialism.' So when came the pleasure, Henry?*

I'm waiting for it.

*You're too late, Henry.*

Maybe I am. But at least I wasn't so deluded as to suppose I could come by it by looking in two places at the same time.

*A pity you weren't. A pity you didn't have the decency to try a little secrecy. You could never keep out of your own backyard.*

It was the only yard I knew.

*That was your fault. I tried to get you out.*

The way you got out?

*A man has one life. He has to see the world.*

So you're admitting this was your home from home.

*This? I've never seen the place before.*

But then you wouldn't tell me if you had.

*Of course I wouldn't. Every heart must have its secrets, Henry —*
T. E. *Lawrence. I learned that from you.*

D. H. Lawrence.

*Whoever.*

# TWO

These warm days!

The old woman's corpse isn't of course rotting, not after only twenty-four hours, but Henry isn't able to stay indoors. Opposite where he lives is a small park which abuts a church. The Little Park, locals call it, by way of distinguishing it from its big brother, Regent's Park. Once the park was the graveyard for the church, now it's a place for sitting and wheeling and watching your children. But it's Thistle Meadow Henry likes best, the part still given over to the dead, a tumble of long-neglected head-stones, barely one of them upright, the names of those they were erected to commemorate eaten away by time and the poisons of the city. Tautology, Henry. Time *is* the poison of the city.

If this were still a place of burial, Henry would think of bringing his parents' bodies down to be closer to him. Get them out of the horror of North Manchester. Give them some of the warm south. In the case of his mother, give her some of the warm south *back*!

But it would be tactless, wouldn't it, questions of faith and practicability apart, to remove them as a pair to this place of betrayal. Stand among the stones and you enjoy good views of the love-nest mansion block; narrow your eyes and the building looks striped from here, pink and vanilla, like Neapolitan ice cream. A pink mist.

Did his father come here, he wonders, and narrow his eyes so that a pink mist was all he saw? Doubtful. His father was not a wanderer among graves the way his son is. Didn't like getting his feet wet, his father, and the earth is always damp between gravestones.

Nonetheless, pink was what drew his father, no doubt about

that. Henry doesn't know why, but pink is the colour he has decided to give his father's mistress. Blancmange pink. He imagines her as a cushion. That's why his father couldn't say no to her. She was of another hue, another substance, of another sort of comfort, to his mother.

Henry is here often for a newcomer to the area. The squirrels recognise him and know not to bother him for food. Another regular visitor supplies those wants, a man with holes in his beard who keeps his breadcrumbs in a plastic bag and clicks his tongue to make the squirrels come to him. Freak! Henry is a non-feeder of animals. He wants the squirrels, and any other of God's creatures come to that, to know just by looking at him that he is on some other errand. That he is above their squalid concerns – eat, shit, eat, shit. He wants there to be no mistake about that. And there isn't. The squirrels do not even start at his footfall. And the birds stay in the trees.

In truth Henry no more cares for getting his feet wet than his father did; but he has things to think about that require the presence of the dead. Walking between the gravestones, Henry believes he has the dead on his shoes.

Anyone watching him crossing and recrossing the high street, going out of his apartment block into the park, then out of the park back into his apartment block, flinging himself against the locks each time, would quickly see what the trouble is. Retirement. You don't have enough to do, old man. What you need is a hobby. Stamps. Grandchildren. An allotment.

Not that Henry is retired. He isn't gainfully employed, but between gainful employment and retirement there is a world of occupation. If Henry were an actor he would say that he is resting. In actuality Henry is in suspense, consequent upon his having handed in his resignation. But that's still not to say he has retired. To all intents and purposes Henry continues to do what he has always done, only without a place of work, without a job description, without students, and without pay.

In which case why did Henry offer to go? A ticklish question, to which the approximate answer is that they made him.

But at least the waitress has woken up to his presence. It's taken six visits in two days – would have been more had the tables not been occupied on some of his essays on her attention – and any number of large tips, since Henry reckons that once you've waded in big to get someone's attention you've got to keep upping your stake. So yes, at eight pounds a Russian tea and a tenner per cup of Viennese coffee she's noticing him now. 'Save your feet,' he has to say every time he orders, handing her a note and making that easy-come easy-go expression with his shoulders which he imagines to be native to people from the old country. It's become a little joke between them – 'Save your feet' – touching on questions of energy and age, and establishing Henry's interest in her person. 'That's if I have any feet to save,' she has said to him this afternoon, signalling with her eyebrows how much she has to do, what with a cricket match at Lord's finishing early, and everybody wanting cold drinks and ice-cream sundaes.

She is wearing white lipstick, unless it's lipsalve, which either way Henry for some reason likes, and her custard hair is tied in an asymmetric left-leaning brush, making her face look lopsided, which Henry also for some reason likes. Scientists of the face say that lopsidedness denotes dishonesty or double-dealing, so that would explain it. Henry prefers women who have secrets. He has a feeling she has been unhappily married, probably more than once, and has teenage children who have left home, either to join the Cirque du Soleil or to beg on the streets in Soho. Her first husband will have been an artist from Budapest who beat her, maybe a failed opera singer, the second a house painter from Norwood, someone she met on the tube, a crackhead. You can tell Henry hasn't lived in London long: he has a lurid idea of what happens in the place.

As, for example, that there is a war of nerves in progress on the streets of St John's Wood between the Muslim and the Jewish communities. Henry enjoys the prospect of the Central London Mosque's stringy minaret at the south end of the High Street, but he wonders if it's a provocation to those who come here to buy bagels and chopped liver. Was it built as a provocation, or were the bagel shops opened as a provocation to it?

To Henry's left, two Arab boys in crêpe de Chine shirts sit drinking coffee and discussing films. They regard each other under soft long lashes, exchanging dark points of light. Henry tries to remember when last anybody looked at him like that. Never. Not ever. He has missed out on beautiful boys, missed out on being one, missed out on knowing one. To Henry's right an Israeli family are fussing over their oldest child. Sammi. Sammi too is dark and beautiful, but he doesn't have the gift of yielding his attention to another person. Sammi might one day win a Nobel Prize, but it won't be for quietude or empathy. Although the sun has shone for days, Sammi has found puddles on the pavement. Henry cannot remember whether it rained last night. In his apartment you don't hear rain. Or see it: the windows of Henry's apartment repel rain. Sammi jumps in and out of the puddles, then marvels at the marks his shoes make on the pavement. 'Abba, look!'

'Those,' says his father, 'are your footprints.'

Without appearing to change their expressions, the Arab boys look long and hard at Sammi's footprints.

Henry orders more Russian tea. It's a good sign, he reckons, that the waitress is not losing patience with him, hogging a table and her time when so many people want serving. The Israelis are just leaving. A Muslim family is waiting to take their place. When the Arab boys move on, a bunch of Jewish kids will sit down.

'This is like the Middle East,' Henry mutters to her as she takes his dirty cup away.

'It's quieter in the Middle East,' she mutters back.

If she has an accent to match her appearance, Henry has yet

to detect it. There is a slight labial flattening out of her 't's which Henry finds attractive, like watching someone pretty slide on ice, otherwise there is nothing to say she is Austro-Hungarian. But what Henry knows, he knows.

Sensing a dog snuffling about his feet, Henry is about to kick out. Another crazy hoping to touch Henry into giving him money? Unusual to get them this far north, but there you are, the madhouse is on the move. What stops him is firstly the possibility that the dog belongs to one of the waitress's children – the one living rough in Soho – and secondly the realisation that although the dog is indeed on a piece of string, it is not some beggar carrying his cardboard home around who is on the other end of it, but Lachlan Louis Stevenson.

'Mind if I join you?' He is carrying what looks like a pair of figurines – Philemon and Baucis or similar – loosely wrapped in kitchen paper towel. And a pair of brass fire tongs in a plastic bag.

Henry repeats his easy-come easy-go shrug.

'Selling off the family heirlooms already?' he asks, since Lachlan has the bad taste to lay them out on the table.

'Readies, that's all. You need readies when you've been waiting for what's yours for half your life. Down, Angus! Angus, stop that!'

Henry feels under the table for what's licking him. He finds a long velvet ear and then the wet spongy innards of Angus's mouth, purple to the touch. It is like putting his hand into warm trifle.

'Don't know if you're planning to move him in with you,' Henry says, cantankerous as befits his years, 'but there's something you need to know about your stepmother's block – it operates a no pets bigger than a goldfish policy.'

'Not a pet,' Lachlan says, swallowing air and banging his chest. 'Sorry, indigestion. He's a friend, this one – aren't you, Angus? I don't imagine they operate a no friend smaller than a wolfhound policy. And you're not going to mind, are you?'

Unable to reply directly, unable to ask a mute for his change or to tell a man with a dog that dogs are definitely not to his taste, Henry steals another look at Angus. The dog rolls his liquid eyes upwards, as though they have never before alighted on anything so wonderful as Henry. Like me at seventeen, Henry thinks. In love with whatever crosses his field of vision. 'Is he noisy?' Henry asks.

'Angus, are you noisy?' Angus twitches a balaclava ear, then scratches himself. 'There you are, not a peep.'

'What is he?'

'What is he! What does he look like? Red setter.'

'Is that good?'

'I'm not sure I understand your question.'

'Is that a good breed . . . a red setter?'

'A good breed?'

'I don't know dogs,' Henry has to explain. 'I never had a dog. I'm just wondering if a red setter is a good one to have.'

'Depends what you want him for. They're excellent gun dogs, but I doubt' – looking at Henry's unweathered complexion – 'that it would be a gun dog you're after.'

'Oh, I'm not after one,' Henry says, wishing he'd never got into this. 'I'm just' – what is he? – 'curious.' Which he isn't.

'Well, I'll tell you what,' Lachlan says, leaning into Henry and inconsiderately bringing up the air he swallowed earlier, 'you can "doubleyou ay ell kay" Angus any night you fancy, and get a feel for him.'

Henry is suddenly vouchsafed a vision of his future. I am to become a dog doubleyou ay ell kayer. I am to become an old codger who doubleyou ay ell kays dogs for another old codger who's got ulcers.

'Is he trained?' he asks.

'Of course he's trained. That's what he's trained for – to wait for his walk. Oh Lord, that's torn it. Now he's heard walk he's going to want one.'

And right on cue, Angus makes a little whining noise, stretches his shoulders and sniffs something on the wind being blown in from the Canaries. 'See,' Lachlan says, doing the same. 'Come on then, boy. Off we go.' He tucks the figurines under one arm and the brass fire tongs under the other. 'Oh, by the way,' he remembers, 'you aren't free to come along to the service, are you?'

'The dog's having a service?'

'No, the old woman's. Day after tomorrow. If you could, I'd appreciate it. No one else, you see. Just me. It would be nice if we could muster something a bit more like a congregation. You won't have to do anything. Just clap.'

'Clap?'

'It's what she wanted. No flowers. No memorials. Just applause. She worked the halls in her younger days. That's her story anyway. "And we all went up up up up up the mou-ow-ow-ow-ountain" – remember that? – "then we all came dow-ow-ow-ow-own again." That's how she got my father, singing him that rubbish. She was past it by then but he couldn't tell the difference. "The higher up the mountain, the greener is the grass. We met a silly billy goat who wouldn't let us pass." That was him – the billy goat. No fool like an old fool. Come on, Angus.'

'And nobody's clapped her since?'

'Lord, no. So I promised I'd arrange it. When the coffin goes through the curtain, a brief hands-together. That's all. No encore. I'll pop a card with the time and place on it under your door. You can come in the hearse with me, if you like. Arrive in style.'

So who'll clap me when the curtain closes, solipsistic Henry wonders. And for what?

Henry knows better, at last, than to go through the list of his achievements. But that's only because he has progressed, in recent times, to counting his mourners. Same sum. Same total.

41

Does Henry feel, then, that his has been a disappointing life? No. Henry feels his has not *been* a life. If Henry had lived a life he would not be able to remember his childhood so vividly; too many other things would have intervened and misted his childhood over. But nothing has intervened. The people he thinks about and whose names he hasn't misplaced are all from *then*. No one else has stuck. Who are they, the people of just the other day? What do they look like? What are they for? Go on, Henry says, impinge! But they won't. The surface of his middle years, rapidly becoming his late years, has grown too slippery. Nothing adheres. There was his childhood – say from zero to twenty-one; all right, say from zero to thirty – then whoosh! (he teaches, he is borrowed by his friends' wives, he resigns, he moves to St John's Wood, he meets a dog) and suddenly it's now.

This is something he would like to talk to his father about. His father managed to extend his childhood from zero to fifty-five, Uncle Izzi, illusionist, fire-eater and origamist, turning up at parties with a stack of newsprint and a travel bag of paraffin-smelling torches, more excited than the infants he was performing for, so that when he died he died, in Henry's eyes, a child – 'Jesus came down to gather flowers / And on the way he gathered ours' – as cruel an instance of infant mortality as any Henry had read about in any Victorian novel. Yet the world mourned him as a man. Such a man! What a man! Some man, Henry, your father!

No one said, 'Some child, Henry, your old man!'

What Henry would like to know from his father, who has had a long time to think about it, is whether he believes he was cheated of a grown-up existence, denied the chance to find out what not being a child was like . . .

*You mean like you, Henry? A little old man from the moment you were born.*

. . . or whether, if his father will allow him to finish, he believes

42

he had the best of it, never growing up to know bitterness and defeat.

*Because I was too busy, Henry, keeping consciousness of bitterness and defeat from you.*

You can see why Henry doesn't want to go home some days, however much he doesn't want to be out. But you can't take over someone else's past and hope to escape a colloquium with ghosts.

So why isn't Henry speaking to his lamented mother? He is, but she understands him too well. When Henry speaks, the sockets of her dry eyes fill with sadness. It's the seduction it always was. If he allows her, she will pull him down with her into the blackness, where she can shield him from all harm. Keep the clanging world away from him. And have him in an early grave.

Was that what they fought over, Ekaterina and Izzi Nagel, was that really the trouble between them – the saving of Henry? Was she rehearsing her version of the truth when the coach crashed? *Your* son . . . And then bang!

Was he answering her, the fire-eater, when his heart gave out? *My* son? *My* son, you call him! And then *oy gevalt*!

To save Henry from the world, Ekaterina Nagel came as close as was within her power – short of jumping him from the summit of the pyramid of Cheops – to stop him being born at all. He should have been the Baby Jesus. As far as the nursing home was concerned he already *was* the Baby Jesus, that honour going to the first child to show its nose on Christmas Day, and little Henry being more than halfway there. Seeing as Henry's nearest rivals were of Singaporean academic and Nigerian diplomatic parentage respectively, and in the Nigerian case were thought highly likely to come out twins, there was undoubtedly some *faute de mieux* favouritism in this. Whatever else there was to say on the subject, at least in Henry the Baby Jesus would be single, white and with a fifty-fifty chance of being male.

So why did Ekaterina hold back? Bombs and spiders. Given

the situation vis-à-vis the aerial war with Germany, Irina Stern had insisted that South Manchester was the only place for her daughter's confinement and to that end had found a nursing home not very many miles from Alderley Edge. Izzi was a young soldier stationed outside Basingstoke, waiting to be sent overseas to entertain other young soldiers with his sleights of hand, and he had no views on the matter other than that he wanted his wife to be safe and his son – though he had a feeling it went against the grain faithwise – to be the Baby Jesus. What no one had counted on was the inaccuracy, not to say the irreligiousness, of German pilots, dropping bombs in the vicinity of Alderley Edge on Christmas Eve while aiming for Ellesmere Port. As soon as Ekaterina heard the explosions she reversed her labour, ignoring all exhortations to push for Christ's sake. In the early hours of Christmas Day, with the prize still there for the taking and the sky clear, Ekaterina did begin to push, but went into reverse again on account of a spider with long sticky legs crawling across her belly. Talking about it later, with a shudder, Ekaterina multiplied the spiders which had taken advantage of her helplessness, increasing not only their number but their size. She wasn't superstitious and didn't hold with omens, she simply refused to bring a child of hers into a world which had such horrors in it. By mid-afternoon her fears had been almost stilled: this was rural England, the countryside, and in the country even the cleanest nursing home could not be one hundred per cent insectproof. As for the offending insect itself, it was just a daddy-long-legs left over from the summer, looking for somewhere warm to hide. 'On my stomach!' Ekaterina cried. 'Shush,' they told her. 'Across my baby's brain!' 'Shush,' they told her. 'Shush and push.' And thus, at four o'clock on a dark December afternoon, the Saviour's birthday, Henry Nagel was delivered, with a brief scream and a cough of blood, into an existence marred by bombs and spiders. But by that time he was too late to make it as the Baby Jesus. The honour of being the Redeemer for the day had fallen to Taiwo and Kehinde Mabogunje, sleeping soundly in a crib decorated with crêpe paper, silver cut-out moons and shepherds.

A family joke for years afterwards, beloved of his father. 'How do you like that? A Yiddeler, two Schwartzes and a Chink. Some choice, eh?'

They brought it out the way you bring out old photographs. Henry remembers the tears of laughter, and maybe of sadness too – regret, horror, who can say? – streaming down his mother's cheeks. Now the family would go to prison just for smiling inwardly at the comedy of colour.

Henry's view is that there was more racial harmony when no one was trying to promote it. But then who of any importance cares what Henry's views are, Henry no longer being in any position to influence events, even in the Pennines.

Take that 'no longer' with a pinch of salt, Henry feeling sorry for his present self – the truth is Henry never *was* in any position to influence events.

Ask what did for Henry professionally and you have to go a long way back. All the way to his not being the Baby Jesus, probably. Takes away from a boy's outgoingness, that sort of thing. Accustoms him, as a matter of aesthetical necessity no less than manners, to holding back.

There are those who would say it was reclusiveness that did for Henry from the off: social reclusiveness in the sense of not wishing to appear too forward, or simply not wishing to appear at all, and political reclusiveness – a sort of intellectual absenteeism – in the sense of not liking the ideas which were being exchanged around him, and therefore not attending to them. A man out of sympathy with his age, eh, Henry? Like Lucretius in Matthew Arnold's understanding of him, who, 'overstrained, gloom-weighted, morbid', turned from the varied and abundant spectacle of Roman life, and 'with stern effort, with gloomy despair', riveted his eyes on the 'naked framework of the world', looking for essences where other men sought appearances, and as a consequence retreating further and further into 'disenchantment and annihilation'. Might sound tosh as applied to Henry, turning from the varied and abundant spectacle of life on the Pennine Way, and toshier still considering that the essences in which Henry sought consolation were the wives and girlfriends of other men, but we can only report on life as it feels to us, and that was how life felt to Henry. The world was a blank to him; he approved and noticed nothing unless he was in love with a woman. Then he approved and noticed nothing but her. It meant you got a good deal if you were the woman. It meant you got a lot of Henry. But of course that was only a good deal if a lot of Henry was what you wanted. And if by a lot you understood intensity rather than duration.

Not so much a little touch of Harry in the night: more a healthy dollop of Henry over the fortnight.

A refined and disenchanted reclusiveness, a principled absenteeism, what you might call a dandified old-fashionedness – modern but not adequate to modernity, was Arnold's summation of Lucretius – and a subtly-fibred sympathy, breathed in from his mother, for women to whom life had been cruel: those were the qualities, anyway, for which Henry, not least as a teacher and exemplar to the young, wanted to be admired. In fact, his fellow teachers thought he was hoity-toity, ludicrous and ill-educated; up himself and as often as not up someone he had no business being up. If you wanted the authoritative account (without the Lucretius) of Henry's academic fall from nowhere to somewhere even lower, then that was it: a pathetic figure without provenance or curiosity, who hoity-toitied and hanky-pankeyed himself out of professional contention, hoity-toitied and hanky-pankeyed himself out of promotion, and finally hoity-toitied and hanky-pankeyed himself out of a job.

Their right to think vulgarly if they so choose, but Henry

sees what happened differently. Henry believes he isn't teaching young persons how to think aloofly any more because young persons have finally cottoned on to the fact that he doesn't like them. As far as Henry is concerned a conspiracy of the childish runs the world – a magic number of the world's most influential children ('We are the Bilderbergies, happy girls and boys') meeting every Christmas and Easter in a secret candyfloss garden on an invisible lemon meringue island somewhere off the sugary coast of Never-Never Land. Irk them and you've had it. Henry engaged their baby wrath by writing one of their number a letter of recommendation without crayoning in a little house bathed in eternal sunshine. Henry forgot the golden rule and made it rain. Or maybe he didn't forget, maybe he just *wanted* rain. He was getting pretty depressed, anyway, Henry, the oldest person teaching in an institution which was the mirror image of his soul – remote, unacknowledged, irrelevant, forgotten. A university they called it – the University of the Pennine Way – but before that it had been a polytechnic, and before that a college of technology, and before that a place for keeping hairdressers on day release off the streets, and before that a Spinners' Institute, and before that Henry had no idea. A playschool for Bilderbergies? Change the name and you change how people feel about themselves, that's the thinking. So by writing a poor student a poor reference, Henry effectively unravelled a century or more of cosmetic nomenclature, thereby adversely affecting not only the student's self-esteem but everybody else's not excluding his own. *Especially* his own. The place was Henry's life. He had been teaching there before the vice-chancellor was born.

Put Henry into a trance and regress him and you'll find that he'd been teaching at the Spinners' Institute even before he was born himself.

Stuck-up, Henry?

Hardly.

47

Just stuck. Stuck in the Pennine mud.

And stuck in his mother. Stuck fast within her resistant womb, stuck fast between her milky breasts, stuck fast in her disapproving mind.

Open the door and let me out, Ma!

Except that Henry has always rather liked it in there.


'Now we're going to make you a professor,' Henry's mother tells him, sitting him on her knee and getting him to read the words she points to with her lovely slender-knuckled fingers. 'First the title . . .'

Little Henry, aged three and a half, over the moon, puts his arm around his mother's neck and bites his tongue. 'The. Awkward. Age.'

'Bravo! Now Chapter One. "Save when it happened to rain Vanderbank always walked home, but he usually took a hansom . . ." What's a hansom, Henry?'

'A two-wheeled cabriolet, Mummy.'

'*Bravissimo*! Now you continue.'

'"But he usually took a hansom when the rain was moderate and adopted the preference of the philosopher when it was heavy."'

'Excellent, Henry. So what do you suppose that philosophic preference would be?'

'Staying in?'

'Good boy. Now let's hurry up and finish this and then we can start on *The Ivory Tower* . . .'

. . . Well, every man who is unhappy idealises his childhood. Henry can't put a name to what he first read with his mother but he is sure it had nothing to do with those ghosts and wizards reputed to be dear to the imaginations of children. Enough that Ekaterina was married to a wizard, and that they would all be ghosts soon enough.

The literature of excruciation, that was Ekaterina Nagel's

gift to Henry. The poetry of alarms and perturbations. Strange, because on her own account Ekaterina was not a timid woman. She had grown up without too many men around, her mother and her mother's sisters sardonically shedding or mislaying them in an early trial run of the century's later phallophobia – nothing neurasthenic about it in their case, simply a contempt borne out by experience, what happened when you met a man from North Manchester, and you always *did* meet a man from North Manchester. Being a girl in these liberated circumstances, where there was money enough to help you hold your head high, men or no men, was exhilarating for Ekaterina. Tall and straight with green eyes and good diction – 'gr-ah!-ssss' and 'rather' – Ekaterina Stern was expected to pursue the logic of her mother's and her mother's sisters' independent braininess, put into practice all their ambitions, and be the first of them to go to university. Professor Ekaterina Stern! It had such a ring that her mother didn't understand why they couldn't skip the qualifications part and just give her the job. Then Ekaterina met a communist, lost her head, maybe lost even more than that, and was sent to cool down with family in the old country just as the old country was facing facts – yes, the Nazis did mean what they said they meant: who'd have thought it? – and packing to go somewhere else. She lasted three weeks, just three weeks fewer than the old country, but long enough for the communist at home to have disappeared. Not that that mattered: on the boat back she had struck up a conversation with a dashing young man, also hotfooting it from a badly timed visit to doomed relatives, who told her his ambition was to be a fire-eater, which she, on account of his coarse North Manchester accent, had misheard as firefighter. By the time she realised her mistake they were already in love. 'Another one!' Irina Stern groaned, shaking her head. But destiny is destiny. Falling for men from North Manchester was what the Stern Girls did, no matter where you sent them.

War stopped Ekaterina finding out at once what being married to a fire-eater would be like. Izzi was soon away, another in the long line of absent men, leaving it to little Henry to hold the fort. By the time he was three, happy Henry was the longest-serving male family member any of the Stern Girls had ever known. Small wonder that they loved him as they did.

As for Ekaterina, the conviction which had assailed her during labour, that she was doing a wicked thing ushering a vulnerable life into a disgusting and terrifying universe, remained with her long afterwards, affecting the literature she encouraged Henry to read. At another time she could have taken the macabre route, allowing the horror of the spider which had crawled across her belly to lead her and Henry into Poe or Kafka. But no one cared for Poe or knew of Kafka and his cockroach then. Instead she went in the direction of *Jane Eyre*. Henry cannot remember how old he was before it dawned on him that *Jane Eyre* was the only book he had ever read. But it couldn't have been all that long ago. *Jane Eyre*, *Jane Eyre*, and nothing but *Jane Eyre*. Even when the work of literature was called something else, it was still, in all its essentials, *Jane Eyre*.

Looking back, Henry is philosophical about it. In the end what other story is there? Reclusive girl suffers agonies because her skin is thin, but finally gets to fuck the hero. Moral: the thinner the skin, the better the fuck.

Wasn't that, give or take, his shrinking story too? Without the bravado – all so much wind, Henry's wife-borrowing talk, all hot air to blow away the evidence of how hard he found everything. And of course without the happy ending.

As for what Ekaterina intended, pushing him in the direction of girlish fragility – who knows? Did she wish Henry had been a girl, was that it? Henrietta Nagel. Alice Harriet Henrietta Nagel . . . Was that why Ekaterina had held him back on Christmas Day, in the hope that the waiting and the disappointment would teach him what it was like to suffer as a girl and maybe turn him into one? Another Stern Girl to add to the collection, except that not one of those girls could hold a candle to little Henry in the fragile-flower department. Home from war, Izzi gasped at what they'd done to his rosebud boy. 'This lipstick?' he asked, rubbing at Henry's pouting mouth. Pampering he'd expected: '*All my love to you, my darling, and to the spoilt one,*' he'd written from the front, or at least from Basingstoke which was as near to the front as they'd send a man who had so much of the child in him. But spoiling was not effemination. 'Why don't you shove him in a frilly frock,' he asked his wife, 'stick pink ribbons in his hair and have done?' But all that did was to make Henry more quivery still, and to plant a confirmation in his mind for later, that the world was full of Mr Brocklehursts, brutes to those whose fine-sprung clockwork showed through their lucent skins.

He suffered migraines as a boy. They suffered them together, Henry and Ekaterina. First she got hers – coronas of pain which lit up her pillows and hurt Henry's eyes – then he got his. Then she called him into her bed.

'If it wasn't for worrying what would happen to you,' she sometimes told him, 'I'd end it all now.'

He stroked her hair. 'Careful,' she said. 'Don't press so hard.'

What caused these migraines? He knew what caused his – the daddy-long-legs ambling across his brain when he lay defenceless in his mother's tummy caused his, she'd told him that, warned him of his terrible beginnings, the psychic indignity, the disgustingness – but what caused hers? And why did she want to end it all?

Was it his father? Henry knew there was a problem of some sort with his father. '*Per se*, he's a wonderful man,' he'd heard Ekaterina say about him. Henry thought he understood what she meant by *per se*. She meant the animal man as opposed to anything the animal man said or did, the husband and the father whose nature was enthusiastic and hopeful, whose face glowed with the adventure of being alive, who had only to enter a room for everything oppressive in it, even the darkness that would otherwise have lingered in the corners, to be dispelled. He made light, Izzi Nagel, even Henry, reluctantly pursing his lips for his father to wipe away the imaginary lipstick, conceded that. Not his mother's sort of light, which went straight to your brain cells and illuminated their ache, but an altogether lighter form of light, weightless light, which made you forget on the spot what it had ever been like to feel heavy.

Midway between his father *per se* and his father *per accidens* was his father the willing but inadequate provider, the upholsterer who made everything too big and charged too little for it. For his part, Henry looked forward to his visits to his father's workshop with its smell of glue and horsehair, its half-finished chairs spilling springs, its huge cards of piping cord – Izzi Nagel was a great piper of furniture, an over-piper if the truth be told – and its view of the Pennines. It suited his father, Henry thought, to be stuffing cushions, carrying bales of Rexine from one part of the workshop to another, humming tunelessly with a mouth full of tacks. It became him to hammer, to be absorbed, careless of what anybody thought of him. How a man should be, Henry decided, secretly selling his mother down the river, relishing the apostasy. But he also knew that not everybody valued his father's upholstery as much as he did. 'It's a great settee lengthwise, Izzi,' Henry remembers a client telling his father in the street. 'The only trouble is it takes up two rooms and the cushions are so high you need a ladder to climb on to them.' 'That's only because the springs are new,' Henry's father explained. 'They'll wear in.' But Henry knew bluster when he heard it. Izzi's armchairs and sofas never wore in. They were built on too grand a scale. Somewhere in his soul Izzi Nagel was upholstering furniture for a tsar.

What most definitely was not comprised by Henry's mother's *per se*, though, was Izzi Nagel the performer, what she (if not he) thought of as the entirely accidental man – the part-time fire-eater, origamist and illusionist. But in particular the fire-eater. At first she had worried about the damage he might do himself. Then she had worried about the damage he might do her. Now she worried about Henry. 'It's just a trick,' he had tried to explain to her at every stage. 'You could do it. Your mother could do it. Let me just show you how cold the flame is.'

'Don't come near me with any of that,' she had warned him. 'Come near me with flame and I'm leaving you.'

'It's as safe as houses,' he'd assured her. 'It's no different from snuffing out a candle, I swear to you.'

'With your mouth, Izzi!'

'But nothing really goes into my mouth. No flame. I'm blowing out. It only looks as though I'm swallowing.'

'We have a child to bring up, Izzi,' she told him. 'You're supposed to blow bubbles at a baby, not flames.'

'He's not a baby. He's a boy – or haven't you noticed?'

'Izzi, no one wants you breathing fire over their children. When were you last asked to fire-eat at a children's party?'

He thought about it. 'So far, never,' he conceded. 'But it just needs one to set the ball rolling. The word has to get out.'

She sat him down and took his hands in hers. 'Izzi,' she said, 'the word's got out. People have seen our garden. They've seen what you've reduced it to. Nothing grows there any more. Nothing ever will grow there again for another thousand years. People don't want you doing that to their gardens. They won't pay you to torch their homes. They want you to come along in a funny hat and a bendy wand, and they want you to fold serviettes. The two things don't go together, Izzi. You can't work in paper and fire. Surely you can see that.' She pleaded with him. 'Please? Tell me you can see that. Please?'

He hung his head. He was a good man. When a woman begged, he gave. Yes, he could see it. But she knew that in his heart he wasn't convinced. If you couldn't work with paper and fire that was paper's fault. She knew what he was thinking. That he would have to find or invent paper which didn't burn.

Otherwise, though, as a couple *per se*, they appeared happy and well matched. He loved her for her haughty beauty and her elocution, and she loved him for his triviality. It wouldn't be quite true to say that he entertained her, for what astonished her initially about his fire-eating, like his paper-folding, was not that he could do it but that he wanted to, a grown man; but without doubt he made the world a toy to her; made a toy *of* her some days, too – she the top, he the whip – dancing and whirling her out of herself. Away from the mothering of Henry, she cut a confident and rousing figure. How could she not? She was a Stern Girl. An exceptional Stern Girl in that she had a man who loved her. On occasions, seeing her abroad, walking briskly, throwing her head back in conversation, shaking her hair, glittering with laughter – *light!* – Henry felt she had betrayed him. Where were the migraines now?

So was it his – heavy Henry's – fault? If it wasn't for him she would end it, she had said, but was she saying what she didn't mean? Was existence a fearful thing to her, to be endured only for his sake, only when she *was with him*. Was that it? Did he draw all lightness out of her? The opposite of his father, was he? The one dispelling all oppression from a room, the other taking it everywhere he went? Certainly when Ekaterina described to Henry some event he had seen with his own eyes, or had heard about from someone else, she made it, as though for his behoof – as though that was the obligation she felt to his oppressive nature – more shocking, more humiliating or depressing, more negatively melodramatic, than it had actually been. She grew physically heavier in the telling it as well. Extremity of expression hung in jowls from her face, inordinacy of vocabulary thickened her neck. 'I thought I'd *die*, Henry,' she would say, gathering him into her offended bulk, actually underlining words with her fingers as she spoke, 'I thought it was the *end* of me. Where this leaves me *now*, I have *no* idea, *none*. Maybe *something* will change the situation. But as God is my witness, darling, I will *never* get over it, *never*.' Ask Henry to name what exactly it was she would never get over, whether it was an event he had seen with his own eyes or not, and he would have been at a loss. Hiroshima? Someone turning up at an engagement party in the same dress as hers? Fog? In the face of her extravagant alarms, the objective world gave up the ghost. Nothing was but as his mother told it, a great halo of migraine encircling everything.

The big question for Henry: did she make him afraid of life, or did he make her?

And then, with a sort of blithe impertinence, as when the sky suddenly clears after a wild storm – bad weather? what bad weather? – she would irradiate him with happiness again, dancing him on her knee, serenading him with songs popular on the radio. He adored her singing. 'Whistle While You Work' especially, with the inexpert whistling thrown in – more humming through the lips than whistling – while she busied herself at the stove, boiling cans of food for him. She had no cooking skills. No Stern Girl cooked. They just boiled cans. Beans. Macaroni. Stews. Vegetables. Soups. If a chicken dinner had come in a can they'd have boiled that. And without ever emptying the can into a pan, for that too would have been esteemed cooking, a concession to the men who were never there. It was the one domestic skill the Stern women passed down the line – dropping cans into boiling water and then forgetting about them until the water boiled away and the kitchen filled with the smell of roasting metal. Eventually the cans exploded – that was how you knew the meal was ready. Sometimes, when his father came home late asking for his tea, Ekaterina would point to the kitchen ceiling. 'It's there,' she'd say.

Then Henry's father would go out into the garden, fill his mouth with paraffin, and burn down more trees.

I have pyromaniacal parents, Henry thought later. They lay

waste to everything. But what he still can't decide is whether they had laid waste to him as well, or whether he had done that to himself.

'Whistle While You Work' wasn't her only song. She also did 'I'm Forever Blowing Bubbles' and 'Ah, Sweet Mystery of Life', and on mercifully migraine-free days, when she wore a turban to keep the odour of molten aluminium out of her hair, 'The Desert Song', performed in the mode of Myrna Loy but with the voice of Jeanette MacDonald. Henry loved nothing more than this, especially when he was feverish and bedridden, watching the patterns on the wallpaper throb and mouth at him – the house alive with the sound of his mother, the cans dry-rattling in their pans, and the whole world safe. Ask Henry, between the age of three and thirteen, what heaven is and he will tell you heaven is his mother at home, singing, burning his dinner.

'How lovely you are,' she would lullaby him in the afternoon, as the Pennine-frilled northern darkness closed in on them, tapping out the tune on his knees, matching the words to the ethereal second movement of Schubert's heaven-sent Fifth Symphony, a piece of music they had listened to together on the Third Programme – Henry's first piece of real music – and which they had made their most favourite piece of music of all time.

'How lovely you are, how lovely-ey-ey you are, how lovely you are, how how how lovely you are.' Set any Schubert loose on Henry now and he will not be responsible for his tears. But he knows that if by accident he gets to hear Schubert's Fifth Symphony, he will not survive it.

You can have too much feeling.

Henry explains many of the strange things he has done in his life this way: he has safeguarded himself against too much feeling. Of course, you can have too little feeling, also. But Henry is not aware he has ever safeguarded himself against that. You can only battle with the nature you have, and Henry's is pap.

Something Henry remembers, from long after the Schubert days when nobody was lovelier than he was: his mother ringing him in his university digs at an odd hour of the night, her voice high and dangerous, to say she would like him to sit down and compose himself (if there is anywhere to sit down and be composed by the communal phone), because she has matter of grave and strange importance to impart, no, no one has died, not exactly, but she has caught his father out, actually seen him with her own eyes – with my own *eyes*, Henry! – going into the Midland Hotel in the company of a woman. 'In broad *daylight*, that's what I can't forgive, the stupidity of the man. At least he owes it to me not to be seen, not to be caught, especially by *me*!'

Henry is surprised to hear himself laughing. 'Mother, what were you doing outside the Midland Hotel?'

'What bearing does that have on the matter?'

'It just makes it the more farcical.'

'I don't know what it is that strikes you as funny. You think this is a farce I'm describing? Well, you're right in one regard. Our marriage *is* a farce.'

'I didn't mean that. I meant that the coincidence of your both being at the Midland Hotel at the same time is comical. Synchronicity is always ludicrous. Did he see you?'

'Henry, I haven't rung so that you can lecture me on the nature of farce. And no, he didn't see me. But I saw him. So what am I supposed to do now?'

'Nothing. He might only have been going in for afternoon tea.'

'It was the morning, and your father doesn't have afternoon tea.'

'Then maybe he was going along to discuss a party, checking one of the reception rooms out or something. Are you sure he wasn't there to *do* a party?'

'Certain. He didn't have his tricks or his torches with him. Nor was it the right time of day. Who throws a children's party at the

Midland at eleven on a Monday morning? What is more he was wearing his suit. He never does parties in a suit. For parties, as you know, my husband – may God forgive me for ever choosing such a clown of a man – wears a top hat and a red nose. For seeing other women he wears a suit. And I'll tell you something else, Henry – he was wearing *odd socks!*'

'How could you tell that?'

'I was six inches behind him. I could have trodden on his heels. One red, one black.'

'There you are, then. That proves he wasn't on an assignation. When a man goes to a hotel with another woman he checks his socks.'

'Not your father. He wore odd socks the first time he took me to a hotel. That's when he gets forgetful – when he's excited.'

Henry hears himself laughing again. (Safeguarding himself against too much feeling, is he?) 'I'm sorry,' he says, 'I just can't treat this with the sort of seriousness you think it merits.'

'You think I'm making it up.'

'No. But I think you should be playing it down. What if you're right – how much does it matter? It's just a morning off.'

'Henry, you don't take mornings off marriages. But then you're a man – what would *you* understand.' For a moment Henry thinks she is going to hang up on him, then: 'Anyway,' she continues, 'it's worse than I've told you.'

'He hasn't run off?'

'Of course he hasn't run off. Your father doesn't run off. He knows too well which side his bread's buttered. He was back here at three the same day, back before I was, asleep on the sofa.'

'Still in his odd socks?'

'Yes, but not on the same feet.'

'Back, though.'

'Oh yes, back and snoring. With that guileless expression on his face. As though he's dreaming of steam engines.'

'Well then . . .'

'Well then what? Henry, I saw him going into the hotel and I saw the woman he was with.'

Sometimes, however urgent the matter, the rhythm of a conversation can make you flippant. 'Anyone you know?' Henry no sooner asks than he wishes he hadn't.

'Of course it's someone I know.'

'Ah,' Henry says. The best friend syndrome, of course. His father would be capable of that. Keeping it in the circle of acquaintance. Kith and kin. Mentally, Henry goes through the possibles. His mother's schoolfriends, the dim girls she tutors privately in G.C.E. English, her hairdresser, the cleaning lady, his mother's cousins, his mother's aunties . . . no, not those, not his father, it is only Henry with whom no member of the family is safe. 'So who?' he asks.

She takes a deep breath, as though trying to suffocate something inside herself. The name, when she delivers it, is stillborn. 'Rivka Yoffey.'

'Old man Yoffey's wife? You're joking.'

'Someone might be joking, Henry. But it isn't me.'

'Isn't Rivka Yoffey Orthodox?'

'Exactly. But the Orthodox, as you know, give themselves latitude. She is also without looks. And without any hair to speak of.'

'Isn't that because Yoffey keeps pulling it out.'

'I would like to think so. But I suspect it's because she's been wearing a wig since she was seventeen. Her head has never seen the light of day. I doubt if much else has either. Until last Monday, that is. But I am not concerned with the whys and wherefores, Henry. I am concerned that your father should take such a plain woman to the Midland Hotel.'

'You think he should have taken her somewhere cheaper?'

'I think he should not make love to women just because they're to hand. I think that if he must be unfaithful to me he should at the very least work hard to find someone worth being unfaithful with.'

Henry puts this very argument to his father in his St John's Wood home from home, where he sits, a bag of dust and bones, on the edge of his old armchair.

Rivka Yoffey, Dad, he says. Rivka Yoffey!

*What about her?*

How could you?

*How could I what?*

What's the appropriate language, son to father? They were always formal with each other. Protectives, Izzi Nagel once advised Henry to be well provided with at all times. Their one and only discussion of the sexual life. Be amply stocked with protectives, Henry. Followed by his blessing. Go forth and don't multiply. Not condoms, not rubbers, not johnnies even, but protectives. So Henry can't say how could you have fucked Rivka Yoffey, Dad? How could you have fucked that poor, sad, ugly, Torah-reading woman?

How could you have taken her to the Midland Hotel, is what he decides to ask instead.

*You'd prefer that I'd taken her somewhere cheaper?*

Funny, Henry remembers, that's the very question I put to Mum.

*I know you did.*

She told you?

*Of course she told me. That's how it is between man and wife — though you wouldn't know that — they tell each other everything. She said you were sarcastic about the whole thing.*

I wasn't sarcastic. I was just amused.

*OK, amused. I have to get the word right, don't I?*

I think it helps. It made me laugh, that was all.

*Yes, she told me that. Some son, she said. I tell him his father is with another woman and he laughs.*

I wouldn't have laughed had I known about here.

*Where's 'here'?*

Come on, Dad. Rivka Yoffey for a morning is one thing . . .

*Exactly what I told your mother. What's a couple of hours with Rivka Yoffey between people who love each other? That was why you were able to find it funny. You knew it didn't matter. And don't say if I knew it didn't matter why did I do it. That's why I did it. Because it didn't matter. A big inducement – a thing not mattering. It removes the barrier of a thing mattering. Though of course you wouldn't know about that when it affected you personally. To you, personally, everything mattered.*

We see things our own way, Dad.

*Dead right we do, Henry. And we do things our own way too.*

Did.

*Did, does . . . You are, you were, no saint, Henry. Letting everything matter to you didn't make you a saint. Any more than it made your mother.*

Leave my mother out of it.

*OK. Just you then. It never made you a saint.*

I never had a second wife.

*Second 'wife'? – nor did I. But then you never had a first wife. Not of your own.*

I never ran a second home, Dad.

*Tauget͜z.*

*Tauget͜z*, otherwise fine, Henry, fine, whatever you say, I'm not going to argue with you. Izzi Nagel's favourite word, often used in pairs – *tauget͜z*, *tauget͜z* – for bringing a conversation to an abrupt but not ill-tempered end. *Tauget͜z*, from the intransitive German verb *taugen*, pedantic Henry surmises, which in its negative form means not to be of very much use. Whatever you say, Henry. *Whadever!* – only who needs 'whadever' when you've got *tauget͜z*, smuggled, *when*ever, in some migrant's luggage to North Manchester, all the way from Berlin via Podolia and the Volga?

Not only Henry's mother who personalised music for Henry's

delight. His unmusical father, too, likes to write his own lyrics. Driving back from an engagement, with Henry on the front seat beside him, still blazing with the shame of being seen to be a fire-eater and origamist's son, Uncle Izzi fits his favourite word to the tune of 'Daisy, Daisy, give me your answer do'. Henry remembers it well and can sing it to this day. '*Tauget*, *tauget*, *tauget* and *tauget* taug / *Tauget*, *tauget*, *tauget* and *tauget* taug . . .'

Not Schubert, but it isn't only lyric genius that makes hapless Henry weep.

Rather than travel with the body of a dead woman he never knew and have people looking sorrowfully at him from the pavement – Henry hates being the object of pity, even when it's undeserved – he makes his own way to the crematorium. He takes a taxi, not trusting himself to the lottery of a bus lane or the discomfort and importunings of the Underground – though cosmopolitan in his soul, Henry is too much of a provincial by habit ever to have mastered the tube, and what is more does not like the idea of being gassed in a tunnel and buried alive, which is what they're all afraid of now – and arrives an hour early. The crematorium is on a hill in north London, looking back towards the city. Henry sits on a bench and enjoys the prospect. Would this do? Could he be happy here? Where best to be dead has been a question for Henry for as long as he can remember, but it is less rhetorical today than it once was. It is getting time he made up his mind. The advantage of this position is its elevation, a fresh breeze keeps the damp away, and the view ensures you would never feel entirely disconnected from the living. Not having damp in his bones is an important consideration. Fear of chilled joints is what has turned Henry off many an otherwise idyllic churchyard. But then this isn't a joint joint, Henry remembers, reminding himself he is in an ash garden and that the bodiless dead seep away like wine here, dust in the wind, dirt in his nostrils. So not for him, then, this pleasing view. Not an available option to Henry, ashes. The Book says you must be ready to meet your Maker pretty much as He made you, nothing added or taken away, and though Henry doesn't in a general way set much store by what's written in the Book, when it comes to death he doesn't cavil. Better to be safe than sorry.

He wouldn't mind having a tree dedicated to his memory, though. Or a shrub. Something light and green and ornamental. A miniature Bridge of Sighs arching over a lily pond, bullrushes at the edges. What about a bridge? Something serviceable. More and more, Henry wonders if death might not be his opportunity to do some of the things he has failed to do in life. Be easy on the eye. Be noticeable. Be of use.

He likes it here. He likes the kitsch. It is like a New Town. A Milton Keynes for the dead. In the past, Henry has thought he would prefer to die antiquely. Suddenly, he is pricked by the deathful possibilities of the present.

A gong sounds, more like a school dinner than a church bell, the signal for the previous mourners to leave the chapel. Henry watches them troop out, bereft of ritual, a steel-haired family group at a loss what to do with their extremities. Grandpa was easy, they could burn him. Knowing where to put your own heads and hands is the hard part. The younger relations just stand on the gravel looking down, as though the gravel might explain it all to them. A few of the older ones take a stroll in the garden, crossing Henry's Bridge, pausing to look at Henry's Ornamental Shrub – *Henrix herbacea*. These would be my visitors, Henry thinks. My admirers. No one looks long or sadly. No one wears a ravaged air. They have burnt to nothing a person they loved once, but no awfulness prevails. In Charnel House New Town this is just another day. After ten minutes they are back at their cars, exchanging directions, and then gone. And now it's Henry's turn. He doesn't want to be hanging about when the hearse bringing his neighbour arrives, so he makes his way into the chapel. But he has to leave and let the coffin proceed before him. Protocol. When he returns, an electronic organ is playing Handel favourites. The coffin is on the conveyor belt, Lachlan is in his seat and a secular officiant with an unlined face – smooth, like the face of a pottery moon – is pacing up and down, consulting his watch. 'Will these be all the mourners?' Henry hears him ask of Lachlan. 'More or less,' Lachlan says, looking round. 'I'd start anyway.'

Henry thinks about sitting at the back, but on a sign from Lachlan shuffles in next to him. 'Fan out,' Lachlan whispers. So Henry tiptoes to the other side of the chapel, a teak vault resembling the inside of a coffin itself, and tries to look like more than one person.

'Norma Jean Louis Stevenson,' the officiant begins, 'was one of those women . . .'

Henry's mind wanders off. Norma Jean . . . who'd have thought it? Did she change her name in accordance with her show-business ambitions, or was she always Norma Jean, in which case what did she think of the other one? The officiant reads from Shakespeare. *Fear no more the heat o' the sun.* Then puts on a record of the 'Warsaw Concerto'. This is not what Henry wants for himself, to go up in smoke to his favourite tunes. Henry wants a man of God to see him off, commending his soul on its final journey, never mind whether it's the hosts of heaven that await him or all the devils of hell. At least make it a journey of dread solemnity – for what else is it, this howling passage from animal to some other form of being we can only guess at, what else, Henry wants to know, if not a passage of the utmost terror and, if we're lucky, if we make it so, if we *insist* on it, of grandeur?

Disturbed from these anticipations of his own passing by a pssst from Lachlan, Henry realises that 'We all went up up up up up the mou-ow-ow-ow-ountain' is playing and that the conveyor belt is on the move. He begins to clap. Lachlan, too, is putting his hands together. Henry wonders if he oughtn't to toss in a 'bravo!' Shouldn't someone have brought a bouquet to throw in after the old girl, a final tribute from the orchestra stalls? As the coffin arcs horizontally into the fires – Henry hears their roar whether or not they're lit yet – the curtains begin to follow it, closing with a juddery computerised hiss which Henry recognises. This is the sound his St John's Wood drapes make when he presses his keypad. Maybe the old lady had the same. Home from home for her then, this. The coffin has not vanished yet, nor has the final chorus of the song, when Henry's ears prick, surely, to more clapping than there was before. A third person has arrived, adding weight to the applause, though Lachlan said there would be no third person. Henry does not look round. He owes it to the deceased to see her turn the corner in her entirety. Sentimental about women, Henry. He has always liked to wave them off. But when it is all over and he can look about him, he sees a woman with the lopsided look he admires, wearing the sort of clothes he goes for too, mourning black with a shorter skirt than is appropriate, slit discreetly, and high merry-widow heels, patent, with scalloped backs.

It tells you something about Henry that he should have taken in every detail of the woman's wardrobe and coiffure – grasshopper brooch on her jacket, demure pearl earrings, inappropriate furry handbag, yak or some such, hair groomed to fall over one shoulder in the manner of Veronica Lake (that dates him), though not quite long enough to be vampish – before processing the much more salient information which is that he knows her. Don't ask him how, don't ask him why, but there, standing very close to Lachlan, close enough to be his intimate, and still absently clapping her bejewelled hands to the memory of the music-hall tune, is the waitress from his patisserie. The one who only a day or two ago owed him three pounds, and now must owe him about three hundred. The one he has been beginning to think about romantically. But who it seems is now, or perhaps always was, associated in some significant way with Lachlan.

# THREE

Here we go again, Henry thinks. He has been had like this before.

'Hovis' Belkin. Osmond 'Hovis' Belkin, his best friend from school, did him identically half a lifetime ago, also, as chance would have it – if there is such a thing as chance – with a waitress. Is the lesson for Henry that he should stay away from waitresses? Or that he should stay away from friends?

They stay away from him, whatever he decides. Or rather, because Henry wishes to be precise about this, and to avoid self-pity, they inhabit space which doesn't have him in it.

Is that barbed wire that surrounds Lachlan and the waitress? Why not hang a sign – PISS OFF, HENRY!

Something that has tormented Henry all his life, something he felt at school, at university, still feels today when he goes to a party, a conference, a concert, the theatre even: how well acquainted everybody but Henry is with everybody else. Leave aside coincidences of sympathy or interest, where do they actually *meet*, at what Henry-free time and in what Henry-free dimension do they make contact, dock, establish intimacy, and agree, without so much as mentioning Henry's name, to exclude him? Let Henry be the first person in a room, it will transpire as soon as the room fills that every single person there except Henry is on close terms with every other. Does it happen when he goes to get himself a drink? Does it happen when he blinks? Or, as seems much more likely, was it all laid down long ago in anterior time? Was there another world before this one, a sort of metaphysical prep school, a preliminary universe, to which someone forgot to send Henry?

It would explain, anyway, much of Henry's strange behaviour towards his friends. I know, he must have thought, aspiring to those intimacies which were such a mystery and such an agony to him – I know, I know how to insinuate myself into their charmed circle and show that I am essentially the same as they are, no less approachable, no less amenable to intimacy, every bit as nice – I'll fuck their wives.

Not that he fucked anyone attached to 'Hovis' Belkin. In so far as there was any fucking between 'Hovis' and Henry, it was 'Hovis' who fucked him.

Unwelcome, this memory. Highly unwelcome. Besides which, Henry hasn't got time to think about the past now, least of all his Belkin-tarnished past. He puts him away, puts him back where he's been hiding him since they were students together thirty years ago and more. Henry's excruciation-span is shrinking and he has reached the age where he can take his humiliations only one at a time.

'Well then,' he says to Lachlan, as they're being harried out of the chapel of rest to make room for the next lot of griefless grievers, 'you happy with the service?'

Lachlan wipes his moustache on the back of his hand. 'So-so,' he says. 'But then anything's more than she deserved. She wouldn't have done it for me. She told me so. She said, "If you go first, Lachie, don't be expecting me to organise you a wake. You'll have to get yourself to the cemetery."'

Henry can't think of anything to say to this, unless it's along the lines of she must have loved you really, Lachie. And Henry finds it altogether too easy to believe she didn't.

'Anyway,' Lachlan goes on, rubbing something from his moustache between his hands, and stamping his feet as though it's cold in the sun, 'that's my duty done.'

And mine, Henry thinks.

And the European waitress's.

He is waiting for Lachlan to say something, perhaps to effect an introduction. Or for the waitress to fill in a few of the blanks – *I'm an old friend of the family . . . Lachlan and I go way back*

68

*. . . I just couldn't help myself . . . He turns my insides to jelly . . .*
*He knows he only has to ask, he knows he only has to snap his fingers*
*and I'll come running . . .* Not that she owes Henry an explanation, Henry accepts that. It isn't as though they are affianced or
anything. It isn't as though he has even asked her out. He doesn't
know her name, for God's sake. Nonetheless, it was his sense
that they had been agitating each other's electric fields, that there
were a thousand tiny crackling unspoken anticipations between
them, and that she has therefore misled him. Not breach of
promise exactly, more breach of expectation, more a violation
of velleity.

'So how come . . . ?' he turns to ask her, making a gesture with
his hands which takes in everything, the whole situation, life,
death, him, her, Lachlan's stepmother, Lachlan. Unsophisticated,
he accepts, like asking someone at a party how he knows the host.
But he's past prolonging agonies. What he needs to know, he
needs to know at once.

She has a way of darting her eyes sideways from under her
hair, which both repels and attracts him. Looking about her,
checking to see whether it's safe to come out, like some frightened creature of the forest. Except that she isn't frightened. I'll
never get a straight answer from this woman, Henry thinks. She'll
always be trying to work out what I want to hear. Which is what
repels him. What attracts him is more or less the same. With the
added attraction that he is repelled by it.

'I came to show my respects,' she says at last, giving her hair
a sideways toss, 'and as a favour to Lachlan – the same as you
did.'

To Lachlan. A favour to *Lachlan*. And what's *my* name, Henry
wants to ask her. I've been tipping you for days, you owe me a
small fortune, what's my fucking name?

But at least – Henry clutching at straws – she didn't call him
Lachie!

He steals a look at him to see if he can make out the lineaments of triumph, but Lachlan is preoccupied with his digestive system, rapping at his chest as though he has an urgent message to deliver to himself, and rolling silent ripples of wind up from his belly. You're welcome to him, Henry thinks, while at the same time refusing to believe she'd want him. She couldn't. Surely she couldn't. Henry's old problem – he esteems himself lower than a snake, but esteems every other man lower still.

A family of mourners, celebrants of the mysteries, attend a coffin on its august passage from the illusory world of the living to the dread solemnity of the dead. Two or three of the younger ones are wearing discoloured trainers. Already a dyspeptic red, Lachlan's face contorts with disgust. 'Common as muck,' he mutters into his chest.

For the first time Henry, though he is in formal black from head to foot himself, sees the virtue of trainers.

A feeling of completion, akin to embarrassment, descends upon their little party. Henry knows he should go and leave them to it. He looks at his watch. From under her hair, the waitress slithers her eyes at him. 'Do you have a car here?' she asks.

'No, I came by taxi. Presumably you'll go back in the hearse,' he says, looking at Lachlan.

Whether because of the trainers, or because he can't forget that his stepmother had told him he would have to bury himself, Lachlan is still livid. 'No fear,' he says. 'They bring you here, but they don't take you back.'

'Well, I suppose that's appropriate,' Henry says.

'What?'

Henry shrugs. 'So shall I call for a taxi for all of us?' he wonders.

'I've got my car here,' the waitress says.

Though he still believes he should call a taxi for himself, Henry doesn't. He wants to go through the awkwardness of seeing who'll sit in the front seat next to her. He also wants to know whether she is one of those women who hitch their skirts up when they drive. He loves that action – the infinitesimal raising of the behind, like a deer at a waterhole, and then the dextrous tug on either side of the skirt, a gesture reminiscent of the tea table to Henry, of tablecloths being changed and smoothed, of doilies being laid, of little fingers extended to lift bone-china teacups. And is she a woman who will be content for however much thigh shows to go on showing, or will she, at traffic lights and round-abouts, be worrying her skirt back down again? Hair-raising, being driven by a woman who is conscious of her skirts. For his part, Henry can't get enough of it. Being driven by a woman full stop, but also being driven by a woman who is thinking more about her body than the road. Crash me, Henry thinks. Crash me at the moment that we are both concentrating on your thighs. And what about her high heels? Is she a woman who drives in high heels, who loves the recklessness of spiking the pedals, or will she keep flatties in her car? A stiletto *and* a flattie man, Henry goes both ways on this. It all depends on how the feet move. It all depends on whether they retain the memory and the promise of spikes.

Nothing in his life has interested Henry more than this. Woman. Never mind the phenomenology or metaphysics of woman, just woman. Just the aesthetic of her. Just the *prospect*. God and all His host could clear the sky and descend from it this very moment, could land in golden parachutes on the memorial lawn of this north London crematorium, could call his name – Henry! Henry! – could offer him that immunity from mortality he craves, yet still Henry would not be able to draw his mind away from the picture that is forming of the waitress hitching up her skirt and depressing the pedals of her car – either with her heels or in flatties, Henry doesn't care which. And what would immortality be worth, anyway, if he couldn't devote the better part of it to attending, intellectually, to such stimuli?

This isn't desire. Henry isn't even sure it has an erotic compo-nent, though it would have had, once upon a time. Now it's more what Henry would call pictorial curiosity.

The best reason Henry can think of not to die – that he will miss the female ceremonial.

And this they called hiding from the world!

So what's his motive for refusing the passenger seat when it's offered him, and for giving it to Lachlan? Does he feel he is in the way enough, just being in the car at all? Does he want to grab a better look at them together? Or does he want to postpone the pleasure of seeing her at the controls of her car at close quarters, savouring the question marks, saving it all up for a future time? Dangerous, Henry, doing that at your age. At your age you never put off until tomorrow what you can do today, given that today might very well be your last.

To be truthful, his deferring to Lachlan is neither altruism nor perversion. He means to catch the waitress's eye, and hold it, in her driving mirror. As someone long schooled in the subtleties of third-person sex – doing the best by the fact of your exclusion – Henry knows what can be achieved in the back seat, through a driving mirror.

'Moira,' the waitress says, turning and extending her hand to Henry. Significant, Henry reckons, that she waits until they're in the car, the doors are closed and he's behind her.

'Henry,' he responds, laughing, leaning forward. Not sure he cares for Moira much as a name – not Habsburg enough for him, he was hoping for something more along the lines of Maria Theresa or Yolande or Margarita of Savoy – but he likes the texture of her hand, warm like a baby mouse in his. He can feel her heart beat through her fingers. He holds them a second longer than he should, squat fingers with red nails, damaged by waitressing, scuffed from scrambling up the egregious tips he leaves, the skin just beginning to come loose on the bone, not promiscuously elastic like a young person's, leaping slavishly to meet every touch, but with some of the give, still, of youth. Always feeling for the life under the skin, Henry. As though dreading the day he won't find it.

What he can't tell is whether she's taken her heels off.

'We ready?' she asks. It's like a big adventure. Three Go Home Through Friern Barnet.

'Not yet,' Lachlan says, belting himself in. 'Let me take one more gander at this place before we leave it. You see that smoke? Do you think that's her?'

Moira gives a little European cry. It makes Henry's heart jump. Straight out of *Fledermaus*. 'That's horrible,' she says.

'You think that's horrible,' Lachlan goes on. 'I'll tell you something more horrible. She didn't even want to be burned. Hated the idea. Always fancied a quiet corner of the Actors' Church in Covent Garden, or failing that Berkshire.'

Moira puts one hand to her mouth, stifling another little European cry. Henry catches her eye in the driving mirror. You've taken up with an animal, Henry's eye says. Happy now?

To Lachlan he says, just to be clear, 'I didn't know you could cremate a person who didn't want to be cremated.'

'If you're the only kin you can do what you like,' Lachlan tells him. 'Unless there's something written to the contrary. And she was too busy spending my money to put pen to paper. Assumed I'd carry out her wishes. A big mistake, in that case, to tell me she had no intention of carrying out mine.'

'Then you have your revenge.'

Lachlan is still looking out of the window, following the plume of smoke. 'I'll never have my revenge,' he says.

The windows mist over with Lachlan's bile. It's like having a ham Malvolio in the car, Henry thinks. It's not the old woman who should be lying in the Actors' Church, Covent Garden, it's Lachlan.

Moira drives for a while in silence, her face pushed forward squintily as though she is negotiating fog. If it looks like fog to her out there, Henry thinks, then why isn't she driving more slowly. Henry hates speed. He is frightened of it. Alarmed by everything, Henry is particularly alarmed by motor cars, wheels, motorways, accelerator pedals, brakes that don't work. This is why he has never owned a car himself. 'You a faggot?' a colleague's wife once asked him, back in his University of the Pennine Way days. It was her theory that only faggots didn't drive. Well, make that only faggots and Henry. All else aside, Henry's ideal ride would be in a battery-powered bath chair driven by Lachlan's stepmother, alive or dead. Crawling pace is fast enough for Henry. What's the hurry? Where's everybody rushing?

Crash me, Moira, is something else entirely. Crash me, crash me, Moira, while both our imaginations are concentrated on your thighs, is purely mental play, as abstract as a death wish, and has no bearing on his hatred of being thrown around in a tin-and-glass bubble travelling at the speed of light.

'Are you all right?' Moira asks him. She can feel him burning up behind her.

'I'm fine,' he says. 'I get a little car sick, that's all.'

'You should have travelled in the front.'

He searches for her in the mirror. 'I prefer it here,' he says. He wants to lock her gaze into his, on the other hand he doesn't want her taking her eyes off the road. 'Anyway, Lachlan's the one that needs looking after. He's had the harrowing day.'

'Oh, you needn't have worried about me,' Lachlan says. 'I'd have been happy in the boot. The open road holds no terrors for me.'

'Nor for me,' Henry lies.

Lachlan turns round to examine him. 'Then why are you holding on to the back of the seat, old man?'

'Would you like to take over the driving?' Moira asks him.

'No, no, I'm fine, honestly,' Henry assures her. He isn't going to tell her he doesn't drive. Enough that she now knows he's terrified. He doesn't need her to think he's a faggot as well.

'You're a keen driver yourself, then?' he asks Lachlan, getting the subject off himself.

'Was. Used to love it in the old helmet-and-goggle days. Even

74

did a bit of rallying in my time. Now it's just up and down, up and down.'

'From where to where?' Moira asks. Funny, Henry thinks, that she doesn't already know. Unless she's feigning ignorance. But then why would she do that?

'To hell and back,' Lachlan says.

'Doing what?' Henry asks. Funny that he too doesn't know and hasn't bothered to find out. Has Henry reached that age where he assumes everybody is like him, no longer with a place of work? Or does Lachlan simply give off the air of being too well connected to need regular employment, outside of flogging the family heirlooms.

'Hogwash.'

'Are you answering my question,' Henry asks, 'or telling me what you think of it?'

'That's what I'm in.'

'You make hogwash?'

'Don't make it, sell it. To farmers. That and other animal feeds.'

'So you drive a big truck?' Moira wonders.

'No fear. I don't deliver the actual feed. Never seen the stuff, wouldn't know it if I walked into a trough of it. I sell them the chemicals. And I've never seen those either. They buy out of a catalogue.'

'Like mail order,' Moira says.

'You've hit the nail on the head there. Soon will be mail order. Then that's me finished. Last of a dying breed. Ask yourself how many animal-feed salesmen you know.'

The car falls quiet while they think about it. Then Henry says, 'I don't know why but I'd have picked you for an antiques man myself.'

'Huh!' Lachlan says angrily. 'Shows, does it? Not surprised. I always did love beautiful things, but you don't always get the chance to live by what you love, do you?'

'You can say that again,' Henry says.

'You have to make do,' Lachlan says, chop-fallen, 'with the cards you're dealt. Antiques are my passion, I suppose because I was brought up with them, pigswill's my penance.'

'Penance for doing what?'

'Ah, that's another story. For being born, I suppose.'

The car falls silent again.

No, they're not close. Henry's impression, studying Moira in the mirror, is that they aren't a pair, not even a potential pair, else she would surely feel herself to be implicated in this last remark, shut out and made desolate by it, at the very least challenged by it into promising to make Lachlan's miserable penitential life better from this moment on. Granted, she's going too fast and changing too many lanes to kiss him, but a squeeze of his hand wouldn't be out of the question, or one of her slithery sideways glances. But Henry discerns nothing, hears not a heartbeat, sees not a flicker. They're not a pair, unless she's cleverer, unless they're both cleverer, than he takes them to be.

It's only when Moira drops them at their apartment block – for it's Lachlan's apartment block too, now – that Henry notices he's been in a BMW. Henry knows nothing about cars, and what he does know he wishes he didn't, but BMWs he recognises because that's all anyone drives around here. Anyone except a waitress, that is. A dented silver Datsun, such as you get when you call a minicab, one of those pitted vehicles that look as though they've driven through an ambush in the Balkans, that's what he thought he'd been in. What he can't decide is whether he'd have been more frightened had he known he'd been in a BMW.

There are two other things he can't decide. Whether Moira and Lachlan are a pair after all, so much not a pair do they seem determined to appear – barely a thank-you from Lachlan, who's a hand-kisser, surely, who you'd expect to slobber over any woman's hand given half a chance, let alone one who's sacrificed her day to the cremation of his stepmother. So how come not?

And what's the other thing he can't decide? Oh, yes. Whether the waitress could have bought the BMW out of the tips he's been leaving her.

'Hovis' Belkin! Christ!

Henry isn't left immediately to his own devices. First he has to decline Lachlan's offer of a dry sherry in the old lady's apartment. 'Hair of the dog?' Lachlan suggests while they're waiting for the lift, which strikes Henry as meaningless since they haven't had a drop yet, unless setting fire to somebody in the sticks whose express wish was to be buried whole in Covent Garden can be considered an intoxicant. Not to Henry, though. Henry is stone cold sober. And wants to lie on his bed with a cold compress pressed to his forehead – you can be sober and still have throbbing temples – and think about the waitress. Moira, yes he knows her name, but he still prefers the anonymity of waitress. Altogether, he wishes he hadn't encountered her in Lachlan's company today, whichever way one reads it. Nothing personal, but he could have done without the contamination of another party. He liked having her to himself. He was enjoying the evolution of the romance at his pace. Over tea and tips. He isn't ready yet to know her name.

And then that other name he would rather he didn't know or remember comes back to him. Belkin. 'Hovis' Belkin.

Henry has studiously avoided the memory of Osmond 'Hovis' Belkin since they shared a room at university, which hasn't been easy given how often photographs and appraisals of Osmond (no mention of the 'Hovis' in latter years) have appeared in newspapers since. But you can know and not know about someone you would rather forget. There is a special chamber of the mind in which you can lock away those not conjunctive to your wellbeing. Occasionally, you hear them hammering to be let out, so you simply turn up the volume of everything else. Now, courtesy of Lachlan Louis Stevenson, 'Hovis' Belkin is at large again in Henry's brain.

Thanks, Lachlan. And thanks, Moira, come to that. Because it took the two of them, didn't it. Always does. 'Hovis' Belkin and accomplice. But in fairness, is it *all* down to the swine-feed salesman and the waitress? Lying on his bed, fiddling with the keypad to the drapes – shaded light is what Henry needs, not day, not night – he admits there is a sense in which Osmond was already due for release. More than a sense. The truth is – and Henry cannot tell a lie – he has been having intimations of his old friend in recent times. Forced intimations.

A funny thing: when Henry thinks of Osmond he catches himself thinking of his father. Not Osmond's father, Henry's. Most people come associated, he knows that. You remember them in strings. Further proof that after a certain age you might as well kick up your heels, since nothing new is going to befall you; the patterns and prototypes are set in childhood and the same characters, or at least the same stories, go on recurring. Osmond Belkin, Lachlan Louis Stevenson – different men, same narrative. So what unites Osmond Belkin and Henry's father, who on the face of it had not a quality in common? Lying on the sumptuously quilted bed it is hard to believe was once his father's bed, Henry keys the fine steel nets to close and the drapes to remain infinitesimally parted. The technology allows for that. If Henry only understood the technology. One wrong button and the bed tilts and the chandeliers go on. That how his father liked it? In the end he settles for total blackout. With which the answer to his question presents itself. Himself. What Osmond Belkin and his father had in common was *him*, Henry. Say their names, say Dad, say Osmond, and Henry feels the same pain in the same organ, that's if there actually is an organ where Henry feels it. Is there a part of the body where shame resides? That's where they separately struck at him, anyway, in the organ of ignominy. Of course he knows he can't be trusted when it comes to mortification. His skin's too thin. And he's read too much *Jane Eyre*. Blows rain on Henry that were never intended to be blows at all. A badly aimed compliment can put Henry's eye out. Nonetheless, if you're mortified you're mortified. No point telling the wounded body that the cut it feels is not a cut at all.

And what exactly was it that Osmond Belkin and Henry's father did to Henry, that shames him now, so long after the events, even where no one can see him, in the enclosing all-consoling blackness of St John's Wood?

They devitalised him. They impugned his masculinity.

They called him a girl.

It is Henry's first day at grammar school, and he doesn't know how anything works. 'Are we allowed to go to the toilet?' he asks the boy next to him. 'Do you have to put your hand up?' 'What time is break?' 'Where *are* the toilets?' 'Are you supposed to write your name on the top of the page?'

The boy next to him is Osmond Belkin. 'How do I know!' he hisses the first time. The second time he kicks Henry under the desk. The third time he says 'Stop asking me dumb questions – you girl!'

Henry turns the colour of damson jam. In his satchel, football boots, a penknife with his initials on it – gifted to him by his grandmother – a box of pencils, razor-sharp, and rare cigarette packets for trading in the playground – the proofs of his little manliness. A new day for Henry. A new start. The world not pishing on him any more. Then slap – *you girl!*

Could anything be worse for Henry? Silly question. Something can always be worse for Henry. On this occasion, teacher-worse. Catching Henry with his hands clawing at his carmine face, and thinking him to be hiding mirth not misery, Mr Frister – 'Fister' Frister – as hair trigger as Henry himself, pulls Henry's ear – 'Something funny, sonny? Something you would like to tell the class about? No, never is, is there? That's what's funny, that nothing ever is.'

At which injustice and misprision the tears spring like miracles out of Henry's eyes. Unseen, unheard, he hopes. But not. Give up all hope, Henry, today. Seen they are by Osmond Belkin, who has girled him once, and who girls him now a second time by passing across the desk a hanky for Henry's fountain eyes.

Asthmatic, half-blind and top-heavy, with a loaf-shaped head (hence 'Hovis') and from a family in which experience of professional or personal failure was entirely unknown – or if known, never alluded to, the failure being sent overseas or thrown into a mental home – Osmond Belkin had his own social pressures to contend with. But by girling Henry when he did, he established an ascendancy over him which persisted throughout their school years and, more importantly for Osmond, won him the respect of other boys. Something schoolboys feel in their bones, power. Tyranny and cringing – that's what little boys are made of. Not that theirs was the sort of school that institutionalised cruelty. Henry did not become Osmond's fag, or otherwise make homoerotic virtue of his defeat. No, on the surface they appeared equals, grew to be friends and rivals, bunked off from games together, smoked when they should have been running cross-country, fought for academic honours – the only ones they valued – and came out, by the usual measures, all square. But the early damage never healed. Henry felt judged by Osmond, under an unflattering scrutiny which, with the pitiless clarity of the too easily hurt, he knew was never to be lifted unless it should turn out to be Henry who made the splash and not Osmond. Assuming it were to go the other way – as it now seems to Henry it was written in the stars it would – Osmond's early verdict would be vindicated. Henry was a girl – no disrespect intended to the other sex – Henry was a softie, Henry was a nothing.

Was it in the company of Osmond that Henry first began to formulate his theory of anterior social space, where everybody except him laid down the friendships and liaisons they would pick up again in the course of life proper? Probably not. The likelihood is that Henry was born feeling left out of it. This can happen when your name's down for the Baby Jesus crib and your mother holds you back. But Osmond certainly intensified Henry's conviction of exclusion, by virtue of his own genius for whatever is the opposite. Think of the word, Henry. Connectedness? Incorporation? Membership? Charm? Poor Henry – how do you call what you've never had?

They were prefects, fifteen, sixteen years of age, boys on the town if you can call being on the town wearing your school blazer with the lapels turned in and having your cap folded up in your trouser pocket like a torpedo. They were allowed into the centre of Manchester a couple of afternoons a week for research purposes, that's to say for going to the Central Reference Library where they snorted at each other across the silent desks, enraging the genealogists and destitutes tracing the whereabouts of their rightful inheritances – where has it got to, where has it gone, my future, my fortune, my happiness? – after being thrown out for which they thought they might just as well slip across to the Ceylon Tea House on Oxford Road for a smoke and a plate of yellow curry. Waiting for a table, Henry marvelled at Osmond's assumption of autocratic disdain, the easy contemptuousness with which he stood immovable in the path of leaving customers, making it difficult for the waitresses to move around him, and yet knowing that they'd give him a good table and serve him promptly despite, or was it because of, that. Henry watched and watched and couldn't work it out. Certainly Osmond had grown tall since he'd cooked Henry's goose for ever on their first day at school together, but he was still a loaf-headed boy with a fat neck and a bad cough. Is it presence? Henry wondered. Is it money, can they smell money on him? Osmond came from a dynasty of surgeons. The least eminent of Osmond's uncles and cousins, the black sheep of the family, had an OBE – so was it that? Did people subordinate themselves to Osmond Belkin, a schoolboy in a blazer, in case they one day ended up beneath his knife? Or was it just the way he wore that blazer? Still Henry watched and watched. On Osmond the maroon blazer with naff blue braiding was somehow transformed into a smoking jacket, he could have matched it with a cravat and got into anybody's tent at Henley. Why couldn't Henry make *his* blazer look like that? Why did Osmond's blazer give Osmond the appearance of a world-weary, twenty-five-year-old aesthete, while Henry's blazer made Henry look like an under-age biscuit-maker from Oldham? And why, although Henry was in truth the better chatter-up of waitresses, had been given lessons in it by his great-aunt Marghanita, shown how to make a virtue of his delicacy and shyness, like Jane Eyre, and knew how to lower his eyes and let his lashes flutter, why, despite all that, did Osmond who was altogether more boorish in his dealings with them, not even bothering to blow his smoke the other way when they came to ask him for his order, changing his mind without apology, being short with them over the state of the ashtrays though it was he who'd filled them – why, explain to Henry why, when it came to an out-and-out contest, he versus Osmond for the hand of any waitress in the restaurant, Osmond would either win it or make sure that Henry didn't?

'She likes you,' Osmond said to Henry, motioning at the girl who poured the tea, a willowy Sinhalese with long brown legs and eyes bigger than dates, at present pouring someone else's, but definitely looking their way.

'Shush!' Henry said, 'you'll embarrass her.'

'Embarrass *you* more like.'

'All right, shush you'll embarrass me.' Making a virtue of his debility, Henry allowed the lovely Sinhalese girl to see the colour play beneath the thinness of his skin. 'A woman appreciates it' – Marghanita's words – 'when a man comes apart for her.' So Henry came apart for her.

'More hot water for my friend,' Osmond called. 'And a cold towel.'

The girl approached their table and bent in places Henry did not know were bendable, and smiled at him. Him, not Osmond. 'Ceylon tea makes you hot,' she said. 'It cleans the pores.' Cleans *his* pores, not Osmond's.

'It's not the tea,' Henry dared to say.

And now she lets him see the colours which swim beneath the fineness of *her* skin.

'My friend would like to know . . . ' Osmond began.

'His friend would not like to know anything,' Henry interrupted, 'which he cannot ask for by himself.'

'So go on,' Osmond urged him. Grinning. Smoking. Blowing grinning smoke rings.

'So what's your name?'

The girl took longer than was necessary to rearrange their tea things. 'Yours first,' she said.

'Henry.'

'OK, I'm Sandra.'

'Shandra?'

'No, Sandra.'

'Sandra? You don't look like a Sandra.'

'Don't I? Well, that's my name. Sandra Weinglass.'

'Sandra Weinglass? From Ceylon?'

She laughed. 'Who said anything about Ceylon? I'm from Didsbury.'

'Wej,' Osmond whispered through his smoke. Back slang. Wej, Jew. Jew, Wej. Back slang and putdown. Because Osmond knows what Henry doesn't. 'She's Wej, you shmuck.'

One Wej is meant to recognise another Wej. It's in the genes. It's to help in the mayhem after the Cossacks have been through. Let me assist you, Wej to Wej, because no one else will. And then at last the obligation becomes a pleasure. Hi, you're Wej, I'm Wej. Let's dance, let's marry, let's have Wej babies. That's how it's supposed to work. Unless you're a shmuck. Unless you're a girl. You girl, Henry. And now Henry is so much of a girl – because you're not meant to confuse Didsbury with Colombo either –

that, all Marghanita's efforts notwithstanding, he is unable to proceed with his suit.

'You're blushing,' Osmond observes, laughing. 'You've gone all pink.'

Pink.

*Why don't you just stick pink ribbons in his hair and have done?*

Henry does not grow up to be a freedom fighter. He lets prisoners of conscience languish in foreign jails. He doesn't save the children, or the elephant, or the planet. But he is on the front line of the war against animadversions on another person's blushes. The beginning and the end of Henry's political system, his Social Contract: you don't tell a person he's gone pink, you don't make a person go pinker than he already is, if you have an ounce of humanity in you, you look the other way, be glad it isn't you, and shut your fucking mouth.

But that is not the end of it. Nothing is ever the end of it for Henry. A week later he turns up at a party at Osmond's house and is let in by the waitress. Sandra. Not waitressing tonight, oh no, but hostessing, at home, a helpmeet, a familiar, and God knows what else to Osmond.

'Hi, Henry.'

And Henry is so astounded, so confused, so put out, so utterly disarranged, that he never does find a way of asking whether Osmond had been back to ask her out, or had done it there and then, under Henry's burning nose, or had known her all along, known her well, known her intimately, even while he was encouraging Henry to make a girl of himself at the Ceylon Tea House.

Henry hasn't seen Osmond for thirty years, but if he were to pass him in the street today, on St John's Wood High Street say, or strolling by the boating lake in Regent's Park, Henry knows in the pit of his stomach that he would feel all the old inferiorities. Though Osmond Belkin has lived in Los Angeles for the whole time Henry hasn't seen him, on Mulholland Drive itself for all Henry knows, the eventuality of such a meeting is not as unlikely as it sounds. Like Henry, Osmond Belkin has quietened down – though where Henry has gone from scarce to invisible, Osmond has gone from extremely prominent to just a little less so. A film man, Osmond Belkin, as he always promised he would be. Producer, director – don't ask Henry, what's the career of 'Hovis' Belkin to Henry Nagel? But his health is not the best, and he has grandchildren he wants to see. Lots of grandchildren. Grandchildren, as Henry puts it to himself, coming out of his fundament.

Cruel, that Belkin should have beaten Henry at having families as well. But that's what happens when you get in first with the insult. Had Osmond Belkin not seized the advantage and established Henry as the failure of the two, would he ever have made it as a film-maker? Suppose Henry had thrown the first stone, calling Osmond 'fat boy' or 'loaf head' or, best of all, 'fatty four-eyes who can't breathe properly' – would it then have been he, Henry, who ended up with the three-swimming-pooled mansion and succession of beautiful wives to go with it, while Osmond languished teaching media studies at the University of the Pennine Way? Such are the eternal questions, centring on the arbitrariness of destiny, a man revolves in his head when the better part of his life is behind him and has amounted to nothing. But they are not now, and probably never were, germane to anything. What matters is that Osmond Belkin is known to be back in England, or known to be thinking of coming back to England, to see his children and his grandchildren among other reasons, and that his children and his grandchildren, some of them anyway, are bound by demographic likelihood to live in or around St John's Wood. Which means that any day Henry could run into him, walking his offspring, wheeling a pram or just jogging in the park with one, or maybe all, of his beautiful wives, and American spring-loaded trainers on his feet.

*     *     *

You liked him, though, didn't you, Dad?

*Did I? You'll have to remind me which one he was.*

The fat one with the loaf head. You liked him because he egged you on. You blew fire for him in the garden.

*I entertained a lot of your friends.*

No, but for 'Hovis' you went that little bit further. You bent nails for him too. And for him you tore the Manchester telephone directory into a hundred dancing girls.

*He must have been an appreciative audience.*

Oh, he was. He roared with laughter.

*Well then.*

Dad, he was taking the piss.

*Yeah, out of you!*

You bet out of me. Out of me for having a father who did what you did.

*I thought you said he enjoyed what I did.*

Think of it, Dad. His father was a surgeon. He had another idea of fathers. When I went to his house his father put on Brahms' Clarinet Quintet.

*So maybe he was envious of yours.*

Think that if you like. It hardly matters now anyway. But you played the fool for him. He paid, you jigged.

*You always had a queer way of explaining a good time, Henry. We had some fun together.*

So now you remember him.

*What I remember is the warped construction you put on everything. I can't explain. You're the intellectual. But it looked like jealousy to me. Maybe you were just jealous of everybody, Henry. Maybe you were jealous of your friend whatever his name was because he amused me. Maybe you were jealous of me because I amused him. What I don't understand is why you were so jealous of people who liked to enjoy themselves, considering how little value you attached to enjoyment. You explain that to me.*

He diminished you, Dad.

*You mean he diminished you.*
Same thing.

Since there's no knowing for sure what's happening between them, Henry has decided to proceed as though nothing is.

They're all on the lonely side, all three of them, that's sufficient explanation for everything. Not nice, not easy to swallow – Henry no more likes the idea of sharing his humanity with other people than he likes the idea of sharing the European waitress – but at least he can do something about the waitress: he can ask her out before Lachlan does, or before Lachlan does again.

And now Henry is in love.

He can't eat. There is an obstruction where the food should pass. He can't drink either, all fluids gathering in a dam halfway down his oesophagus. Intermittently the dam bursts, leaking acids into Henry's system. This is how you know you're in love when you're Henry's age. It feels like indigestion. So anyone observing Henry and Lachlan when they meet on the stairs would guess they were competing to see who could hit his own chest harder. Some mornings they do no more than burp at each other as they pass.

When Lachlan has Angus with him, the dog folds himself even tighter around Henry's leg, waiting for the aftershock of the convulsions which shake Henry's frame. For Angus, too, associates bad digestion with love.

But it's not Angus with whom Henry is in love. Tough on the dog, but love's cruel that way. More than ever Henry doesn't want Angus's hairs on him. He's got new clothes. He thought he had his dressing right before he came to live in St John's Wood. He was dressing into his age, he thought. Big loose cardigans, voluminous corduroys, though not of the farmer's sort, russet colours – greens, browns, ochres – becoming the autumn of his life and the profession he no longer enjoyed. But that's not how a man is supposed to look down here. In the shops on St John's Wood High Street Henry finds clothes that defy age. Not the tennis shorts, he hasn't gone that far. Italian shirts with deep collars suit him though, worn open to show a lot of sternum, to establish that his chest hairs haven't yet turned completely white, though that doesn't deter them in St John's Wood either. And he's in Valentino jeans – he, Henry, a man who has scorned denim all his life. And soft ankle boots with square toes. This, of course, for the daytime. For nightwear it's Armani, no questions asked. Midnight black, made of crêpy materials which flatter his bulk, the shirts creamy with high collars that make his head look as though it's buried in his shoulders, like his autochthonous neighbours in the Pennines – but that's the fashion. The shoulder bag he's still thinking about. It's a bit of a jump, the shoulder bag, for the son of a northern fire-eater. But he knows, watching men in their seventies and eighties even, parading arm in arm, braceleted and medallioned and shoulder-bagged – and these are the straight men, these are the husbands and fathers – that it's only a matter of time. Sad? Well, who can say. It's sad that a man has to lose his shape, that his abdomen has to thicken and that his joints must grow stiff. But you have to wrap it all up in something. And what's the alternative now that at sixty you are still up and about, however precariously? How are you supposed to look? There's need of a new couture, without doubt, to meet the new demand for geriatric chic, but until it comes along Henry has to settle for looking like one of the grandfathers of the Mafia.

And the waitress seems to like it.

Moira Aultbach, that's her name. Sounds better when you run the two halves together. Still not Elisabeta-Adelheid of Saxe-Coburg, but an improvement on just Moira. She gives Henry her card when he puts the proposition to her at his favourite pavement table. Yes, she'll go out with him, but he ought to have her number, just as she ought to have his, in case either needs to change the time. That's good: she's put flux on the table.

Everything swirls in Henry's head. She flushes, seeing him go morally at the knees, pulling at her lopsided hair as though she is trying to centre it. Henry hopes that doesn't mean her overall crookedness was purely predatory and that she is going to straighten herself out for him now they've fixed a time and a date. Except that they might not have fixed a time and a date, which makes him feel heady again.

He isn't sure how the etiquette of tipping is changed by what he's done. Do you go on tipping a waitress you're taking out? And if you do, oughtn't you to tip her more? But how much more *can* Henry tip? A tenner for a Viennese coffee's about the limit, isn't it? Just this once, as a sort of foretaste of the munificence she can look forward to, he gives her twenty. 'Save your legs,' he says.

She smiles at him and shakes her head. 'Take it back,' she says. 'Today the coffee is on me.'

Can a waitress do that? It's only when he is across the road in Alfredo's, trying on belts, that it occurs to Henry to recall that the patisserie is called Aultbach's.

So he's been tipping the proprietress. Is he a girl or what?

# FOUR

She's still married.

'I don't know if that puts you off,' she says.

'Why should it?' Henry asks.

'Well, some people don't want the baggage. Aultbach's no problem. We get on fine, he's got a girlfriend, and we both felt it would be a shame to break up a successful partnership.'

'You mean the marriage?'

'No, the patisserie.'

'He still works there?'

'He makes the patisseries.'

'The strudel too?'

'Everything.'

'Well, it's good strudel,' Henry allows.

'Everything Aultbach does is good,' she tells him. 'He even made a good husband for a while.'

Henry has never been sure about women who invoke their husbands by their surnames. He can't quite put his finger on the offence. Cuteness? The dysfunctional family version of talking about yourself in the third person? But in this instance he is more forgiving. He likes the faint trace of a lisp with which Moira pronounces Aultbach, the rabbinic lapping of the t.

'So what changed him?' he asks.

'I changed him. Or rather I changed me.'

'What did you do?'

'I fell in love with one of my students –'

'Hang on,' Henry says, feeling that she's pinched his line, except that he didn't exactly 'fall in love' with his students, not Henry, more, well, whatever it was he did. 'Hang on, are you telling me you're a teacher on top of everything else?'

He thinks he might be disappointed. He doesn't want her to be a teacher. He's done teachers.

'What everything else?'

'Well, waitressing and proprieting and looking beautiful and everything.'

She inclines her head. Why thank you, Henry. 'Just pastry-making,' she says. 'I teach it a couple of nights a week at a college in Camden. That's how I met Aultbach. He was a student too.'

Henry is relieved – she isn't a teacherly teacher, then – but also astonished. 'That's amazing,' he says. 'My mother taught cakes.'

'She was a pastry chef?'

'God no. She wasn't any kind of chef. She didn't know how an oven worked. She just showed people how to decorate cakes.'

'Ah,' Moira says, letting Henry into a world of precise distinctions and hierarchies, 'cake decoration is another thing again.'

'I know,' Henry says, quickly pulling an anti-grandiosity face on his mother's behalf. 'It was an entirely unconnected activity. Her skills began and ended with decoration.'

'You're saying she didn't bake at all?'

'Not so much as a biscuit. She had been brought up to stay out of the kitchen. Couldn't even remember where it was most days. Then out of the blue she discovered she had this talent for armatures and icing. I had already left home so I'm not witness to what exactly happened, but family legend has it that she was expecting friends round for tea and dropped the cake she'd bought. As there was no time to go out and buy another, her range of choices was limited to doing without cake altogether or repairing the one she'd damaged, in which latter course –'

'*In which latter course!*'

'I was an academic. Not your sort of teacher. Nothing useful. That's how we used to speak. *In which latter course* she succeeded to such effect, in her view, that it looked a damn sight better when she'd finished with it – the cake, I'm still talking about – than when she'd bought it. It was like a blinding light. Suddenly she wasn't frightened of food. The next day she enrolled in a class and what seemed like a week later she became a teacher.'

Moira points her face. 'It takes longer than that to train as a pastry chef,' she would have Henry know. 'Almost as long as it takes you to finish a sentence.'

Henry rides with the compliment. 'I'm sure it does. But my mother was in a hurry. My father was leaving her alone a lot and she needed an interest.'

'What was he doing?'

Always hard for Henry, this. 'Well, he began life as an upholsterer. Then someone burnt his workshop down and he became a fire-eater.'

'He didn't!'

'He did.'

'Professionally?'

'Well, in the sense that he called it his profession. But not in the sense that he earned a living from it. And don't ask whether it was he who burnt his workshop down. The police looked into that. It wasn't. His bookkeeper burnt the workshop down. A coincidence, though, I grant you. But then life is coincidence. Look at you and my mother.'

She does, falling silent for a moment, apparently not certain what she thinks about coincidence in this particular.

They are in a dark panelled booth in a Hungarian restaurant in Soho, eating dumplings. A heavy *ancien régime* meal had seemed just the ticket to Henry. He wanted to nail her down. Eat a light meal with a woman on your first date, and she'll be polishing off seconds with someone else before the night's over. Toast her in ox blood, bog her in goulash and dumplings, and chances are — if she lives — she's yours for ever.

'So you were telling me about your life,' Henry says, trying to call her back from wherever unwelcome synchronicity has taken her.

'Was I?' She is rooting in her furry bag for a handkerchief. She must have a collection of furry bags, Henry thinks, for this one seems unfamiliar to her, a thing of depths she has never previously plumbed, full of objects she appears not to recognise. Henry too believes the hairs to be longer and more quilled than on the one she carried at the crematorium. Anteater? Aardvark? Or is he confusing the bag with the way she is snuffling through it?

'You were telling me what happened when you fell in love with your student.'

'With Aultbach?'

'No, the other one.'

She dabs her nose, as though she is staunching a wound, with the little handkerchief she has finally found but which she gives the impression of never having seen before. 'Which other one?'

'Ah,' Henry sighs. So there's a list! He feels fluttery in the stomach suddenly, as though his insides have fallen away. Which is extraordinary, considering how much he's eaten. But retrospective jealousy – a list without him on it – does this to him. 'Well, let's just stay for the moment,' he says, offering to be urbane, 'with the one who caused Aultbach to stop being a good husband.'

'Michael. He was Greek. Very beautiful. But very dependent. He wanted a mother more than he wanted a lover.'

'And you?'

Another dab, pitched somewhere between nostalgia and provocation. 'I just wanted Michael.'

'Hence Aultbach's . . .'

'No, Aultbach didn't mind. He has very modern views, Aultbach. He would sell me into slavery for a night and not bother as long as I'm there to open the patisserie in the morning.'

'You call that modern?'

'He isn't possessive.'

'So what happened?'

'I crashed his car.'

I knew it, Henry thinks. I knew I should have called for that

93

taxi. 'I see,' he says. 'Presumably you were going to see Michael at the time.'

'No. I had Michael with me. But Michael wasn't the problem. The problem was the car. Aultbach had just bought it. A brand-new lemon Porsche with personalised number plates. He cried like a baby when he saw what I'd done to it.'

'And Michael?'

'He also cried. I broke both his legs. Did I tell you he was a footballer?'

Henry opens wide his eyes in alarm. 'Stop,' he says. 'I'm not sure that I'm in the right league for you. I don't do cars. I don't do football. I don't do personalised number plates. I don't do slavery. I don't even do pastry. In a few months I will be eligible for a senior railcard. All I can offer are cut-price trips to the seaside. Shall we call a halt to it now, before pity enters?'

She twists a smile at him and puts a hand on his wrist – part placatory, part flammable. Henry likes and fears the size of her hand, half as big again as his own; he also likes and fears the weight of her jewellery: a gold bangle he hasn't seen before, a huge silver watch with a third of its face scooped out moonily, not unlike hers, and a row of rings she presumably removes when she is waitressing. Though Henry loves a woman to have a past, sometimes a past can be too much for you. He's too old. It had to happen, and now it has. Whatever the jingling weight of her jewelled hand on his wrist says to the contrary, he is past it.

'What's age?' she asks.

'Age is what kills you,' Henry says. 'That and your driving.'

She slaps his hand. Naughty boy.

And in that second Henry goes from wondering whether he is up to it to wondering whether he *wants* to be up to it.

The old faint Henry heart. There's something wrong with his machinery. Always has been. His cogs slip. At any time in a friendship or an amour the reason for proceeding will suddenly escape him. Decency requires that you go on, he knows that. You can't keep walking out in the middle of things. But then if he does go on, there will be that dire sensation of pointlessness afterwards, of spirit expended to no explicable purpose. Nothing to do specifically with sex, any of this. Henry is not a tristesse merchant. If anything, he understands better after sex why he has bothered than he does after almost any other activity. At least in sex there's sex. But what is there in friendship again? What's that for?

He is not his father's son. *You never know when you'll need a friend, Henry.*

Don't you, Dad? I rather thought it was the other way round, that your friends always knew when they needed you – which was all the time. Who was that blind old bastard who got you to walk him half a mile to the Variety Home every morning for fifteen years, promising he'd leave you his ceremonial origamist's robe, then made you pay a thousand quid for it on his deathbed?

*Seven hundred and fifty.*

And how come you stayed on good terms with the bookkeeper who burnt your workshop down?

*Harris? He didn't do it deliberately. He was upset.*

And what about your Austin A40?

*That he did burn deliberately.*

But you stayed his friend.

*He was still upset.*

And Finkel?

*What did Finkel do wrong?*

He tried to steal your wife, Dad.

*This from you?*

I never stole. I borrowed.

*Finkel too borrowed.*

Yeah, your life savings.

*Well, that's better than your wife.*

His mother, on the other hand, was like him. She tired of people. After a brief intimacy she couldn't see the point of them. Company gave her migraines. It's very likely, Henry thinks, that she couldn't see the point of him in the end. Is that possible? Can a mother run out of interest in her child? Henry suspects it happens all the time. But that doesn't mean he's happy about it in his own case. If he became uninteresting to his mother, wasn't that her fault? Hadn't she *made* him uninteresting? Her Jane Eyre boy. Of course he bored her. Who wants a Jane Eyre boy? But she should have thought of that sooner.

Heart-heavy with ox blood, goulash and self-reproach, Henry focuses on the positive aspects of the waitress. Her custard hair, her asymmetric looks, the something ironical about those demure pearl earrings, the way she laps the t in Aultbach, the fact of her still being married to Mr Aultbach, the feelings she had for Michael – 'Michael, I wanted Michael' – her red-and-gold hands, nicely aged, which he imagines gripping the wrists of the men she teaches in her kitchen – this is the way to beat a batter, not like that, like this – her spiked shoes, the thought that she might be carrying on with Lachlan. Then he invites her back to his place.

Still doing it. Senior railcard in the mail and he is still asking women back to his place.

Is he mad or what? Was he always mad?

At a sherry party at the closing of the first day of his new job, his first job, his only job, at the Pennine Way College of Rural Technology (later to be a polytechnic, later still to be a university, but always a tech in Henry's heart), Henry asks the wife of his head of department (Liberal Studies – so why not?) to go back to his place. It's only when she astonishes him by agreeing that he remembers he doesn't have a place.

Maybe she knew that.

He escorts her out, under the Pennine moon, kisses her clumsily, then says, 'Now what?'

'You're asking me?'

A difficult one for Henry. What's worse – pretending to have lost desire, or admitting to not having a place? He does neither. He suggests they spend the night in nature.

'Out here?'

'Not out here exactly, more out there.' He points to where the moors begin, just beyond the library. The advantage of a moorland tech.

That's when she astonishes him by agreeing again.

And that's also when Henry first realises how utterly miserable everybody's wife is.

'How old are you?' she asks him.

'Twenty-four.'

'Do you know how old I am?'

'Thirty-four?'

'Forty-four.'

'You'd never think that,' Henry says.

She spreads her jacket under her. 'Thank you. When you're my age, how old will I be?'

Henry thinks about it. 'Sixty-four.' Then feels he ought to add, 'but I'll be forty-four.'

'And who will be sitting on my jacket with me then?'

'Probably lots of people,' Henry says.

'People?'

'Men. Lots of men.'

She begins to cry, or at least to do something that reminds him of crying. 'So that's what I've got to look forward to, then, is it? Being a whore in my sixties. A whore on a moor.'

'Who said anything about being a whore?' Henry says. 'You don't feel you're being a whore now, do you?'

'Of course I do. Isn't that what you've brought me here for?'

'No,' Henry assures her.

'You've brought me here because you respect me?'

'Yes, actually.' Something tells him not to add, and because I respect your husband.

'It's a funny way of showing respect, Mr Nagel. Sitting me in this damp.'

'Call me Henry.'

'I'm not sure if I *can* call you Henry.'

'Why's that?'

'Because my husband's name is Henry.'

Of course it is! Henry wonders if he ought to have thought about this earlier. Tactless of him, making love to the wife of someone who shares his name. And it isn't as though he didn't know she was married to a Henry. He, the other Henry, was Henry's tutor at university, some would have said his mentor, maybe even – though this might be stretching it – his friend. It's thanks to the other Henry that Henry has landed this job.

Tonight is the first time, however, that he has met the other Henry's wife. A nicety which, by the subtleties of Henry's reasoning, removes all moral obstacles.

'Then call me Mr Nagel, or just Nagel, if that makes you more comfortable,' Henry says.

'I can't call you Nagel. Sounds like some Jew in a Bloomsbury novel.'

'I am a Jew in a Bloomsbury novel.'

She peers at him in the dark. 'All the more reason.'

'Don't call me anything in that case.'

He puts his arms round her and kisses her ear. She gives a little shudder. 'I don't like that,' she says. She has long breasts. Not full, but elongated.

'You feel lovely,' Henry whispers.

'I see,' she says. 'So this is to be one of those straight-to-business nameless fucks, is it?'

'Well, it won't be if you tell me your name,' Henry says.

'Jane.'

Henry feels for her in the dark. 'You have exquisite breasts, Jane,' he says.

'Oh God, no,' she says, fending him off. 'I can't have you

calling me Jane, not while you're weighing my breasts. Henry does that.'

'Which?'

'Which breast?'

'No, which don't you want me to do – weigh your breasts or call you Jane? Which is it your husband does?'

'I think that's strictly between me and Henry, Henry, don't you?'

'Of course it is,' Henry agrees, remembering the marriage vows. Let no man put asunder. 'Absolutely is. I'm just trying to ascertain, between us, whether it's the Jane or the weighing of the breasts that's the problem.'

'Both.'

'So neither would be permissible even without the other?'

'That's too long a sentence and too complicated an idea. Why don't you just try me, Mr Nagel?'

He weighs her breasts.

'Stop,' she says, pulling herself free of him. 'Please stop that.'

'Sorry, Jane,' he says.

'Stop,' she says, 'I'd much rather you didn't call me that. What I think would be best is for you to have your way with me quickly and in silence and then to drive me home.'

Henry hasn't the heart to tell her that he doesn't have a car.

Older women, Henry. Older women, invariably attached. Invariably having to go home to another man. Borrowed older women. Explain that.

He can. He doesn't want the responsibility. 'Want' might not be the best word. He can't *handle* the responsibility. And he isn't certain of his own judgement. If they're older that means they have the wherewithal to make an informed choice and to take that burden away from him. It must also mean, *ipso facto*, that they are durable. And if they're attached that means someone other than him desires or has desired them, which confirms and vindicates, or at least seconds, his interest in them.

Not very courageous, as Henry is the first to accept. And in practice not very nice. But the diffident never are very nice. He'd have been a sweeter man altogether, Henry, kinder, more pleasant to be with, more generous in the aftermath, had he known what he wanted and grabbed it single-mindedly. Like his father, with a second wife in St John's Wood, and possibly a third and fourth, for all Henry knows to the contrary, somewhere else. So certain was his father of himself, so indifferent to what anybody else thought of his preferences, he was prepared to be seen taking Rivka Yoffey to the Midland in broad daylight, a woman with a dress down to the ground and a wig that looked as if it had been ripped off a drunk. Would Henry have risked being espied squiring Rivka Yoffey, who met two of his essential stipulations, after all, in that she was both durable and otherwise accounted for? He feared not. Particularly if there was the remotest chance of Osmond Belkin – the fly in Henry's ointment from way back – being the espier.

But it wasn't only because he lacked certainty in all matters pertaining to the heart that Henry needed a pre-existing second opinion about a woman. It was also because he doubted his capacity to look after anybody, to be 'there for her', in contemporary parlance, to bear the burden of making her happy until death did them . . . Death being the hardest part. Though even in the matter of helping out should she cut her finger or get something in her eye Henry knew himself to be unreliable. Too squeamish. Unfitted to be of use to anybody in discomfort, let alone in pain. If another man were on the case then the other man could take care of the problem – the wound, the fly, death; for they were all on the same continuum. Take care of it practically and emotionally. *Face* it. Henry sometimes thought that if he could only reconcile himself to death, as a fact of his life, then he would be better able to accept it as a fact of someone else's. Until then, he was in no position to commit. Only to borrow. Women died, therefore Henry could do nothing for them.

Looking back, Henry can't imagine how he could have organised this aspect of his moral history differently. Maybe had he not stayed teaching in the Pennines so long, he would have outgrown his morbidity. 'What are you doing burying yourself up there?' friends in fairer places used to ask him. 'You're supposed to be a life man.' This an ironic reference to the course entitled Literature's For Life which Henry obdurately ran while his colleagues in Liberal Studies and then Media Studies and then Women's Studies were shedding the lot, both Literature *and* Life, in favour of the frost of theory. 'We all do death our own way,' was Henry's reply. 'They teach it; I only live it.' But the real answer to the question – 'What are you doing burying yourself up there?' – was 'Rehearsing'. He had, after all, to get reconciled to being buried somewhere. Face burial, and you can face death. So yes, he was running through his lines.

'No motion has she now, no force / She neither hears nor sees / Rolled round in earth's diurnal course / With rocks and stones and trees' – those were the lines he was running through.

And of course, 'The rest is silence.'

Not by nature a nature man, Henry: he feared what he had in common with rocks and stones and trees no less than he feared the humanity he shared with text-messagers and honkers. No motion have they now, no force – fine if you're a rock, but if you're Henry the thought of possessing neither force nor motion (notwithstanding that he has forced nothing of more moment than the lock on his briefcase, and moves, when he moves at all, only very slowly) freezes the little blood you still have. Getting away, coming south earlier, would only have been a postponement of the problem. Whereas so long as he stayed, who knows – perhaps he would learn to love the forceless rock he was destined to become. So he watched the seasons change, impatient with the summer because that was easy, feeling the earth warm beneath him, standing outside his plain-faced pittance cottage like a fieldsman in the early evening, enjoying the sun sinking into the Pennine embrace, cosying into the valleys, making even shadows things of hope. Lovely while it lasted – children's singing coming from the next village, skipping from hill to hill, a radiance of sound no less than light – but no help with death, no preparation, not for Henry. Whereas the winter, which came soon enough, God knows, and hung on twice as long as any winter anywhere, smashed every illusion of happy perpetuity. Better to be in town, drowned by traffic, pestered by the poor, than to have these vistas of nothingness, rolling moorlands which mock time because time has made no impression, unless you call a chimney or a shoe factory an impression. Now if Henry could make a friend of *this*, Henry would be saved; and so could take himself a woman his own age, with no strings attached, and promise to look after her until death took them both away. And lie with her, thereafter, like two pencils in a pencil box, for ever and ever and ever.

Until the Resurrection, when Henry would rise again.

The thing about older women once you've reached Henry's age is that there aren't any.

What happens, Henry has discovered, is that you go on thinking of women of a certain age as 'older', go on entertaining the idea of an 'older' look – nice little collection of shrewd lines beneath the eyes, wonderful resolution of the mouth despite some wobbling of the chin, long teeth, sad neck, striated bosom – regardless of how old you are yourself. A wonderful provision of nature, this, for bamboozling lovers of mature women such as Henry – who would otherwise be in despair – into believing that nothing has changed.

What you do have to be careful of, though, as a man of almost sixty, is mentioning your preference for older women while looking into the eyes of a woman of forty-five.

Henry is pleased with himself for not making any such blunder with Moira.

And yet it's true. She *is* the older woman. He looks at her sitting, with her legs crossed and her mouth skewed, on the edge of what he thinks is meant by an ottoman – fancy his father having knelt at the feet of a woman who owned an ottoman! – and for all the world he's the baby of the two. It's as she said to him over goulash at the Happy Hungarian, 'What's age? You're as old as you feel, Henry,' and Henry feels he hasn't been born yet.

He would like to lick her face. She is the colour of banana and limes. A glacial yellow, like the Baltic Sea in spring, he fancies, though he has never been there. Her profile like a ski slope, a smooth gently sloping ride but for the two camel bumps in her nose. He hasn't asked her where precisely she's from yet. You don't do that with people who speak perfectly good English and aren't carrying baskets of yams on their head. He never liked it at school. So where did your parents originate, Nagel? Poland? The Ukraine? Stetlsburg? St Anne's Pier? But he knows she's from the old country. The two are almost synonymous for Henry – older and from the old country. Some people will only look forward. It's recommended, particularly after the twentieth century. Not Henry. Henry doesn't like what he sees forward. Backward is better. Backward has happened. And the old and the old country are the proof of it.

She's going to sort him out. He can tell from the way she has started to edge a look at him, giving him the three-quarters profile of her bumpy nose. As though she knows it's not going to be easy, but considers herself the woman for the job.

'You were quite strange with Lachlan coming back from the crematorium,' she tells him.

He is pacing the Persian carpet. Like a cat with sticky pads. A step at a time, not bringing down his full weight, hoping she'll take the hint and keep her voice low. Lachlan is next door. The walls are thick, but what if Lachlan's got his ear to a glass? It was a risk bringing her here. His fingers had fumbled the keys in the locks. Nerves. He hadn't wanted Lachlan coming out on to the corridor and seeing them. Inviting them in for a snifter.

'Was I? Strange how?'

'You don't seem to like him, yet you went to the crematorium.'

'He asked me. He said there was not a soul on earth but him to applaud her into the flames. I could hardly refuse an appeal like that. There won't be a soul on earth to applaud me. Then you turned up. I thought *that* was strange.'

'How could I not turn up? I knew her.'

Ah. She knew her. Nothing to do with Lachlan. It was the old lady she knew. Why hadn't he thought of that? Would have saved him heartache. But then again . . .

'So if Lachlan knew you knew her, how come he asked me?'

'He didn't know I knew her. Just as I didn't know about him. She'd always told me she had no one.'

'Ha! Well, you can see what she meant.'

She narrows her eyes at him.

Henry narrows his back. 'So you met him for the first time at the crematorium?' he continues.

'No. At her apartment. I went round, as usual, to deliver her pastries, and discovered that the poor woman had died.'

'You deliver pastries?'

'Only to her. She used to have tea every morning at the patisserie. Then she wasn't able to make it across the road any more. Her hips went. We were fond of her. She behaved like an aristocrat. She had a rude word for everybody in the neighbourhood. And she loved our cakes. So once she couldn't come to us we took our cakes to her. Lemon tart every Tuesday. *Millefeuille* for the weekend. She had a *millefeuille* only the day before she died.'

'You're telling me that the sensual pleasures go on until the end? I can't decide if it helps me to know that. I'd always imagined they fell away, bit by bit, so that you didn't mind or didn't notice you were going. Just think – she's probably lying there, dry-mouthed, missing *millefeuille* even as we speak.'

She shakes her head. 'Hardly. We burned her, remember. But what is it with you, Henry? What's this death thing?'

'An old lady has just died. My neighbour.'

'I bet you'd barely spoken to her.'

'How little is barely?'

'Did you know her name?'

He thinks about it. 'Norma Jean.'

'Did you know her name *before* the cremation?'

'Do you have to know someone's name to mourn them?'

'You're in mourning for her, are you?'

'Yes. No. Listen, what is this? You think I'm affecting something I don't feel?'

'I think you're wallowing, yes.'

It's a bit cheeky, he thinks. Never mind how well do you have to know someone before allowing her death to get to you, how long do you have to know someone before you allow her to accuse you of wallowing? Longer than this.

She comes over to him and puts her face close to his. He expects her to give off a smell of limes and she does. He expects a slight Baltic chill to blow off her also, which it does. But he doesn't expect her to put her hands up to his cheeks and then to take him by his ears. And that too she does.

'You need a bit of straightening out, fellow-my-lad,' she says.

'Do I?'

'You most certainly do, yes.'

'And you reckon you know someone in the neighbourhood who can do it?'

'I most certainly do, yes.'

Whereupon Henry kisses her.

Which Moira takes to be assent.

But look, she's also fun to be with. She shows him around St John's Wood, even the parts he knows, telling him tittle-tattle, who owns that shop, who lives there, walking him into shop doorways where she feels him up, the minx, or getting him to ride the deep chaste escalators in St John's Wood tube station with her, up and down like hooligans, except that hooligans don't stop to admire the bronze lights and the arches and the echoing flagstones and the coats of arms – 'Look, Henry, isn't it beautiful in here, don't you love it? it's like being in a ship' – making it an adventure for him, getting him to loosen up, to express enthusiasm, to love what's close to him, what he can have rather than what he can't. Sometimes, if they are out and Henry is being Henryish – huffy, heart-burned, mawkish, morbid – she opens her mouth and shows him that she hasn't swallowed her food. Look, Henry! Like a child. Or like someone entertaining a child. She does it once when Henry is arguing with a waiter. And another time when he bumps into someone he vaguely knows from the building and takes too long getting rid of him. Behind the person's back – Look, Henry! She likes revealing herself to him in this way, taking him by surprise, coming back from the ladies room looking elegant, for example, clip-clop in her stilettoes, and then showing him that her mouth is full of food. It is meant to make him laugh. To render him helpless with embarrassment and mirth. And sometimes it does. Just not always.

One evening, at the theatre, she opens her jacket and shows him a breast. God knows who else sees. This gesture is more to rouse him than to make him laugh, but she isn't afraid of blurring the distinctions. Coming down a staircase in a house to which they have been invited, as dinner guests, she raises her skirt and shows him she is wearing no underwear. A glacial blur. He gasps. Then she opens her mouth which is still full of food from dinner. She loves it that he is utterly confused, frightened of what she might do next. In Regent's Park with him, she gets him to take a bench immediately opposite to hers. Then she opens her legs. By now he doesn't expect her to be wearing pants.

'My God, Moira,' he cries, looking away. 'There are children about!'

'Yes, you,' she says.

He doesn't know her. Never seen her in his life before. He quits the bench in what he takes to be a natural manner, walks towards the lake, engrosses himself in duck life. Swans, herons, Canada geese. Fascinating. When he returns she flashes him again.

She has coaxed him back into the car, promising not to go over thirty, even on the motorway. Hitting eighty she tries to fish his member out of his Valentino jeans. 'These are too tight,' she says.

'They're what's fashionable,' he tells her, 'on older men.'

'You're not an older man. Look at that.'

'Don't you look at anything but the road,' he says.

'I can do both,' she tells him. 'I'm a woman. I'm multi-tasking.'

'Then slow down and put my dick back.'

'I'd rather go faster and take it out.'

'It's not worth the risk. Not for old sperm.'

She sidewinds him a look. Who was talking about sperm. But she has to put him right about one thing. 'Sperm doesn't age, Henry. Sperm renews itself.'

'Mine doesn't. Mine's old man's sperm. Old wine in an old bottle. It's tired. It even looks tired.'

'This'll perk it up,' she says, accelerating.

He searches for something to hold on to. But there is only his seat belt. 'Moira, I beg you to slow down! Remember what you did to Michael.'

'Michael? Who's Michael?'

'The Greek.'

'I know no Greek.'

And now his dick is out. Old and petrified, but out.

See!

She's showing him. Things are not the way they convention-ally seem. He's been pushing, trying to get her to stay the night with him, trying to get her to commit, fall for him, become his mistress, all that sixties and seventies stuff; now, at eighty miles per hour on the M1, she is demonstrating that it isn't always he who's asking and she who's saying no.

'If you're so frightened,' she asks him, 'why's your cock like that?'

'It's how I show fear.'

She swerves suddenly across three lanes, as though she's got a puncture, and effects a controlled career into the hard shoulder. 'Then let's rid you of your fear,' she says, turning off the engine and unbelting herself.

He doesn't know whether to open or to close his eyes. 'You can get arrested for just looking at a map here,' he says. 'God knows what sentence a blow job carries.'

She sidewinds him that look again. 'What makes you think you're going to get a blow job?'

The tease she is!

He puffs out his cheeks. 'Which are you trying to do, Moira,' he says, 'scare to me to death or disappoint me to death?'

'Neither and both,' she laughs. *Both*, the h almost silent, the t protrusive, tapping at his nerve endings.

Then she's off, out into the traffic again.

Henry closes his eyes.

But this is how she likes him – full of trepidation. Never knowing what she's going to do, how she is going to shame or confound him, next. He is perfect for her. Heart-in-his-mouth Henry.


'What are you so frightened of, Henry?'

How many times has he heard that said in his long life? It was the way every relationship with a woman ended. 'What is it you fear is going to happen to you, Henry?' Though the woman, of course, would have told you the relationship was already ended. Hence the question, since it appeared to be Henry's fear that always ended it.

What was he supposed to say? Until I can face that I am earth and will be returned to earth — and you the same — I cannot continue to go out with you? I cannot risk your cutting your finger?

It wasn't as though he went out with them exactly anyway. Too risky, a man in his position, and the women married to someone else. He snuck, as they said in those American novels Marghanita had persuaded him to study, but which he isn't quite so stuck on now — he snuck up, snuck off, snuck around, and then snuck home. The moors were good for this. Would have been better had he owned a car, but it added to the romance to walk a little. Eat sandwiches by a little brook. Seek shade in summer under a tree, if you could find a tree. Climb to a water tower inscribed to a local engineer, where you could kiss and have plenty of warning if anyone was coming. Quite a nature boy he became in his first years at the Pennine Way College of Rural Technology, or whatever it was then called, considering what a nature boy he wasn't. Entwined as they were with the heart, with *his* heart anyway, he even grew to love the moors and to find a sort of consolation in their antique persistence. Nearly, nearly it made sense to live obscurely here and to die unremembered. Nearly there was nobility in it.

But when that didn't work, or when it rained, he called a taxi and snuck away, scarfed-up and companioned, in that. Lunch in a quiet pub, not a poly pub — yes, it was a poly now — on the Yorkshire side. Love over pie and ale. And sometimes a room.

Lying under wordwormed beams, Lia Spivack (Henshell Spivack's wife) had a go at getting him to roar like a tiger. Grrrrr, Henry. She clawed his chest. Bit his neck. Grrrr, Henry, grrrr. He couldn't do it. Stiff bastard.

'I'm no good at animals,' he told her.

'Not even a snake in the grass?' she said, not yet retracting her claws.

He knows when he's upset a person, Henry. But he also knows

when someone has upset him. 'A snake's a reptile not an animal,' he explained in a quiet voice, lighting them both a cigarette. In those days cigarettes were intrinsic to sex, regardless of how successful or unsuccessful the sex had been, no matter whether animal or human. Henry was so addicted to the combination he had to light himself a cigarette even after he'd finished merely thinking about sex. 'But look,' he added reasonably, 'if you want to rip me apart you can, it's just that I'm too self-conscious to make the noise. It could be a faith thing. I have a feeling we are prohibited from imitating whatsoever flyeth in the air and whatsoever creepeth on all fours, which must include tigers. It's one of the ways we knew we had put totemism behind us.'

'Bullshit, Henry. I'm from the same faith you are. I've got an uncle who's a rabbi. He did rabbit imitations for us when we were kids.'

'A rabbi who did rabbits? Well, a rabbit I am prepared to do.'

'Go on, then.'

So Henry, cute as a button, twitched his nose. But even that not convincingly.

'Considering how difficult you find it to shed your inhibitions,' Lia mused, blowing smoke into the rafters, 'don't you think it's surprising how easily you shed your trousers?'

Henry wants to say that sex has always been his only chance, the one area, for some reason he can't explain, where he can find a little ease. It's his theory that many men who have been thought of as predatory sexually have wanted peace, that's all, a period of relief, not from sexual tension, but from reserve. Did they all start out as blushers, Bluebeard, Don Juan, Casanova, Byron, did they all pink up the moment someone spoke to them? 'You girl, Casanova!' Did some eighteenth-century Venetian 'Hovis' Belkin set that whole shooting match in motion with a careless remark of that kind? 'You pansy, Giacomo!' After which no maiden on the Adriatic could count her virginity secure.

But to Lia, Henshell's wife – Henshell his second-best school friend after 'Hovis' – Henry wants to make a more simply factual rebuttal of her charge.

'I don't easily shed anything, Lia,' he says. 'It isn't true. And I am not a snake. If I did, if I were, if you knew me to be, why would you be here?'

She smiles at him. He has known her for years. Henshell's bird. Henshell was still in the sixth form when he started taking Lia out. The first of them to have a regular girlfriend. They teased him about it. Fancy going steady, fancy talking about engagement rings at his age. Bought the pram yet, Henshell? Opened an account at Mothercare? Got your pension plan sorted out? But secretly they envied him. He wasn't having to go out on the prowl every Friday and Saturday night. He had in regular supply what they found it difficult to get their hands on even intermittently. And Lia herself – forgetting the impersonality of the supply idea – was a treat for all their eyes, all except 'Hovis' Belkin's that is, for Belkin measured by a different standard, was already out of there in his imagination, gazing beyond far horizons, and set no store by local beauty. A beauty she was, though, Rubensesque, as undulant as water when she walked, always animated, black-eyed, with bright red swollen lips and bright red swollen tonsils to match, they joked, in allusion to the way she threw her head back when she laughed, and with a mind, of course, to whatever other use she put her throat to for lucky Henshell.

She smiles at him. Funny fellow, Henry. More serious than Henshell's other friends, she remembers, more hot and bothered, the least likely, had she been asked to prognosticate, to turn into her lover. But then she hadn't expected she would make a lover of any of them. Henshell was plenty, Henshell was enough for her, Henshell always would be enough for her, she thought, not imagining when she crept into his digs at Brighton and talked politics late into the night that she would one day be the wife of someone who owned six pharmacies and thought of nothing but the seventh. 'You were a biomolecular scientist with a heart once,

Henshell, you were going to make a significant pharmaceutical intervention into the Third World, now you sell shampoo.'

'And house you in undreamed-of luxury,' Henshell reminded her.

She smiles at Henshell's one-time friend. 'I'm bored, Henry,' she says. 'I'd be here, whether you were a snake in the grass or not. You could just as easily say that I'm the low one. I wouldn't fight you. We've all grown up to be not nice.'

'Not nice is another thing again. I resent the suggestion that this is what I do – serially.'

'That's your reputation, Henry.'

'Where?'

Her smile turns into a laugh. Not the old swollen tonsil laugh. Long gone, all that. 'Where's where?' She makes a flamboyant gesture with her arms, all breasts, like a heroine of the French Revolution on the barricades, taking in this little everywhere. 'Wherever you are talked about.'

Tough one, for Henry. *Wherever you are talked about.* It almost doesn't matter what they say, does it, so long as you are talked about as universally as *wherever you are talked about* sounds as though you're talked about. From the mountains to the sea, wherever men and women gather to talk about Henry . . . Choke on that, 'Hovis' fat-head Belkin.

But no, in the end it does matter if all they're saying is that Henry is a dope who drops his pants – what was her expression? – sheds his trousers – without compunction. Not nice for his parents to get wind of. Not nice for his mother particularly. Not nice for his grandmother who thought she'd slain the curse of North Manchester man which had been laid upon her family. Not nice for Marghanita, who wouldn't want to think that what she nipped in the bud the night he carried her cocktail shoes in Wilmslow was nothing but serial endeavour.

'No,' he tells her, 'no. I don't believe it. I don't have a reputation.'

'Ask your students.'

Lia has become one of his students. Part of that mature intake which the poly, having become a poly, is suddenly indecently eager to attract. Bring out your old! Someone's done a paper. Discovered that there's gold in them thar hills, old gold, any number of the hard of hearing and the all but past it, languishing in Pennine towns and villages, who would jump at studying Drama and Movement, or the Torment of Sylvia Plath, or even Literature's For Life with Henry, if they were only given the chance. Now in they stream, tapping their sticks, as though into a hospice for the terminally curious. Perfect for Henry. All attached, all older than he is. Not Lia. Lia is attached and the same age. But one out of two will do for Henry. This is how he has come to meet her again, anyway, after all these years. Eight, is it? Ten? He lost interest in Henshell, needless to say. Lost track of what their friendship was for. Now he remembers. It was for Lia.

'And what will my students tell me?' Henry asks. 'That I seduce them in return for good grades?'

'No. I have heard no mention of your giving good grades.'

'That I seduce them in return for bad grades, then?'

Grrrr, Henry! Why doesn't she ask him to be a tiger now?

'No,' she says, 'I wouldn't swear I have even heard the word seduce. They're more interested in the fact that everyone you sleep with is older than you, married or going out with someone else. The psychology of that arrests them. They're not stupid, Henry. They're curious as to why this is. Why, for example, you never seem to have a girlfriend of your own – not just of your own age but simply of your own, for you only. Why you're always scavenging round the edges of other people's relationships, as though for leftovers . . .'

'Like yours, I suppose? Do you see yourself as a leftover.'

'Like mine, yes. Definitely like mine. And do I see myself as a leftover? Yes. Yes, I do a bit.'

'A bit?'

'Don't be smart with me, Henry. I'm not complaining. I know the score. Something on the side suits me as much as it suits you. But everything you have is on the side. Which prompts some of us to wonder why you don't want anything that's – what? – in the middle, at the centre, a main course in itself.'

'And the fact that I appear not to explains why I am always shedding my trousers?'

'Maybe. Because it's as though you've finished before you've started. As though you know you're not going to get what you want the minute you embark, so the next one is a necessity, a foregone conclusion. If you could invert time, Henry, you'd have the next one before you had the last.'

'And that would help me to keep my trousers on?'

She sighed. 'Nothing will help you to keep your trousers on, is that what you want to hear me say? I don't know. Maybe nothing will. It's not for me to judge. I'm just your student. And your old friend's wife. Though no doubt . . .' She trailed away.

'No doubt what? No doubt that's what I'm in it for? Because you're married to Henshell?'

She began to put her clothes back on. Growing weary, like the light. 'Well, I'm not going to say that's not an element, Henry. I'd be a fool not to think about it at least. But I'm not accusing you of spite or anything like that. I'm sure you don't mean to do Henshell down. That's probably more my motive than it's yours. But this is new to me. You've been here before, Henry. By your own admission this is your thing.'

Henry hated these Pennine afternoons. The light not so much withdrawn as swept away, as though a smudgy hand had reached out and in one motion wiped a blackboard clean. Listen and that was what you heard, the blackness drying over the white, obliterating all trace, all remembrance even. Look out and nothing beckoned. As a boy Henry had kept the moors in the corner of his eye, a promise not of glamour exactly, not of Belkin's Hollywood or Bel Air, but of some glimmering Englishness whose quietude was strange to him, and which one day he would try to penetrate. Now he was on them, everything they'd promised, the glimmer and the quiet – the quiet as a property of the soul, he meant – was gone. What he'd seen was an illusion. He is standing on what was never there.

He didn't want Lia to go yet. She probably had it right, he was ready for the next one, but he still didn't want her to leave. 'The mistake people make about me,' he said, 'is to think I see myself as a lover.'

'And you don't?'

'No, I don't. Not a lover in the heroic sense, anyway. I don't have that much interest in the grand scope and narrative of erotic love, I don't have the confident brush strokes. I'm more a miniaturist. If Don Juan is Rubens or Titian, then I'm Vermeer.'

'You do interiors, is that what you're saying? You don't like going out?'

'Correct, I don't like going out. But I mean something else as well.' He was sitting by her on the bed, stroking her arms, absently pulling hairs from her sweater, thinking about what he was. 'I think I'd like to say,' he said, 'that I'm an intimate proximist. Taking an intimist to be someone who has a preference for the smaller, nearer view, as against the broad sweep of the panoramic, then I'm one stage closer in. I'm besotted with the proximate. You remember "Hovis" Belkin – of course you do, Henshell hated him – well, he was the very opposite. "Hovis" was only interested in what was remote.'

'He was never particulary nice to me, if that's what you mean.'

'No, he wouldn't have been. You were altogether too familiar to him.'

'But you always seemed distant yourself, Henry. None of us thought of you – don't be offended – as a warm friend. You were never really in the hutch with us.'

He's hurt. Not even in the hutch with Henshell, his second-best friend?

But he doesn't want her to see he's hurt. 'No,' he says, as though the charge is a familiar one to him. 'But that's only because I didn't know how to do it. The haughty are always people who just lack the trick of intimacy. Invite them to your homes and make them cocoa and they're pussy cats.'

He does a pussy cat for her. The nearest Henry gets to tigers.

'So if Henshell had made you cocoa you wouldn't now be here fucking his wife?'

He laughed. What else was there to do? 'I think it started earlier than Henshell,' he said.

'Oh no, not your parents.'

'Afraid so.'

'They didn't love you . . .'

'Or they loved me too much. Mothers, for their own reasons, keep you in thrall to the proximate, fathers are meant to push you out into the world.'

'And yours didn't?'

'Well, he tried. But maybe he was too influenced by my mother in the end, maybe she kept him in thrall as well. Who knows? Take bloody "Hovis" – he wasn't afraid of what was out there and his Dad was so aloof he only spoke on Yom Kippur, and that was to remind "Hovis" of his sins. To all intents and purposes he had no Dad. Half the time he coveted mine. Yet this didn't stop him going for distance. So where does family psychology get you? I'm sorry, I've forgotten how we got into this.'

'We? *You* got into it by way of explaining why you can't play tigers.'

'Ah yes, and why tigers notwithstanding I can't keep my pants on. I hope I am no longer a disturbing mystery to you.'

She was muffling up, afghan coat, suede boots, woolly gloves, two scarves, what you need to brave a Pennine winter. She was shaking her head over him. 'Why are you so frightened of leaving things to chance, Henry? Why do you feel you must make your

116

version of yourself prevail? You should trust other people more. You should risk their opinion of you.'

'Other people?'

'Yes. Me, for instance. About whom you haven't asked a question all afternoon. Not even how are you, Lia. It's a bit rich, Henry, all that loving what's close, all that intimate proximist stuff, when you wouldn't notice another person if she was sitting on your face.'

'Try me,' he suggested.

But she couldn't be bothered taking all those clothes off again.

It didn't last. Mia, Jane, whoever. Nothing ever lasted. In so far as that had anything to do with Henry – and it didn't always – the reason wasn't callousness or cold feet. Order, that was the problem. 'Save me from chaos,' Henry pleaded with every older someone-else's woman he met. Without a woman in his life, Henry was like the world before God created it. Nothing but flying fragments. At the mercy of hunger, boredom and his dick – when he could tell the difference – not understanding where he ended or the void began, unless he *was* the void. Then, if he was lucky, the woman came, parted the dry land from the sea, stuck up a firmament, blew light upon him, and arranged him into order. Trouble was – order is death. Chaos life, order death. This had nothing to do with Henry wanting to throw his socks about the bedroom floor. In fact, Henry had always been a neat person with a side parting, who kept his clothes in drawers and his papers in a filing cabinet. So there was nothing hippyish about his pronouncement that order was death. What he meant was that the moment women did what he needed them to do, they set in motion the process of deterioration. There was this to be said for the world before God created it: there was no death in it. That which is not created cannot die. Chaotic, Henry could have lived for ever. Ordered, as he longed to be, he could smell his flesh rot.

Maybe when he grew up it would be different. You need to be mature to be ordered. You have to be accepting. But so long as he stayed chaotic, how could Henry grow up?

How did you manage to grow up and yet stay chaotic, Dad?

*Taugetz, Henry.*

# FIVE

'*Taugetz, taugetz, taugetz* and *taugetz taug* / *Taugetz, taugetz, taugetz* and *taugetz taug* . . .'

Henry's father, the paper-magician, happy and blithering his favourite song. '*Taugetz, taugetz,* give me your answer do . . .' Beside him on the front seat, Henry, the misery-magician, not happy. How old is Henry now? Thirteen – thirteen going on three hundred, according to his father's calculations.

They have been to what Henry's father has recently taken to calling a gig. Another humiliation for Henry. Gigs being what rock musicians do – even rockless Schubertian Henry knows that – and are not to be confused with tearing up newsprint into pretty shapes for a bunch of four-year-olds who couldn't give a shit. Henry has been helping out, the paper-sorcerer's apprentice, now that he is of an age to be useful. He carries the cases. Makes sure they've packed enough newspapers and serviettes, not to mention the torches, the fire extinguisher, the blanket, the bucket of water. Come the performance, he holds one end of whatever his father wants one end holding. He is the butt of his father's mirth. 'Here you are, Charlie, catch' – that's his stage name, Charlie – 'oops, couldn't catch a cold, could you, Charlie?' And he does the navigating, getting them the length and breadth of the county, from one kindergarten gig to another. Tonight they have been to Liverpool. Hard town, Liverpool, his father had warned him before they set out. 'How can it be hard, Dad,' Henry wanted to know, 'when the person whose party it is is five? What are they going to do, knife us?' 'You'll see,' his father told him. 'You'll see.'

And his father was right. They *were* hard. Old lags in short pants, potato-faced, thug-nosed, jelly-spitting mafiosi with piggy proletarian eyes, who booed when they should have clapped, and heckled when they should have marvelled, who belched and farted and shouted 'Fucking rubbish!' – and that was only the little girls – and who, when Izzi presented them with a dancing paper dolly each, screwed them up and threw them back at Henry.

'Told you, Charlie,' Izzi whispered to his son. 'Only one thing for it – you'll have to go and get the other stuff from the car.'

'What other stuff?'

'You know.'

'Ah, Dad!'

'Just go! And as for you' – to the under-age delinquents – 'I've got something that'll keep you quiet.' With which wild boast he swept them up behind him like the rats of Hamelin, down into their cancered concrete garden, a place of rusted bloodbaths, broken bicycles with tampered brakes, seatless swings and ruined roundabouts, promising them real magic this time, blood and thunder, death and dissolution, inferno. Yeah? – we'd like to see it! Yeah, well, you're going to see it. Yeah? – well, where is it? Yeah, well, it's just coming. And two minutes later back it came – Henry with the bags of torches. Him? No, not him. Yeah – well, it had better not be him. And of course it wasn't him, not Henry, no one ever produced Henry if the call was for blood and thunder.

In no time, no longer than it took him to unzip a bag, pour paraffin, light a match and summon up a mouthful of spittle, Uncle Izzi had become volcanic, gargling lava, bouncing fireballs off his lips like balloons. Head back, throat open, smiling – for smiling pulls the lips away from danger, that much even Henry knew – he addressed his baby audience in flames, the fiery words evaporating when he breathed, exploding and vanishing as though they'd never been spoken. Or he would swallow fire – *seem* to swallow fire, there was the trick – sucking it into his stomach which must have been as one of the boiler rooms of Hell.

You like that, kids? You like that better?

Without doubt they liked it better. Offered the choice between paper-folding and a man with his face on fire, how could you not prefer the man with his face on fire. These, Henry reminded himself, were the children of arsonists and incendiaries, pyromaniacs and safe-blowers. They had grown up with sticks of dynamite in their cots the way other children had grown up with dummies. They were heat-resistant. They felt no pain. They had no *imagination* of pain.

Their eyes burned with excitement. Now you're talking, now you're cooking with gas, this is what you call a children's party. If only Henry's father would set fire to Henry as an encore, they'd suck their thumbs and go to beddy-byes content.

Smelling the paraffin, hearing the children's shouts, seeing the sky light up, the entire proletariat of Henry's reading and foreboding came out to look – missing persons, rent-evaders, men in hiding, IRA men, men with prices on their heads, dodgers, defaulters, defectors, defecators, escaped convicts, wife-beaters, spies, snoops, grasses, bigamists, bombers, whisky priests, welfare cheats, distillers of illicit hooch, contrabandists, drug dealers, inbreeders, squatters, illegal immigrants, under-age runaways, child-molesters, tower-block prostitutes and their pimps, men who slept with their mothers, neighbours who hadn't spoken since their blood feud first broke out in another country in another century, creatures not men, creatures with iron claws for hands, creatures with bullets for teeth, creatures who knew what they wanted, took what they wanted, what they borrowed never returned, inexpugnable, shatterproof, immortal. Whoosh, went Izzi's breath. Whoa, went the estate. Could they have been thinking that Henry's father had been sent by the council to burn the disgrace that was their habitation to the ground? Were they hoping to collect on the insurance? Who cared why they roared. Not Izzi. At last – an audience appreciative of his genius *at last*. Boiling hot, like a blacksmith, two scorched circles on his cheeks, like Old Nick, he blew four more fire rings at the moon, then took his bow.

See. See what happens when you're given a chance. My first ever Gentile gig, Henry.

You've done loads of Gentile gigs, Dad.

My first ever *über*-Gentile gig. What does that tell you?

Henry knew what it told him: never to come to such a place again.

But to his father it told a different story. From now on, paper for the Yiddlers, fire for the goyim.

That could have been the moment, Henry now realises, when his father decided to take a second wife.

Hence happy in the car home. '*Taugetz, taugetz* . . . Didn't I tell you?'

'Didn't you tell me what?'

'That Liverpool was a hard town.'

'You did.'

'And didn't we show 'em?'

'You showed 'em, yes.'

'Was I good or was I good?'

'You were very good.'

'Shame we didn't bring your mother.'

Silence from Henry.

'She'd have liked it, don't you think?'

'Dunno.'

'You don't think so?'

'Not sure.'

'Maybe you're right. Maybe not. The excitement would have been too much for her. What do you think?'

'I think so, Dad.'

'Yeah, me too. And you? You all right?'

'Me? Absolutely. Yeah.'

His father steals a sideways look at him. Concentrating on the road ahead. Not much traffic, but there's a light rain falling, making conditions treacherous. 'Oil and water,' he says. And then, returning to what's on his mind. 'So why the long face?'

'I haven't got a long face.'

'You have. It starts there and ends there.'

'That's the shape.'

'*Taugetʒ.*'

'It is. That's how I'm built. It's how I came.'

'Who you came from, you mean.'

'Well, I came from you, Dad.'

'Yeah, indirectly.'

'Is there any other way?'

'You should get out more.'

'I'm out. I'm out with you.'

'I mean with your chinas.'

Henry says nothing. Problems with his chinas, even then. Some dissatisfaction. Not knowing what friends are for. Wanting a little girlfriend, yes, but that's different, and not what his father means by chinas, anyway.

And also not knowing what his father's for . . .

He would have asked, had he dared, had the hour been right. 'Dad, what exactly do you get out of this?'

*Driving?*

'No, not driving. This . . .' But he couldn't spoil the party.

So ask it now, Henry. No, Dad, not the driving. This . . . that . . . Go on, Henry, spoil the party now. That fire-eating and stuff.

*I enjoyed it. It gave pleasure. You saw that with your own eyes. You saw the expressions on those kids' faces.*

Should Henry say that had his father set about the estate with a blow-torch, that too would have lit up those kids' faces? No. Stick to what he wants to know. Which is not why *they* enjoyed it, but why *he* did.

*Why the hell shouldn't I have enjoyed it? Fun, Henry. Remember fun? No, you wouldn't. Not you with your endless sick notes from your mother in your pocket. You wouldn't remember anything about taking risks either. Or the joys of expressing a little wildness. Feeling your blood heat. Ever felt your blood heat, Henry? No. I thought not.*

*And all right, I admit it, enjoying the attention. Is that so terrible? There was a song your mother liked — 'I don't want to set the world on fire, I just want to start a blaze in your heart.'*

Different things inflame different people, Dad. Had you wanted to start a blaze in my heart, you'd have tried alternative methods.

*Such as what? Burning your books? You'd have liked that. Then you could have called me a Nazi. No, Henry, I didn't want to start a blaze in your heart. I knew my limits. No one was ever able to set you alight.*

Too damp, you think?

*Too frightened.*

I wasn't frightened of the fire-eating. I thought it was ugly.

*Well, that was your opinion, Henry. Other people have always found fire beautiful.*

I'm not talking about the fire. It's what you did with it. The smell, the paraffin, the putting things in your mouth, all that.

*You didn't like the smell of paraffin, I didn't like the smell of ink. But I didn't say your homework was ugly.*

He could have, though, Henry thinks. Given what Henry's maps and tables looked like, given the spider-scrawl Henry called writing, he'd have been within his rights. But then that's the line down which his own ugliness has travelled. Patrilineal, the mess Henry made with a pen — must have been, given the beautiful hand his mother had. Not that any of this is to the point. Nothing, of course, is to the point now. Should all be left dead and buried. Unhealthy, all this disinterring. Dispiriting. Like his father's fire-eating. Dispiriting. Soulless. Leave him alone.

*Soulless? Don't start me off, Henry. Your soul was a luxury we made available to you. Not everyone had your advantages. No one sat me on their knee and read me books. I had my hands, that was all. Big hands. There's Izzi, the geezer with the big hands. You make the most of what you've been given. I had this friend called Aaron Eisenfeldt, who kept egging me on. I bet you can't knock this nail in this piece of wood with your fist. So I did. I bet you can't rip a tele-*

*phone directory in half. So I did. I bet you can't put your hand in fire. So I did.*

It was a good job, then, says Henry the Pious, that this Aaron Eisenfeldt didn't bet you you couldn't kill the headmaster with your thumb.

*You're dead right there, Henry. He became a High Court judge in later life.*

And you, Henry thinks, became a children's entertainer.

But just because someone dared you to do something, he says, it didn't mean you had to do it. Least of all that you had to *go on* doing it.

Nothing his father says makes any sense to him. He is flesh of his flesh, but they might as well belong to separate species. Henry knows what he'd have said to Aaron Eisenfeldt had Aaron Eisenfeldt come to him with fire.

Fuck off, Aaron!

Eat shit, Aaron!

But why blame Aaron. Just because, it doesn't have to mean –

*I agree with you. It didn't have to mean that.*

And just because you put your hand successfully in fire once didn't mean you had to put your tongue in fire for the rest of your life.

*Who said I was successful? If you want to know, I burnt it.*

Ah, so that's it. So now you have to prove yourself for ever.

*Taugetz. Was that the psychology they taught you at university? We wasted our money, in that case. No. I got a taste, the same way you got a taste for books. I don't say to you that you read books to prove yourself, because once you couldn't finish one. I did it because I liked it. I liked the illusion part of it, I liked the gadget part of it, I liked the danger part of it – but don't tell your mother that – and I liked amazing people with what I could do. I ask you again, was that so terrible?*

Henry thinks about it. No, it was not so terrible. Except that it was so terrible because it was so common. That's the word,

Henry is afraid. Common. He knows he ought to have thought differently of it. He should have tried thinking it was exotic instead, tried telling himself that he was luckier than most boys who had dentists or accountants for fathers. My father is a fire-eater! What a start for a boy! What a beginning to what is meant, after all, to be a great adventure. Thank you, Dad, he ought to have said, for lifting me, by your example, out of the common. For it is not a common profession for a father, a fire-eater. Could Henry name one other boy who had a father who ate fire, or who ate anything but chopped liver on bagels, come to that? He could not. So he must have been using common in another sense. He was. He is. By common, when he employed it of his father, Henry meant low, lacking grace and sophistication, of little value, low class (unlike 'Hovis' Belkin's family), inferior, *goyische*, unrefined. On account of which commonness Henry was ashamed to be his father's son. And hung his head.

Driving home from Liverpool, scene of his father's greatest éclat to date, he sits, hunched quietly, looking into the headlights of the oncoming cars.

And then, out of the blue, in a ditch of its own making on the other side of the road, a car on its back, exquisite like a sculpture in the yellow-fever moonlight, a thing designed for speed become utterly still, except for one of its rear wheels, spinning, spinning with infernal beauty, as though powered by a battery designed for that very purpose.

Some sights, however inconsequent, you see for ever. Henry still sees that spinning wheel, though in his memory he suspects he turns it slower than it turned in actuality, and bathes it in more yellow moonlight than there really was. Milking it. Smoking it. Or maybe just wanting to invest it with greater significance than it warranted. Never sure, Henry, whether he is doing enough or too much justice to event. Perhaps because he draws too big a distinction, unless he draws too small a one, between event and him. Is this an uncertainty which is bound to follow when you take no interest in world history?

But then his father took no interest in world history either, yet to Henry there never seemed to be an event that didn't have his father at the centre of it. Mr Busy. Forget Superman: it was Henry's father who was always first on the scene. And who always knew what to do. He was one of those men, Henry's father, who are born to make a human bridge of their own back, to be the rope down which the injured slide, to hold crumbling apartment blocks apart, to scoop unconscious babies from under the wheels of runaway trains, to take Rivka Yoffey to the Midland. Did the bastard breathe fire, Henry sometimes wondered, only in order to put it out? Was *that* it?

Mindful in disaster, he didn't slam on his brakes, not with oil and water on the road – oh no, not Henry's father – but slid gently into the verge. That's the way to do it, Henry. Suit the driving to the conditions, even in an emergency – correction, *especially* in an emergency. Then he was off, across the road almost before he'd stopped, his paper-magician's jacket with its big patched pockets flying behind him. And he was strong. If need be he would right the upturned vehicle with his own hands, then peel it open like a sardine tin. He was wrenching at a door and all but had it off by the time Henry was out of his seat. Henry not one of those in whom catastrophe finds a hero. Henry more circumspect, weighing up the pros and the cons, not wanting to make a bad business worse.

Cometh the hour, cometh not Henry.

Your fault, Dad, you were always there before me.

*If we waited for you, Henry . . .*

Don't rationalise it. You were always there before me because you wanted to be there before me. Had I run you'd have raced me.

*There were people dying, Henry.*

There were always people dying. And you were always the first to find them.

*You think I should have left it to you find them? You were just a boy.*

So how was I ever to learn to be a man?

*Not by seeing people decapitated in their cars.*

Ah, that! Thanks, Dad. At least no one can say you never called a spade a spade.

Henry only got to hear about people with their heads missing at the inquest where, red and incoherent, he had been subject to cross-examination – asked questions anyway, which was tantamount to a cross-examination as far as Henry was concerned – in the matter of what he'd witnessed. To which his answer, probe him as they might, was precisely nothing. In our family, Henry tried to explain, it is my father who does the witnessing.

For the moment he had joined his father at the ruined car, its wheel spinning, smoking in the night, his father had clapped a heavy hand across Henry's eyes and twisted his head from the scene. Not for you, Henry. Not for you to behold what's happened here.

'Wave a car down,' he'd said, 'quickly, go on, now!' His voice urgent, in command, but from the immeasurable depths of adult sorrow. Henry knew the sound. Keep the sight of death from the kid – *that* sound. Used on Henry before, first when poor Anastasia decided to give up the ghost while they were visiting her mob-handed in hospital, suddenly, as though that was the only way to get rid of them, the grey creeping across her face like the afternoon light passing from the Pennines; and then again when a neighbour popped in to get his breath and without a word of explanation collapsed on their living-room carpet, his lips fluttering as though in final indecision. On both those occasions, and with a tenderness which surprised and doubly saddened Henry, his father had covered his eyes and led him away.

Never the women who did it, never his mother, always his father.

In this way Henry had got to thirteen with death all around

him, with death nudging into the peripheries of his vision, but without ever having actually seen – actually been allowed to rest his eyes on – a dead person. And now here he was again on the East Lancashire Road, denied another golden opportunity.

He was grateful at the time. He consented. He let his head be turned away. He wasn't sure he could have coped with anything horrible anyway. And someone had to flag down a car. Because that too was being grown up – standing in the road and flagging down a car.

But there has to be a first time, doesn't there? You can't go on being protected from mortality for ever. And yet that seemed to be his father's intention – to keep him out of the club.

Until when? Until exactly when, Dad?

*Until you were old enough.*

And you were the one who said I was tied to my mother's apron strings.

*Not the same thing. You'd be dealing with the dead in good time. There was no reason to hurry it.*

Wasn't there? Do you know what it felt like? It felt as though you wanted the big stuff all to yourself. I couldn't get near. You wouldn't let me near.

*Trust me, Henry, it wasn't a competition. I'd have been only too glad for you to have taken over, gezunterheit, but you were too young. I found my sister dead in bed when I was six years old. My grandmother, God rest her soul, died with her arms round me when I was ten. She died in my face, Henry. I swallowed her last breath. I couldn't have wished any of that on you. But I didn't want more for myself, I can promise you that. I'd had my fair share. More than my fair share.*

Maybe those events were the making of you.

*They weren't.*

How do you know?

*I know.*

You'd have been a better man without?

*I'd have been another man without.*

129

Dad, you might not have been a man at all. You might have ended up like me.

*No. You're the Stern Gang's doing.*

And then, the day Henry leaves home to go to university, it happens again.

Both his parents are intending to take him to the station to see him off – along with his grandmother Irina, and his surviving great-aunts Marghanita and Effie. But that's too many. It will embarrass the boy, the Girls see that. So it's down to just his mother and his father and then, at the very last minute, his mother cries off.

'It will upset me too much.'

Izzi Nagel open his arms to the heavens. 'Why should it upset you seeing your son off to university? It's what you've always wanted.'

'That's why it will upset me.'

'How can getting what you've always wanted upset you?'

Ekaterina exchanges looks with her son. What a husband! You marry a man from North Manchester and this is the subtlety you have to live with. He eats fire and thinks getting what you want must make you happy.

'You take him. Just see he gets a nice seat in a comfortable compartment.'

'Look,' Henry says, 'I don't want any of this. Let Dad drop me at the station. That'll be fine.'

On the way out of the house he hears his mother whispering to his father. 'Don't dare drop him at the station. Go through with him. Make sure he's got his ticket and settle him on the train.'

He hugs his mother. These are not yet kissie-kissie times. Love you, Mom / Love you, son has not yet been imported from the United States of Schmaltz. In matters of human relations the English are still clinging on to dignity, the Nagels more tightly than most. 'Enjoy yourself,' she says, patting his cheek. 'And don't forget you are as good as anybody.'

'I will. I won't.'

'But don't be too much of a snob either. Try to value other people's talents.'

'I won't. I will.'

'And write.'

'No choice, it's an essay a week.'

'No, you fool, I mean write to me.'

Henry wishes, though he knows she means nothing by it, that his mother hadn't called him a fool on the day he leaves home to go to university. *Fool.* Does he want that to be the last word he hears her say? But then he is upset, wavering, his insides rattling around in his body, his voice not firm. This will be further from her than he has ever been. Love you, Mom.

More matter-of-fact, being seen off by his Dad. No word problems, because between his father and himself there are no words. Words will come later.

'You got everything?'

'Yep.'

'Ticket?'

'Yep.'

'And you know where you're getting off?'

'Yep.'

Goodbye then, handshake, wink, maybe a bit of rough stuff around the shoulders – that should have been it. But his father decides to see him on to the train. Mr Busy. 'Here,' he says, motioning to Henry's bags, 'let me take those.'

Never a sight Henry likes to see, whether he already has reason to be distressed or not, his father carrying another person's bags, even when they're Henry's. A distinguishing feature of the man, of course, no doubt about it, the alacrity of his public spiritedness. Got a bad back, can't move your furniture, need a push because your car won't start, want your party to go with a bang – call Izzi Nagel. Demeaning, isn't it, Dad? Demeaning to be at everyone's beck and call?

A question he means to ask. Why did *you* have to be the butler for all and sundry? Who appointed you dogsbody of all Manchester? But he will need more than his usual amount of courage for that one. You don't demean the demeaned.

Sometimes Henry thinks he can actually smell it on his father's breath. Servitude willingly suffered. Vassalage. Sour and a little too warm. So that's what slaves smell of – egg and onion toasted in petroleum.

On to the luggage rack his bags go, anyway. Neatly stored. Little Lord Fauntleroy with his manservant (who also happens to be his father), Izzi.

With all the fussing, the train is filling up around them. Henry finds a table with just one sleeping person opposite. He'd have preferred nobody, but at least this person is wearing railway employee's uniform and so might be getting off shortly. Might even be planning to drive the train when he wakes. Henry's father makes sure Henry's settled comfortably.

'You won't forget to write to your mother.'

'Nope.'

Then he pulls a small packet from his inside pocket. 'Something for you to read,' he says awkwardly. Not Henry's father's sort of sentence. Nor Henry's father's sort of gesture. Is this the first gift they have exchanged, without the intercession of Ekaterina, man to man? Henry is so astonished he thinks he is going to cry. A book, a book from his father!

But before he can say so much as thank you, his father does what he is always doing and claps his hands over Henry's eyes. 'Quick,' he says, 'come on, off the train, quick.'

Oh, shit! Henry thinks. What now? What this time? What tragedy has he conjured up for me today?

And everything happens so quickly – for Henry of course does not struggle, but goes quietly, putty in his father's hands – that when he next opens his eyes he is on the platform, and his father is in urgent conversation with the guard, and everyone is up out of their seats, looking, wondering, and people are running, and an urgent request for a doctor is going out over the Tannoy, though as Henry knows from experience, a doctor will be too late. Kaput, whoever you are, once Izzi Nagel has found you.

'The man opposite me?' Henry asks, as though he needs to.

'Yes,' his father tells him. Compassionately. That old deep adult sorrow, keeping from Henry what must be kept. 'A heart attack, I'd say. Probably died in his sleep.'

Then Henry remembers that the man did look a little green. So has he seen a corpse at last? He doesn't think so. He didn't really look. And he didn't really know the man was dead. It can't count as looking upon death, can it, if you don't know it's death you're looking upon.

Thus, on my first foray into manhood, Henry thinks, does my father deny me once again. The ghoul he is, the fucking ghoul!

For a moment it occurs to Henry to wonder whether his father planted the dead man there, has always been planting dead men there, as milestones marking the stages of Henry's freedom from dependence. Except that there have been no stages of Henry's freedom from dependence. He will die dependent.

Once the body has been removed, propped up in a station wheelchair, like unwieldy luggage, the train gets underway again. To be on the safe side – his father's idea – Henry is in another compartment. Henry concurs with this. He doesn't want to catch anything. Malaria, rabies, bubonic plague – whatever the dead infect you with.

A mile out of Manchester he unwraps the gift his father gave him. It's a picture book, with diagrams. Henry suspects the first picture book with diagrams he has ever owned. *Origami – Let's Fold*, it's called.

It bears a brief inscription on the title page, in childish writing. '*For Henry, on the occasion of you going to university, Dad.*'

The next corpse that comes Henry's way is his father's. Struck down by a hammer-blow of guilt and sorrow. Nothing to stop Henry this time. Carte blanche. No one to shield his eyes or to usher him into another room or to order him to flag down a passing car. Now's your chance, Henry. Go on. Go on, do it. Go contemplate the awful majesty of death to your heart's content.

His mother, too. But his mother has been damaged and he knows that's beyond him. Whereas his father, they tell him, has an air almost of serenity and looks like a young boy again.

And his breath? Henry wonders. Will his breath still be sour?

Forgetting there won't be any breath.

Either way, it's far too late for Henry now. He isn't man enough to look.

# SIX

Although Henry is always the first person in the country to get a flu jab, he is also always the first person in the country to get flu.

Without the jab, he tells himself, it would have been even worse.

In fact, Henry likes having flu. It reminds him of being jealous. The same aching of the limbs, as though his bones – his clavicles, his femurs, his humeri (words he's looked up in an atlas of the human skeleton) – have overheated and become new centres of the senses for him; the same lazy throbbing of the temples, like warm jets of water flushing through his brain cells; the same submission to the caprices of the body and its blood. When he is jealous, Henry can barely move his head, so drowsily heavy, like a sunflower at evening, does it become; and so it is when he has flu. For these reasons, Henry has always preferred jealousy and flu to any other sexual activity.

He imagines, Henry, that he looks rather spectacularly hollow on his pillows, the rims around his eyes purple, his lips faintly parted, his cheeks blazing. Not as beautiful as when he was young and the bones showed their burning tracery through his flesh, alarming whoever cared for him at the time, but he has a grander backdrop for his sufferings today, a softer and more billowing bed, an altogether more elegant bedroom with its row of seven little windows – one for each dwarf – looking out, not over the deathly Pennines, but the park, the West End, the City, an extruded horizontal of teeming London, a fluttering letter-box diorama of the metropolis from which, for a cruel day or two, flu has parted him. If you have to be ill, Henry thinks, this is the place to be ill in. He tries to imagine his father unwell here, but he cannot connect him with the pillows, cannot picture his cheek upon them. Which just goes to show that a person is not a person full stop, but changes with his habitat. As Henry's habitat is changing him, like a hand constantly soothing his brow. So if this had been my place of birth, instead of up *there*, what would I have been, Henry wonders.

Happy, for one.

Successful, for two.

No one I recognise, for three.

On Sunday morning Moira brings him strudel in a plastic container. She lets herself in now, with her own key, then makes him tea. 'Fluids are essential when you've got a cold,' she tells him.

'I haven't got a cold, I've got flu.'

She fluffs his pillows. 'It's a little early in the year for flu. People don't get flu in August. You've got a cold.'

'I'm too weak to argue with you,' he says. 'Which proves I've got flu.'

'And I am not prepared to humour you, which proves you've only got a cold.'

'Feel my forehead.'

'And?' she asks.

'What temperature is it?'

'Hot.'

'See.'

'Henry, your forehead is always hot. You're a hot-headed person.'

'That's because I've got flu all the time.'

No, she could say, but doesn't, that's because you're jealous all the time. Yes, she has noticed it. They have been going out for three or four weeks, no more, but already he is jealous of his own shadow. When they pass a shop window which offers them their reflection he pauses so that he can admire them together. Henry in his dotage and a woman young enough, almost, to be his daughter. That's when she observes that he is jealous of himself for being with her.

He has an antique tray which moves up and down his bed on oiled brass tracks. The opulence of this place! On this tray, Moira lays out strudel for him and strong tea. And of course aspirin.

'You take too many of those,' she tells him.

'A man of my age can't take too many aspirin. It prevents the blood clotting. The only reason I am not having a heart attack now is aspirin.'

'Fine, Henry, so long as you don't prick your finger.'

'Why, what will happen if I prick my finger?'

'You'll bleed.'

'Of course I'll bleed. If you prick me do I not bleed?'

'To *death*, Henry! Think how thin your blood must be by now. It'll drain out of your finger in seconds.'

'All of it?'

'Every last drop.'

He thinks about it. 'I can't stop taking aspirin,' he says at last, cutting into the strudel, 'I need them for my migraines.' Then he tells her about the spider, the daddy-long-legs which sat on his brain while his mother laboured to hold him back from a disgusting world.

'And you've had migraines ever since?'

'On and off.'

She is sitting by his bed in a tasselled chair which must have intrigued and baffled Henry's father, so dainty is it, so unlike anything that ever came from his workshop. 'What is this?' Henry imagines his father saying when he first saw it. 'A sofa for fairies?'

Moira is no fairy, which might be why she appears uncomfortable in it, on the edge, fiddling with her earrings.

She shakes her head at Henry. 'I seem to have spent my life,' she says, 'undoing what mothers have done to their sons.'

'Well, one must suppose you wouldn't accept the job if you didn't like it.'

'Who said I've accepted it?'

'You're turning me down?'

'Don't personalise everything. When it comes to remothering I'm turning you all down, I've had enough of it.'

'Who's "all"?'

Their eyes meet. Hers very Baltic this morning, Henry's rheumy, the colour of strudel. Then she turns her face from him and gets up, going to the window, where the world of men undone by mothers stretches further than the eye can see.

'For a start, Aultbach has suddenly developed a limp,' she says.

'I thought the strudel wasn't quite perfect today,' Henry says. 'But what's that got to do with his mother?'

'It's got to do with me, it's got to do with me having to mother him.'

'I thought he had a girlfriend.'

'He has, but she doesn't mother. Then there's Lachlan, then there's you . . .'

'Lachlan? What's Lachlan been asking you to do?'

'Same as you. Tuck him up in bed. Spoon him cake and give him aspirin.'

'Tuck him up in bed? You visit Lachlan's bed?'

She remains at the window, her head averted. He loves the back of her. The front of her too, but the back of any woman Henry cares about is more poignant and therefore more sensual to him. When you've got jealous flu the receding parts of a woman are what you want to look at.

She is wearing a cream suit, well tailored, the waist nipped in, the skirt straight with an insolent slit at the back, not just a parting in the material but a wilful slash, a touch of tartiness which the elegance of the cut otherwise belies. The way Henry likes it. On her feet high-heeled summer shoes, a lattice of fine straps, her painted toenails showing. Her weight is on her left foot, unbalancing her, giving her an impatient look, as though she would rather be somewhere else. But she must also know that when she stands like that her skirt tautens across her buttocks, and therefore she cannot want Henry to want her to go.

'You're all ill, you men,' she says at last. 'It's a beautiful summer's day out there and you've all got something wrong with you.'

'That's because we're all old,' Henry says. 'But there's no reason to be irritable with me just because you've been visiting Lachlan's bed.'

'I haven't been "visiting his bed". He isn't well, you're all not well, and he asked me to bring him round some patisseries.'

'The way you used to do with his stepmother? Is he planning to resurrect the tradition? Including cremation?'

'I don't know what he's planning.'

'But you took him some.'

'How could I refuse? He's recently bereaved. He's a customer. And I was coming to see you anyway.'

'You mean you delivered him patisseries this morning, on the way to me? You're telling me you've already been there? You've done him first?'

'It's not a crime, Henry.'

'That depends on how long you stayed –'

'I didn't stay.'

'– and on whether he got fresher strudel than I did.'

'Well, you've nothing to worry about on that score – he doesn't like strudel.'

'So on what score do I have something to worry about? Croissants? Or do *millefeuilles* run in the family? Let me see if I can guess how he likes them – confectioner's cream, I'd say, I doubt he's a custard man . . . yes, confectioner's cream. Which just leaves the method of delivery to be determined . . . By tongue, I'd say. Am I getting warm?'

She turns to face him, denying him her back. In anger, her face loses its lopsidedness, as though it is contentment which makes her crooked. 'Grow up, Henry,' she says.

But how can Henry grow up, given the eye of the storm of her skirt, its still point, where the horizontal tension meets the vertical, that eloquent square of fraught silence which only an engineer or a philosopher of space possesses the science to explain? Let Hell freeze over while Henry's standing in it, discoursing with the Devil, and let a woman scurry through the icy flames with that square of silence screaming from her skirt – Henry knows which phenomenon will engross him more.

'Come here,' he says, reaching out for her, bravely, despite his fevered state.

But before he can touch her she has quit the room – skewering his carpet with her high heels, her hair tossing like a pony's, the slit of her skirt gaping more lewdly than Henry in his influenza can bear – leaving him trapped under his antique tray, the crumbs and the cold tea. 'Call me when you're feeling better,' she shouts as she opens the door. 'And you should know that we don't use confectioner's cream at Aultbach's. That would have been your mother.'

Aultbach's – t,t,t. Her lapping of the t his final torment.


His poor mother.

Not enough she used confectioner's cream, but now, in death, where she cannot defend herself, she must be derided for it. What's Henry's duty here? He has never known. Stand up for your mother every time another woman speaks slightingly of her and the truth of it is you have no women left.

She'd warned him how it would be. 'They'll make mincemeat of you,' she'd prophesied. 'You won't know how to resist. They'll twist you round their little finger. They'll get you to cut my heart out to prove how much you love them, and you'll do it.'

And she was right. How could she be otherwise? Who knows women better than a mother? And who better knows her son? First chance he gets, Henry is fist-deep in his mother's innards, scalpelling out her ventricles and whatever else they fancy while he's in there. Aorta, anyone? Small intestine? Pancreas? And then he's off, running, running, dispensing maternal organs like a second Mother Teresa let loose among the bloodsuckers. Whereupon he stumbles, whereupon the heart falls from his slippy grasp, whereupon, of course, of course, the heart cries, 'Are you hurt, my son?'

Christ! These mothers!

And what does Henry, in the dirt, do then?

Attacks the pulp of pumping muscle, that's what, throttles it, berates it, cries 'Will you shut the fuck up, Ma!', then remembers himself, his task, his sacred duty, and resumes running to the woman, the women, just as his mother said he would.

The women who don't give a shit how hurt Henry is.

Was that another reason, yet another among hundreds, she held him back from the world, kept him inside her as long as she decently could, and then bound him in ribbons to her side, reading to him of callous men and girls with skin as fine as angels' wings – because she knew he would have no choice but to knife her once she let him go?

It would help if he knew more men. He could ask them. Is this what you did too, is this what we all do? Is this what we essentially *are*?

But he's got rid of all the men he knew. Friends. What do you do with friends? Hang on to your friends, someone should have told him – maybe the wife or girlfriend of one of the friends in question – hang on tight to your friends, Henry, you'll need them when you're old. But then he'd have fallen for her, wouldn't he, loved her for her foresight and intelligence, worshipped her for her wisdom and acuity, and asked her to have dinner with him – and bang would have gone another chum.

His father's no use. His father was a brute, crashed like a herd of elephants through the fine web of undergrowth which bound Henry to his mother and then, when he was finally called upon to feel his way gently, felt too much – felt too much too suddenly – and let his own heart give out. What sort of example was that?

Henry's heart could give out, too, remembering the desertion of his mother. It's cake talk that does it. Confectioner's cream. He sees it as a measure of her loneliness, the extent to which he and his father had abandoned her, that she should have been reduced to that. She could talk of nothing else the weekend he nipped across from the Pennines to see her and found her in the kitchen — a room in the house she had once upon a time claimed she needed a guide dog to help her to locate — up to her ears in piping nozzles and spatulas. 'What are you doing?' he had asked, afraid her sensitivity had finally tipped her over the edge. 'I'm scrolling, Henry,' she told him. 'Look — it's like decorating a church. It's like sculpting. I love doing it. You've no idea. It's like a whole new world. I just love it.' She seemed possessed, inordinate. 'Did you actually bake that thing?' Henry asked, seriously frightened for her now. 'Don't be ridiculous! When did I ever bake a cake?' 'When did you ever scroll, Ma?' She kissed him, pulled him to her so he could smell the marzipan in her hair. 'The cakes, I buy,' she said. 'Dead plain. Nothing on them. The rest I do. See this? It's called a crimping knife. Guess what I do with it.' 'You crimp?' 'Exactly. I crimp, Henry! I flute, I pipe, I letter, I emboss. Aren't you proud of me?' What could he say? That he would have been had there been less hysteria in the enthusiasm? That it had always been under-stood between them that they were too civilised ever to embrace a craze, that they were professional sufferers and bleeders, nothing else, and that they had only to look at her husband, his father, if they needed to be reminded what a hobby did to you?

It was the undividedness of her zealotry that betrayed her. The wild bacchante look in her eyes, the almost proselytising fervour. How long, he wondered, before she'd be buying him a little set of icing scrollers and extruders of his own? This was not his mother. This was not how she operated when she was herself. Yes, her vocabulary had always been extreme, but when she was truly engaged she was vaguer, less upfront, more ambiguous.

Henry recalls the time she discovered Nietzsche. He had gone to Paris on a school trip and returned to find her sitting up in bed in a nightgown and wearing reading glasses he had never seen before, with *The Genealogy of Morals* held out before her as though in some soft-porn parody of a sex-starved teacher enticing her students with German philosophy. He stood at the foot of her bed, waiting for her to ask him about his holiday. She peered at him over her lenses. 'Have you read this?' she asked. He shook his head. 'Probably best you don't,' she said. 'Not yet. But then again, maybe you're old enough. I don't know. He's a profound thinker. Rabid, someone called him, morally contagious, maybe too contagious for someone your age. But no Jew should go through life without reading him sometime. With a pinch of salt, I grant you. But with an open mind as well. Anyway, how was Paris?'

It was the idea of there having been a slave revolt in morals which interested her. According to Nietzsche this was a Jewish revolt, the Jews, a priestly people, having hacked away at the aristocratic edifice of those manly virtues of war and chase and gaiety, and ushered in an era, in which we still live impoverished today, of equality and democracy. Those whom the gods had loved for their daring were henceforth damned; only the unfit were blessed. In the place of power, beauty and nobility, were now enthroned poverty, ugliness, intellection and suffering. A change in our entire system of valuation effected by the terrible potency of envy.

Henry, tired with travel, wondered whether his mother was thinking of what her husband had done to her, the vulgar demos of North Manchester pulling down the aristocratic gaiety of the South. But that interpretation failed when he tried imagining his father as a priest.

Or as potent in his envy.

'Is that why we all wear glasses?' he speculated instead.

She looked at him strangely. 'We don't all wear glasses,' she said. 'You don't, your father doesn't, and I have only just started wearing these to read philosophy.'

'No, but you know . . . I might not wear glasses but I wear a scarf. We all wear glasses or scarves.'

'Henry, I don't know what you're talking about.'

'We put something between ourselves and the world. Is that what Nietzsche means, that we have removed ourselves from nature?'

Ekaterina took off her glasses and called her son to her. '*We* don't do anything,' she said, patting his hand. 'There is no we. And if there were it wouldn't include us. Now I'd like you to forget everything I've told you. I warned you it was contagious. I won't mention the subject again.'

The trouble was she had mentioned it far and wide already, not least to her mother and her mother's sisters. Over Friday dinner at their place – tinned chicken soup, tinned chicken, tinned syrup sponge – the Stern Girls, by then depleted by one, and only to that degree less indomitable, quizzed him about it.

'How long has your mother been reading this person?' his grandmother wanted to know.

'Nietzsche,' Marghanita corrected her, with a quick, precise stare at Henry.

How did she do that, Henry wanted to know, how was she able to make even a dead German philosopher sound like an adventure between them? OK, Nietzsche's name had a buried z in it, but she could embroil him no less successfully in secrets with Hawthorne or Melville, or Emerson even. Was it her? Or was it him, simply what happened to him when he heard the names of writers?

He shrugged. 'I can't remember seeing her with anything but *Jane Eyre* in her hand,' he told his grandmother. 'Always a novel, anyway. This philosophy business seems to have come out of the blue.'

'It's not one of your books?'

'No,' Henry said.

'You haven't been told to read him at school?'

'No. Look, this hasn't come from me. But I have to say it sounds interesting enough.'

'Interesting!' Effie exploded. 'Do you know your mother's reading Hitler's favourite writer?'

Henry wondered where it would have left them had Hitler's favourite writer been Charlotte Brontë, as for all he knew it was. 'She doesn't believe every word of it, you know,' he said, as much in his own defence as his mother's. 'I think she's just toying with it.'

'You don't toy with fire,' his grandmother reminded him.

Henry shrugged again. 'My father does,' he reminded her.

'Yes, well, that's what we are wondering,' Effie broke in. 'Could it be that there's a problem between them?'

'Do you mean is she reading Nietzsche because Dad's away a lot? I suppose that's possible. But then you could argue there are worse things to do when your husband's out.'

Always supposing you can keep a husband, was the implied slight which Henry intended them to hear in that. He was annoyed with them. On his mother's behalf largely, but also because he hated the way they would suddenly close ranks and close their minds – even Marghanita – the moment the world beyond threatened to impinge upon their privacy, and thus destabilise, as they saw it, their meticulously contrived anonymity. They read books and played music and looked at paintings, they embraced the arts of civilisation, they loved to talk, they cultivated feeling, yet at the same time they cultivated ignorance. Why does no one ever try to interest me, Henry wondered, in what is happening at this moment? Not to him, not to them, not to the family, and not even to the tribe, but out there, in the world, *to* the world. He didn't mean politics, specifically. He didn't quite know what he meant, since he was describing the absence of a presence for which he had never been given the word. That was his beef. That he hadn't been kept informed. That he didn't know what he was missing, only that he was missing something. The way things worked, was that it? The operations of the universe? The physics of being?

But the physics of being as recently understood. Not as decreed on a mountain top on Sinai five thousand years ago.

His father was his father. Uncle Izzi, children's entertainer. And Henry wasn't going to look to a children's entertainer for enlightenment. His father lived out of time, not in the past but on some other plane where there was neither past nor future. His father's parents had barely learned to speak a word of English though they'd been born in Manchester and lived there all their lives. Yiddish did them. Yiddish sufficed. In Yiddish they thought they were invisible to their enemies. Like the ostrich. Which certainly made them invisible to Henry, at whom they stared in deep anxiety, the few times they saw him, as though he might be about to report them to the authorities, and as though the penny they gave him, pinching his cheek, would buy him off. But his mother and the Stern Girls were different. They weren't in hiding. They weren't afraid. So why didn't the times pulse audibly in their veins? Wherefore, at the last, were *they* bemused?

Sometimes Henry wondered whether it was all an effect of being in the north. Too cold up there, too dark, too backward, for anything but your own immediate wants to engross you. But always he would come back to believing that the fault – if fault it was – lay more particularly with his own people. They had come north in order not to know or notice; they were up here precisely because it was like being nowhere.

Was this why Marghanita pressed American literature on him? In America the Jews had taken on a version of the national iden-tity, had made the American cause their own, had even shaped it, sometimes dangerously – tempting fate, risking a backlash – in their own image. Not in England, not in Manchester, not on the Pennines. Yes, they were dutiful citizens; they paid their taxes, fought in wars, performed charitable deeds, gave service to the community – but only for the right, at last, to be left alone to notice nothing. And not be noticed noticing it.

The catch for Henry was that he, too, found this half-absence from the world alluring. By Henry's lights, if anything was civilised, this was – knowing nothing of event, forswearing effect, attending only to the still sad humanity of your own heart. 'You and your ivory tower version of civilisation,' his Gentile school-friends used to twit him, Geoff the geographer who understood the economic underpinnings of Henry's street, Ned who could compute the distance of a star from how bright it was, Dick who debated capitalism versus socialism with numbers – how many privileged, how many deprived, how many slaughtered or gone missing, how many enriched – all stuff Henry knew absolutely nothing about. But that's my point,' was Henry's invariable reply, 'civilisation *is* an ivory tower.'

Except that it didn't look so civilised on days like today, with the Stern Girls manning every exit, and his grandmother in the forecourt with her torch, reminding him why it was necessary, on occasions, to round up stragglers and turn the key.

'Yes, there are worse things to do when your husband's out, Henry,' she said, 'though not very many. You know we don't go in for old world superstition or fanaticism here. We are free thinkers. But if there's one freedom of thought we don't need just at this very moment it's the freedom to accuse the Jewish people of poisoning civilisation. *That* we can think about again a hundred years from now.'

Ah well, Henry supposed he agreed with that. Or if he didn't, couldn't remember why he didn't. Jew talk embarrassed him. At school it was frowned on by Jewish and non-Jewish boys alike. It felt old hat. Wej talk was different. Back slang the fact of your being a Jew and you did something witty with it. Joking was fine. Otherwise leave it. As for Nietzsche, he was old hat too. The world he'd set alight was no longer even smouldering. The most interesting part of it all, for Henry, was seeing his mother fired

147

with intellectual passion, reading without migraines, not merely to rub at the itch of her sensitivity – could that have been the reason for the migraines? – but seeking for truth in that penetralium of mystery, philosophy. It made him proud of her. *My* mother understands philosophy, what does *your* mother understand? But he also suspected it would pass. He was confident of the soundness of her mind. She was too sensible to be a fanatic.

And at length, of course, it did pass. One day she was talking about 'slave ethics', the next she wasn't. Just like that. Possible that the Stern Girls had put the screws on her, but he doubted it. Much more likely to have been the firmness of her character. The sane are fickle. When it came to cake decorating, though, he could see that something had changed. Her natural soundness had been undermined. She couldn't stop doing it. Couldn't stop reading about it, couldn't stop showing him her sugar pastes and wire flowers, couldn't stop going on courses, couldn't stop giving lectures and demonstrations. Once, he walked into Lewis's in Leeds (never mind why he was in Leeds) and saw her with a semi-circle of women around her, doing something with royal icing. He was relieved he was on his own. Not because he was ashamed of her, no, if anything he was thrilled to see how smart and assured she looked, how well she held her audience, how roundly she rang her voice. Sometimes you need to observe your mother in a public place, at the centre of a world which excludes you, to grasp her separateness. At least Henry did. So that was his mother! So that was what she actually looked like! Amazing. But upsetting too. His mother become a kitchen person. His mother in an apron. She who had sat him on her knee and got him to read to her from *The Awkward Age*. She who had put her mind to Nietzsche and the idea that there was once, in some city of the mind, a slave revolt, not in marzipan but in morals. Demeaned. Diminished. And all because the men in her house had left her to her own devices, marooned her at home where at last she had grown homey.

Is he to allow Moira, a mere pastry chef who as like as not has never opened Nietzsche in her life, to demean the memory of his mother further? Does being with a woman who fishes for his member on a motorway matter that much to him that he would cut his mother's heart out on her say-so?

Well, does it?

Well?

What Henry needs is a man to talk to. Is this what you do? Is this what we all do?

Then it occurs to him that Lachlan is only next door.


'I've still not entirely got rid of the witch,' he tells Henry, pouring port. He is in a pink candlewick dressing gown, presumably hers. Around his throat a Highland scarf, worn like a cravat. His legs, Henry notices, are badly veined. Like many men his age, he will soon be able to pass for an old woman. And in me, too, Henry wonders, is the old woman in me too beginning to show?

As for the persistence of the other old woman, Henry is in no position to have an opinion. 'I've never been in here before so I wouldn't know,' he says.

Lachlan wafts the air. 'Can't tell if it's death I can smell or her thirty years of illegal occupation.'

Henry doesn't have the heart to tell him it's the dressing gown.

He looks around the room. The apartment is the mirror image of his own. If Henry understood more about the architecture of mansion blocks he would realise that the two flats were once one, extending the full depth of the building. But other than in shape and proportion, they do not resemble each other. The old lady's place is all heirlooms, heavy, dark, patina'd with the mustiness of a long invalidism. Pictures of flowers on the walls, a bad painting of an elderly gentleman looking stern (Lachlan's father, Henry presumes, before Norma Jean got her playful hands on him), and a small amount of Robert Louis Stevenson memorabilia: 'Requiem' in a chipped brown frame –

Under the wide and starry sky,
Dig the grave and let me lie.
Glad did I live and gladly die,
And I laid me down with a will.

– and a photograph of the grave itself, the famous sepulchre built, as the author had requested, atop Mount Vaea, in a jungle of flame trees and banyans, and snapped so that you can see down to the blue waters of Samoa. On a bronze plate, the poem. *Here he lies where he longed to be; / Home is the sailor, home from sea* . . .

Sad, bardic Henry sighs. He has a soft spot for the graves of writers. Words and death, there's no beating the combination.

'Signed by him,' Lachlan says, noting Henry's interest.

'Signed by whom?'

'The old boy himself.'

'Your father?'

'No, not my father, of course not my father – what would that be worth? – by RLS.'

Henry peers at the signature. Illegible. Then realises it's nonsense. 'How could he have signed a photograph of his own tomb?'

Lachlan makes a noise in his stomach. Umbrage. 'That's his signature,' he says. 'Know it anywhere. We've got letters from him. See that S, see that funny L, leaning backwards – his without question.'

'Spirit writing, you're saying?'

'They buried him according to his wishes, who's to say he didn't design the tomb before he died. Brain haemorrhage, you know. Terrible thing.'

Very likely, Henry thinks. Designed the tomb, erected it on the top of a mountain, pointed the camera, wrote 'wish you were here' across the print, and haemorrhaged in his servant's arms. Though he has never been to Samoa, Henry can see it all in his

mind's eye. Who needs to travel when you have a lively imagination.

He shifts his attention to the marks on the walls, handprints
almost, trails, anyway, leading from one doorway to the next and
stopping at light switches, where the old lady must have paused
to get her breath and see her way.

'I know what you're thinking,' Lachlan says. 'Sad, the poor old
girl, living on her own, having to save on heating and lighting.
Don't let that fool you. She slept with the heaters on in summer.
See these?' He shows Henry the blackened linings of the curtains.
'Scalded from the heat. And she never turned off a light. There
are light bulbs here that are welded into the sockets, they've been
on so long. I'm still waiting for some of them to cool down. She
didn't need to worry, you see. It wasn't her money she was
burning.'

Henry would like to sit down, but he has spotted Angus curled
like a cobra in love in his wicker basket. He eyes the dog. The
dog eyes him back, lost in the melancholy of sexual desire. Only
reduce yourself, the dog says, only meet me halfway, on the couch
if not the floor, and I will give myself to you.

'Maybe she didn't realise what she was doing,' Henry says.

'Didn't realise! I think you realise when you're going through
someone's inheritance.'

'I mean maybe she didn't realise how you felt about it.' Henry
wants to say maybe she didn't realise your desperation, but there
are some liberties you can't take in the matter of another person's
fortune, however indiscreet that other person is himself. The
other thing Henry wants to say is what the fuck does any of this
have to do with me.

'Oh, she realised how I felt about it,' Lachlan assures him. 'She
made me check the balance of her account every day and then ring
her up and read it out to her, so she could *hear* how I felt about it.
Think of that – every single day of the week. The only time she
let me miss was a bank holiday. When I came up to visit she insisted

we go to the bank together so she could *see* how I felt about it. She wanted me to count it dripping away, penny by penny. And she wanted to be there while I counted. There's a word for that.'

'Sadism,' Henry ventures.

'Sadism. Thank you.' He secretes bile. Henry can smell it. Hear it. Like the central heating switching on. 'Sadism. Yes.'

Henry shakes his head. It's difficult for him, in Lachlan's presence, remembering how to make his face show sympathy, so he just shakes it to be on the safe side.

'Have I told you about her suite in the Imperial in Torquay?' Lachlan asks.

'Not that I remember,' Henry says.

'Ten years she had it. Concurrently with this place. How do you like that? Two homes while I had none. Best view in that building as well. She used to invite me up for tea, to show me the sea and make me eat what was owing to me in scones and cream. "Have more, Lachie," she'd say. "Don't deny yourself. Your father wouldn't have wanted you to go without. I'll ring up for more cream." I was so down on my uppers I used to have to work there myself in high season.'

'Nice place to work though, isn't it, Torquay?'

'Might be if you're collecting deckchairs, but I'm talking about the hotel.'

Henry tries to imagine Lachlan working in a hotel. Guest relations? Baggage? The kitchens? 'As what?' As a waiter, Henry decides even as he asks. He must have been a waiter. One of those who never lets you catch his eye, unlike Angus who lives for nothing else.

'As a gigolo.'

Henry's mouth falls open. At least he hasn't forgotten how to do surprise. 'You were a gigolo?'

'I was better looking in those days.'

'I'm sorry, I didn't mean that. It's just that I've never met a man who has actually slept with women for money.'

'Slept? Chance would be a fine thing.'

'So what did you do if you didn't sleep with them?'

'Waltzed with them.'

Henry is disappointed. 'But after the waltz,' he says. 'Presumably there were occasions . . .'

Now it's Lachlan's turn to shake his head. 'Never. Too old, most of them. It was hard enough work just getting them back into their chairs.'

'You're a good dancer, then?'

'Was. All the Louis Stevenson men danced. "Can't call your-self a complete man if you haven't got twinkle toes," the old boy used to say.'

'Robert Louis Stevenson said that?'

'No, my father did. And look where that motto got him.'

'But if you didn't sleep with them,' Henry goes on, 'how did you get your money? Did they pay you per dance?'

'Good God, no. What do you think I was – a prostitute? The hotel paid me. But since the old woman was keeping the hotel afloat anyway, I was just getting my own money back. Makes you bitter, you know, dancing your life away with old bats for nothing.'

Oh, I don't know, Henry thinks.

Normally, he would like to be off now. By his standards this is a preternaturally lengthy conversation. But he is gripped by the spectacle of a man more disgusted with his life than he is himself. When Lachlan talks he appears to be staring into an abyss. Henry is curious to see whether he intends to fall into it this afternoon.

He notices that Angus has gone to sleep. 'May I sit down?' he asks.

'Of course,' Lachlan tries to say, making a sign of apology. He is temporarily unable to talk for something lodged in his oesophagus. His life. He is choking on his life, Henry thinks.

'You never talk about your mother, your real mother,' Henry says, once Lachlan has cleared his passages.

Lachlan's eyes water like Angus's. 'Too long ago,' he says.

'I'm sorry,' Henry says. He doesn't want another of them falling in love with him out of loneliness. 'It's just that I am thinking a lot about my mother at present.'

'She alive?'

'No.'

'Dreadful business, I know,' Lachlan says. But what does he know? Nothing. He is not listening, not concentrating, gone somewhere else. London Bridge, circa 1958. The time he threw his bowler hat in the Thames. Kicked the dust of his family off his heels. Watched the hat float away on the tide, then strode off, free, into the future. Except that there was no future. He tries to collect himself. Then tells Henry all about it.

They were in sugar. In molasses, to be exact. In molasses big. Does Henry know anything about molasses? No. Few people do. And those that did would not have known what Lachlan knew. Lachlan was born into molasses. Louis Stevenson – did the name not mean anything to Henry? *Treasure Island*, obviously. But to some the name was even more synonymous with molasses. Louis Stevenson treacle . . . No? In a sense, the island that provided Lachlan's branch of the Louis Stevensons was even more of a treasure island than Long John Silver's. Treasures poured, anyway, however fanciful the comparison, into the pockets of Lachlan's great-great-grandsires, as it was meant to pour, when his time came, into Lachlan's. He had been prepared for nothing less since his earliest age. Taught the trade. Taught the history. Taught the geography. Taught the chemistry. Taught the economics. Taught the shipping. High-masted schooners which brought molasses back from the Indies bore the names of Lachlan's great-aunts, and one day would bear the name of Lachlan's wife. Except that by Lachlan's fifteenth birthday his father and his grandfather were employing tankers to transport their molasses, which meant that Lachlan's wife, whoever she was destined to be, would have to make do with having her name on one of those. Less romantic,

Lachlan thought, but as his father told him, progress was progress and no one with a sweet tooth would ever know the difference. Make no mistake, Lachlan was proud to be the heir of Louis Stevenson syrup and treacle and however many dozens of other products besides. He loved enumerating to his friends at public school the sweets and chocolates which would never have been what they were had his family not had an input into them. But for the plummeting of the price of sugar after the First World War, he told them, they wouldn't have been able to suck on anything that he wasn't in a manner of speaking responsible for. But for colonial exploitation you wouldn't be at this school, some of the smartest of them retorted. Which hurt a bit, though he was versed in the arguments to refute that sort of sentimentality. No molasses, no jobs. No jobs, no money. No money, no self-respect – so up yours, Engels Minor. What hurt more were the prosaic tankers, and the storage terminals which had been built to receive them. Lachlan thought he remembered barrels. Maybe he'd only seen photographs of barrels, or heard talk of barrels, nevertheless the idea of barrels was part of the heritage of his imagination. One day he would go over to the islands, share a rum with the natives on his plantation, and sail home, in a boat named after his beloved wife, with the molasses slurping about in barrels. Some who couldn't wait to have their molasses tinned and bottled and sold to them in the normal way would be standing on the quay expectantly, their jugs in their hands, their lips moist, knowing they could draw from the barrels the moment the ship was still. That was how he had always pictured it. Hand to mouth. Now, there were thousands of feet of pipeline enabling the molasses to be pumped directly from the ship. Suddenly it had become an industry. And just as suddenly, Lachlan had become a City man, no trips to Jamaica or the Antilles yet, but only shipping routes to get to know, warehousing, tank sizes, pumping velocities, mere ledger work no matter how it was bedecked in the language of high finance. 'Not what I want,' he told his father.

'But then what you want might not be what I want,' his father told him in return. 'I'm all unexpended energy, Dad,' he said. 'Then go on unexpending it,' his dad told him, 'you'll need it one day.' 'I'm not a bank, Dad.' 'Oh yes you are.' Hence Lachlan, one bright metropolitan morning, striding along London Bridge in his pinstripe suit – no pirate shirt, no pantaloons – reaching a decision which would affect the whole of his life. Enough. He'd had enough measuring and counting and pen-pushing. He was twenty-three, a young man, not a bank, the white sun-tipped town humming about his ears, the great brown river of promise rolling beneath him. So off with his hat, off with it, a gesture of such liberating boldness that he remembers himself singing as he performed it – 'Burlington Bertie' or 'The Man Who Broke the Bank at Monte Carlo', something like that, though it's also possible he didn't sing at all, so contracted was his heart with fear. Away went the hat anyway, in a lovely fearful parabola of freedom, up and away like a black balloon, tumbling and spinning and almost, *almost* floating, until it landed brim down in the river and sailed away, a little boat with Lachlan's prospects in it.

In his sleep, Angus cries a lovelorn cry.

'And?' Henry wants to know.

'Oh, there's no "and",' Lachlan says.

'You didn't get to the Antilles?'

'Never tried. Got myself entangled with a woman instead. Took a job as a clerk in an antique auction house for the time being – it's always for the time being, have you noticed? – fell for the secretary and married her. Dreadful mistake. She thought I was moneyed. I have the look, you see. Or at least I had it then. She thought I was idling until I came into my fortune. After I told her I'd thrown my fortune off London Bridge she didn't talk to me for three years.'

'But you married for all that?'

'We already were married. It was our wedding night when I told her. Damned silly, I suppose.'

'You still married?'

'Officially, but we don't communicate. I hit her with a fish and that was that.'

'Your life seems to be marked by large gestures,' Henry notices.

'I don't know about large. Futile more like.'

'So why did you hit her with a fish?'

'Years of ill treatment. She spoke ill of me and ill to me. Couldn't forgive the molasses. Couldn't pass a tin of syrup without abusing me. Sometimes you just snap. It was a kipper actually. I think that made it worse, that it was a breakfast fish.'

'You like to make your runs for freedom in the morning?'

'I hadn't thought of that. But yes, you're right. I believe I can change things in the morning. Or I did. And it was a bit like the bowler, the kipper. I felt the same lightness afterwards, for ten minutes.'

'And your mother? Had you stayed in touch with her?'

'We wrote. But she was disappointed in me. I imagined she'd see my point of view, you expect that of mothers – fathers equal business, mothers equal the heart, all that nonsense – but she thought I'd been an ass, walking out and marrying a secretary who wouldn't talk to me. She had a point, too. In the end it was my father who came round, though by that time my mother had passed on – cursing, I was told, cursing all of us on her death bed – and Louis Stevenson molasses were suffering in the City. Tanker problems – there's a joke! The old boy was ready to make a gesture of his own, you see, and saw me as an ally. I'd thrown my hat in the Thames, he was about to throw away his life, or what was left of it, on a woman who'd sung in the music halls. Funny the way it turned out – he made a better job of being flamboyant than I did.'

'Oh, I don't think you should see it like that,' Henry says, gesturing to the room, to the idea of St John's Wood beyond, to the principle of London with all its bleak emancipations and amenities. It was something he'd always imagined for himself, being washed up and cynical at sixty, a free and bitter spirit, proof that nothing pays or matters, that you can persist beyond happiness. In this way they are bedfellows – he born into spiders, wee Lachie born into molasses – the fellow-fallen, but each with a nice apartment.

So *Oh, I don't think you should see it like that* is on behalf of both of them.

Lost on Lachie, though. 'I'll tell you what sticks in the craw,' he says, redundantly Henry thinks, since everything sticks in his craw – 'the fact that I've come full circle, still dependent on molasses money, what's left of it, and still selling the stuff.'

'I thought you were in pigswill,' Henry says.

'Animal feeds. As it happens the pigs don't care for sweeteners, but sheep and cattle love it. It's an important source of good-quality carbohydrate. Easily digested, not too high in nitrogen content, and cheap to produce. I should know.'

'Then that's all right,' Henry says, not being a conversationalist in the matter of animal feeds, and not wanting to stir Angus from his sweet sleep with talk of din-dins.

'Not all right with me. If I'd thought I was going to end up selling molasses, I'd have stayed, wouldn't I? Kept my hat on. As it effing is, pardon my French, it's all been for nothing.'

Hmm. Time to go, harumphing Henry thinks, refusing another drink. Time to return to his own disappointments. But not before it has crossed his mind that they have something in common, Lachlan and Moira – she the pastry chef, he caramelised in history and grief. Sweeteners.

Henry has been alive a long time; he knows how much small things count, what tiny fibres of like-mindedness bind the lonely. He himself is merely a failed teacher, arid, an amateur cake decorator's son, with at best confectioner's cream in his veins. Between Moira and Lachlan flows, whether or not they yet know it, molasses.

He should let Lachlan have her. Give something back. He's

borrowed from other men all his life, now's the time to make some recompense. Moira isn't his to give, he knows that, but if she were he should part with her. Give someone else a chance.

'Before you go, old man,' Lachlan says at the door, not quite putting his arm round Henry's shoulder, but nearly, disconcertingly *nearly*, 'do you use whores?'

Henry's jaw drops. Actually slides out of his possession. He is aware that he has reddened. 'Not exactly,' is the best he can think of saying, 'though I suppose there have been times when they've used me.'

They laugh at that, together, if you can call the noise they make a laugh.

Yes, Henry decides, he should definitely let Lachlan have her. Lachlan's need being by far the greater. And by that token, his capacity to love and cherish being the greater too. It would be a kindness all round. If nothing else, that would at least leave Henry with the eminence he once enjoyed, as the most miserable person in the building.

But he loves her. And you don't give away what you love. That much he has learned. So there you are.

# SEVEN

'I've cocked up my life,' Henry told himself, early on the first day of his first term as an assistant lecturer at the Pennine Way College of Rural Technology. That was not simply a description of what had happened, it was also a statement of intent. Henry conjugated verbs differently from other men. 'I've cocked up my life', as Henry inflected it, also contained the meanings 'I will cock up my life', 'I will have cocked up my life', and 'There was never a time when I wasn't going to have cocked up my life'.

A future imperative, past determinative tense, all Henry's own, perfect, unconditional and punitive.

So who was Henry punishing? Ah, if Henry only knew the answer to that!

As for why he was punishing whoever he was punishing, that is much easier. Henry couldn't forgive him/her/them for making him so frightened of life that all he could do was teach it. In the abstract Henry admired teachers and didn't hold with the smug wisdom which said that those who could did, and those who couldn't taught. Teaching was as much doing as most things, Henry thought, and in many cases more. Those who really could were proud to pass on the trick of it – for pedagogy was a species of philanthropy – while those who couldn't clothed their incompetence in selfishness and went into banking or politics. The parasitic professions. That being the case, Henry should have been proud to be a teacher. But he wasn't.

This was partly the fault of the profession itself. Or at least the fault of the profession at the time Henry as a pupil encountered it. By believing it could effect wonders as an influence for social change, not just enlighten but liberate, teaching became the architect of its own demise. It educated boys like Henry into inordinate ambitions for themselves, created the most grandiose expectations, of which the least was staying where you were and passing on the baton of learning.

When it came to mapping out their futures, Henry and his school friends, not excepting the stellar 'Hovis' Belkin, had all been unthreateningly vague, wanting to do well, hoping to make a name, meaning to be of use, expecting, at the very least, to be creative. Beyond that it was felt to be crass to declare your career path. The only people who knew what they wanted to be wanted to be train drivers. The world was all before them, that was how they felt about it; they were educated to believe they could be and do anything. Anything but teachers. That was their single specificity. Whatever other choices we may make, we will none of us choose teaching. It was almost a blood oath. An obligation to their collective idea of themselves, past and future, sacredly binding each to each. We will make the world sit up or we will not, but we will never so help us God be stuck stuttering in front of a class of boys like 'Fister' Frister, or go quietly to the funny farm like 'Fat Frieda', or break down and weep like 'Bunny' Hensher, in commemoration of whose congenital rabbit twitch Henry's classmates sat a carrot on their desks at the beginning of every lesson.

Thus by becoming the only one of them to renege on his oath, Henry had let not only himself down, but all his friends. In a queer way he even felt that by becoming a teacher he had let his teachers down.

Complicated, the labyrinth of loyalties a boy bears to his school past. One way or another you're always letting someone down. Henry remembered 'Fat Frieda' with such a toxic mixture of embarrassment, allegiance and regret, such consciousness of treachery, that what he felt for her was almost love. Something of him belonged to her, that was the only way he could understand it; something of him pertained to her, which he was duty-bound, if he were to make any progress giving his own nature the slip, flatly to deny.

Biology, she taught. Whatever biology was. Henry never listened. Biology, physics, chemistry, maths – whatever explained the way the physical universe worked was of no interest to Henry, who preferred not to know. You look in a mirror and you see yourself, that was knowledge enough for Henry. All refraction did was explain what didn't need explaining and give him migraines. Molecules were less obvious to the eye, but made him queasy for that very reason. Face that life was molecules, rather than words, and suicide was the only logical conclusion. In fairness to it, biology lacked the hard-edged cruelty of the other sciences. Biology was more like a ramble through the park, looking for catkins, than an actual subject. 'Oh, and what is it we see here?' No point asking Henry; Henry hadn't seen anything. None of the teachers ever lasted very long either. Often Henry's class was without a biology teacher altogether. Not that Henry minded that. Who needed biology? So desperate was the school, however, to take on anybody who could be induced to teach biology for more than a term, whether or not they knew any more about it than Henry did, that at last they flew in the face of a century of tradition, not to say wisdom, and hired a woman. Miss Hill. Spherical, owlish, low on the ground. Her bad luck that there was already a Hill on the premises, Fred Hill, also seriously fore-shortened, a podgy lab assistant in a discoloured white coat which smelled of stink bombs. By the end of her first day she was 'Fat Frieda', echoing 'Fat' Fred, and assumed to be 'Fat' Fred in disguise, a money-saving ruse on the part of the school attested to, above all, by the fact that Fred and 'Frieda' Hill had identical moustaches.

Whenever 'Fat Frieda' asked a question, Henry's classmates made aerials of their arms, like the antennae of caterpillars, and shouted, 'Sir, sir – oh sorry, Miss.'

Then they held their noses, the way they did when 'Fat' Fred entered the lab.

Henry couldn't understand why she wouldn't learn from experience, since she was a scientist, and give up asking questions altogether. He also couldn't figure why the headmaster didn't squash the ribald speculations by parading Fred and 'Frieda' Hill on the platform at the same time, as in the final act of *The Comedy of Errors*. Failing which, he wondered how long it would be before Miss Hill fell apart, leaving them without a biology teacher once again, but more importantly, leaving him without the wherewithal to control his features. Henry was only ever marginally able to police his face. If 'Fat Frieda' went in his seeing, he knew he'd go with her.

Then, towards the end of one muggy Friday afternoon, that afterthought hour when biology was always to be found, like a drowned man lashed to the shipwreck of the week, Henry was brought back from his mental wanderings by the noise of the rest of the class jumping on to their desks, scratching their armpits, and making like monkeys. 'Ooo, ooo, ooo!' Poor Miss Hill. He shook his head over her. She had no instinct for self-preservation. Zoo animals, for God's sake. With boys! Hadn't she learned yet that the only safe subject with boys was the broad bean? But he pricked his ears, nonetheless, to something he half-heard her say, her voice quavering as ever, as though there were perforations in her voice box. *The skin of apes and monkeys remains dry even in a hot environment* – was that it? 'Ooo, ooo, ooo!' Yes, that was it. Dry even in a hot environment – like school. He was a profuse sweater himself, Henry. He was wet all day. He had been wet all week. His difference from apes and monkeys could have been explained had apes and monkeys lacked the means to sweat. But they didn't. As he understood it – and he was listening hard now, harder than he had ever listened to anything that was not poetic fancy – they were possessed of the same two categories of sweat glands, apocrine and eccrine, as himself. Eccrine glands were absent from the majority of mammals, but not from chimpanzees and gorillas. They may have had fewer than he did, every living creature had fewer than he did, but the big thing was that they had them at all. For biologists taking the long view, this suggested that intense thermal sweating in man was an answer to some new prompting. Henry reckoned he knew what that prompting was. Shame. In that instant he formulated his own theory of the ascent of man. What impelled man forward, sophisticating his glands and separating him at last from the apes, was disgust and embarrassment with himself. The whole story of our evolution is the development of our capacity to know shame, and the cutaneous transpiration of mortification into pearls of sweat which roll glistening down our chests and backs, and not down the backs and chests of gorillas, is the visible evidence of it.

Ergo – civilisation *is* shame.

His mother was right. She should not have given birth to him.

His eyes met 'Fat Frieda's'. He was the only boy not jumping up and down, scratching his armpits and bellowing. Was that a smile she found for him? Through all the fear, a glint of gentle recognition, and maybe even gratitude?

Henry knew what he had to do. He leapt up from his chair. 'Ooo, ooo, ooo!' he went. 'Ooo, ooo, ooo!'

And was never able to look her in the eye again.


So who could say that teaching wasn't his punishment?

They screwed a polished wooden board to his door with his name on it in swirls of gold lettering.

### HENRY NAGEL LECTURER

He stood in front of it a long time, balancing grief with pride. It wasn't quite the same as teacher, lecturer, was it? Lecturer denoted something else. Lecturer meant soon to be professor, which definitely denoted something else. Or did it? Would the distinction have cut any ice, to choose a name at random, with 'Hovis' Belkin?

Knowing that the board with gold lettering would please his

mother and the Stern Girls, he invited them (but not his father, who would breathe on it and burn it down) to sherry in his room.

'Henry, the board!' his grandmother cried.

'Board?' Henry wondered. 'Is there a board?'

They kissed him in turn, Irina, Effie, Marghanita, his mother. He'd done it for them. And for the memory of Anastasia. He had penetrated an England which, for all their culturedness, had hitherto eluded them. He was a soon-to-be professor. He had opened up the spice route to the institutions of the English mind. He wanted to weep, they had it so wrong.

Madness, wasn't it, listening to 'Hovis' Belkin, the enemy of his soul, when he could have taken the word of the women who loved him, and considered him a success? But that was the way of it, for Henry. Only those who thought badly of him counted.

How long it was before the waters of the college closed over him, Henry can no longer remember. He fancies he was a drowning man from the day he took his first class, clicking his fingers and cracking his knuckles and pulling hairs out of his beard, an excruciated boy in a leather jacket, his voice not a voice he recognised, the preposterousness of his being a figure in authority all he could think about, he, hangdog Henry, who only the day before, it seemed, had been sitting on his mother's knee, reading aloud to her from *The Awkward Age*. But the truth is he went under only gradually. Didn't even have the balls to dive straight in, Henry.

It was the women who finally dragged him down. Not the womenfriends or the womenrelatives or the borrowed women-wives of his best friends, but the women in his department, the bookwomen in whose name literature, as a sort of evidential documentation of persecution, or, when not that, a palimpsest of resistance, was now being universally understood. He should have been prepared. He should even have been at home. If ever a man had been brought up to be one of them, a girl among girls, it was Henry. What was so different about their way of looking at things from his own? Literature was the history and lexicon of their oppression; well, wasn't literature also the history and lexicon of his? Jane Eyre, Mrs Dalloway, Henry Nagel – take your pick.

He could have done without a father. Left entirely to the mercies of his mother and the Stern Girls, Henry could have made his way nicely through the newly effeminated humanities. He joked about it in a rare letter to 'Hovis' Belkin, by then in America. '*Textually, or I might even mean textologically, I am entirely in my element. All I need to do is wear a frock and cut my dick off and the prize is mine,*' he wrote, and no sooner posted it than wished he hadn't. Tactless, tasteless, damaging to himself, to be confirming 'Hovis' of all people in the very view of Henry's masculinity which 'Hovis' had been the first (not counting Henry's father) to promulgate. Did Henry *want* 'Hovis' to think of him as frocked and dickless? Had he always wanted it? In a rare letter back, 'Hovis' skipped the dick but was surprised to hear (but then again not surprised to hear, the Pennines being the Pennines) that they were still in frocks and not yet in dungarees and overalls where Henry was. But not surprised, Henry noted, to hear that Henry was thinking of wearing one. Would anyone have been surprised? The question stirred the dormant pond of genes bequeathed to Henry by his father. Be a man, Henry. Be a man and stand up for men. His voice deepened from belated boy soprano to something closer to light baritone. His beard grew bristlier before he shaved if off altogether to manifest dark stubble. He trimmed his lashes. He adopted the mannerism of scratching behind his ear when any of his women colleagues spoke, a downward raking of his neck, as though he meant to draw his own blood, which he'd seen someone do in the movies and which he thought denoted a fine masculinist contempt. He breathed fire. Going in to empty the ashtrays after staff meetings, in those days when Henry bit back his bashfulness and went to war on behalf of the waning phallotyranny of fathers everywhere, the cleaners believed they could smell paraffin.

Nothing so pathetic as a dragon without a bite. Having set himself against the girls, Henry couldn't come up with anything to cheer the boys. Men in books? Henry didn't know of any men in books. Yes, there were odd male interlopers, incidental swashbucklers even, about whom the heroines might and then again might not, but the fictional strategy, not to say the underlying semiotic, was against them. Henry wasn't convinced by all the talk about the conductibility and viscousness of women's writing; he couldn't feel the deep maternal blood flow, let alone go with it; he missed the goo; but in all the novels that were important to him – even those by the author of *The Ivory Tower* – the poetics invariably confirmed the sensibilities of women. The form was theirs. Its structure chimed with the almanac of their frustrated powers. He made a brief excursion into *Tom Jones* and *Roderick Random* and *Ivanhoe* and *Peveril of the Peak* and *The Last of the Barons*, but he could no more take the historiography than the facetiousness. He even canvassed a course in which anything with Henry in, would Henry teach. The Henrys of course, *Henry IV* (*Parts 1* and *2*), *Henry V*, *Henry VI* (*Parts 1*, *2* and *3*) and *Henry VIII* (which Henry himself had never read), *Little Dorrit* (for Henry Gowan), *Northanger Abbey* (for Henry Tilney), *Mansfield Park* (for Henry Crawford), *Emma* (for Henry Woodhouse *and* Henrietta Bates), *A Pair of Blue Eyes* (for Henry Knight), *The Fox* (for Henry Grenfel), the poetry of John Berryman whose Henry set the benchmark for suicidally unhappy Henrys everywhere, and, bending his own rules, the earlier short stories of O. Henry and the later novels of Henry James. This, however, struck the department as differing in no essential from what Henry normally taught, except in so far as it came clean at last about the solipsism, which wasn't necessarily a recommendation.

So he settled finally – was allowed to settle, that's to say, in the spirit of its being his goose, so let him cook it – for a comparative and evaluative course of study (you had to announce if there was going to be any evaluation, you had to issue a health warning, and you had to include a sub-clause offering students the option not to) entitled Literature's For Life, implying that it wasn't just for Christmas while at the same time echoing life as in Lawrentian 'life', a religious entity with masculinist overtones, and also the last line of *Washington Square*, 'for life, as it were', which as everyone knows refers to the cold fate of a betrayed woman. That's what he would really have liked to call it: Literature's For Life As It Were, but he knew without asking that it would take up too much space in the Handbook. In meetings on the curriculum or when trying to interest incurious students at the beginning of a new academic year, he pronounced it North Manchesterly – Literature's For Laff – to evoke, as well, the idea of muscular expansiveness and mirth. But when all was said and done – Life or Laff, however you cared to interpret or pronounce it – his course comprised the same texts as everyone else was teaching: *Pamela*, *Amelia*, *Clarissa*, *Henrietta*, *Sophia*, *Cecilia*, *Evelina*, *Belinda*, *Emma*, *Shirley*, *Sybil*, *Venetia*, *Ruth*, *Eleanor*, *Marcella*, *Mary Barton*, *Mrs Dalloway*. Only with the occasional consolatory Henry thrown in, and taught, as Henry liked to think, with more sinew.

Lit's For Life, was how the students referred to it, whatever Henry liked to think. Lit's For Life – like the motto on a T-shirt. Shows us your tits, show us your lits. So much for Henry James and D. H. Lawrence.

He became a spider, spinning in the dark. Five years into his appointment, and still uncertain of tenure, he was moved to the end of the corridor, and then into another wing of the humanities building altogether.

'The students can't find me,' he complained to his then head of department – the previous incumbent, Jane's husband, having moved on, taking Jane, who wouldn't let him weigh her breasts on the moor, with him. Mona Khartoum the name of the new one. Brought up in Sussex and Baghdad. Dr. Lilac and orange hair, time at the Sorbonne, author of a work on the sexual economics of prosody (assertive cadence a tax on women, an actual emotional revenue, administered and gathered in by men), and a way of pursing her lips – almost homoerotically, Henry thought, almost like offering a rectum – when kissing her colleagues. Even to Henry, whom she wanted dead – an otiose ambition in the circumstances – she presented the little puckered O of her rectum mouth.

Henry made a chivalric cherry of his lips in return. And planted it on her cheek.

Years later, still waiting for promotion, he remembered his failure to reciprocate Dr Khartoum's obscene greeting. Not that he believed she took him to have turned her down, or had sufficient interest in him to care even if he had. No. His mistake had not been sexual but political. He hadn't adequately abased himself. He hadn't acknowledged gynocracy. But it was also true that promotion waited on publication, and Henry had published nothing. Virtually nothing, anyway. And academics who had published virtually nothing were in no position to be picky where they pressed their mouths.

'Have you considered the possibility that your students might not *want* to find you?' she asked him.

'No, I haven't,' Henry said. 'Do you think I should?'

'No. No. But there are very few things we do that we do not mean to do.'

'Like getting cancer and being run over?'

She put her head to one side, as colourful as a parrot, a single lilac braid looping from her hair. 'Those too,' she said.

Then mean to do both, Henry thought. But what he said was, 'I'd settle for a wooden finger by the main departmental noticeboards, pointing them my way.'

She thought about it. 'But then wouldn't everybody want a finger?' she wondered.

To which lily-livered Henry was not prepared to chance an answer.

He was like the mad wife in the attic, only he was in the cellar. When inspectors or external examiners came to the college, they were not shown Henry. He was their terrible secret, the last man teaching literature, or at least the last man teaching it the old male way, as though language were achievement rather than trace.

They appended a Mr on his name board –

## MR HENRY NAGEL LECTURER

– in order to hammer home that he would never be a professor, that he was an amateur, a mere unlettered dabbler, but just as importantly to dissociate the department from his gender. No one else was Mr. Either they were Dr or they were nothing. But Henry needed defining. *The views expressed in this room are not necessarily the views of the department* – that was what they were telling students and whoever else stumbled, in the blackness, upon Henry's room. *In here language is considered an achievement not a trace – be warned!*

'Why don't you rename your course Literature and Invasiveness?' Drs Grynszpan (Cerisse) and Delahunty (Rhona) asked him, pissed, at an end-of-term party. He was the only man they had to talk to, else they wouldn't have bothered.

Henry fiddled with the sharp points of his tie. Never without a suit and tie, Henry, whatever the occasion. The suit caused consternation, he could tell, by virtue of its symbolic refusal of flux and chaos, and the tie – well, a tie's a tie. He smiled his sweetest. 'Because I don't know anything about it,' he told them. 'Cup and mitre, I'm the cup.'

Dr Grynszpan stood on one leg, like a stork. She was wearing a parody short skirt, slightly starched like a ballet dancer's, over opaque black Hamlet tights. Short skirts on Drs flummoxed Henry. He never knew where to look that did justice to the doctorate. 'You've gone immediately into defensive mode,' she said, turning her grey eyes on him.

Henry looked into those. 'Centuries of repression,' he explained.

'So now you're getting your own back?' Dr Delahunty wondered.

She was easier for Henry, visually, a Dr who dressed in what Henry thought of as rehearsal clothes, like a mime artist's, with a violent splash of red lipstick, almost as electric as Henry's tie. Logocentric Henry hated mime, but at least Dr Delahunty concealed her body.

'No, surprisingly I don't feel vengeful,' Henry said. 'And certainly don't teach vengeance. Rather I see myself in a demystifying role. Like you, I understand that as a teacher of the syntax of oppression, it is my job to fracture it. There's where we find ourselves, we of the margins – now in the fissure, now in the fracture. We fracture away down there in my little room.'

'It must be a sight.'

'It is. You are welcome to observe it. You'll need to being your potholing gear, though.'

'But you are still talking to your students about genius, I hear,' Grynszpan said. She had a way of swirling around him, like a little girl showing Daddy her new frock. What there was of it.

'They've reported me, have they?'

'No. But the word crops up in their essays. They have to have got it from somewhere. We figured it was you.'

'We?'

Delahunty nodded. '*We*.'

'Then you both figured right,' Henry said. 'I'm a genius freak. Especially I get freaky when the genius in question is female. It's how I was brought up. I am constitutionally impressed by the intelligence of women. I am by yours.'

'Well, we do both have PhDs,' Grynszpan reminded him.

'I am at all times mindful of those,' Henry said, holding up the hand of peace. 'I can't begin to imagine the disadvantages you must both have had to overcome to get where you have got.

When one thinks of how it was for those poor governesses in Charlotte Brontë . . . '

'It has, however, nothing to do with genius, which, along with *plaisir du texte*, is a masculine concept,' Delahunty told him. 'And ascribing it to women doesn't undo its violence, just like that. You perpetuate an injustice to those women writers you teach if you miss the subtlety of their subversion. It was never their intention simply to become proxy men.'

'You're not a proxy man just because you write well.'

She arched her mimist's eyebrow. 'You are,' she said, 'if all you understand by writing well is the smooth didactic surface of the patriarchal logos.'

*Taugetz*, Henry thought. A great wave of nostalgia for home passed over him. What you give up when you go to a university or wherever, what you forfeit doubly when you go to teach at one – the seasoned scepticism of people not deranged by the politics of their specialisms. *Taugetz, taugetz, taugetz, taugetz* . . .

But all he chose to say was 'Look, I just teach the kids to read what's there. OK?'

'Ha!' they said together. '*There!*'

He looked into his drink. 'You seem to have forgotten this is a party,' he said, excusing himself.

But they hadn't done with him. 'Still *there*, is it, Henry?' they would enquire, laughing, wherever they ran into him, slumped over his Pennine shepherd's pie in the refectory, wandering the library stacks in search of a novel with a man in it, stumbling in the direction of the lecture theatre, emerging blinking from his spider's hole beside the print room, coming out of the single male lavatory the department provided for men, particularly *then*, the lavatory – 'Still *there*, is it, Henry?'

He was no match for them. They wore him down. He couldn't keep it up. Whereas they could go on for ever. Was that the power of gibberish over language proper, the female semiotic, as they called it, over the male symbolic, the flux over the mastery – that

there was no stemming its flow once it started? 'Ooo, ooo, ooo!'
Unless it wasn't gibberish. Unless it wasn't *all* gibberish. Henry's
big mistake, he now realises, is that he left them to it. He thought
they would go away. He thought *it* would go away. Thought it
was a fad. What goes around comes around. I'll continue as before,
he decided, enjoying the thing that's written rather than the thing
that isn't, and all will be well. One day he'd wake up from the
nightmare of their horrible unintelligibility – all right, their grace-
lessness, then, their vile verbal discordances – and they'd be gone,
and in their place once more nice people like his mother and her
aunties, book lovers and Henry-appreciators of the old sort. So
he never kept up, never read them or their womby sources, never
sought to understand them, never even tried, intellectually, to meet
them halfway. Grew lazy instead, knowing what he knew.

No better than his paternal grandparents, he now realises, who
stuck with Yiddish though they'd been born in an English-
speaking country, because in Yiddish they felt at home. I too,
Henry thinks, though born in a gibberish-speaking country, took
the coward's way out and spoke only English because in English
I felt at home. Would it have killed me to have picked up one or
two words of the other along the way? Since gibberish was the
currency of communication, didn't it behove me at the least to
buy a phrase book?

Couldn't do it. Not in the genes to contend with those who
spoke a foreign language. Safest to hide and not let them embroil
him in conversation he didn't understand.

And meanwhile history rolled with them, burying Henry with
his love of the thing that's written rather than the thing that's
not, until he was just a squeak in the darkness.

*Taugetz!*

His father turned up once, Henry can't even work out when
that would have been – twenty years ago, twenty-five? – turned
up unannounced, rapping on Henry's door when Henry was in

the middle of a seminar, proud, embarrassed, shit-eating grin on his face, ha, who'd have thought it, Henry the mother's boy, who would rather run away from home than ask for his threepence back, heartfelt Henry a big man all of the sudden, with a roomful of girls bending their pretty giraffe ears to everything he said.

*No boys, Henry? Did you never teach a boy?*

There were no boys, Dad. Not in my subject.

*I blame your mother for that.*

She wasn't in charge of the intake, Dad.

*She was in charge of you. You could have done something else.*

Why does it matter? Why needed there be boys?

*To keep your mind off the girls.*

Then if that's all, you don't blame Mum. Chip off the old block, Dad.

I should leave him alone, Henry thinks. Honour thy father and thy mother. I should remember him as *I* wish to be remembered, justly, which is to say variously. I should remember how sweetly he smiled on me that day, holding up his hand to show that he didn't mean to interrupt, hadn't realised, mouthing roundly in a booming sibilant stage whisper, 'I'll wait outside,' which he did, pacing the corridor for half an hour, for there were no chairs where they'd put Henry, just grey-green linoleum on the wind-tunnel floor and something institutional like asbestos, almost certainly asbestos, newly fitted — choke the bastard out — on the near-lightless ceiling. So upsetting, Henry thinks, and thought at the time, the sight of your father waiting for you, waiting for YOU, killing time, at the mercy of your busy schedule. Such a reversal of the proper order of things. Your father a petitioner, and petitioning makes a vassal of anyone.

If there were a dead man out there, Henry thought, dismissing his class — same time next week, same book, same judgement-aversion — would it be me shielding my father's eyes now, or would we both revert in an instant? And which way would I want it?

No one ever upset Henry the way his father did. Rivers, Henry wept and weeps for his mother and her clan, those marvellously punctuated women who left him one by one, going down almost it seemed as it suited them, without a word of explanation, except for Marghanita who had her tragedy to explain to Henry before she too quit the scene. But for his father, even while he was alive, Henry felt a piercing grief. People had choice. People were responsible for what became of them. You owed it to people to believe that, at least, unless their circumstances were exceptional. Henry's father's circumstances were not exceptional, not until his wife's accident they weren't, anyway, yet Henry packed him round with enough extenuating circumstances to empty Hell. What happens to you, Henry thought, should not happen to a dog; but he could not have begun to explain what he meant by that, what exactly it was that befell his father that was so terrible. Carting Rivka Yoffey off to the Midland? Did that *befall* his father? A second home in St John's Wood, as he now knows, with mermaid's breasts to lean against whenever he retired to the quiet of the lavatory? Did that *befall* his father? It made no difference. None of it made a difference. His father broke his heart, whatever reason there was to be critical of him. Something to do with the way he floated just above the surface of things, folding his paper napkins and breathing his fire, as though the errand he was on had never been explained to him. Am I like him, then? Henry wondered. Was it him I was being when I couldn't retrieve my threepence from the Yoffeys? Was that why he wouldn't leave me alone about it – not because I was diffident like her but because I was baffled like him?

He took him to the students' cafeteria with a view beyond to a field of sheep, baby sheep, mummy sheep, daddy sheep. Introduced him on the way in to Grynzspan (Dr), who did a little twirl for him and shook his hand. 'Ah, the patriarch! So you're the cause of Henry?' she laughed.

Henry's father was beguiled. 'I hope you're not saying that because he's the cause of trouble.'

She gave him her grey eyes. Drown yourself in these. 'Henry? No. Not half the trouble you'd be, I bet.'

Henry watched his father wish he'd brought his torches with him. She'd have adored that, Grynzspan; she'd have clapped her deadly little hands, egged him on and lit his wicks, the way 'Hovis' Belkin had. They loved Henry's Dad, Henry's enemies.

'Nice woman,' he said, after Henry had dragged him away and sat him down.

'You think?'

'Yeah, I think.' She'd gone now, but he was still looking in her direction, as though seeing the twirling umbra she'd left behind her, like a candle's. 'You and she . . . ?'

'You must be joking! We'd both rather have rats gnawing at our innards.'

'She knocked you back, did she?'

'For God's sake, Dad, keep your voice down. And try to remember that pique is not the only motive that drives the universe.'

*Taugetz*, Henry could see him thinking.

'These are radical feminists,' Henry went on. 'They don't behave, up here, the way they do at home. They don't toddle off to the Midland with you just because you ask them.'

Henry saw the light die from his father's face. That again. The old refrain. Why do I do it? Henry wondered. Why can't I leave him alone?

His father dunked a biscuit in his tea, his hands too big for so delicate an operation. Henry had forgotten how hard his father found it to hold a cup, the handles always too small for his fingers. In order to get a cup to his lips, Izzi Nagel had either to become a feeding bird, dropping his head after checking that no one was watching, or to make a sort of mechanical grabber of his hands, downing the tea in a single gulp. Hence the dunking: that way he could at least leave the cup where it was and suck the tea out of the biscuit. Except that biscuits fell apart in Henry's father's fingers faster than they did in any other man's. Faster and further afield.

After which the toothpicking. A family joke, Izzi Nagel's toothpicking. Or at least a Stern Girl joke. 'I have never seen anyone make such a song and dance of being discreet,' Henry remembered his grandmother Irina saying, luring Henry into laughter which he feared was treacherous, one side of the family against the other, the girls against the boys. 'Someone must have told him it's good form to shield your mouth, but they omitted to mention that you aren't meant to go on exacavating for the duration of the meal. What do you think he's doing behind that hand – taking out his dentures and cleaning them one at a time?'

The action reminded Henry more of someone undressing in a public place, a showgirl slipping noisily out of her undies behind a screen. Marilyn. Mae West. Come up and see me some time.

His poor father. Everything such a performance. Picking his teeth, knocking up a settee, burning down the garden, visiting his son – same difference.

Finished with his mouth, he looked around the room, taking in but not taking in his son's world. The clatter of student trays, the pinball machines, the sheep in the fields beyond. Why had he come?

Why did you come, Dad?

'So what's a radical feminist?' he asked at last, not interested.

And equally not interested, Henry told him. Though the description was unlikely to have been one any radical feminist would have recognised.

'You should be at home here, then,' his father said.

Henry took it. Tit for tat. 'You'd think, wouldn't you.'

So why have you come, Dad?

They made small talk, driving themselves deeper and deeper into the unbearable inconsequence of family. He breaks my heart, but I can't think of anything to say to him, Henry thought.

Who knows what his father thought.

Just before he left, he told Henry that he had hoped to have a conversation with him about his mother, but another time maybe.

'Nothing's wrong, is there?'

'No, no, nothing.'

'Her health's OK?'

'Absolutely. There's nothing to worry about, I promise you.'

'She still decorating her cakes?'

'Well, you know that, you saw her last week.'

What Henry wanted to say was that though he was bound to his mother, migraine to migraine, with filaments of steel, and would have known had anything been the matter with her, because it would immediately have been the matter with him, talking about her to his father made her seem a million miles away.

You render remote my mother, Dad – I could hardly have said that to you, could I?

*You could have tried it. And with the words in their more familiar order, who knows, it might have helped.*

Helped what?

*Helped make you a little less remote.*

What Henry did say, and this too sounded strange, was 'You two all right?'

'Yes, we're all right.'

Was there a hesitation?

'Sure?'

'Yes, sure. Look, I'll talk to you next time.'

But of course there wasn't one.


Amazing, Henry thought, how a single mistake can claim you and that's your life over. The mistake of his becoming a teacher, he meant, not his father's visit in broad daylight to the Midland Hotel.

He didn't just think it, either; he observed it, sat in his cellar and watched his life running through his fingers the way a child wanting to make a fist of sand watches it seep from his grasp.

That face you make when you are in a lift with people you don't know and don't want to know, that face which is in fact the disappearance of a face – Henry learned how to make it in his first years on the Pennine Way and never learned to make another.

Unable to conceive of anything else to do, and seized by the irresistibly self-perpetuating logic of inertia – why bother when you can effect no change, how can you effect change when you lack the force to bother – Henry sank into middle age, a disgrace to himself, a shame to the collective idea of success he had shared with his friends, the longest-serving and least-published member of an institution he despised. Many a time it seemed that they would sack him, for learned publications, not teaching and invigorating, were the measure, though God knows they could have sacked him for the latter as well, so lacklustre had his seminars and lectures become. His own joke against himself, that he slept on his feet while lecturing some days, slept and snored and kept on talking, while his students, faithful as always to the letter, wrote 'Zzzzzzzzzzzzzzzzzzzzzzzzzz' in their notebooks. But though Mona Khartoum called him in a couple of times during her tenure, puckered up her O for Henry to salute, cautioned him against overuse of the concept genius and wondered if he wanted her to suggest a research topic, or introduce him to an editor, for a salaried academic couldn't expect to do nothing with his professional life except read and reread *Jane Eyre* and yet never publish a syllable about it, no step was ever taken to remove him. Perhaps they liked having him there as a warning and a specimen, like the mock-up of the woolly mammoth or the mastodon you find in the entrance halls to provincial museums, evidence of the life that once roamed the planet but which, due to some fault of character or design, some incorrigible predisposition to male-centred humanism, some congenital incapacity to publish, is now extinct. Tyrannosaurus Henrix.

Which could also have explained how come he was permitted to live a semblance of a man's life at the poly or the uni or whatever the fucking place was called, throwing himself on the mercies of friends' wives when they happened to turn up as mature students, and otherwise, in his early years there at least, putting it freely, if disconsolately, about. See how pathetic — was that it? See how harmless when not allowed to roam in packs?

Look on this work, ye Mighty, and despair.

# EIGHT

He has agreed to w-a-l-k Angus.

It seems to Henry that if he is not prepared to r-e-l-i-n-q-u-i-s-h Moira, w-a-l-k-i-n-g Angus is the least he can do.

Lachlan comes knocking, only hours after their conversation, begging Henry to get him out of a hole. His pretext is an aspirin. Does Henry have? Of course Henry has. Henry has half of Western Europe's stock of aspirin. As Lachlan must have known, because Moira must have told him. But the real reason is the dog's exercise. Lachlan isn't up to it, doesn't know what the matter is, a virus of some sort, and poor old Angus who's been in all day is getting desperate. It's your fault, that's what Henry takes him to mean. It's your fault for getting me to tell you my life story and upsetting myself. The other implication is that it's Henry's fault for engrossing the dog and keeping him indoors.

'Bless you,' Lachlan says when Henry agrees. 'I'll fetch him.'

But Henry doesn't want Angus in his apartment. There are ghosts where Henry lives and he doesn't want the dog frightening them, or vice versa. So the handing over takes place, hugger-mugger, on the landing between them.

'Just the dog,' Henry says, when Lachlan starts to explain the contents of the little tartan bag that goes with him. 'Nothing else.'

'Yes, but you'll need some of these if —'

'Just the dog,' Henry says.

'Suit yourself,' Lachlan says. 'But he can't go out without a lead. Do you want me to attach it to the collar now or will you do it when you get him down?'

Henry looks startled. 'What does getting him down mean? Do I have to wrestle him or something?'

'No, just down the stairs. He doesn't like the lift. Afraid of it, the silly sod.'

'Do it now,' Henry says, looking away. 'You do it, here, now.'

The dog's tongue is making a lapping noise which Henry doesn't like. He has a triumphant air. He may love Henry but he also has his measure. He knows that there is a battle of wills afoot and that he is winning it. He meekly offers his throat to Lachlan, in parody of obedience. See this, Henry? Well, you won't be seeing this quality again for a while.

'What you've got to watch with this clip –' Lachlan begins to say.

But Henry stops him. 'You just sort it,' he says. 'I won't be touching any mechanisms.'

'No, but you'll need to know how to unclip it when you let him off.'

'I won't be letting him off.'

The dog pants, eyeing Henry with consternation. Unless its ironic consternation.

'He needs an r-u-n,' Lachlan explains. 'He's an old dog, but he needs his r-u-n.'

'How old is he?'

'How old are you, Angus? Twelve, I'd say, at a pinch.'

'How old's that in human terms?'

'Seventy-two, maybe seventy-five.'

'Then I'll r-u-n with him,' Henry says.

What he doesn't say is that he has never w-a-l-k-e-d a dog in his life. Let alone r-u-n with one.


Not counting the country daddy-long-legs which crawled across his unborn brain, little Henry was never allowed an animal of his own. The usual reason. Who would feed it.

Together with the perhaps less usual reason: who would dare look upon it.

Nothing short of metaphysical, Ekaterina's horror of

incalculable living things, into which category she placed the entire animal and insect kingdom. She had been given a rabbit when she was a child – Natalia – a lovely golden floppy creature, more hare than rabbit, with soft liquid eyes and a white patch on her chest, which Ekaterina thought of as an apron of the sort worn by the lady who came to do the dusting and make the beds. It helped Ekaterina overcome her initial fear of the rabbit to think of her as a maid. Two weeks after her arrival, maid or not, Natalia mysteriously fell pregnant. Not wanting to burden her daughter with the finer points of Natalia's earlier life in the pet shop, Irina explained that rabbit-pregnancy was an airborne spore which had come in on the wind and invaded Natalia while she was busy nibbling her lettuce. Ekaterina marvelled at this and waited with her heart in her mouth for Natalia to deliver herself of bunnies. Are they here yet? Will it be this afternoon? Will it be tomorrow? They were exquisite when they came, balls of the warmest fur Ekaterina had ever touched, their hearts pumping through her fingers, one golden like its mother, two black, two brown, and one dirty grey. The next morning, when Ekaterina went to look at them, she noticed that the dirty grey was not moving. And the morning after, both the blacks. Had Ekaterina not seen Natalia pick up one of the browns in her mouth and dash it pitilessly against the side of the hutch, Irina would have let her believe the deaths were due to natural causes. As it was, burying them under a tree at the bottom of the garden, she felt she had no choice but to try to convey to Ekaterina the idea of post-natal depression. Down to just the bunny that was the same colour as herself, Natalia appeared to settle back into the serenity of motherhood. But then one day the golden favourite disappeared altogether. Rather than get the inconsolable Ekaterina to accept that it was in its mummy's tummy, Irina told her that she had taken it out of the hutch and set it free, to give it a chance in life. But by that time Ekaterina was off rabbits altogether.

Which left, if the emotional instability of animals was to be a consideration in the matter of Henry's having a pet, only fish. Henry remembers dimly the ornamental goldfish in the pool in the back garden, over which his mother sometimes shook a drum of what looked like pepper. Were they his? He never thought that they were his. But they didn't last long, whoever they belonged to, on account of his father frightening them to death in the course of practising his fire-eating. That was his mother's guess, anyway. They'd been fine and suddenly they weren't. Izzi had gone out to exhale flame in the open, since he wasn't allowed to do it in the bedroom, and the next day there they were, all six of them, floating bloated on their backs. Their eyes turned up. In shock.

'If they're in shock they're alive,' Henry's father said.

'By in shock I mean suffering the aftermath of shock.'

'How do you know it was shock?'

Ekaterina was adamant. 'So what else do you think it was?'

'Fish die. That's life.'

'Not six, all at the same time, Izzi.'

'I think I've read,' he said, 'that the death of one fish can deprive others of the will to live.'

She laughed at him. 'And where would you have read that, you who have never read a sentence in your life?'

Not true. He had read a dozen books on origami and fire-eating from cover to cover. But it wasn't in his interest, just that minute, to cite those.

So Ekaterina's theory won the day. The fish had been going about their business, opening and shutting their mouths, when the flames had shot across them. Ekaterina put herself in their place. On her back, looking at the sky, she heard the bombs fall, saw the shadow of the flames, smelt the smoke and the paraffin, and said no to life.

Soon afterwards they drained the pool and dumped sand in it for Henry to play in. But Henry wasn't a sand boy. No matter how colourful the spades and buckets his father bought him, no matter how many moulds of Norman keeps and castles, or flags to fly above their ramparts, Henry was no sooner deposited in the sandpit than he fled it. Look out of the window and there he'd be, sitting under a tree, nursing his thin skin, reading *The Awkward Age*.

What happens when you don't get a boy a pet.

He has a plan to ring Moira the minute he is out of the block, and get her to w-a-l-k Angus with him. It will be a try-out for them, an earnest of their future domesticity. There is a particular way of being together that couples out with their animals have, which Henry has always envied. An absent-minded complacency, an absorption in their separateness which is not to be confused with coldness, as though the reason for their being together, the abstraction of their union, is bodied forth in the ball of fluff charging around in front of them. The ectoplasm of their love.

But she can't make it.

'Are you still angry with me,' Henry wants to know, 'because of before?'

'I'm not angry with you.'

'I've only agreed to exercise the little bastard in the hope I'd see you.'

'You should be pleased to be doing Lachlan a favour.'

'I am. Of course I am. That's the other reason. To show you I have overcome my jealousy.'

'Well, that's good, but I can't. Enjoy your walk.'

Only when he rings off does it occur to Henry to wonder whether this is a ruse, hatched up between them, to get him, and the dog, out of the way.

Thus does the dog become the ectoplasm of his insecurity.

'OK, Angus,' Henry says, 'you and me.' At which Angus, padding like a horse, looks up at him with eyes of longing.

Henry can't remember whether his favourite park, the one with all the graves in, is out of bounds for dogs. But he does know that parks are places where dog owners converse, and he doesn't want any of that. He might be walking the dog but he is not dog-associated. So the High Street is the safer bet to be going on with, though he has forgotten how many shops are still open, how many people are about, and how conspicuous he therefore feels. Except that conspicuous is not the word. Searching for it, he rejects unaccustomed and awkward and even embarrassed in favour of humiliated. Is he insane, or what is he? Humiliated, *humiliated* to be walking a dog!

And wherein lies the shame? Silly question to ask of Henry. Wherein *doesn't* lie the shame?

But he can tell you wherein lies the *specific* shame. In being seen to be reduced to the affections of a dog. Not mine, Henry wants to say. Nothing to do with me. Doing it for a friend. Allowing that the friend has nothing to do with him either.

Henry is reduced to the affections of no one.

Which seems to be the clue for Angus to piss against the tyre of a BMW.

'Hey!' someone calls.

Neither Henry nor Angus takes any notice.

'Hey! I said hey!'

Henry looks up. They are outside Bar One or something similar. A man in a shiny metallic suit and of Middle Eastern appearance, could be Israeli, could be Lebanese, could even, Henry supposes, be Italian, is standing in the doorway, pointing rhythmically. He is on his mobile phone, and expects Henry to put up with his half-attention.

'Your tyre?' Henry wonders.

'My wife's tyre.'

'Well, I'm sure she drives through worse,' Henry says. He does not intend to apologise. Not on Angus's behalf. For Angus, Henry will now lie on a bed of broken glass.

The man goes on shaking his finger. 'You should know you're not meant to let dogs foul the footpath.'

'That's not the footpath. He wants the gutter, but your wife's car is in the way. And on double yellow lines.'

'In the way! You shouldn't be walking him here at all.'

'I take my dog,' Henry says, 'for walks where he wants to walk.'

'And my wife parks where she wants to park.'

'Then your wife and my dog have much in common.'

'You're a very rude person, you know that,' the man says. Then, into his mobile, 'Did you hear that? The arsehole!'

Henry wishes, as he has wished all his life, that he had the insouciance to go over to the man and crush him and his mobile between his hands. If Henry had crushed more people between his hands in his fifty-nine years he would be a happy man now – happ*ier*, anyway – whatever his other disappointments.

Instead, he shrugs. 'Come on, Angus,' he says. 'Let's see who else we can upset.'

He has started to hum to himself. It is almost like carrying a gun, he has decided. Walking with a dog, at least when you have never walked with one before, is like being armed. No wonder people who walk with dogs *and* guns bear themselves with such swagger.

'I ought to get one,' Henry thinks. 'I ought to have one of my own.'

A dog, he means.

But he would also have uses for a gun.

It is possible Angus is able to feel what Henry is thinking through the lead. So far he has stayed close to Henry, keeping within the slack. Now he begins to put distance between them. If Henry is thinking about other dogs, then Angus will think about other dogs as well. And do it better.

Head down, he noses out an urgent trail along the pavement, his jaw like a hovercraft, floating upon the aroma, or aromas, coming up from the flagstones. Could there be several? To Henry's eye it appears that Angus is caught between two rival and parallel temptations, now breathing in the one, now breathing in the other, sometimes, with a worried shake of his ears, attempting to breathe them both in at once. Whether they each veer into the doorway of the shop, or Angus has made his choice, Henry cannot tell. But having got here, Angus has another piss.

'You've just done that,' Henry says.

'Hey!' someone shouts from the shop.

This time Henry doesn't stop to slug it out.

Then it's off on the trail of other dogs' piss. There are rivers of the stuff. Who would have thought it? What to Henry looks like dry desert slabs of cement and stone, are to Angus raging torrents of dog genealogy. And every trace engrossing. That's what Henry can't get over – how indiscriminately *interested* Angus is in everything he finds. Go on, Henry wills him, light upon a smell that leaves you cold, turn your nose up, say no to something. You're seventy-five years old, you've been there, you've done it, there can't be a surprise left. But there is. To Angus the world of dogs is as intriguing as it must have been the day he was born. Now there's a stain at the foot of a parking meter, a congealed downward trickle burnt into the foot of a lamp-post, a telling discoloration of the bricks on the wall of a bank, just below the automatic teller, where, as always, there is a queue. Never mind waiting your turn, never mind people's feet, Angus has to get to what he has to get to, it's essential, absolutely beyond question, else he will miss – what? The site of a famous piss-in? Evidence of a spray-for-all which Angus cannot bear to have forgone? A haunting faecal memory? Is everywhere Pompeii for Angus – a normal dog day of another era, frozen for ever? What kind of life is this, Henry wants to know, where piss is all you ever think about, piss the centre of your every waking moment, and maybe of your every unwaking one as well, piss to sniff, piss to taste, piss to ponder, piss to piss on. A dog is meant to be man's best friend, the animal world's nearest approximation to us, not counting the eccrine-glanded chimpanzee, but any man who behaved one-hundredth as grossly as Angus would be locked away for life. Aren't there said to be men who get off on sniffing girls' bicycle seats? There had been rumours at Henry's school linking the headmaster, Olly Allswell, MA, to a ring of degenerates who circulated among themselves soiled underwear belonging to women of the lower orders. Several of Henry's friends had seen the postman delivering the parcels. To the school, would you believe that! 'He's probably sitting there with his face in them right this minute,' Henry's classmate Brendan O'Connor reckoned, 'at the same time as he's writing our reports.' 'Or with them on his head,' Osmond Belkin guessed. 'Or with our reports on his head,' Henry jumped in. 'You don't suppose, do you,' Brendan O'Connor wondered – Brendan, the handsomest boy in Henry's class, eyes black as coals, but who would later waste his fires on the Catholic priesthood, perhaps as a consequence of this very conversation – 'you don't suppose he wears them for school assembly?' No end, no end to the crimes you could ascribe to a pervert. Yet what was any of it compared to the improprieties of which Angus, without the slightest consciousness of shame, was routinely guilty?

And this is just the piss part. No sooner are they out of the high street into rural St John's Wood Terrace – for he is sick of the shops now, Angus, and wants a residential street to defile – than they encounter what Henry at first takes to be an albino dwarf, but is in fact a miniature bull terrier with a blind face, sitting as proud as an heraldic lion on a wall, sheathing and unsheathing his penis. Henry pulls at Angus, hoping to get him to cross the road. But Angus is riveted. The bull terrier squints, unsheathing his penis, a cigar coming out of its wrapper. To Henry it is a windless early evening, still as the grave, but the albino dog can smell breeze. He tilts his head, blindly nosing the air for it, calling it to him; then when he finds it, relaxes his shoulders, spreading his limbs, allowing it to fan his cigar alight. Angus stares. There is none of that mutual embarrassment of which

Thomas Mann speaks, nothing of the constraint which he believed obtains when dogs meet for the first time. Take me as you find me, the bull terrier appears to be saying. And Angus is mulling it over. Henry can hear him pondering. That's good. So he is not entirely beyond reflection. To dogs, too, has the Almighty granted free will. With what there is of his, Angus reaches the decision to sit and unsheathe his own penis. It's like a beauty pageant. First it was the bull terrier's turn, now it's Angus's. What next – evening gowns? Already Angus is upping the stakes: not content with showing the judges his penis, he must show how well he licks it. Nothing elaborate or fanciful. Nothing you could even call sexual. More like Henry's father cleaning his teeth. Now this side, now that, now in and around a bit, the tongue conscientious and searching, but the mind elsewhere. A hygiene thing, Henry takes it to be, putting the best gloss on it, an act of dog-to-dog consideration, given where they both know they've been. Whatever it is, the bull terrier looks unmoved in his impure whiteness. Finished with himself, Angus gets begrudgingly to his feet, his age showing, and approaches the bull terrier's penis with the sole intention – what else can it be? – of licking that. Rather than allow which abomination, Hebraic Henry hits the roof.

Are you allowed to strike another man's dog? You shouldn't strike anything aged over seventy, but then over seventy should act over seventy. Henry has picked up the wisdom from somewhere that you punish a malfeasant dog by rubbing his nose in his malfeasance, but given that Angus's malfeasance is the bull terrier, that wouldn't be much of a punishment. Removal, that's the thing. Violent removal from the scene. Grabbing him by the collar, Henry pulls him away from St John's Terrace like a dog on wheels, down Charlbert Street whimpering, along Allitsen whipped, then back on to the High Street, like a sled. Home, that's where Angus is headed, home for three Hail Marys, a shower and a thrashing. He knows he's done wrong. He can't help nosing out more piss as they go, his love of the smell of other dogs' piss as ineradicable as Henry's love of the smell of other men's women, but at least, Henry allows, he has the decency to hang his head. Periodically, he slows, looks up at Henry with pain in his eyes, and shrinks into himself, as though he wishes the earth would open up and swallow him. Which to Henry is a clear sign that he is capable of remorse.

Against Angus's wishes, Henry slows at a hole in the wall of a bank. A couple of Americans, presumably from the American University around the corner, are discussing world politics while waiting for their money.

'Rule one, always plan your exit,' the older of the two explains.

'Yeah, but exit to where?' the other asks.

'Doesn't matter. Just be ready. That's why I never pass one of these without making a withdrawal.'

Good thinking, Henry thinks, fishing for his card. In these dangerous times you cannot have too much money about your person.

Angus pulls at the lead and whimpers.

'Yes, yes, just wait,' Henry tells him. 'I have to plan my exit.'

Outside Bar One, the man of Mediterranean appearance is still on his mobile phone. Angus recognises him and stops. Again, he looks pleadingly at Henry. Does he want him to say something to the man? Apologise? Twit him a second time? 'No, Angus,' Henry says. 'We've done here.'

But Angus hasn't. Unable to contain himself any longer, he squats on the pavement and defecates.

It is only when he hears the man shouting, 'Now *that* you will do something about, you filthy pig!' that Henry finally realises how good a joke on him his life has been.

# NINE

'I've looked you up,' Moira tells him, 'on the Internet.'

'In which case,' Henry says, 'you don't have enough to do with yourself.'

'That's a laugh,' she says, putting her flattied feet up on his knees. 'I've been running all day.'

They are in his apartment, at home, as he likes to think of it, lolling. Henry has never lolled, but Moira is teaching him. 'You want to lighten up,' she has been telling him. 'You're coiled as if waiting for something to happen. Look at your shoulders. And why are you always in a jacket? What are you expecting?'

'Nothing,' had been his answer. Which was a lie. Like Mr Micawber, Henry is always expecting something. The difference being that Henry is expecting a blow, not a windfall.

'Then relax,' she'd said, helping him out of his jacket, undoing his tie, and putting her feet up on him.

So he's trying. But he'd rather not be reminded that there is an index of achievement called an Internet out there which contains not a mention of him.

'Oh but it does,' she informs him. '"Western wind, when will thou blow?"'

'That's not by me.'

'I didn't say it was by you. It's a favourite poem of yours, though. I know that much.'

'It says that on the Internet? You look up my name and it tells you my favourite poetry? Just like that?'

'No, not just like that. I looked up your name and that took me to the site of the University of the Pennine Way, and that gives the name of academic staff and their specialities.'

'I'm not a member of their academic staff any more.'

'It'll be out of date. Everything on the Internet is out of date. I'm down as offering courses every Monday and Thursday. I haven't done a Thursday for three years. But why haven't you read me "Western wind, when will thou blow" if it's your favourite poem?'

'It isn't. It's just the shortest.'

'Recite it to me, then.'

'You've already recited it.'

'Is that all there is?'

'No. There's a bit more.'

'So . . .'

So, not to be a niggard, Henry recites it.

> Western wind, when will thou blow,
> The small rain down can rain?
> Crist, if my love were in my arms,
> And I in my bed again!

'That's beautiful.'

'Yes. And short. Poems should be short.'

'It's more nautical than I'd have expected of you. He is a sailor, isn't he?'

'Or a soldier. A traveller, at least. To be honest with you I've never worried about that aspect of it – I just always associated the wind and the rain with the Pennines. "Western wind, when will thou stop," was how I read it.'

'Wouldn't that change the meaning?'

'Not at all. It was still about being somewhere you didn't want to be. And wishing you were home.'

'So where was home? Where was the bed you wanted to be back in?'

Henry looks up at dimmed lights of the chandelier. 'Ah,' he says, 'you have me there.'

'And who was "the love"?'

'And there,' he says, 'you have me again.'

She wriggles her feet on him. 'Come on, tell me. Who were you missing when you made it your favourite poem?'

'If you really want to know, I was missing men.'

'"Crist, if my love were in my arms" – a man!'

'No. I was missing men to whom I could talk about how much I was missing women.'

'Why couldn't you just tell the women?'

'They were the wrong sort of women. Maybe all women are the wrong sort. You need men to discuss longing with. That was why I put it in on my Literature's For Life course. A subsidiary module on longing – Angst and the Man. Hoping it would attract the boys. But it didn't. It just attracted more of the girls, on whom, of course, it was wasted.'

She throws him one of her twisted looks. 'My sex does not understand longing?'

'Well, it didn't understand this version of it. They kept wanting to talk about it from the woman's point of view. How *she* felt.'

'And you weren't interested in that?'

Henry is very tired suddenly. Some battles he no longer has the stomach for. He has just made a joke. Or maybe it was life that made the joke. It doesn't matter. But in relation to four brief lines of unbearably exquisite male yearning, the idea of a woman's point of view is lunatic. *How she felt*. Laugh, Moira!

He shouldn't have been inveigled into reciting it to her. It is a deceptively treacherous piece of verse. Read it with your arms around a woman you love, and you cannot avoid remembering wrapping your arms around another woman you loved. It is a corridor of mirrors, infinitely receding, each enactment of the thing you longed for issuing in remembrance, and each remembrance leaving you longing for the longing before.

Or it could be that it isn't the poem which is deceptively treacherous, only Henry.

Laugh, Moira!

Henry, full of grief for what was and what was not, remembers Marghanita. Crist, if my love were in my arms. She never was, though, and that's the truth of it. Never was and never should have been. But does that make the subjunctive memory the less or the more painful? Crist, if only she had been!

And now it's clear to him why he is thinking of Marghanita. Laugh, Moira. Laugh, as Marghanita had laughed, at the very idea, with the Western wind not blowing and the small rain down not raining, of seeing it from the woman's point of view. She had visited him at the institute, as it must still have been called then. Henry is not master of the chronology, but he is fairly sure she had stopped calling on him by the time it was a polytechnic, and was dead before it became a university. So does Henry measure out his sorrows. Not her first visit, the one he is thinking of, nor her last, but vivid to him perhaps because of the poem. She had sat in on one of his classes. She liked doing that. His students would not have known what to make of this elegant elderly lady with the tragic expression, whom Henry passed off on them as an inspector, as though any inspector would have turned up in the Pennines, however freezing, with a fox around her throat.

She sat at the back, smiling her elegiac White Russian smile, her head not as high as it had been, just a touch shaky now, but that perhaps only visible to Henry who scrutinised mercilessly those he loved. Better not to be loved by Henry, that's the lesson. And many had learned it. But Marghanita was family, flesh and blood, so there was no question of not being loved by him, or of not loving him in return – Henry, the marvellous boy, in whom so many of her ambitions, and the ambitions of her waning sisters, were realised.

Explain that. Henry will go to his grave not understanding. There she was, a woman with the music of the capitals of Europe in her soul, wise with the wisdom of the Volga, yet blind to the overwhelming provinciality of Henry's professional life, a barely tenured teacher in a barely illuminated institution in a barely breathing Pennine valley. Wonderful, what he was doing, she thought. Wonderful for himself: a privilege to have your soul filled with literature all the long day. And wonderful for others: those who came to listen to her great-nephew, and learn. There is a variety of views on everything, one man's meat etc.; but can there be divergence of opinion in the matter of what is life and what is death? Henry was the corpse. Ask him. He was the one lacking in any of the usual presumptions of animation. Yet to Marghanita he was not merely living, he was a creative force, the reason that life is in others. If it turns out that she'd been right all along, that he'd led a privileged, energising life, what does that say about Henry? Wouldn't that make him doubly a dead man?

'"Crist, if my love were in my arms . . ."' Henry read to his class. With feeling. His arms out, cradling air.

Which was when they raised the question – What about the woman?

There is no woman, Henry told them. Marghanita sad, smiling from the back.

There is no woman in this poem. The poignancy of her resides precisely in her absence.

Dangerous word, absence. Henry's students had written essays about the absent woman in world history. What is absence, Mr Nagel, they asked him, if not presence in its most eloquently telling form – the woman objectified in her removal, possessed and reified *in abstracto*, assumed without question to be the man's property, the object of *his* desires, to be enfolded in *his* arms, in *his* bed? Passively waiting for him while he gallivants about the globe, no doubt colonising it.

What if the woman didn't want the man, had Henry thought about that?

He had, and could recommend any number of works on the subject. Just not this.

What if the small rain down did rain and he came home to

find her with another man, or better still another woman, he, she, they, in her arms, not she in his, hers, theirs. What then? What then, Mr Western Wind?

Then we'd be reading a different poem, Henry explained.

Then let's, they told him.

So he read them Berryman –

> There sat down, once, a thing on Henry's heart
> só heavy, if he had a hundred years
> & more, & weeping, sleepless, in all them time,
> Henry could not make good.

But they weren't satisfied that the woman's point of view was adequately attended to in that either.

You are the collective thing that sat down once on my heart, Henry wanted to tell them. You are the thing I will never, not if I have a hundred years and more of weeping, make good.

Not true, of course. The thing that sat on Henry's heart predated student feminism.

'Where do they get this stuff from?' she laughed afterwards, Henry's great-aunt Marghanita, still lovely enough at God knows what age to melt Henry's só heavy bones. Laughing.

Laugh, Moira! Laugh like Marghanita!

Lying with Marghanita in his arms, however, had such a thing been – been allowable, or, being allowable, happened – he would have fretted (because fretting was what he did) that her laughter was maybe the tiniest bit too loyal. Too much in agreement. Not sufficiently dialectic or dialogic, if those are the words he's after. For he is fastidious, Henry, in the matter of loyalty, and believes there can be too much as well as too little. Precise in the matter, also, noting that while too little can frustrate a man and, who knows, build up a tumour in his brain, too much directly invades his nervous system, and makes him feel that spiders are crawling across his flesh. All this is supposition. He never did lie with Marghanita in his bed. The one person who did, for whom she had held herself in chaste reserve, waiting and waiting for the Western wind to blow him to her – Crist, that she were in his arms – allowed himself, if only temporarily, to forget her, for which offence Marghanita refused, if only permanently, to forgive him. It was the story of her life. *The Deceiving of Marghanita.* An evergreen melodrama which described herself to herself, not one single line of which suffered diminution of black sardonic pain in all the years of its playing. It went everywhere with her, like her handbag, or like a writer's first manuscript, *The Deceiving of Marghanita.* Sometimes Henry saw her lips moving to the famous soliloquies, saw her lovely cheekbones moisten, and on occasions – who knows, perhaps anniversaries – tears spring like geysers from her eyes. So she, if anyone, might have embraced the woman's point of view. Hang on, Henry, let's just think about this. You're right, of course you're right, and funny, of course you're funny, and they are preposterous, of course they are preposterous, but the woman waiting, Henry, the woman waiting . . . After which correction to his prejudices, dealt fairly and understandingly with, but not indulged, it has to be assumed that Henry would have been content to lie with his arms about her – all else being equal – and not ache with melancholy for those other ones in the corridor of mirrors, those of the past, and those who were yet to come, those who overlaughed and those who under-laughed and those who didn't laugh at all. For that must follow, Henry, must it not? That you were only ever waiting for every-thing you liked, the right amount of this and the right amount of that, to come together? Your bed, then, and only then, the perfect paradise.

Crist!

Henry sat with Marghanita as she lay wet cheekboned on her own bed of perfect peace, and discovered he was weeping for his mother. How hard it is to be discrete. How hard, in the end, to be certain you can tell one person from another. Death the great leveller, but what about life? In Henry's experience, life too eventually rolls out all undulations. Unnecessary for King Lear to have called upon the all-shaking thunder to smite flat the thick rotundity o' the world. It was always going to happen anyway.

But Henry doesn't want, today, tonight, to think about Marghanita smote flat, unprotrusive on her bed.


'The second thing I found out about you that I didn't know ...' Moira says, slithery like tofu in his arms, but he won't let her finish.

'I'd rather find out about you,' he says. 'Tell me what you hated most at school.'

She doesn't hesitate. 'Hockey.'

'What didn't you like?'

'The cold. I was always on the fucking wing.'

'I didn't realise it was colder on the wing.'

'Well, it didn't have to be. But no one passed to me. So I just stood around with my feet getting more and more numb.'

'You could have run about anyway.'

'I was too cold to run about.'

Her kisses her hair. Smells school playing field in it. 'Fancy you being a winger.'

'Why, don't I look like a winger?'

'I don't know. Just fancy you being anything. Just fancy you having been a girl.'

He was delighted. He loved hearing about the girlhood of girls. Infinitely touching, in the woman, the evidence of girl. Especially before sleep. Better than counting sheep for Henry, the traces of girl in a borrowed woman.

'And remind me again,' he says, after a moment of reflection, 'this was school in Prague?'

She aims an imaginary blow at him. 'Hemel Hempstead,' she says, 'as you know full well.'

But Henry doesn't know anything full well. 'I am in charge of the whereabouts of your childhood,' he says.

'And I of your whereabouts on the Internet,' she teases. 'The second thing I found out about you that I didn't know is that you're a film critic.'

He looks bemused. 'I'm not. I just don't like films.'

'Not any?'

'Not many.' He is breathing in the odours of her neck, just below her ear, where she is mentholated.

'I cry a lot in films,' she tells him.

'Me too,' he says. Not adding that these days he cries a lot everywhere.

'Well then?' she says

'Well then what?'

'Well then why don't you like them?'

'What's crying got to do with anything? Anyone can make anyone cry at the drop of a hat. We all go around carrying our tears in our pockets like loose change. The merest reference to our fragility sets us off. Say mummy, daddy, baby, love-you, dead, goodbye – and that's it, you've got the whole auditorium snivelling. And this is before you throw in the amplified music and the widescreen Technicolor grave, ten times the capacity of your house. To me, going to the pictures is like lying down in front of a pantechnicon and marvelling that you've been moved.'

'So what were you doing,' she asks, 'writing for *Movie Tones*?'

Henry turns cold. If we're to be scientific about it, his actual temperature has soared – nought to a hundred before the clock starts – but he feels cold, clammy cold, the perspiration freezing on his back.

'That's on the Internet?'

'Not what you actually wrote. Not the words. But it's mentioned. And why are you so hot?'

'Does it say what it's about?'

'Some English director. Why are you so hot?'

'Does it name him?'

'It must do. But I can't remember, I'm sorry. Henry, why are you burning up?'

'Shame,' Henry says. 'I am oversupplied with eccrine glands which can pick up and process shame before I even know I'm feeling it. I like to think this proves how far evolved I am. Civilisation equals shame – have I told you my theory? The end of civilisation will come, if I'm right, when we're all too hot to touch. I advise you to remove yourself soon to your own side of the bed.'

'I have my own side now? That's good.'

She has swivelled girlishly on to one elbow, treating him to the best of her profile, her neck taut, its veins like blue striations in rock, the angles of her face sharp and askew. She is a lovely colour, icy gold. What Henry wouldn't give to have ice in his blood!

'I am to take it,' she goes on, pretending to warm her hands on the heat radiating from him, 'that you are not proud of your film criticism.'

'No, I am not,' he tells her. But that is all he tells her.

He wakes in the night, relieved to find she is still with him. No one in London's sleeping well, but that's not Henry's worry. It's history that's got the rest of them in a state, fear of a plane dropping out of the sky, or someone squirting smallpox through their letter box. There are rumours that there are Japanese people on the floor below Henry's who will not leave the building, who have built up food reserves sufficient to keep them alive for five years and who wear biological suits fitted with oxygen masks at all times. Some days, Henry thinks he can hear them rattling about in their foil clothing, unless what he's hearing is the sound of them counting their cans. Henry has not bothered to stock up. The threats to Henry's life are not of a sort you can take precautions against. Besides, Henry reasons, the nearby mosque must surely act as a deterrent to any attack, despite the otherwise rich pickings of NW8.

Moira has taken his advice and rolled over as far as she can to her side of the bed without falling out of it. It's a miracle he hasn't drowned where he is. This is how it has always been for Henry. He sleeps in pools of perspiration of his own making, one recollection of ignominy succeeding another. Tell him death will be dry and he'll feel a lot better about going there.

He would like to get up and wring out his pillows but he is afraid of waking her. He likes listening to a woman sleep. Tell him death will be dry and there'll be a woman sleeping beside him, and he'll give up the ghost tomorrow.

Tell him *this* woman will be sleeping beside him and he'll give it up tonight.

Moira snores the way Henry imagines a young boy snores. Sudden gasps, like implorations, as though the day has been physically hard and the body is replenishing itself, succeeded by an even, insect hum, testifying to the innocence of the labours if not the sweetness of the dreams. Snails, earthworms, pollen hanging from the stamen of a flower. Had he been a father, he would have liked to hear his children snore. Lying still, determined not to wake her, he gives in to fatherly feelings for Moira. She has not given him permission for this, he knows. She hasn't intimated she needs looking after. And he hasn't listed fatherliness among his needs. Twist my heart and in return I'll try to be good company, that's the deal. She looks askance when he tells her that he sees the Danube dancing in her eyes. It's a lot for one woman to provide – and she only a pastry chef – all the corruptions of a vanished empire. But she gets the rest – that he wishes to be hurt, however she chooses to hurt him, by her past; that he wishes to be agitated, however she chooses to agitate him, by the future; and that he would like her to be conventionally nice to him in between. Now she has to be his daughter, all of a sudden. Typical of Henry, just when he's getting what he wants, to start fiddling with the agenda.

But he's sore tonight. No fault of hers. She wasn't to know what looking him up on the Internet would stir up. Any more than she was to know that his article for *Movie Tones* was his darkest hour, his deepest shame, his lowest moment.

Maybe it would have made him feel better had he come clean with her at once. My love, my little one – that article you unearthed, my single essay at film criticism, my sole publication, the one thing I would not wish to be remembered by, but now, you tell me, the *only* thing I will be remembered by, I have to confess to you was pure vendetta.

How would that have sounded? Kissed him better, would she? Wrapped her arms around him? Absolved him? Who's to say not. And who's to say a better sleep would not have been his reward for honesty. A woman's forgiveness can do wonders for a man.

Should he wake her now and tell her?

Do you hear me? Pure vendetta – conceived in hatred, motivated by malice, driven by envy, and couched in primness. Not even my own primness, at that. 'I am persuaded,' I wrote, 'that this director does not think as he ought on serious subjects.' Pick up the allusion? Fanny Price, *Mansfield Park*. What's Fanny Price doing in a piece of twentieth-century film criticism? Good question. But there you are. That's what happens to you when you give your life to teaching the literary history of girls. You become one. In fact, I am by no means the first to have written criticism in that spirit. There have been worse than me. But my particular sin is this: the English film director, now living in Hollywood, the recipient of innumerable awards, whose reputation, as I maintained, was grossly overblown, whose films were claptrap, stagebound, artificial, unctuous and self-pleasing, and who did not think as he ought on serious subjects – but I won't rehearse my arguments again, not tonight, not to you, not here – does happen, *did* happen, to have been my best friend. Not Alfred Hitchcock, no. Christ, Moira, how old do you think I am? No, and not David Lean, either. Osmond Belkin, I'm talking about. *Belkin.* I'm glad you haven't heard of him. But that doesn't alter the offence. I have been guilty, though it was twenty years ago or more, of dishonesty and small-mindedness and, most unforgivably of all, pique. Do you, *can* you, still love me?

He doesn't wake her. She is sleeping too peacefully, her breathing steady, like a high-speed train, from time to time falling quiet altogether as though she is going through a tunnel.

I have done some good things in my life, Henry thinks, and not waking her is one of them. Another is to have tried to forget the words I wrote about 'Hovis'. If you really don't wish a thing to have been, whether it's a lie or an adultery or a betrayal, if you wipe it from the slate of your memory, then that's almost the same – isn't it? – as its never having happened. You can't will away a misdeed, Henry accepts that, but if you will it away hard enough you almost can. Like the dot into which your picture used to disappear when you turned off your old cathode ray tube television: always there somewhere, you felt, receding into infinity, but to all intents and purposes – provided you are not a metaphysician – gone.

Of the compunctions he suffered at the time of writing the article, most were suppressed beneath the conviction that Osmond had better things to do with his time than read *Movie Tones*, or to care, even if he did happen to fall upon the relevant edition of that high-minded journal, what a long-forgotten failure of a shmuck of a friend, buried brain downwards in an obscure teaching institution in the Pennines, had to say about him. Later regrets Henry dealt with by reasoning that the article was of its time, in the spirit of what people did then, and contained arguments which – again bearing in mind contemporary expectations – needed to be heard. Like bear-baiting, Henry's indiscretion had to be put down to the prevailing barbarism of the period. Anachronistic to criticise him. Like accusing Moses of Zionism, or Medea of bad parenting, or Prometheus of violating fire-safety regulations, like that other anachronism, Uncle Izzi.

Thus, over time, Henry's delinquency – going, going, going, going . . .

Not his fault that the fucking Internet has suddenly to pop up and revive it all.

Hot in his bed – in his father's bed, it helps him to remember, spreading the blame, sins of the fathers and all that – Henry wonders if it would aid his cause to come clean about other offences while he's at it. Have them taken into consideration, as they say, and – who knows? – thereby get his sentence reduced.

The women, does he mean? The friends? The wives of friends?

No, not the women, not the wives. And not the friends. He's done friends. Hand on heart, he's told the court all about 'Hovis' Belkin.

Unless there's more, just one eensy-weensy little detail more . . .

When was it that Catherine Grigson, the departmental secretary, knocked on Henry's door with the first of the xeroxed Guidelines governing relations between staff and students – 1973, 1974? What and what not to say on a student's essay. What and what not to say when disagreeing with a student on a matter of critical judgement in a public place. How to recommend a particular course of reading to a student without thereby compromising his or her intellectual liberty. How to behave when faced with a verbally aggressive student – don't back him or her into a corner, for example, don't punch him or her in the face, don't tie him or her up or otherwise imprison him or her in your room (especially yours, Henry), don't make promises you can't keep.

Henry liked Catherine. Liked the pale skin flecked with red, and her bronze hair in which, if you were so minded, you could see your own reflection. Effortlessly overweight, a mere half-stone or so, and always flushed, as though caught out that very second in a minor misdemeanour, she belonged to another age and idea of women, a major's daughter or something like that, raised to look after men, to bring them tea and take their boots off and otherwise ease their passage through a world made brutal by war and insurrection. Catherine wore too many clothes, all of them too long for her and too loose, so that in between dispensing guidelines she was forever reaching for straps which turned out to be the wrong straps, struggling to put back jackets whose fallen shoulder pads she had first to punch back into shape, tucking away undergarments to which Henry could neither give a name nor ascribe a use. That this chaos of too-muchness around her wardrobe was meant to make life pleasanter for brothers, fathers, uncles, persuading them of their own compactness and efficiency, and preparing them, if necessary, for the rigours of colonial conquest, Henry did not for a moment doubt. But seeing the ruse did not make it a jot less efficacious. The hottest and most ineffective of men, Henry cooled and became competent the moment he was in Catherine's company. If he had a complaint about her it was only this: that she enquired after his well-being with so much concern etched on her face and so much sorrow in her voice – 'Are you OK, Henry?' or 'Is everything all right with you today, Henry?' – that she made his eyes water. 'I'm well, I'm fine, I'm great,' Henry would reply, knowing that he couldn't possibly have been any of those things, else she wouldn't have asked the way she did. 'I'm terrific, I'm fantastic, I'm off the planet,' he went on in desperation, wilting under her consideration.

Sweet. Sweet that someone cared.

Over the years he discovered that she had the same effect on everyone. As soon as she asked people how they were, they felt terrible.

The day she brought in the Code of Spatial Practice document, she made Henry feel it had been written specifically with him in mind. Normally she just dumped the updated weekly Guidelines on his desk, asked him how he was, and left. This time she sat down in a billow of slipped straps and fallen petticoats and took him through the most salient provisions. *Do* acknowl-

edge students' individuality and right to their views, she read –
as though there were some danger he wouldn't. *Don't* communicate, either directly or indirectly, in a way that maligns others –
as though there were some danger he would.

He shrugged, checking himself out in her hair. Fair enough.

*Do*, she went on, frame your responses in a considered and
magnanimous manner. *Don't* initiate rumours, whether to students
or to your colleagues, which may be damaging to the reputation
of either.

Aha, Henry said. Fine. Fine.

And *don't*, Catherine continued, raising her flushed eyes to
meet his, arrange to meet students alone, whether on the campus
or off it. *Don't* instigate relations which may be deemed intimate
or in any other way inappropriate or misleading. *Don't* show or
express favouritism for one student over another. *Don't* touch the
student or crowd his or her personal space. A gesture which seems
to you encouraging or consolatory can easily be misinterpreted.
If a tutorial situation necessitates your seeing a student alone, *do*
send a memo to the head of department in advance, explaining
the situation, and *do*, in those circumstances, contrive to keep a
distance of approximately one metre between you and the student
throughout.

'Catherine, stop,' Henry said. 'I'll read all this in my own time.
But you have nothing to worry about. I'm in my thirties, pushing
forty. And when you're pushing forty you're pushing fifty. People
are taking early retirement at my age. In my head I'm working
an allotment – in slippers. I'm no threat, believe me. I'm past
invading space.'

And he was. Let the no-touchies rulings of the middle seven-
ties proliferate all they liked, nothing could have been easier for
Henry to comply with, because by that time there was no one
Henry wanted to touch.

One metre! I have to get to within one metre! Too close,
Catherine. Too close by a door, a corridor, an institution and a

county. Too close by however you measure the distance between life and death.

It had been different when he was twenty-five, or thirty, but now that he had begun his headlong decline into the second half of his life he was no longer attracted to the young of any species, least of all his own. He never had been much, now he wasn't at all. He didn't like their wet mouths, their casualness, their trainers, the pride they took in everything they didn't know, their assumption that the old were interested in, or envious of them, the way they glottal-stopped, the way they said 'gid' for good, their failure to understand that education was an escape from popular culture not a platform for it, the tuneless head-banging songs they hummed – *Hit me with your rhythm stick, hit me, hit me*, no Charlie Parker riffs of the sort favoured by his pals at school, *doodleoodleoooodleoo*, no Gigli either, no Fischer-Dieskau, no Schubert, and whoever lives without Schubert does not live at all – and most of all he didn't like their slack sexualism, born of the pill, a loss of shame, the decline of Christianity, and an insufficiency of that bodily fastidiousness without which sex isn't worth performing. Sooner than reach out to touch or tap a student, sooner than put his arm around a student, whether as a gesture of encouragement or consolation, Henry would have snuck into a nest of vipers. Indeed, he did from time to time wonder whether his bodily revulsion from those whose intelligences he was paid to sharpen wasn't itself a more serious breach of the new codes of conduct than intimacy of trespass. Staff are not expected physically to loathe their students, nor to start from them as from a leper, so *don't* throw up on their essays or otherwise manifest nausea without a third party being present – there'd have been more sense in Catherine getting him to take on board *that* injunction, than worrying him, had-it Henry, with warnings of inviolable space which he had not the slightest urge to violate.

But though he was spatially impeccable, judgementally he wasn't. He went where he should not have gone. He judged.

Ask Henry for a reference or a letter of recommendation and you took your life into your hands. Every student knew this. Henry warned them in advance. I don't like writing references, he explained, and the only way I am able to reconcile myself to the chore is by treating them as art. My model is the character sketch of the seventeenth century. Clarendon, Halifax, Sir Philip Warwick, none of them writers of whom you'll have heard. Judicious, dramatic, unflattering, starting from the centre and working out. If you do not choose to trust your character to my pen, then don't ask me for a reference. Otherwise, take your chance, hope that I have seen what value lies within your nature, that I have truly measured your accomplishments, and all might yet be well. Someone might be persuaded to employ you. Then again someone might not. My only obligation is to the truth.

For a while it was possible to get away with this. A reference was a reference. A considered verdict delivered by an expert. Even if the expert happened to be a pompous prick like Henry. But little by little the times they changed around him. First, the authority of the teacher was called into question. Who was Henry, who were any of them, to suppose their opinion was qualitatively better or truer than anyone else's? Then came human rights, the expectation enjoyed by every student to be well-spoken-of, to be free of anyone's opinion of him or her should that opinion happen to be unwelcome, the right never to be the object of comment that could be construed as negative. And following hard upon the heels of both, news from the United States of America that students at the sharp end of a bad reference, regardless of its justice, were successfully suing the institutions on whose notepaper the reference had been written.

'Here are the new Guidelines for Writing References,' Catherine said, dropping them on Henry's desk. 'I particularly draw your attention to page 9, paragraph 14 – "Please ensure that you provide only factual information as opposed to personal opinion."'

'I don't know the difference between factual information and personal opinion,' Henry complained. 'They write an essay, every-thing they say in it is shit. Is that a fact or my opinion? I say it's both. My opinion has to count as fact. That's why I am trusted to teach.'

'I didn't write these,' Catherine reminded him. 'And by the way, how are you?'

Seeing Catherine's concerned expression, Henry went into immediate decline.

As for references, the only safe course now was to give up writing them altogether. Or failing that, to get students to sign a waiver in advance, indemnifying the referee from prosecution.

A third, unspoken option, the anodyne option, in which you unearthed something complimentary to say of every student – how kind to animals they were, how punctually they handed in the shit they wrote, how innovatively they tied their shoelaces – was closed to Henry who found it hard enough to speak well of someone who deserved to be spoken well of.

Page 10, paragraph 6, settled it for Henry. 'If you aren't certain, DON'T WRITE THE LETTER.'

Music to his ears: fair enough: he wouldn't.

So what on earth suddenly made him let his guard down and ignore the guidelines, not only denying a student the words of enthusiastic commendation to which she'd been born entitled, but offering it as his judgement that she had a poor mind and an even poorer attitude – slovenly was the word he used, a slovenly intelligence – thereby abusing her human rights, defaming her character, exposing himself to the charge of negligent misrep-resentation and the University of the Pennine Way to the possi-bility of a damaging lawsuit, and thus bringing his illustrious career to an ignominious end?

How come, Henry?

Explain yourself.

Who was she? What had she done to deafen you to that exquisite music – DON'T WRITE THE LETTER – and make you depart from your usual precautions? And what would have led her to believe, if you had so low an opinion of her, that she could count on you to speak up on her behalf? Was she someone to whom you owed an obligation of some sort? Was she otherwise known to you? And if so, should you not, in common decency, have advised her to look elsewhere for the recommendation she sought?

He isn't sure he can go ahead with this line of self-interrogation. He turns on to his side, being careful not to wake Moira. Her snoring soothes him. If you can make a sound when you are not awake, then there is life beyond the pains of consciousness. That's where Henry would like to be: somewhere else, somewhere he can fall into ignorance of himself without ceasing to be altogether. A halfway house. Not quite death, not quite life.

Sleep does it for some people. But sleep isn't quite what Henry means. The state Henry craves hasn't yet been discovered.

Besides, Henry can't sleep tonight. Too many people in his head tonight who do not think as they ought on serious subjects.

So he lies there, straining his ears for the sound of traffic, the outside welcome tonight, more welcome than the inside at least. The disgrace of it, he thinks. The disgrace of it! Nothing specific. Just the disgrace of life before and – whether he falls into blessed ignorance of himself or not – the disgrace of life hereafter.

# TEN

'Guess what?' Lachlan says, looking from one to the other. 'She kept diaries.'

'Really,' Henry says.

Moira kicks him under the table. 'What?' his eyes ask. 'What have I done?' But he knows what he's done. He hasn't shown sufficient interest. He's off and away, somewhere else. 'Sorry,' he says, bringing himself back, attending to Lachlan properly this time. 'Who kept diaries?'

'The old biddy.'

'Really,' Henry says. Moira again kicks him under the table. This is the trouble with having a woman friend. If you have a woman friend she likes to know where you are, even when you're with her, and that means having to come back from the dark backward of abysmal time, where most of what is interesting to you, if you're Henry, is to be found.

They are in Henry's favourite restaurant, the Tallin Palace, to which Moira has only recently introduced him but which fits the bill for Henry, exactly. What a restaurant should be. Pink tablecloths, arched entrances from room to room, arched alcoves, arched mirrors, an air of anxious plenty, as though those who eat here are not beyond imagining a time when they may never eat again, but in the meantime every sort of meat and fish – though only the meat is important to Henry – served by men, not impossibly Cypriots, in wigs and black bolero waistcoats. And *where* a restaurant should be, too, attached to a mansion block, almost the mansion-block canteen, invisible to the eye of mere passers-by, but just a five-minute walk from the High Street.

'Why don't we have all our meals here?' Henry had suggested, after his first visit.

'Because I'd be twenty stone in a month,' Moira told him.

But she was pleased he liked the place. She is enjoying being his Virgil through the underworld which is St John's Wood. Though Henry offers to be jaded, he marvels easily. He vanishes from her side sometimes, floats away like the shade of a dear-departed, but a new restaurant always brings him back. In time she'll be out of restaurants, she knows that. She'll have taken him to every one there is. And then, the chances are, she'll lose him. It's like waiting for the dawn to come and the first cock of the morning to crow – signal for ghosts to start like guilty things upon a summons, and be gone. She feels she's borrowing him from something or from someone, she just doesn't know from what or whom.

Tonight there are three small parties in progress at the Tallin Palace. Intermittently, with well-calculated consideration for those who are not celebrating a birthday or an anniversary, the lights are dimmed and one of the waiters comes in with a cake. Next to Henry's table a dozen people are gathered for a golden wedding. The wife is birdlike and triumphant: fifty years ago they said it wouldn't last. The husband is mottled on his hands and face with the brown stains of death. Little by little, starting from the inside, it's seeping through his flesh. He is so decrepit – though there's been nothing wrong with his appetite, Henry's noticed – he does not have the breath to blow out a single candle. At the other end of the table a great-niece, maybe a great-great-niece, stands up, rolls out her chest and extinguishes it for him. Everyone applauds. Only the wife is displeased. 'We should see you more,' she tells the great-great-niece.

'Families,' Henry says, thinking about the cake. 'But you were saying' – to Lachlan – 'your stepmother kept a diary.'

'Not a diary – dozens of diaries. Going back to the twenties as far as I can tell, and only finishing when she did. Do you know there's even an entry for the morning she passed away.'

'What does it say?' Moira wants to know.

'"Not feeling well."'

Henry laughs. Moira kicks him under the table.

'That's upsetting,' Moira says.

Lachlan bangs his chest. He is not the best person to be out eating with. Every morsel of food has to be chased down his oesophagus, a punch more or less wherever there's a button on his shirt, every six or seven seconds. Then air has to be coaxed back up, at similar intervals.

It's only a pity, Henry thinks, looking away, that my father isn't here to pick his teeth behind his hand. We could leave them to enjoy each other's company.

Why Lachlan is eating with them at all, Henry isn't sure. Moira's doing. She is sorry for him. She thinks he's lonely. And since she and Henry are not in the slightest bit lonely now they have each other, there is no reason not to make the occasional gift of themselves – a proof of their superabundance – to their friends. Friends? All right, neighbours then. Henry suspects her interest in Lachlan goes beyond pity. He is a mystery to her. She has already remarked several times how much she admires the way he wears his clothes. Not necessarily the clothes themselves, which have nothing of St John's Wood Italianate about them, aren't tight about the hips, or open at the throat, but the way he carries them. They look as though they belong to him, as though he's grown them, she said. Observe him when he sits down in his suit, she ordered Henry, he looks like an old bear enjoying the slackness of his skin. She also likes the smell of them. (The countryside, she said. Angus, Henry corrected her.) And she is intrigued by the gold pocket watch he carries on a chain, fastened by a fob chain to a buttonhole in his waistcoat. She thinks he's aristocratic, a laird or Highland chieftain. Though she doesn't admit to being a foreigner herself, laughing off Henry's conviction that she is Viennese or Czech, insisting she was born in Borehamwood or somewhere like, this to Henry proves conclusively she's from somewhere else. Only a foreigner would be intrigued by Lachlan, or think him aristocratic. He is like beefeaters and Chelsea pensioners and the changing of the guard – picturesque only to the eyes of a tourist.

Lachlan himself is less upset than Moira is by his stepmother's diaries. 'Dear old thing . . .' he says, comical in the pause, ' . . . I don't think.'

Henry is anxious not to have his meal ruined by another Lachlan monologue on the subject of his stepmother.

'Find something nice to say about her,' he says. 'It's better for your heart. Speak well of people and you'll live longer. Speak well of the dead and they'll watch out for you.'

'That's very positive, from *you*,' Moira says.

'I'm practising.'

Lachlan says, 'You're sounding like her. Every day she tried to write down something in her diary that would cheer her up. I thought seeing me without a penny did that, but apparently not.'

'So share with us some of her wisdom.'

'Oh, lor,' Lachlan says, closing his eyes. 'Well, there is one I remember, probably because the old feller used to recite it, though I can't say I know whose it was first. "If you would be happy for a week take a wife; if you would be happy for a month kill a pig; but if you would be happy all your life plant a garden."'

'Funny,' Henry puts in, 'that was one of my mother's favourites too.'

'Lot of nonsense, if you ask me,' Lachlan says, 'Should read, "If you would be miserable for a week take a wife; if you would be happy all your life bury her in the garden."'

Moira slaps his hand across the table. 'That's not very nice,' she tells him.

'Strange,' Henry says, ignoring the pantomime. 'I could never understand what any part of that meant to my mother.'

'Ah,' says Moira, 'Ekaterina the cake builder and decorator.'

'Leave her alone,' Henry says. 'She isn't here to defend herself.'

Moira ruches her lips at him. For a moment Henry thinks she's going to show him a mouthful of food. Or bring a breast out. 'I only say it,' she says, 'to annoy you.'

'Don't annoy me.'

'I only annoy you because I love you. Has no one ever told you how handsome you become when you're annoyed?'

'Who's Ekaterina?' Lachlan wants to know.

'Henry's mother. She was a maker of architectural cakes. Henry doesn't like me joking about her.'

'Quite right. Nothing funny about a mother. Nothing funny about a stepmother either, but there you are. Nice name, Ekaterina. Russian, was she?'

Henry nods. Let's not get into that. Given the amount of drink that's going down, Lachlan will be talking Jewesses soon.

'So go on,' Moira says, quickly, 'why could you never understand what any part of it meant to your mother?'

'Part of what?' Lachlan wants to know.

Angus would be better company, Henry thinks. 'Part of what we've just been talking about. What interested her about it. She was never going to take a wife, she never saw a pig, and she never went into the garden.'

'Maybe she was aiming it at you,' Moira says.

'Wife bit, yes, you could be right, though she universally warned me off women. And planting a garden was something we talked about. I used to tell her I couldn't bear the idea of being buried, and she said I needed to learn to love the earth. Rich, coming from her, but there you are. The pig, however . . .'

'The pig's me,' Lachlan says. 'The pig-food salesman.'

'So how does that work? I'll be happy for a month if I kill you?'

'Not for me to say, old man. Do you recognise any such inclination in yourself?'

'None that I would admit to.'

'Then I'd better watch out.'

'Your dog, however –'

'Poor Angus. I don't know what you did to him.'

'It's what he did to me.'

'He came home –' Lachlan says to Moira, enlisting her sympathy.

'Is this Henry or the dog?'

'The dog, the dog. I can't speak for Henry. He came home, went straight into his basket, and didn't leave it again for a week.'

'Canine shame,' Henry explains. 'He knows I have his number. Piss-sniffer, ball-licker, shit-eater.'

'Would you mind!' the woman at the next table says to him. 'This is my golden wedding.'

'So sorry,' Moira says for him.

'I'm not sorry,' Henry says, but not loudly. 'If people don't want to hear about dogs . . .'

'They should what?' Moira wants to know.

'They should . . . I don't know . . . Stay in.'

'It's actually my dog he's talking about,' Lachlan leans across to explain. 'So I'm the one who should be upset.'

'My golden wedding,' the woman says, 'and you're the one who thinks he should be upset.'

This is why Henry likes it here. It's almost a club. Everyone has something in common. If it's only that they are all dying.

A club for the mordant.

And actually, Henry realises, it's more than that. Everyone here is not only dying, but finds the idea of death disgraceful. There's no letting on, of course, and Henry would be hard pressed to prove this, but here, among his people, among this particular manifestation of his people, the St John's Wood branch, so to speak, where expectations have been less pinched than in the north, there is a shared apprehension of the disgrace which death brings. As though not to have beaten it yet, not to have found a way round it, not to have exceeded the common in precisely the sphere of operation where the common is so indiscriminating, is to have failed, in the end, failed disgracefully at the only worthwhile task that's been set you.

And so they sit eating red meat while blackly joking, a community of separated souls, each consumed with self-reproach.

When Henry floats back to the table, he finds that Moira and Lachlan have resumed their conversation about the old lady's diaries. Moira has been asking whether they are newsy and informative, whether they are publishable even, since there is a great interest in those whose lives coincided, more or less, with the beginning and the end of the twentieth century.

'Oh, she doesn't talk about politics much,' Lachlan is quick to explain, 'not in the ones I've looked at so far, anyway. It's more people.'

'People are what people like,' Moira says.

'Are they?' Lachlan is looking disconsolate now. Once the food has been thumped down the oesophagus and settled into his stomach, the sadness follows. Henry understands this. Like friends, food. After the initial excitement it all seems pointless.

'You couldn't round us off with another of your stepmother's positive proverbs?' Henry asks. 'Something to raise our spirits before we leave?'

Lachlan rubs his fists in his eyes. No doubt, Henry thinks, Moira finds this gesture of helplessness aristocratic.

But then he remembers one. 'I might not have this right,' he says. 'But it's something like, "We should consider every day lost on which we have not danced at least once. And we should call every truth false which was not accompanied by at least one laugh." Neetzer, I think.'

'Nietzsche,' Henry says.

'I approve of that, yes,' Moira says. 'We haven't danced today, Henry.'

'Then that's another day lost,' Henry says.

But he isn't thinking what he says. He's away. Floating. *If you would be happy all your life, plant a garden.* Funny. He can hear his mother saying it, her delivery mischievous, as though she knows she is mouthing advice she has no right to give. And yet the memory of it conjures up a garden. The garden she didn't care about. The garden which his father laid waste with his torches, giving the ornamental goldfish heart attacks, after which the sandpit that they hoped would miraculously turn Henry into a little boy like other little boys. The sunlit, Schubertian garden of his childhood, where it was never cold, and never dark, and he was never anything but happy. So she was right. It works. If you would be happy, plant a garden. And for a moment or two he does, and is.

Funny how youthfully he remembers her, whistling while she worked. He can see her things, the most inconsequential of them, the round straw box in which she kept her thread and needles, though she was the world's worst sewer; the blue airmail writing pads she liked to use, with faint grey lines across the page; the pile of books she kept on her bedside table, all with folded pieces of paper sticking out, marking passages she wanted to read aloud to him; her *Pocket Oxford Dictionary*, of which on her account Henry was always a little bit ashamed, because it implied limits to her curiosity.

And now Nietzsche.

The following day, he goes looking for somewhere to be buried. He has an *A to Z* in his pocket. The burial places circled with a red marker. He'd like Moira to go with him. A day out in the country, is how he puts it. But she's busy. Has to be at the patisserie in the morning, and has a class to give in the evening. Life, Henry. Life. So he goes on his own.

Nowhere special. He has no plans. Which must mean he isn't looking for an exact place to be buried yet, isn't expecting to come to any definite decision, more trying to get ideas. Like slipping along to an Ideal Home Exhibition when you're wondering what to do with your kitchen. An Ideal Burial Exhibition. The death you've always dreamed of. Earls Court, 22 Dec, the year's midnight, for one day only – all you need to plan your own extinction. I could open it, Henry thinks. Henry Nagel, renowned author of the previously buried critique of the films of 'Hovis' Belkin, will be in attendance.

Almost-country churchyards are what he's thinking about today, nothing civic, not cemeteries but church-sheltered semi-rural plots, all within a bus ride or two from St John's Wood. He's read that there's an ancient yew in Downe in Kent. He likes yews. He isn't always sure he could pick you one out, if other trees were present, but he likes the idea of them, and indeed likes the thing once another person has identified it for him. 'There is a yew tree ' – William Wordsworth. Reminiscent of 'There is a willow' – William Shakespeare. The matter-of-fact topography of anguish. Where trees are, human trouble is. If someone enters a room with the words 'There is an oak', or 'There is a laburnum', start running.

Not running anywhere, Henry has always had a soft spot for Wordsworth's yew tree, standing 'single, in the midst of its own darkness'. It is like an epitaph in itself. HERE LIES HENRY – SINGLE IN THE MIDST OF HIS OWN DARKNESS. He'll settle for that. Not as good as HERE LIES HENRY – WHO NEEDS NO INTRODUCTION, but then what man is remembered the way he'd like to be?

The yew, Henry recalls learning at school – was it from 'Fat Frieda' he learned it? – was a favoured churchyard tree because of the superstition that its roots grew into dead men's eyes. That frightened him at the time. By rights it should frighten him more now, the closer he gets to finding out for himself, but accommodations crowd in when you least expect them. Why *not* be blinded by the yew? If your eyeballs feed the roots, does that not mean your seeing will live on in the tree's branches? Not according to the superstition it doesn't. The reason you wanted the dead blinded was so that they couldn't see and covet the world of the living, and then be tempted to return as spirits. More effectively than the stone lid to your grave, the yew finished you off and kept you in your place. But that's only the superstition; there's no saying it works. And no saying that the dead aren't watching from every dark green leaf . . .

Such a consciousness junkie, Henry. Wanting to live for ever, wanting to watch for ever, unable to bear missing out on anything. So characteristic of a man, he remembers Esmé Papping, his friend Lawrence Papping's missus, telling him soon after he'd told her he loved her and could not contemplate the idea of her so much as drawing breath where he was not – so untrusting of the flux, Henry, so controlling. Esmé's favourite yew, of course, was Sylvia Plath's –

> And the message of the yew tree is blackness –
> blackness and silence.

After her, after Sylvia, the deluge.

Let it go, Henry. Let it finish.

Sweet Esmé, another one putting him right. Another one who failed, for Henry is still here, not letting it go, not letting it finish.

But the Downe yew is too distant. Kent, for Christ's sake! He wants Moira to be able to come and visit him on a whim. Maybe bring a flower. Maybe bring Lachlan. Have Angus piss on his grave.

He catches the number 13 bus from Finchley Road, heading north, meaning to go as far as it will take him, then catch another if he has to, according to the red circles in his *A to Z*. But the 13 only goes as far as Golders Green, in which case he might as well stroll up to Hoop Lane and take in the great crematorium, where the burning started in earnest for Londoners. It looks vaguely like a monastery, with red-brick Tuscan chapels and cloisters, memorial plaques on every inch of wall, and, behind, a wedge-shaped garden, a meadow he guesses it should be called, on which sheep would not be out of place, though the grazing wouldn't be of the best, this being what a discreet notice describes as the Dispersal Area. How many have been shaken out here? Henry wonders – the body and soul of man reduced to the contents of a pepper pot.

He is quickly tearful. Tears creaking in his forehead, at the apostrophes of his eyes. The creak of tears – where does that come from? A poem? A woman's novel? Not his phrase, he is sure of that. One he'd needed to appropriate. Too apposite to be without. The skull like an old unsteady boat, at sea, tear-drenched, and the timbers creaking.

I'll have that, Henry had decided.

Not for himself, the creaking tears, but for everybody. Every body. He reads a memorial stone to Shirley – he knew a Shirley once – *Addio mia sposa brava*. Though he has never had a wife, goodbyes to wives have always struck Henry as too sad to bear. Second in unbearableness only to goodbyes to children. And second not even to those if you are the erotic sentimentalist Henry is.

*Sposa brava*. Wherein the bravery? he wonders. In Bunhill Fields, another of Henry's favourite gardens of interment, there is a memorial to Dame Mary Page, relict of Sir Gregory Page, Bart, who 'in 67 months was tapd 66 times, had taken away 240 gallons of water, without ever repining at her case'. Was Shirley, too, a non-repiner? *Sposa brava*. Hard for Henry, in the exquisite abstract, the suffering of women. Man is different. Man is born to suffer and not repine. Henry himself a case in point. But wives in pain – the soft liquidity of *mia sposa brava*, like water over pebbles, its dying fall, its too too tender salutation, says all there is to say about the unnatural cruelty of such things.

Is it going to happen to some woman Henry knows? Is this why he has been preparing for it in his imagination for so long? And oughtn't he, if that is the case, to let Moira go now, while she is still safe? Mulling it over, Henry gets to enjoy the anticipatory frisson of parting, at no cost, gets to mourn freely in his mind her brave passing, the schmaltz merchant that he is.

Some couples are 'Reunited at last' in a rose bush. Would he like that? He and Moira feeding the roots of a rose? 'After a short time apart, together again.'

Together again, together for ever – Henry has no resistance to the banal poetry of for everness, and has to go and sit on a little bench by a little wall and put his fingers to his forehead where the creaking has started up again.

Ah, yes. He remembers now. Henshell Spivack, Lia's husband. Once Henry's second-best friend. Hensh the Mensch. That's whose tears creaked. Until they stopped altogether. Nothing to do with Henry. By no means was it because Lia lay with him in the Pennines that her husband Henshell, who'd taken up angling all of a sudden, walked with purpose into the reservoir where he fished. They weren't even any longer a pair, Hensh and Lia. He had been married to another woman for a decade. So why? Henry thought it was to stop the creaking. Lia, less fancifully, said it was a combination of business failure and the fact of his ever having gone into business at all, he who'd meant to make the world a better place – literally better, better in the druggist's sense. She'd written to Henry, all those years after he'd failed to be a tiger for her, first to tell him about Henshell, and then, another year or so after that, to ask if he'd like to meet her at Heaton Park, where Henry and Henshell had horsed around as kids – rowing on the boating lake, winning toffee apples at summer fairs, rolling down grassy banks together – to help her dispose of her half of the ashes. A surprise to Henry, a sort of impiety, he thought, that Henshell had stipulated cremation. (What sort of a Jew was he – first angling and now burning?) And a bigger surprise still that the women had divvied up his remains. Civilised, he supposed, honouring the variousness of the dead's affections. So why no smidgen of ash for him, Henry, Henshell's erstwhile pal? Well, that was Lia's point. Let's scatter what we've got together. Not in bad taste, Henry wondered, given everything, given Henry's habitual borrowing and the like? No, taken all round, she thought not. So they'd met and hired a rowing boat, and Henry had done the rowing, and she'd emptied the grey matter over the side, like fish food, and then they'd sat there in silence, moored to the little island, listening to the ducks, and the cries of the living, and the creaking timbers. And Henry had not been able to think of a single thing to say.

'That's that, then' – Lia's words, at last. 'Gone for ever.'

And Henry had put a hand out to touch her, then thought better of it and touched himself instead – two fingers to his temple, where the pain was.

Too big an idea for Henry the borrower – for ever.

Always was, always will be.

Enough. He can't stay here. Burning is too final. He will not be piped into a furnace and dispersed. Not in a meadow, not on a lake. He wishes, Henry, if he can, to keep himself to himself. On the way out he sees that Bud Flanagan has been burned here, and Tubby Hayes and Ronnie Scott and Bernie Winters and Nellie Wallace and Marc Bolan, whoever Marc Bolan is, and Hughie Green – 'You were the star that made opportunity knock.' Several generations of popular entertainment up in flames. *Addio*. No place for Henry.

Across the road – despite himself – the Jewish cemetery, Spanish and Portuguese to the right, Ashkenazim to the left. The Ashkenazim prefer their gravestones upright, like mantelpieces, whereas the Sephardic dead are remembered horizontally, in sarcophagi above ground. Mizrahi, Benezra, Benosiglio, Saady, Sassoon, Dellai – who are these people? A mystery to Henry, these lilting Jews from sunny places who don't have the dour music of Eastern Europe in their blood. '*Geliebt und unvergessen*' it says on the first Ashkenazi stone Henry bends his attention to, and lo! the magic still works. The native language of Jewish grief. Fucking German! The cruellest of all ironies to befall an ironic people. Falling in love with fucking German. Different if you're a Benzecry or a Saatchi. More restless in their white stone coffins they are, too, uneven, turgid and confused, as though the earth is stirring with them. Expectant, are they? Impatient to be off, to be up and gone to where the sun shines on burning desert, the moment they hear the bugle call? Half close an eye and Henry reckons there is definitely movement on their side of the cemetery. As turbulent as the lurching sea they look to Henry. Alive still, as near as damn it. Unreconciled. One thing for sure: a messiah in a hurry would wake these before trying for some response from Henry's lot, succumbed to cold, long given up the ghost, buried deep, in front of their silent mantelpieces.

Jewish burial! Not what Henry wants. Not the Polack way nor the Portuguese. Why can't it come down on one side or another? Serene or clamorous. Either return me to the quietude of earth, or kick up a racket for me. Why are there no angels here? Why no declamations of defiance? If a garden isn't really what you want, if the trees are merely incidental, and the grass there only because something must separate one plot from another, why not more gesticulating marble?

He remembers unveiling the stone to his parents, a year after he had put them in the ground, his anger overtaking his distress, so mute the ceremony, so bare the symbolism.

Of the close family, only Marghanita was with him. They leaned on each other, weeping.

'We should have done better,' Henry said.

'There is no better,' she told him. 'The better is in your heart.'

He shook his head. 'Not good enough. My heart will die. There should be better here, where it can be seen.'

He knew the arguments. Admired them even. They threw the myth of Jewish showiness and materialism back in the teeth of those who hated Jews. In quietness we pass away. Decorum in obsequies and entombment denies the privileged their last advantage. In death, everyone is equal. The poor man as *geliebt und unvergessen* as the rest. Great democrats, the Jews, as Nietzsche had observed – though from Nietzsche that wasn't unadulterated praise.

As it wasn't, always, praise from Henry either. The pursuit of democracy was an attempt to improve on the inequities of nature. Everything the Jews did was an attempt to better nature. Subdue the natural man, encode him into obedience, and you have civilisation. Well and good. Henry was all for that, as how could he not be, all trace of natural man having been squeezed from him in the womb. But it left you high and dry, he reckoned, when it came to death. The only way to make sense of dying was to see it as a return, but once you've turned your back on nature, there is nowhere to return to.

'It's not the seeing,' Marghanita said, 'it's the feeling. They are remembered by how we feel about them.'

'Yes, but look how banal the feelings,' Henry said, reading from the nearby stones. '*Sadly missed. For ever in our thoughts. To know her was to love her*. Trivial. If all you are is sadly missed you might as well not have lived.'

'You can't blame people for not being poets.'

'Can't you? I think you can. I think there is an obligation on us to be poets when the occasion calls for poetry and nothing less. It's laziness of the heart, or maybe I mean cowardice of the heart – faint-heartedness – that stops us. We'd rather be commonplace. It takes less out of us.'

'Henry, people find comfort in the commonplace. You know what they say about a sorrow shared. What we all feel the same about is easier to bear.'

'Is it?'

And it was true, in so far as he and Marghanita felt the same about Ekaterina and Izzi. They sobbed plainly in each other's arms. And it *was* easier to bear.

But when his turn came and somebody supervised the carving of *For ever in our thoughts* on his tomb, supposing there was anyone willing to supervise anything, what would he think and feel then? That death was comprehensible because he lived on as a sort of afterthought in some unpoetic person's thoughts? Better a marble vault.

He jumps on another bus. And immediately falls to thinking about his father. It was after the unveiling that Marghanita made her point by planting a story in Henry's mind which he would never forget, and which would indeed serve as his father's memorial. And his mother's too, because it was from his mother, Marghanita explained, that she had originally heard the story. And his mother had wept when she told it. 'It makes me want to forgive him everything,' she had said to Marghanita, 'except that I can't.'

*Mia mama brava.*

It was a Passover story. Not one of the usual ones. Nothing to do with Moses and Pharaoh. There are people who think everything is to do with everything – Henry spent a lifetime teaching in the spaces they allowed him – but this is not an allowable assumption in the context of Passover, for during Passover, of all festivals, nothing is as it usually is or resembles anything else. 'Why is this night different from all other nights?' asks the youngest child. Henry had asked that question in his time, though he has long forgotten the answer. Izzi too, when he was the youngest, asked it. Hard for Henry to imagine that. He must squeeze his eyes to do it. And even then he only sees himself.

Difference was of the essence, anyway. Passover is a night unlike all other nights. A boy will understand that as he may. For Izzi the reason was clear. This night was different from all other nights because it was his birthday. That's what they told him anyway. They messed his hair and pinched his cheeks and muttered Yiddish over him. *Vos draistu mir a kop?* What are you twisting our heads with all these questions for? On this night, *Got tsu danken*, you came into the world. *Mazeltov!* Now eat your egg in salt water. Only a moderate lie, as Marghanita pointed out. It was

227

your father's luck – who's to say whether it was his good luck or his bad luck? – to have been born within a few days of the period in which Passover usually falls. Your grandparents, as you know, were poor as mice. They had no money for birthday celebrations. A Pesach dinner, however, you have whether you can afford it or not. No Jew goes without Pesach. Was it such a crime, then, to allow Izzi to believe that Passover was for him, that the dinner was his birthday party, and that everyone was gathered in their best clothes to celebrate it in his name?

Yarmulkas instead of party hats, matzo instead of cake, and more remembrance of plagues than games of pass the parcel – but still, a party's a party.

No, Henry thought, a party is not a party. A deceit is a deceit but a party is not a party. So, yes, since she asked, he believed it *was* a crime to let his father believe what wasn't true.

Marghanita, older, wiser, and in the unfamiliar role of apologist for her brother-in-law's family, thought not. She quoted Graham Greene at him. 'In human relations, Henry, kindness and lies are worth a thousand truths.'

No, Henry said. That doesn't apply. It wasn't as though they were sparing him bad news. He didn't have cancer. They weren't going to sell him. And anyway, what's with the Graham Greene? Are we Catholics suddenly?

Oh yes, they *were* sparing him bad news, Marghanita believed. They were sparing him the news that they couldn't otherwise afford to do a single thing for him. It was Pesach or Izzi, so they did what was intelligent and lied and made it both.

And when he found out what sort of trick they'd played on him?

He'd laugh. Or at least he'd be old enough by that time to understand and to forgive.

Trouble was, he found out sooner than he was meant to. 'Izzi, go next door and borrow some salt' – that was what did it. They forgot that what he'd find next door, at Maxie Eisenklam's house, was an identical party – same songs, same matzo, Maxie Eisenklam being made a fuss over for asking the same questions – and Izzi knew it wasn't Maxie's birthday. Though he asked, just to be on the safe side. 'What, Maxie, is this your birthday party too?'

'Not to be thought about,' were Ekaterina's words to her sister. 'Unimaginable, their laughter. Unimaginable, what he must have felt.'

But Henry can imagine it. Henry can hear it in his head, the shame being piled on shame. The conviction that there will never be a single day from now on when you do not think of this and burn up with the disgrace of it.

Marghanita meant him to remember his father in this story, but he would have wished to remember him some other way. The sadness which once befell a parent is like no other. The humiliation of a parent when young is a historic pain a child should be spared all knowledge of.

Who knows, it is possible that Ekaterina was more upset for Izzi than Izzi had been for himself, and that Marghanita was more upset for Ekaterina, and that Henry is even more upset for all of them.

Is that what lives on longest, the sadness? The proof of our being weak, not the proof of our being strong?

Is there such a place where Henry can be buried, where every grave commemorates a weakness or a shame? A graveyard of the humiliated? Here lies Henry who had thin skin. Sadly missed for being sad. To know him was to be embarrassed for him.

He stays on the bus until it reaches its terminus, then does the same with whichever bus comes next, until he feels he's far enough. Totter Down, he arrives at. 'Is there a church here?' he asks a girl with a stud in her navel. She shrugs her shoulders, showing more belly. 'Dunno.' A black street sweeper astride a giant vacuum cleaner points him in the right direction, past the golf course, past the other golf course, past the pub. 'Does it have a graveyard?' Henry asks, not wanting to labour, in the heat, for nothing. The street sweeper laughs. Maybe Henry has the air of a man intending to bury himself in Totter Down. 'I think so,' the street sweeper says. 'You walking?' Henry nods. 'Then you'll need it by the time you get there,' followed by another laugh.

Henry doesn't like Totter Down. It's for the motor car – not another soul, once he's hit Totter Down Village Lane, out walking. The houses are expensive and gated. They have no natural way of looking. They are all approximating to some idea of some-where else or some other time. He can smell bad money. Gangster money. Football money. Opportunity knocks money. You make your pile and then you barricade yourself against the world in a house that isn't anywhere. So who's the misanthropist here, Henry asks, me or them? At least I'm living in a mansion block that looks like a mansion block with a pigswill salesman for a neigh-bour. At least I'm keeping company with a waitress.

The road arches and twists. The traffic roars past, honking at nothing. From behind the gates a dog snarls. Country life.

It takes him half an hour to find the church. Just beyond a row of Spanish villas he sees the spire, and then, if he's not very much mistaken – and no, no he isn't – a yew. There's a find! An old yew, too, he thinks. He has read – or was it 'Fat Frieda' who told the class? – that yews can live to a thousand years or more. He has no way of knowing if the Totter Down yew is as old as that, but it appears to be petrified with age, its bronzed bark twisted like Laocoön, pitted with barnacles as though it has been at sea for five hundred years, at its heart a whorled hollow, black and damp, resembling an entrance to the underworld. Abandon hope, it mutely warns, all ye who enter me. Henry walks round and round it. From no angle is it a comforting or companionable tree. It sucks in the light, just as Henry once feared he sucked away his mother's lightness, converting it to gloom – not only single in its darkness, as Wordsworth saw, but single-*minded*, having no other will or purpose but to send down darkness, so there should be absolutely no mistake, not a glimmer of expectation, not a chink of lighted hope, to where the sightless dead lie. No eyes on these branches. No one watching. Not a soul. But at least there is no confusing death's meaning here. *Always in our hearts*, be blowed. Gone, that's what. Gone away, gone under, gone for ever.

Henry takes a turn around the graveyard, not looking, his mind closed down.

And then, just as he is leaving, a figure appears from behind the yew, for all the world a visitant from the nether regions come up through the lightless trapdoor in the tree. Harrowed with fear and wonder, Henry starts. Not because the figure is ghostly in the sense that he is vile and loathsome like Hamlet's father, rotten, rotting, scabby from having dwelt among the dead, vengeful, jealous of the living, a disgrace. But because he is ghostly in the sense that he is Henry's best and oldest friend, not seen for thirty years or more – Osmond Belkin, unless too many graves have robbed Henry of his wits . . . Osmond 'Hovis' Belkin to the very tips of his soft smoker's fingers.

# ELEVEN

Henry's heart hammers in his chest. Is this happiness? Is hammering Henry happy suddenly?

He throws open his arms. '"Hovis"! My God! What in hell's name are you doing here?'

The man steps back from Henry's wild embrace.

'I'm sorry,' he says, 'you have the wrong person.'

Henry peers at him. Loaf head, well-kneaded flesh, squeezed sardonic eyes, top-heavy, but confident that the space he occupies in the world is his by right. '"Hovis",' Henry repeats. It is almost an entreaty. '"Hovis"!'

The man returns him a half-apologetic expression. Meaning, I would be if I could be. But also meaning, you are a bit of a girl, aren't you, not knowing who you know and who you don't.

How long does it take Henry to realise what he has done? Five seconds, an hour, a year? Stay, illusion! But the illusion is time itself. The man before him cannot be more than twenty-five or thirty. Henry has forgotten that Osmond is sixty or thereabouts and will not look now as he did when Henry saw him last. No, it wasn't, isn't, happiness. A great depression seizes Henry. That nausea of returning consciousness, as after fainting. It is as though half his life has been taken from him in an instant, been peeled from him, during the few moments he has been asleep, like loose skin.

'I'm sorry,' the man says again, seeing his distress.

Henry looks him over. He is wearing linens, well pressed, a cardigan about his shoulders, good Italian casual shoes – if he is out walking, he is not intending to walk far – a large expensive watch, an unnecessarily sleek belt, and aftershave almost certainly by Georgio of Beverly Hills. Rodeo Drive clothes, unmistakably, but worn as Henry has seen their equivalent worn with similar swagger in earlier days in Manchester. He is in no doubt now who he is talking to. And why the name 'Hovis' might not ring any bells with him. No man tells his family everything.

'Me that should be sorry,' Henry says, extending a hand. 'I used to be a good friend of your father's. You're Osmond Belkin's son, don't even bother to tell me you're not. I'm Henry Nagel.'

The young man takes his hand. Not as warmly as Henry would have hoped, but a shake's a shake. 'I think I've heard of you,' he says. 'I'm Mel Belkin.'

Henry is disappointed. What did he expect to hear? That Osmond had called his son Henry?

I'd have settled, Henry thinks, trying to be grown up about it, for the boy's at least knowing who I was. *Henry? Not Henry Nagel? Not 'the' Henry Nagel? Come, let me embrace you. I've never heard my father speak of you with anything but love and admiration.*

'And what,' Henry says, opening the palms of his hands, as though to measure the inappropriateness of Totter Down to their encounter, 'you live in these parts?'

'Dad's taken a house up here.'

'He's in the country, then? I had no idea.'

Mel Belkin bites his lip. He pulls a cigarette from his shirt pocket, not offering Henry. Osmond used to do the same. He lights it like his father too, virginally, as though it is his first and very probably his last. 'Yes, he's here,' he says in a precautionary way. Meaning, if Henry understands him right, he's here but doesn't want that to be generally known. 'And you,' he asks, not without alarm, 'do you live round here?'

'No,' Henry says, pointing back over his shoulder to where he thinks London is. 'I'm in St John's Wood. I'm just here' – why is Henry here? – 'to take the air.'

'You're a long way from home.'

'Am I? Sometimes I jump on buses and see where they take me.'

'Quite a coincidence, then.'

'It certainly is. But I am very glad of it.'

'And you like graveyards?'

'I do, yes. Yourself?'

'Yes. I'm working on a vampire script.'

'I thought for a moment,' Henry says, 'that that was what you were.'

'A scriptwriter?'

Henry laughs.

'Oh, sorry, you mean a vampire?'

'Well, more a spook.'

'Was that before or after you thought I was my father?'

Henry laughs again, though he doesn't know why. Unless it's simply funny, meeting your best friend's son for the first time, the dead spit of his father, and not liking him much. 'We were very close in our time,' Henry says. 'I'd love to see him.'

The young man stretches his jaw. 'He isn't well,' he says.

Henry looks into his eyes. 'How not well?'

Another pause, another pull at the cigarette. 'Look,' he says, 'is there some way we can contact you? Do you have a card or something?'

A card? Henry? Some joke. A man has a card when he knows who he is and what he does. And when he believes his future is worth investing in. Occasionally Henry has thought about getting himself a card, but what's the point? He'll have a thousand printed, use three, and the rest will be found in their little box by his executor. Not that he has an executor either.

He frisks himself, anyway, for the form of it, at a loss to understand why, of his usual stack of cards, not one is about his person.

'I'll write my number down,' he says, tearing a corner off the back page of his *A to Z*.

The young man holds Henry's number at a distance from his

face. He seems faintly disgusted that this is the best Henry can come up with. It's even possible – since he's a Belkin – that he disapproves of the numerals.

'And you,' Henry says, 'do you have a card?'

But it is as if Henry has not spoken.

'I'll tell Dad I've seen you.'

Henry looks down, not wanting to see the deadness in his friend's son's eyes. 'How not well?' he asks again.

Mel Belkin taps the torn-off corner of the *A to Z*. Meaning – well, meaning whatever it means. He shakes Henry's hand again, but with no more warmth than the first time. If anything, with less. 'Sorry,' he calls back after they have separated, 'what name should I say it was again?'

Riding the buses back, Henry remembers how he and Osmond were suspended from their junior prefects' duties for a term, for wrecking a production of *Twelfth Night* mounted by their sister school. In fact, they had not really wrecked the play, merely masterminded a disturbance which brought it to an earlier conclusion than was usual, before all the mistakes of identity had been cleared up, before any nuptials had been entered into, and before Malvolio could make his chilling promise to be revenged upon the entire cast. In this way, Osmond argued to the headmaster, Olly Allswell, MA, they had been responsible for an entirely new reading of Shakespeare's hackneyed comedy, one which was neither too conventionally happy nor too problematically black, but rather where irresolution and uncertainty were allowed to go on teasing and troubling the mind.

'You are not yet too old or too big, Belkin,' Allswell had retorted, 'to be given six of the best.'

'Sorry, sir,' Osmond Belkin had said. 'Just trying to put a decent gloss on our behaviour, sir.'

But it was Henry who was unable to stop himself snorting with mirth, and it was Henry who ended up getting five strokes of the cane.

'Thanks a lot, turd,' Henry said as they left the headmaster's office.

'Don't blame me,' Osmond told him. 'You were the *meshuggener* that laughed.'

Causing Henry, still in the headmaster's hearing, to burst out laughing all over again, remembering 'Hovis's' justification for what they'd done.

In fact, Henry had been more responsible for the disturbance at the girls' school than Osmond. Together they had egged on their party – comprising everybody doing fifth-form English at the boys' school, even Brendan O'Connor who was already contemplating the priesthood – to cheer when the scenery wobbled, to clap the moment someone forgot their lines, and to wolf-whistle as Viola, pretending to be a man, stroked her false beard and slapped her thighs. But it was Henry who made the more noise, shouting 'Behind you!' and 'Oh, no you don't!' whenever the play descended into pantomime, which was most of the time, and 'Not funny!' whenever Feste (Fiona Shatzkes) shaped one of his laborious jokes, and 'Pervert!' whenever Olivia (Sally Rotblat) looked longingly into the eyes of a person doubly the same gender as her own. He was overexcited. He had never been inside a girls' school before, never been surrounded on all sides by girls, and never seen so many girls in doublet and hose on one stage at one time. He couldn't help himself. It was like discovering within him a person he had never known was there. He had been brought up to be retiring, to be considerate of the feelings of others and to appreciate Shakespeare, and here he was, all at once, being none of those things.

'I am everything that's bad,' he told himself as it was happening, 'and it is marvellous.'

What made the liberation marvellous, of course, for a boy Henry's age, was that it wasn't a little bit sexual or even a lot sexual, but that it was completely sexual. At a bound Henry had gone from shrinking diffidence to exhibitionism, to libertinage, to violation, to ravishment, to *ejaculatio praecox*, to wanting to do it all over again. Had someone told Henry he hadn't just fucked the play he had fucked the entire girls' school, he would not have demurred. That, exactly, was how it felt.

From henceforth, he told himself, I shall be a man.

But at next morning's assembly when the headmaster announced a black day in the history of the school, citing behaviour that would have been unacceptable at a prison for the criminally insane let alone at a direct-grant grammar, it was Henry who was the first to blush.

'You're giving yourself away, Henry,' Osmond whispered into his ear. 'You're lighting up like a lamp-post.'

Henry dug his knuckles into Osmond's arm and twisted. But that only spurred his friend on. 'He knows it's you,' he whispered. 'He's looking at you right this minute. You're stuffed, you shmuck.'

In fact, they were all stuffed. Later that morning everyone doing fifth-form English lined up for an identity parade in the gym, their heads down, their hands hanging like empty nooses by their side, waiting for Miss Rawlins, producer of the play, to come across from the girls' school and pick out the guilty. She wasted no time. 'All of them,' she said. 'But this one,' extending a finger, 'most guilty of them all.'

The person at whom she pointed – and here was the surprising thing – being Osmond 'Hovis' Belkin.

Changing buses, Henry is surprised to discover the power this recollection still has to upset him. Osmond, of course, protested his innocence vociferously. 'What did I do?' he wanted Miss Rawlins to tell him. 'What did I do that was different from what we all did?'

'That's enough, Belkin,' Allswell warned him.

'I don't mind answering that,' Miss Rawlins said. She was a

237

ripplingly voluptuous woman in her forties, large-breasted, pulled in at the waist, her hips rounded, only the heaviness of her legs stopping the boys falling in love with her – though when she pointed her painted finger and said 'But this one', who cared about the legs?

Osmond Belkin, bred to be unafraid, looked at her evenly.

'What this one is guilty of,' she said, looking just as evenly back, no matter that she was addressing him in the third person, 'is letting down his family. I know the Belkins. I know their standards. Of those who should have known better' – and there is no mention of Henry here, no glance in his direction either – 'Osmond Belkin should have known better than any.'

And what could Henry say to this? What about me? Shouldn't I too have known better? And didn't I, though knowing better, as I most assuredly did, not only wreck your play but fuck your entire school? Credit where credit's due, Miss Rawlins. It's me you should be pointing at. I'm the ravisher.

Henry gives the pound coin he's been holding to the bus conductor, who has to juggle it in his hands, so hot is it. 'Where have you had this, mister?' the conductor asks.

'In the fires of Hell,' Henry says.

Credit where credit's due, Miss Rawlins. This could be the only play I ever wreck. Have a heart.

'Pisses me off,' Henry had said to Brendan O'Connor after the line-up.

'What she did to Belkin?'

'I'll say!'

'You're a good friend,' Brendan told him. 'When she said "Of those who should have known better" I was certain she was going to point to me. And then when she didn't all I could feel was relief. And there you were not thinking about yourself at all, but worrying for Belkin. You've taught me a lesson in humility.'

They shook hands. It would have taken Henry too long to disillusion him. And anyway, he liked being bathed in Brendan

O'Connor's liquid stare. The pools of black that were his eyes, the extraordinary lashes. If he does become a priest, Henry thought, I'll confess to him like a shot. Just not today.

Since she was going to find out about the fracas anyway, Allswell having warned the boys he was writing to their parents, Henry took his mother into his confidence.

'Well, I won't tell your father about it,' she said, 'but it's possible you were nothing like as naughty as you thought you were.'

'I wasn't naughty, Ma, I was *bad*. I ruined the first night of that play. Half the girls left the stage in tears. Some of them will never act again.'

She made him tea directly from the strainer. Hot water over a cold wodge of tea leaves. Sometimes the same tea leaves sat in the strainer for a week. 'I understand what you're telling me,' she said. 'But I know what you're like. You shouldn't have done what you did, that goes without saying, but you shouldn't take all the responsibility either. I know how susceptible to outside influence you are. You've always been easily led, Henry. That's why I worry about you. The first girl that comes along –'

'Ma, listen to me. Nobody led me, I led them. That's what I find so unjust. I do the work, "Hovis" gets the credit.'

'It's hardly credit, Henry. It sounds more like blame to me.'

'That's my point. I'm the bad one and he gets the credit for the blame.'

She smiled at him. '"The credit for the blame" – that's good, Henry.'

'Ma, I get cheated out of everything. Is that because no one notices I'm there?'

'It's the best way to be, Henry.'

'What if no one *ever* notices I'm there?'

'Then you'll live a happy life and die a happy man.'

In the end, he'd have been better off talking to his father. Though his father would have belted him for getting into trouble, then stormed off to the school to get justice for him. And who knows, might have ended up running off with Miss Rawlins. Would have eclipsed Henry, anyway, whatever he'd have done.

To make things worse, Osmond Belkin took him aside the next day and said, 'Coward!'

'Me, coward? Who wrecked the fucking play?'

'You didn't say that though, did you? You didn't stand up for me, when the fat cow pointed her finger.'

'You were enjoying it, that's why.'

'And why do you think that was?'

'Because you're a greedy turd who likes stealing the limelight.'

'And you're a coward.'

'No I'm not. I'm your friend. That's the difference between us. *I* didn't want to steal *your* glory.'

'I'd like to see you try.'

Henry threw his hands to heaven. 'Which way do you want to play this, "Hovis"?'

'All ways.'

And he did.

One week later, pressed and polished in their best shirts, Henry, 'Hovis' and all the other offending fifth-formers turned up to see Miss Rawlins, each carrying a bunch of bluebells. Henry's idea. He had read that bluebells connoted sorrowful regret. 'Hovis' had wanted orchids. Too sensual, Henry had argued. We aren't here to flirt. You might not be, 'Hovis' said. But if it was Henry who carried the day – mainly on account of bluebells being cheaper – it was 'Hovis' who delivered the sorrowing address. 'What we would also appreciate,' he said, rubbing his nose in patent duplicity, though no one but Henry seemed to see it, 'is the opportunity to appear before the whole school so that we can apologise personally to all the girls we upset.'

What Henry had not read was that bluebells wilt soon after they are taken out of the ground. 'Hovis' made the best of this, bearing his drooping posy as though it were a clue to the condition not only of his wallet but also of his heart. A poor boy spending the last of his pocket money on his conscience. A waif of remorse.

It was 'Hovis' who delivered the apology to the girls' school as well, a masterpiece of abjection in the manner of Anthony Aloysius St John Hancock, of whom all the boys could do passable imitations, though it was a toss-up whether 'Hovis' or Henry did him best. But today 'Hovis' had the stage. Henry remembers the ovation his friend received. And the invisible kiss, blown like a smoke ring, from Miss Rawlins.

Hidden among the others, Henry felt his soul shrivel to the size of a peanut.

And thus, says Henry aloud to himself on the bus, did Osmond Belkin steal the credit for the credit as well as the credit for the blame.


'So how was your day?'

Moira is waiting for him when he gets home, a bottle of wine open, olives in a bowl, squares of cheese.

'I thought you were teaching tonight,' he says.

'I was. I've finished. Now I can concentrate on you.'

Henry looks at his watch. It is later than he thought. How long they extend, these days of summer, when ghosts get hold of them.

'When you're not concentrating on me,' Henry asks, 'are you aware of me?'

'Do you mean am I thinking of you?'

'Yes. Am I there, a constant, or do I go when I'm gone in person and you have other things to occupy you?'

She thinks about it. She is dressed, the way he likes her, for going out. Heels, skirt with a taut quiver, hair up so he can see her neck. They have agreed that she should keep a housecoat here, or a kimono that matches Henry's, but Henry feels not yet. This is not domestic caution. Henry is not fussy about personal space. He simply isn't ready to dispense with the image he has of her, as a person of the city. The inside he can do himself; Moira's role is to carry the hum of the streets about her person.

'Yes,' she says, 'I am aware of you. I might not be thinking of you, but you're there like background music.'

'Muzak, you mean? As in a lift or a supermarket.'

'No, not Muzak. More like, I don't know – a distant waltz.'

There you are, Henry thinks. She *is* Viennese.

He smiles at her. 'Thank you,' he says. Coyly for him. He likes being a distant waltz.

'And me?' Moira asks. 'When I'm not there . . .'

'My dear, you're always there.'

'No, come on. I answered you fairly. Now you me.'

He paces the carpet. Has she been there with him today? At the gravesides, yes. A figure weeping over his remains. Bent, clearing away weeds, scraping moss from his stone, so that his name can still be read. And not simply as a spectator either. She has been dead alongside him also, plant food, reunited at last in the roots of a rose bush. But in the way he wishes to be told she thinks of him, a vibrant presence, no, it hasn't been her best day. Belkin's fault. Belkin empties his mind. Always has. And more, Belkin turns him against his own. If he is to be honest with himself he must admit to a faint sense of relief, no more than that, that Moira didn't accompany him today to Totter Down. Why is that? Because he doesn't want to be judged and reported as an engaged man by Belkin's son? Because he doesn't want Mel Belkin to meet Moira and form an opinion of her? Strange. Can he really have allowed the negative influence possessed by Osmond Belkin to be passed on automatically to his son, a person Henry has never met until this day and has no reason to respect for his judgement about anything? And more than that, what's so wrong with Moira that Henry should be reluctant for a Belkin to see her?

I fear cynicism, Henry has often admitted to himself. I fear cynicism more than I fear anything. I fear the judgement of one who thinks the world amounts to nothing. More specifically, I fear the judgement of one who thinks I amount to even less. He knows what he has done with Belkin. He has invested him with that power of cynicism, chosen him, rightly or wrongly, to be the one who sees through everything. In Belkin's eyes, Henry Nagel ceases to be. But it is always possible, he accepts, that Belkin neither wants this part nor fits it. And that the cynicism Henry dreads is his own.

So is it he, Henry, who is obscurely ashamed of Moira, for no other reason than that it is he, Henry who is nothing, who has chosen her?

'You are taking one hell of a time to answer,' she tells him.

'Am I?'

He can see that she is momentarily frightened. Whereupon, flooded with the most intense love for her, he folds her in his arms.

But they both know that isn't an adequate response to her question.

'Has anybody called?' he asks her in the morning.

'You're here. You'd know.'

'No, I mean last night, before I got in.'

She shakes her head. But is curious to be told, her face a question mark, whom he is expecting a call from.

Another woman? Even when it's not spoken, the question angers him. Always the same, always their first thought.

She feels the irritation stiffen his body. She knows what he thinks he knows she's thinking. 'Don't blame me,' she says. 'It's your doing. It's what you do. You create foreboding.'

'I make you feel I'm waiting for a secret phone call? If it were secret why would I ask about it?'

'You're shifty,' she says. 'There's always a bend in your trans-actions.'

Interesting. He thinks there is always a bend in hers. She has a bent face. It's what he loves her for. So do they love the same in each other?

'I'm waiting to hear from an old friend,' he tells her.

She waits for more. Which old friend? Why are you waiting? What has occurred?

But he is not going to tell her that it's the old friend she'd found on the Internet, the one he'd denounced in print. He's too bent to get into all that.

She makes him coffee. He has tried to interest her in tea from his samovar but she doesn't find the ceremony as cute as Henry does. 'This tea's as weak as piss,' she told him. Fine. Henry lets her make coffee. He has always been like this. He will change his habits for anyone. They are only borrowed anyway. Such accommodatingness makes him easy to live with, he believes. But also, as Moira has explained, frightening. The man who is accommodating to you will be accommodating to someone else. 'I like a man to be rooted,' she told him.

'Then root me,' he said.

She has to be off. Her stint at Aultbach's . . . t,t,t.

He kisses her, trying to apprehend her tongue with his teeth. 'Don't Ault – t,t,t – me,' he says. So she does.

Queer, being so in love. It is not unknown to him, quite the opposite, but being in love *again* is strange, stranger each time, because each time is necessarily new territory – he has never been in love *this* many times before, and of course never at so advanced an age.

So how not well is 'Hovis'?

Sex and death. Brutally obvious, but there is nothing Henry can do to fight it. The more in love he feels, the more his thoughts tend to 'Hovis' Belkin, and the more he thinks of 'Hovis' not well, not well at all, he gathered, the more intensely alive because in love he feels.

So how not well is 'Hovis'? And how not well would Henry want him to be?

After coffee, Henry needs his samovar after all. Piss-weak tea, a morning of it. Tangy – pissy, she is right – on the teeth. Awash with the past, as tea famously always is.

You liked him, Dad.

*Which one is he, again?*

Oh, enough of that. You liked him, that'll do. And now he isn't well. You know, really isn't well.

*How old is he?*

My age?

*So older than I was.*

Dad, most people are. They cheated you. But 'Hovis' will no doubt be thinking they're cheating him. No one gets enough.

*Well, you look well, Henry.*

And feeling it. But what ought I to do, what ought I to feel about my friend?

*If you don't know, he isn't your friend.*

Henry thinks about that.

Well, we had our differences. But I still don't like it that he's ill.

*For him or for you?*

For him. For me it could be OK, that's part of what I don't like. The growing callousness.

*Growing? Henry, you were always the same. Who was that other one?*

That other one who what?

*You know . . .*

I don't.

*Snuffed it.*

There have been several.

*No, the one who snuffed it while you were still at school. Werner somebody, was it?*

Warren.

*That's him.*

Warren Shukman. I'd forgotten Warren.

*There you are.*

Dad, Warren died forty-five years ago.

*Yes, but that's not the time it's taken you to forget him. You forgot him in a month, you said so. You cried and said you had no feelings.*

We weren't that close.

*So why were you crying?*

Because I had no feelings.

Henry hears his father's laughter. He loved making his father laugh. It was such a surprise to both of them. When Henry made his father laugh it was as though his father had just found a ten-pound note in an old pair of trousers.

So do the dead laugh at the hard-heartedness of the living? Better that than lying there weeping for yourself. Hardness is all – will that be the lesson? Someone, make me hard, Henry thinks. Make thick my blood. Though with Warren, when hardness came easy, he'd asked that someone make him soft.

They hadn't been close, that was how Henry had explained it to himself. Nowhere near as close, say, as he'd been with 'Hovis'. Though the fact of Warren's hating 'Hovis' and once attempting to strangle him in the playground made for a closeness of its own. 'You'll end up naked in the gutter, a no one, an arsehole, swallowing your own sick,' Warren had foretold of 'Hovis' after they'd finally been pulled apart, 'and you won't have anyone to help you then, because you'll be too disgusting to touch, even more than you are now.'

'We'll all end up in the gutter,' 'Hovis' had replied, rubbing at his neck, 'but at least I'll be looking at the stars.'

'Meaning I'll be looking at what?'

'Meaning you'll be looking at your own shit.'

'Well, I'd rather look at mine than yours.'

'Good, because you'll be eating mine.'

Which only encouraged Warren to start strangling him again.

Henry reckoned 'Hovis' had a point about Warren Shukman and shit. Morally, Warren was the filthiest boy in school. It was

Warren who introduced Henry's class to onanism, getting a self-help group together, a good year before there was any reason for any of them to go public on the matter. It was Warren who told them about fellatio, which Henry found it difficult to credit, and cunnilingus, which 'Hovis' refused to countenance, though Henry was easier with that, suspecting he'd been doing it spiritually all his life anyway. And it was Warren who, at the age of thirteen, came to school swinging a full Durex. A sight which remained with Henry for many years, troubling his mind's eye not only on those occasions his father brought up the subject of protectives, but also on the afternoon he stood head bowed with his class-mates, watching Warren's coffin being lowered into the ground while his father and his uncles wailed.

Extruded rather than tall, unclean in that way of the obses-sionally clean, as though there's unstoppable seepage from the mind into the body, with a pernickety person's jaw and Adam's apple and a translucent nose in a permanent wrinkle of disap-proval (you actually could see orange light through his nostrils), Warren Shukman gave off such an air of sexual distaste that it was mysterious to Henry why he should have chosen to exper-iment sexually at all, let alone so widely and so soon. His ascetic profile reminded Henry of a rabbi's, and indeed there were rabbis in Warren's family, not to mention, somehow or other, a couple of turncoat charismatics and a Roman Catholic priest who wrote books settling the problem of pain which Brendan O'Connor read. Later, when he read Dostoevsky, Henry came to understand the connection between fastidiousness and lubricity, and even tried to introduce a module on the subject at the University of the Pennine Way, though that failed at the hurdle which was Mona Khartoum. ('Honestly, Henry, there should be a law against you!') But at the time, Warren baffled him.

'Tell me when you need me to fix you up with a hum job, Henry,' he remembers Warren offering, twitching his nose as though his own last hum job was something he would rather forget.

'Yeah, all right, but I'm not rushing,' Henry had replied.

'Oh, so you do know what a hum job is?'

'Sort of,' said Henry.

'Bet you don't.'

'It's when you do it with the radio on.'

'Bollocks!'

'It's when you do it with the radio on but very low.'

'Double bollocks. You haven't got a clue.'

'All right, I haven't.'

Warren Shukman advanced his mouth to Henry's ear. 'A hum job is when a bird puts your balls in her mouth and hums while she's chewing them.'

Henry felt as though the Devil himself were whispering vilenesses to him. 'Why would she do that?'

'Which part of that?'

'Any part.'

'Because you ask her to, you moron.'

'But why would I ask her to?'

'Because you haven't had it.'

'But why would I *want* it, Warren?'

For a moment the question seemed to floor even him. 'I don't know. Because it's like Everest, I suppose. Because it's there.'

'Yeah, but only because you put it there,' Henry said, resentful that henceforth he was going to be troubled by a desire for something which until now he hadn't even known existed.

In the time that has elapsed since Warren's death, Henry has never again heard of a hum job and must reasonably assume, therefore, that Warren invented it. But whether he had heard of the practice and taught somebody to do it, or whether it was an invention from top to bottom – the performance *and* the practice – Henry doesn't know and will never now find out.

Was it *all* a lie? Catching the bus to town on a Saturday morning to go buying second-hand records, Warren showed Henry the hotel to which he boasted he took married women. Tonight, for example, he was taking two.

'How can you afford two rooms?' Henry asked.

'One room, shmuck. And anyway, they pay.'

'They pay?'

'Sure they pay. They love it.'

Married women would pay to go to a hotel with Warren Shukman, aged fourteen! Two at a time!!

And what is more to a kosher hotel!

It was beyond Henry.

But a rumour began to circulate that while Warren did indeed go to hotels, he went on his own, signed in as Mr Smith, and spent the night tossing off. 'Hovis' Belkin was the chief instigator of this rumour. 'One of my uncles has just removed the gall bladder from the father of the hotel clerk's girlfriend,' 'Hovis' told him, 'and he swears –'

'Hang on, who swears?'

'The hotel clerk. He swears that Shukman comes in on his own and goes out on his own. It's the God's honest truth.'

'How can this clerk be sure that the birds don't come along later and leave earlier?'

'Because he does the night shift. And on some nights the hotel is completely empty – but for Shukman.'

'He's the only person staying?'

'The only one.'

'So why would he sign in as Mr Smith?'

'Because he doesn't want anyone to know who he is.'

'Why not, if he's there on his own?'

'Why do you think! Because he doesn't want it to be widely known that he goes there for a J. Arthur Rank.'

'Can't he have one of those at home?'

'Hovis' didn't even bother to think about it. 'Not in a clean bed he can't, and not as Mr Smith he can't, no.'

'And you reckon he needs to change his name to masturbate?'

'You tell me.'

Hum-jobless Henry scratched his head. What did he know? Except that it was beyond him.

A month later, Warren Shukman, alias Mr Smith, was dead of a heart attack. Discovered, the rumour mill had it, on the floor of Birnbaum's kosher hotel on Cheetham Hill Road.

'Proves it,' 'Hovis' said. 'He wanked himself to death.'

'You can't be sure of that,' Henry said.

'Yes, I can. There's no other explanation.'

'That's crap. There are a million explanations for a heart attack.'

'At our age?!'

'What are you telling me? – that at our age only wanking kills!'

'Wanking and depression, yes.'

'So how do you know it wasn't depression?'

'It might have been.'

'There you are, then.'

'No, there *you* are, then. You tell me why Shukman should have been depressed.'

'I don't know. Because he was a shithead.'

'A good reason, I grant you. The only trouble is that Shukman didn't know he was a shithead. Give me a better reason.'

'I can't.'

'Yes, you can. Why do you get depressed?'

'I don't get depressed.'

'Bollocks. I know you get depressed. You've admitted it.'

'Only after wanking.'

'Hovis' Belkin threw his arms in the air in triumph. 'My point precisely!'

When the headmaster addressed the shocked school with the news, 'Hovis' Belkin winked at Henry and made the sign of Onan with his hand, shaking it and rolling his eyes like a lobotomised cocktail waiter.

Finding mirth easier to deal with than grief, Henry decided to go along with 'Hovis's' explanation, fully expecting to see an obituary in the local paper – *Shukman, Warren. Passed peacefully away 17 March, while playing with his dick. Will be for ever missed by his disgusted parents and nauseated friends.*

Later, Henry learned that Warren had been born with a hole in his heart and must have known he was on borrowed time. Hence the rush.

All the same, he accepted that Warren could have chosen another way to make the best of whatever life was left to him.

As Henry now intends to do.

# TWELVE

A week passes, and then another, but there is still no call from 'Hovis' Belkin.

He could, of course, be too ill to call.

Or he could be too well. Well, 'Hovis' has managed fine without calling Henry for decades. And has no reason to call now.

Or, all questions of health apart, he could be too angry with Henry to ring, having read and not forgotten, or even read and long forgotten Henry's article, forgetting not being the same as forgiving.

Or the son could have failed to pass on the message.

Or 'Hovis' could be both ill and well, could be ignorant of Henry's article, could know that his son had encountered Henry underneath an ancient yew, could know that Henry had expressed concern about his health, and still could be indifferent.

Or, or, or . . .

Or 'Hovis' could hate him for the hateful reference he wrote his brother's cousin's nephew's niece or whoever the hell she was, the girl with the slovenly mind who put Henry's career that never was to bed at last. The which being the case, it was Henry, surely, who ought to have been aggrieved, not 'Hovis' – but there you are, there never has been nor ever will be justice when it comes to families, or favoured girls, especially when the family's name, and the favoured girl's, is Belkin.

He had never liked her. Too gamine for Henry's taste, too compact in her ruthlessness, altogether too well aimed and smart a bomb. They are all ruthlessly ambitious now, to Henry's eye, but at least some of them have the decency to spill, to show a little uncontrol, whereas this one came all tied up and packaged, slovenly of mind but neat of purpose. What she was doing in the

Pennines, a Belkin, Henry could not imagine. Maybe she was the first crocus of the spring, the sign that the season was changing. Chic, all of a sudden, to get your education at one of those institutions your uncles would never have been seen dead in. Proof of authenticity. There she suddenly was, anyway, gleaming like a silver bullet, marching to the top of her class, a friend and confidante in no time of Drs Delahunty and Grynszpan, eyeing Henry archly, saying nothing, until at last he stopped her in the corridor and commented on her name. Yes. Osmond Belkin, yes. Her father's uncle's brother's whatever it was. She narrowed her coal-black eyes. You knew him, didn't you, at school, my father's uncle's brother's . . . Yes, she'd heard that. And poor Henry, still blushing at the end of his life, blushed then to think that 'Hovis' had mentioned, maybe even recommended him. ('Go to Henry Nagel, my dear, if it is wisdom you want.') Then blushed again in shame for blushing, recalling the inequality of that friendship and how grovelling, till kingdom come, his gratitude.

Not that she had 'gone to him'. Not for Nancy, on arrival, Henry's Look at the Lits on That. Not when she had Delahunty and Grynszpan to beef up her credentials.

So why, against the grain and out of the blue, did she show up in the front row of his lectures on *Pamela* and *Clarissa*, and the following term roll along to his classes on appetence and yearning? Why did she start writing him eager essays though he wasn't at all sure she had even officially enrolled for his course or had any appetite let alone aptitude for the subject as taught by him? (Longing? Nancy Belkin? Don't make him laugh!) And why did she then ask him for a reference?

Was it a test?

Of his loyalty to a friend as against his loyalty to an academic subject?

Or was it a test of her? She must have known he didn't like her. People not liked by Henry always knew it. So did she want to show that she could turn him? Demonstrate that even he, the

last man of principle standing in the Pennines, was no more principled than a porcupine? One smile from a determined girl with
coal-black eyes and a little bottom, Henry, and you're putty.

Except that he wasn't. Nothing puttyish about him at all when
push came to shove. Quite the contrary. Adamantine, if anything.
Henry, Man of Stone.

Henry's motto: A man must stand for what a man must stand.
And while Henry didn't stand for much, he did stand for not
capitulating to the calculations of a minx with a taste for theory.

Unless the real reason he held out against her was that she was
a Belkin, and that Henry still had things to prove with Belkins.

In which case, principle was not the word for what had motivated him at all. Oh no. In that case, principle was the last word.
Even if he did, in a hail of high-mindedness, put his job on the
line for it. But then it isn't entirely unknown for people to put
their jobs on the line for spite, is it? Evil impulses are no less
destructive of their owners than virtuous ones. Not unlike Henry,
not exactly alien to his character, to have spited himself out of
work.

Or, or, or . . .

Be sorry for Henry. He only wants to know why he hasn't
heard from his best and oldest friend.


Moira would like him to go with her to Eastbourne. She is teaching a weekend course at the Grand and would appreciate his
company.

'Actually on the course?'

'Well, you're welcome, if you have a pinny to wear and five
hundred pounds to cough up. But I was thinking just to be there
when I finish in the evenings. To smell the sea with me and
accompany me along the promenade.'

'Will you take your highest heels?'

'Not for walking along the promenade, Henry.'

'I meant for bed.'

'I'll take whatever you want me to take.'

'Will you wear no underwear?'

'Not for teaching pastry-making, Henry.'

'I meant for walking along the promenade.'

'Whatever you want.'

Is she real? Sometimes Henry has to pinch himself to make sure he's still among the living. In Henry's world women do not say 'Whatever you want'. No woman that Henry has known personally in the last twenty-five years, or that Henry has heard tell of in that time – no fabled woman about whom men whisper to one another over drinks, no ignis fatuus of any realistic man's imagination – is accommodating in the way that Moira is. Not that she is yielding, or subservient – quite the opposite. The policy of taking Henry in hand, which she instituted from their very first evening out together, remains in strict force. There is work to be done on Henry, alterations to be made, they both know that. And who's to say that Henry isn't already a nicer, sweeter, happier person than he was? But the wonderful thing about Moira is that she does not believe that change always has to be painful. If Henry enjoys himself in the process of becoming a different man, that's fine by Moira. It's like bringing up a child. You give a bit to get a bit. Which is fine by Henry too. She wears her highest heels and no underwear, and he does what he's told.

On her part – this is how Henry understands it – it's an act of material intelligence. Call it bourgeois, call it Viennese, call it Moira's genetic inheritance, call it what you like: what Moira understands is that there's no satisfying the inner man until you've soothed away the frustrations of the outer. There is no hierarchy here, no higher being and no lower. The tactile pleasures of the world need no apologising for.

It might also be her calculation that if Henry is ghostly half the time, giving her the impression that she's only borrowing him from someone else, that soon he'll be on his way again, drifting,

drifting from her, then anchoring him in the material things he loves is wise all round.

Is no underwear a material thing? Perversely, yes. It is.

Material enough to get Henry to agree to accompany her to Eastbourne anyway; the thought of Moira naked underneath her clothes in an unaccustomed place, her skirts in a losing tussle with the salt winds, all the persuasion he needs, though he is otherwise happy where he is in St John's Wood and doesn't feel in want of a holiday. After the Pennines, St John's Wood *is* a holiday.

'One other thing that occurs to me,' she says, the day before they go away, 'do you think it would be fun to take Angus?'

'No,' Henry says. He is already packing his case. Or rather, because he did most of his packing yesterday, he is repacking. He likes to look ahead, Henry. He likes to go to sleep knowing that everything is taken care of. Come the call, Henry will be ready.

'That it? Just no?'

'When you say Angus do you really mean Angus or is Angus a euphemism for Angus and Lachlan? Because I definitely do not want to go to Eastbourne with Lachlan.'

'Of course I don't mean Lachlan.'

'Good.'

'So are you all right about the dog?'

'No. I definitely do not want to go to Eastbourne with Angus either.'

'It would be nice for you, you could walk him while I'm teaching.'

'Moira, the last time we took Angus anywhere he lay in the back of the car whimpering and being sick.'

'That was because you'd locked him in the boot.'

'Only because he'd been lying on the back seat whimpering and being sick.'

'He isn't used to travelling, the poor thing.'

'Yes he is. Lachlan takes him everywhere. What he isn't used to is travelling at 140 miles per hour in built-up areas.'

'I'll go slower.'

'You won't. It is not in your power to go slower. Nor would I want to travel with Angus even if it were. A car is too confined a space for me and a dog, and I do not want to walk behind him in Eastbourne, picking up his shit every hundred yards. I don't pick up dog's shit, Moira. That was never in God's plan for me. No adult human should stoop to pick up a dog's shit. Some get a buzz out of it, I know that. Homosexuals and the like. In another era they'd have licked lepers' sores and been called saints. Now they pick up dog shit. But Leviticus prohibits it. Whosoever stoopeth to pick up dog shit, yea even with a plastic spoon, shall be stoned; it is an abomination.'

'So that's a no, then?'

Henry goes on with his packing, repacking what he packed yesterday, and re-repacking what he'd repacked this morning. He doesn't say what he is thinking, that Eastbourne is an opportunity to go looking at some new graveyards – plots where the dead may sniff the sea – and that he doesn't want a dog tailing after him between the graves, digging up bones.

Boring into his back, Moira's eyes signal a terrible promise. She will have him picking up dog shit, and loving it, before she's through with him.


He has never been to Eastbourne. He knows it by repute, for some reason or other, but he can't remember why. Did a person of his close acquaintance come from Eastbourne? Has someone dear to him retired to it? Or school friends – was there a summer school in Eastbourne, one of those camps to which Henry was never invited and where everybody else laid down those intimacies from which he was thereafter excluded? Eastbourne, Eastbourne . . . It rings bells. Unless he knows it only from Henry James, as a place where adulterers more twisted than Henry Nagel bought golden bowls or brazened it, arm in arm, at country-house weekends. Except that James liked to send his adulterers to cathedral cities, and Henry doubts there is a cathedral in Eastbourne.

Moira busy in the hotel conference centre, miked like an airline pilot and kneading dough, Henry ventures out. Of the same mind, the doughty old. Not knowing what to wear any more, confused by what is and isn't in the shops, denied their sensible flat caps and stout shoes, they are reduced to baseball hats and trainers. Only the sticks remain the same, and the swollen ankles, and the prevalence of widowhood – a dozen blue-bobbed hobbling dames to every rheumy gent. No more adulteries for this lot. You whiff the sea and if you're lucky you remember. And that's that.

Henry watches a survivor – one of the eligible, own limbs, own car keys, own car even – negotiating himself into his vehicle. Gingerly, first the left leg, testing, testing for unfamiliar obstacles, testing for distance to the pedals, testing that the car still has a bottom, then, no less gingerly, the right, as though entering foreign space, a lift shaft maybe, afraid that the lift has long gone, and there is only darkness and a long drop now. Braver than Henry, anyhow, who was frightened of cars at eighteen, never mind eighty.

The world's your oyster, old boy, Henry thinks, watching him pull out into the traffic, all his lights on, his indicators flashing, his window wound down, for him, too, one more whiff of the sea.

Henry isn't sure what he thinks of the sea hereabouts. Not worth looking at from this part of England, the sea. It holds no promises, wafts on its currents no aromatic seductions from far away. It's only France out there. Or Belgium. Politics apart, the Eastbourne sea – the Channel, is it? – might just as well have been concreted over, so little of what you want a sea to do for you does this sea do. But he likes having it at his shoulder, a drop into nothingness, as he ambles in the direction of Beachy Head, the promenade gradually turning into cliff, the vegetation becoming saltier, stranger and more tenacious, on edge, like a hermit's garden.

By Henry's standards the walk is quickly turning into a climb. He stops to inhale the salt air, and almost faints. In his Pennine days air was not a problem to him. Sometimes he stood outside his cottage for no other reason than to breathe it in. I am, after all, a man like other men, he would tell himself. I live on air. But that was then. Now, after however many months away, his lungs have grown accustomed to the BMW fumes of St John's Wood. He steadies himself against a bench, not wanting to sit down, because if he sits he probably won't want to rise, and looks back the way he's come, back over the groyny beach, the bandstand and the pier. It isn't pretty, except in the sense that all signs of life are pretty when viewed from a distance. This must prove, Henry reckons, that God, if there is one, is benign. You cannot take the distant view of humanity and not be touched by it. Ask those who walked upon the moon.

He can just see the flags of the hotel. Somewhere there Moira is in her flatties, contorting her profile, rolling pastry. His heart is so touched by her, simply by the idea of her existence, by the abstract thought that she has being, that Henry is brought to tears. The breeze dries them on his cheek, where they sting as though some tiny summer creature has tried to bite him.

It isn't only Moira. Maybe the sea, too, upsets him after all, wiping out the horizon, bleaching the day.

Moira, the sea, and something else. Henry screw up his eyes. What's the something else? The becalmed yachts? The sound of shingle submitting to the sucking of the tide? The smell of seaweed? The warm air buzzing with insects, the odd wasp dying? No, none of those. Or maybe all of those but none of those in particular. Then he realises. It's the benches.

Henry doesn't think he has ever seen so many memorial benches on a single walk. At the best of times he is a sucker for a bench with someone's name on it. In memory of So-And-So who loved this coastline, loved this garden, loved this park. Inexpressibly sad, Henry finds it, remembering a person for what they loved, especially when what they loved was the coastline or the garden or the park in which you're standing as you read about them. Disconcerting, such a perpetuation of sedentary innocence – a bench memorialising a person who loved a bench. At least a gravestone marks a difference. No 'Here Lies So-And-So Who Loved This Grave'. What's fine about the grave, if anything *is* fine about the grave, is its promise of release. After life's fitful fever he sleeps well. It's the next stage. A moving on. Whereas the bench, which does not acknowledge life as fever – not bench life anyway – continues where the dead left off.

A single bench is normally adequate to Henry's daily diet of melancholy. But here on the Eastbourne heights, where there is an infection of benches, where there's barely room to drop a stone between one bench and the next, and where they are kept in tip-top order, varnished and revarnished, the colour of blood some of them, and occasionally reconsecrated with a sprig of heather, Henry gorges on morbidity. It's not his fault. Blame whoever permitted this orgy of remembrance.

Meticulously, as though he owes it to himself no less than to the dead, he reads every inscription. IN THANKS FOR THE LIFE OF IRENE H. JAFFREY. JOAN, WIDOW OF JACK, TOGETHER AGAIN SIDE BY SIDE. MICHAEL O'NEILL FOR THY SWEET LOVE REMEMBER'D SUCH WEALTH BRINGS, JE T'AIME – YOURS JANET. ALFRED BONE – MISSING ON THE SOMME. ERIC J. NEEDLE – AT PEACE WATCHING THE SEA. GP PETER JONES WHO SO LOVED THIS TOWN AND THIS SHORE. KITTY OCKENDER – COMMEMORATING MANY HAPPY TIMES SPENT IN EASTBOURNE. ROSEMARY SOUTHOUSE WHO LOVED LIFE AND LIVED IT TO THE FULL. Lived it *to the full*, Henry!

He takes them all in, pausing, like a dutiful son, at each. Gladys Holman, Lucy and Will Dibb-Fuller, Dorothy Conway, Reg Vincent, Bolly Middlemiss, Arnold and Florence Billam, Frances May Clancy, Bernard Pasche, Don Wakeling, John Green, Fred Green, Daphne Skelton, Gladys Bamber, Bob and Maud Packham, Archie Parrish. Lillian E. Sale ('a remarkable lady'), Joyce Worger,

Ellen and Arthur Bew, Biddy Bradfield, Ena Palmer (hers under a stone shelter, doubly provided), Lt. Col. Norah Smythe, Albert de M. Fleury, Roma Romanowska, Ola Amos, Elsie Dove, Mattie Banks, Phyllis Sageman (MA), Jack Owlett, Constance Penney, Gwen Humphreys, Lil and Len Morris, Beatrice Grace Willsmer, Gladys Woods . . .

All those Lils and Mauds, all those Freds and Regs, names gone, fallen out of fashion, like whatever the old wore before they were forced into trainers.

He cannot decide who upset him the most – the Romas and Olas far from home, single it would seem in their exile, or the couples like Joan and Jack, together again, hand in hand, staring out to infinity. Unbearable either way, but Henry reckons it must help to have a friend.

Variations on the same story, told again and again and again.

The repetition is too much for Henry. He drops on to Harold and Agnes Lawrence who loved it here – they all loved it here – and hangs his head. He is aware that his lips are moving, that other walkers are observing him, an ageing man reduced to talking to himself. Doesn't the poor bastard have someone he can text?

How long does he sit, pushing letters of the alphabet about with his lips, making words he has no control over? Long enough to feel his back go. He rises, afraid that if he doesn't he will set in this one position and become a monument himself. He is badly oiled, creaking, his lower back in spasm, giving him a stoop. What a sight I am, he thinks. He cannot decide whether to go back the way he is, and risk Moira seeing him, or to keep walking in the direction of Beachy Head in the hope of straightening himself up. Walking, walking he thinks is best, but with a little less attention to every bench. Maybe he should concentrate on what's still growing here, rather than on what's stopped. There are rockeries, he will tell Moira, full of things that don't object to too much salt. Speedwell, catmint, torch lily, thrift. Thrift, thrift,

Horatio. Sea campion, fleabane. Lichens, are they? Heather? What does he know. Botany was never Henry's subject. He just reads the notices. Something to discuss when he gets back, how lovely, rather than how dead. On he goes, getting higher, the path sometimes opening out to small gardens, viewing areas, greens, where the benches proliferate more hysterically yet, and where even a seat made of planks on concrete blocks and a single backrest nailed into cliff bears someone's name. It is fertile up here, the air drowsy with the dungy sweets of summer death. Stretching back into town, the groynes look ill-assorted, like pieces from a difficult jigsaw puzzle. Henry mops his brow and holds his back. Below him some sort of amphitheatre has appeared, a sign pointing to Holywell Retreat. Should he come to live here? Spend the rest of his days polishing benches and committing their messages to memory? He can't stop reading the occasional brass plate, but others he lets go unrecorded. He will do his duty by them next time, when he takes up residence. Impossible to say what his principle of selection is, why he reads this inscription and not that, but a higher hand must be guiding him. Else why would he find himself, with his heart beating at the walls of his chest, before a bench dedicated to his mother?

His mother!

IN MEMORY OF EKATERINA NAGEL WHO FOUND PEACE HERE.

Jesus Christ!

His mother found peace here! In Eastbourne!

Impossible. He closes his eyes and shakes his head. Must be some other Ekaterina Nagel. But he has only to entertain that thought for it to vanish. How many Ekaterina Nagels were there? How many in the whole world let alone in this country? And it has her dates right. 1919–1976.

So when was this that she found peace in Eastbourne? And in what circumstances?

Had she come specifically looking? And if she had, how was it that he knew nothing about her search?

In which case, who did? Who sponsored this bench in her name?

His father – that would be the natural supposition. His father the furniture-maker. Appropriate, as a gift from Izzi, a bench. Though it would have killed him not to be able to upholster it.

But you cannot kill what's dead already. Henry's father was not left to mourn or think about memorials. Couldn't face it. Couldn't bear it. Couldn't contemplate life without her. And no, there hadn't been time for him to leave a bench to her in his will, even supposing he had wanted to, or knew where Eastbourne was, or understood the meaning of the word 'peace'.

Had they spent time here together, peaceful time, before there was such a person as Henry to noise their lives up for them? Had they wheeled him along this walk when he was too small to know about it? He'd have heard tell, surely. His parents were great historians of themselves, were always recalling in mirth or melancholy the mishaps associated with holidays and outings, and even if, for some reason or another, they had not verbalised Eastbourne to Henry, they were bound to have shown him photographs, curly-edged black-and-white age-of-innocence snapshots with the place and name and date written on the back in Ekaterina's hand – her robust, round-bellied copperplate, the ink black even in the days when everybody else's ink was blue. She had been painstaking about every photograph and keepsake, ordering her memories, keeping tabs on the narrative of her life and loves, however disappointing. This had always upset Henry about his mother – the journal of the heart she kept, as conscientious as an archivist in a burning city, as though what wasn't transcribed would fade away like smoke on a summer's afternoon.

But wait – just suppose that Eastbourne had been witness to some time of peace his mother and his father shared and wanted, for whatever reason, to keep secret, why then wasn't the bench dedicated to his father too?

It bewilders him, and hurts him more, his mother's memory commemorated separately from his father's. The bench asserts a rupture which wasn't true to the facts. But a bench with a little plaque on it *is* a fact, insists for ever its version of events. How many thousands of people will now pass, have passed already, to whom the one great incontrovertibility of Ekaterina's life – her love for Henry's father – will remain unknown?

It is as though, Henry thinks, my father has been wiped out of her life. It is as though this bench as much excludes him as it perpetuates her. A monument to the not-thereness of his father.

Henry runs his fingers through his hair, halfway to distraction, wondering whether he should go the whole hog, and begin howling at what they've done – whoever they are – to his parents' memory. It's a decision, whether to go mad or not. He has always been sure of that. And it's a decision, whether or not to go to pieces. You lose control or you don't. It's in your hands.

In the end, he decides against. He doesn't have good enough cause. Never properly paired himself, he has been a sentimentalist of pairs all his life. And that, surely, is all that's operating in this instance. Sentimentality. Wanting to see his mother and father, who died apart, while one of them was on an errand of sorrow and suspicion, united in love for ever. Sentimentality, pure and simple. Which is not an adequate justification for going mad. A quiet tear would be more appropriate. *Una furtiva lagrima*. And a sprig of something – thrift, fleabane, herzschmertz – to tie to the backrest. So he plucks a little purple flower he finds growing between stones, and lacking any of the ways of nature, attaches it, just above his mother's name, with one of his shoelaces. Not pretty, but nothing Henry does is pretty. 'There,' he says, 'from me and Dad.'

After which he is not fit to do anything but squat down on his haunches, whatever the stiffness in his back, and sob his heart out with grief, with strangeness, with everything he doesn't know and doesn't want to know.

The *furtiva lagrima* become a raging torrent.

Henry's sky fallen in.


Another of the reasons he loves her: she likes finding a solution to a problem. Uncertainty for Henry comes in swarms which he allows to buzz around his face. Moira's tactic, on the other hand, is to take a swat to them.

'Who is responsible?' Henry has been saying all morning, as he was saying all the night before. 'Who did it? Who put it there? And why?'

'I'll ring and find out.'

'Who will you ring?'

'The council.'

'Which council?'

'Eastbourne Council, Henry. Which council do you think?'

'Will they know?'

'I'm going to ring them and find out.'

'When?'

'Now.'

And she does. Without slowing her step – they are strolling along the promenade, in the direction of the pier; no more benches for Henry on this trip – she actually rings directory enquiries on her mobile, and then the council.

Henry looks on in amazement. First of all, how does she know to ring the council; second, where does she find the resolution to ring the council? For these skills alone he'd marry her, assuming she'd want to marry him, which is by no means a foregone conclusion given that he has never had the first clue who to ring on any matter, nor the will to make the call when someone tells him.

'Cleansing,' she repeats. 'OK, I'll try them. Can you put me through?' Then to Henry, in case he hasn't heard, she mouths, 'Cleansing.'

When Cleansing answers, she hands the phone to Henry who fumbles it, as though afraid it has a poison bite. 'I don't suppose you can help me,' he begins, at which Moira snatches the phone back from him. 'Negative bastard,' she says, then has to explain to the person in Cleansing that she doesn't mean him.

In fact Henry is right in his supposition. Cleansing isn't able to help him. Not immediately, at any rate. You can't just go around asking the authorities who donated such-and-such a bench on the cliffs at Eastbourne.

'Why not?' Moira wonders.

Data protection.

'Can you tell me whether the person who donated the bench specifically asked to be data-protected?' she asks.

No.

'Why would that be?'

Data protection.

But they are prepared to countenance special circumstances. If Henry writes in to Cleansing, they tell her, and explains what he wants to know and why, they will consider his case on its merits.

'Then I'll write,' Henry says.

But Moira knows about the future tense when Henry uses it. Future never-never. She buys a postcard of the front at Eastbourne, sits Henry at a table in a café, wipes it expertly, passes him a pen from her furry handbag, and says, 'Write!'

'I can't send a card of Eastbourne to Eastbourne council,' he says.

She takes no notice of his epistolary niceness. 'Write!' she orders him.

No disrespect to Moira, but he needs Marghanita.

What is all this, Marghanita? Was it you? Did you and she come here when she was fed up with Dad? Was that the peace she found in Eastbourne? Relief from him? Relief from thinking and worrying about him? Relief from the triviality? Relief from the insult of his restlessness?

Actual peace, was it? Simply a cessation, for a while, of his demandingness? Forget the mistress or the mistresses – simply a holiday from the torches and the origami?

It isn't so much an answer that Henry wants – this is where Moira, with her love of solutions, gets it wrong – it is more the wallowing in the questions.

And Marghanita was the best of all people to wallow with. Towards the end, when intimacy between them held no ambiguities, she was forever calling him over to her side to whisper another secret in his ear. For the most part he didn't know the people she was divulging secrets to him about, the majority of whom had been dead and gone long before Henry had arrived on the scene, that's if they had ever enjoyed independent being outside of Marghanita's imagination at all. But that didn't matter. What stirred him was the heat of the confessional, the animal warmth of a soul ridding itself of all it knew. Come, Henry, she would say, crooking a finger. Almost *komm, kommst du*, the Yiddish into which all Jews, even the least Jewish, even the most white like Marghanita, must eventually fade, as Henry himself will when the time comes, *wenn es so weit ist*. How comforted he felt when she beckoned him to her, like a small animal nuzzling into the heat, enjoying the warmth and the odour of the straw, absorbing the unutterable voluptuousness of family.

She saved the best to last, Marghanita. When she was very ill, Henry stayed with her, sleeping on a couch she had ordered him to bring close to her bed, her hand in his, passively, like a child's. Spurred on by morphine, demons crowded round about her in the dark, waking her suddenly with cries which she could not distinguish from her own. She fought them from her, picking them from the sleeves of her nightdress. 'Don't bother,' she told Henry when he tried to help her, 'they aren't really there.' So in the end, despite his doubts, she seemed to know the difference after all between her real assailants and the false. Which made him more disposed to believe her when she told him that her woes began earlier than he supposed, earlier than she'd ever told him, far earlier than her great disappointment in love. 'My hopes weren't so much dashed exactly, Henry, because strictly speaking I never had hopes. A better explanation is that things turned out as they were bound to.'

This was Henry's greatest dread – hearing from a woman on her death bed, when it was too late for him to help, that her life had been a wasted tale, a blight foretold. But at least this time it wasn't his fault. Or was it?

He listened, not saying anything. Whenever he tried to speak she held his wrist. Just listen, Henry.

Did he never wonder, she asked him rhetorically, at the vast age discrepancies in the family, she so much younger than the other Stern Girls, so much younger, especially, to choose a name at random – she smiled at him, her eyes still bright, though her cheekbones wasted – than Effie.

Funny, Henry thinks, remembering, how much of what you don't know, you do. Does that mean he knows more than he thinks he knows about his mother's bench? Will someone one day say, 'Did you never wonder, Henry . . . ?' And he will recognise in a flash all it has been about?

Maybe. But who is that someone likely to be, now they have all gone?

He knew what Marghanita was going to tell him, anyway, knew immediately, as you know when someone comes hammering at your door at four o'clock in the morning, that everything was going to be different now; and yet not, because all the characters remained the same, only the plot had changed, and a plot is nothing more than the way things turn out, a mere arbitrary intrusion into the game of life, causing the pieces to be shifted right enough, and some even to be swept from the board altogether, but not affecting the overall shape of the contest, or the pleasure you take in playing. It is still chess, or snakes and ladders, or happy families.

Marghanita was Effie's daughter – that was her flabbergasting news. Flabbergasting, but then again not. Of course Marghanita was Effie's daughter! How could she not have been? And when had Henry really thought otherwise?

As a general fact of life, Henry had heard the story a hundred times; he just hadn't heard it told about his own family. From what had passed the lips of Henry's school friends and from gossip overheard in his own kitchen, he'd deduced that there were illegitimate daughters of Marghanita's age all over Manchester, secreted in broom cupboards, handed on to the safekeeping of institutions, bartered, bandied, passed off as the offspring of their grandmothers, become their mothers' sisters. Victims of the great provincial shame. Partly it relieved Henry, after all this time, to discover he had secrets in common with the rest of humanity; though it perplexed him, too, that the Stern Girls, with all their apparent aristocratic insouciance, turned out to be as conventional as everybody else.

But that was sex for you. Sex ironed out everything.

Henry tried a joke. 'Was that why you all moved to North Manchester?'

But in sex there are no jokes. Not when it's family sex. 'Of course,' she said. 'There was never any question of staying in the south with Effie's belly getting visibly bigger with me, and the man unacceptable.'

'On religious grounds, I take it.'

'Hardly religion. Tribal is more like.'

'Shame, I'd fancied our family was free of that.'

'Ha!' Marghanita said. Not a laugh, an expostulation. 'But in fairness he was also married to someone else at the time. And three times Effie's age.'

'So the tribalism was the least of everybody's worries.'

'Never the least, Henry. But it's sweet of you to try to think the best of us.'

'It's a way of trying to think the best of myself.'

'Well, I can't say I don't understand that.'

A pause between them, the present too feeble to keep pace with the past. Henry felt he could hear one of them trickling away into the other, but he wasn't sure which was trickling into which. 'So you were born on this side?' he finally said.

'While no one was looking, yes.'

He leaned over to stroke her forehead. Unbidden, the recollection of stroking her breasts, that foolish and exquisite evening when he held her shoes. 'How disappointing,' he said. 'I have always thought of you as a Wilmslow girl.'

'Well, I am. I was conceived there.'

'Ah, but I thought of you as a Wilmslow girl who had been conceived in St Petersburg.'

She smiled at him – lovely still, her smile, sadder than summer – leaning into the pressure of his soothing hand. 'That's you all over,' she said. 'Forever wanting more than you can have. I suppose you'd like my unmentionable father to have been the tsar.'

'He wasn't?'

'He was a teacher.'

'Languages?'

'How did you know?'

'A guess. Effie's language teacher, presumably?'

'Of course. We always revered learning in our family.'

Another passage of silence between them. Learning – tick, tock. Henry the professor. The silence long enough for Marghanita to make it known to him, because she remembered how papery his skin was, that he hadn't let them down. The sight of her expending the little energy she had on his wounded self-esteem wounded Henry still more. Did she know, then, did they all know, the bad opinion of himself he entertained? How terrible to think he'd been imagining he was sparing them when all along they'd been sparing him.

Why, had he known that he might have left the Pennines and sought fulfilment as a bookie's runner or a shoeshine boy. He had only become a teacher in the first place to please them.

'Yes, it's our weakness,' he said.

'No,' she said, shaking her head at him, 'it's our strength.'

'So did you ever meet him?'

'My father? No. Your great-grandmother forbade it. And Effie never wanted me to either. We wiped it out as though it had never happened. We moved here where nobody knew us, I grew up as Effie's sister, and in the end we believed our own lies.'

'Eminently sensible.'

'Yes and no. Maybe if we hadn't kept everything secret I would have understood it all better. Maybe become a wild girl, who knows, or a nun.'

'We don't do nuns, Marghanita.'

'No. We don't do wild girls, either. We just do wronged women. And as the daughter of one, I stepped into the role myself as neatly as if I'd been measured for it.'

'Like my mother.'

She looked at him. And Henry remembers that she didn't agree or disagree, just kept on looking and then closed her eyes.

When she opened them again it was to correct any impression she may have given that she was sorry for herself. 'It hasn't been a ruined life, Henry, I'm not saying that. In many ways I've been more privileged than most. But I think what happened knocked the stuffing out of us. It's possible these secrets gnaw away at your insides, I don't know. Certainly the more conscious you are of having to conceal a shaming secret, the more front you have to put on.'

'I loved your front. I loved the sight of you marching out to right some wrong.'

'Usually yours, Henry.'

'Exactly. Usually mine. You were my champions.'

'Like so many Don Quixotes.'

'Hardly. You were always better shod than him.'

'But every bit as mournful of countenance.'

She thought about that image, smiling to herself. Then,

following an inner logic of her own, she said, 'The situation was sadder than it needed to be, that's what I'm saying – for all of us.'

Henry didn't want to hear it. Not sad. Please don't say sad.

'Well, you were all my example, anyway,' he said.

'Exactly,' she told him. 'And look how sad you are.'

So she knew.


She was Henry's first corpse. The one he'd been saving up.

At her request he stayed with her throughout the night, kept awake for most of it by the morphined demons that swarmed around her. In the early morning she woke suddenly, sat up in bed, the pale light bleeding her hair of all lustre, her eyes ground hollow as though by the knuckles of someone's fist. 'The poor child!' she cried.

Henry went cold. 'Hush,' he said.

She was frantic, looking about her, the tears pouring down her cheek. 'The poor child!'

'Hush,' he said, taking both her hands.

But she wouldn't let him have them. She needed her hands to make space in front of herself, a swimming action, taking her away, or a gesture of rage, hitting out at whoever was hindering her.

Then she looked deep into Henry's eyes. 'That poor child!' she cried. 'That poor, poor child!'

He didn't ask her who she meant. Couldn't bear to hear the answer, supposing she had an answer in her. Wanted it to be no one, no one she knew, no one he knew, no one at all.

She fell back on her pillow and began to snore deeply. Tired out, Henry dropped into sleep himself. When he awoke, an hour later, he realised she was silent. He could feel the cold around him.

He wanted to do something for her, smooth her hair back, kiss her lips, shut her eyes the way they did in books and films. But he wasn't able to look, afraid of seeing an expression on her face which would break his heart, dreading the texture of her skin, dreading discovering that she had begun to crumble like old stone, or become as papery as parchment, already. Above all he was terrified that his father had been right all along to keep this from him, because his father knew him, and knew he wasn't up to it.

*I was, Henry. I was always right about you. A father knows.*

So he stole out of the room – understanding that if he failed to hold himself together he would come apart for ever – and rang the doctor.

The disgrace of it.

And never saw her face again.

# THIRTEEN

He doesn't want to go home yet. He would like another day.

'Not if you're going to be morbid,' she tells him. 'Not if you're going to go on about benches.'

He promises her he isn't. He just wants to be with her, beside the seaside.

'I'll have to ring Aultbach, he's expecting me in the shop tomorrow.'

'Ring him.'

'And we are supposed to be going out with Lachlan tomorrow night.'

Such a wild life they lead.

'Then ring him as well.'

He doesn't mind. He has always liked the woman he is with, on borrowed time, to be busy with other men. It releases him a little of the burden. Means he won't be their only mourner. Means his won't be the only tears. And, yes, makes him a little jealous.

Not that he is in need of the stimulus of sexual rivalry in Moira's case. On his own account he can't have too much of her. He has reached that stage in a love affair, what some would call its climacteric, when everything about the woman fascinates you, when any angle you see her from enhances her beauty, when you attend so closely to the way she makes herself up and dresses that it is as though you are on the other side of her – not just under her clothes but under her skin, become as subtly conjunct to the movement of her body as cartilage – and when you cannot imagine how existence was ever possible any other way. The seaside is partly, though not entirely, responsible for this. Henry has always been more in love by the seaside than anywhere else. It could be the air, or the sensation of being driven to the brink – the seaside being as far, topographically, and therefore erotically, as you can go. Or it could be associational – Henry remembering how much he missed not having a little girlfriend in the days when his parents took him to Southport and Morecambe and New Brighton. What age was he then? Five, six? It starts early, started early in Henry's case, anyway. He was a worry to Ekaterina and Izzi, he remembers, so downcast did he become the minute they took him away. 'We could have left you behind, Henry, would that have suited you more?' – his father speaking. 'Come on, darling, brighten up, we're only here for a few days more!' – his mother. But he could hardly have told them, could he, that there was nothing the matter with him that a fuck wouldn't have put right. Did he mean a fuck? He couldn't have. He was years from knowing what a fuck was. But there is a premonition of sexual intercourse from which you can suffer when you're five or six. You know you want the warm proximity of a girl. You know you want to exchange the liquids which swim about in her eyes with the liquids which swim about in yours. You know you want to vanish into her and suffer obliteration – even though you don't necessarily know the word for it – at her hands. And you anticipate the pain you will feel when the heart she gave to you she gives now to another. Put it this way: limited as was little Henry's knowledge of romance at that age, everything he wanted then, together with everything he feared, did indeed come to pass more or less as he'd anticipated it would.

Now, as he moves in on his second childhood, his idea of sex is returning to that earlier, more primitive form. Talk, holding hands, companionability, the condition of being chums, before or after or even in the absence of coition.

Ask Henry to enumerate his reasons for loving Moira and it will be a long time before he gets on to bed or bodies considered carnally. He loves holding hands with her. Lacing fingers, crooking thumbs, swinging as they walk. Hence the particular advantage of the seaside. You can stroll with your hands laced

and swinging for miles, whether on the beach, or along the promenade, or up and down the pier. As a child he knew with certainty
that that was what beaches and promenades were for. Hence the
cruelty of his single state, aged five.

He loves putting his arm around her shoulder. Perhaps stroking
her custard hair, perhaps not. Just leaving it on the clavicle can
be enough.

He loves feeling her neck. The tracery of veins and whatever
else. He doesn't know what's in there. The body, as a machine,
isn't his subject. But he loves feeling life being pumped through,
the messages to and from the brain trembling his fingertips. Her
neck being long and slender, the skin very fine, Henry is just
about able to decipher with his touch what the messages are saying.

He loves nuzzling her. Stopping mid-walk and burying his face
in her shoulder, blotting out the light, blind to anything but her
smell, or blowing in her ear, which she starts from, laughing, skit-
tish, ticklish. Make a person laugh and you part them from themselves. Henry loves doing that to Moira – uncoupling her.

And she uncouples wonderfully, like a starburst. All the air
around her, peopled by her.

He loves sliding his arm around her waist, encircling it,
possessing her slenderness, having her, almost as though he's
wrestling her, which of course he isn't, on his hip.

He loves walking so close to her that he can feel the warmth
of her thigh against his. She is cooler at every point than he is,
so limb on limb he ought not to be able to feel her heat, but he
can.

He loves coming up behind her, if they've been parted infinitesimally, and putting his hands on her hips, or, moving further
in on her, placing the flats of his palms on her belly, feeling the
declivity either side – the ilium, is it? Ilium with its topless towers
– the wad of flesh on the bone which is shaped like an ear, and
which he reckons, if he blew into it, would also make her laugh.

He loves buying her an ice cream and unwrapping it for her –

his boyish gift, all his pocket money gone. Or he loves it when she says no to ice cream but darts at him suddenly, like a predatory bird, to steal a lick of his, looking up at him from under his chin, the scene of the theft, her eyes smiling, her lips wet and cold, enjoying the unaccustomed angle.

He loves that – looking down at her. And also looking up at her. Though that's moving closer to the carnal than he is willing to do in this enumeration of what he loves.

He loves slipping his hand inside the back of her cardigan, or a little way down the waistband of her skirt, or into the cuffs of her shirt if she's wearing a shirt, or under the narrow straps of her summery top, or into the sleeves of her jacket. If she's lying across him, with her feet up, he loves feeling about in her shoes, and if her feet are bare, loves making forays between her toes.

He can't stop playing with her. This is how he would have been at five or six had the right girl only given him the chance, but since then he's enjoyed the company of many women close up, and worked with countless numbers more, few of whom he hit it off with, it's true, but still, they were women – so why, suddenly, is *this* woman such a novelty to him?

He loves fiddling with her rings when she's sitting idly, staring at seagulls, with her hand in his. He loves unfastening her watch strap and then fastening it again. He loves taking off her earrings and absent-mindedly feeling their weight, then clipping them back on – assuming he hasn't broken them by then. He can't keep his hands off her or her things. At any moment he expects her to turn on him and tell him to leave her alone, to keep his filthy interfering mitts off her and her jewellery, to give her a moment's peace; indeed it sometimes occurs to him to wonder whether he isn't doing everything in his power, perversely, to provoke such a rebuff; but it never comes. She doesn't shock him by opening her mouth or showing him rude parts of her body as much as she used to – they know each other a little too well now for that

– but every so often she does revert to her old tactics, as when today, in broad daylight, posing for his camera at the end of the pier, she whips her top up a fraction of a fraction of a second before he clicks. And she wouldn't be doing that – would she? – if she wanted him to leave her alone.

As for his even possessing such a thing as a camera, who can explain that? Henry hasn't owned a camera since his parents, thinking to cheer him up and make him interested in things outside his head, bought him a Brownie 127 and binoculars in matching leatherette cases for his sixth birthday. In the intervening years Henry has had no need for any sort of recording device. No camera, no tape recorder, no Walkman, no video, no DVD, no nothing. 'What is it I'd want to preserve?' he would have answered anybody surprised by this asceticism. The prig he was. But now Henry is preserving like a mad thing, snapping Moira at every possible opportunity, hoping to record her every mood and movement, even asking passing Japanese if they'd be good enough to snap the pair of them together – Henry who has always been too embarrassed to ask anyone for anything, fearing the sting of refusal.

He is even the owner of a photograph album, the first of his adult life, into which he affixes her, remembering to write the name, the place, the date, on the back of every photograph. Not beautifully like his mother. Henry is not in possession of the idle calm of copperplate. Spider-scrawl, befitting the spider he has been – that's Henry's hand. Words written to make words indecipherable. Explain that. Has anyone investigated the psychology of a bad hand? The hurry of it. A man of words who cannot get the words out of his fingers soon enough. Even Henry's signature is stillborn. Explain that.

But if it's an instinct for death, he's fighting it. An album after all, however you deface it, is a vote for sempiternity. And he is trying to slow his hand down, releasing the pressure on the pen, clasping the other hand about his writing wrist, hunching his back, biting his lip, forming each letter like a little drawing in itself, the way he was taught to do at primary school.

He is a boy again. She has done this for him. She has given him back the verve he never had.

'Life,' he exclaims, ascending or descending stairs with her, enjoying escalators where he can stand behind or in front of her, feeling their bodies exchange stature as they go up and down, now him higher, now her. 'Protean life, everything in flux, nothing ever the same.'

'Jesus, Henry,' she says, 'can't we ride an escalator without you becoming a philosopher.'

'Just be pleased,' he tells her from the lower step, whispering into her neck before it rises from him, eluding his breath, the small of her back now level with his lips, and even that escaping him, vertebra by vertebra, 'just be pleased you make an old man happy.'

And is she? Well, it beats having him like Hamlet's father's ghost, starting like a guilty thing upon a summons, hardly anchored to the earth at all.

A doting lover beats a spectral one any time.

Now all she has to do is convince him his happiness is not the proof that he is at death's door.


Though he has promised not to involve her in the morbidity of benches, they do occasionally have to rest their legs and sit on one; but only on the understanding that she will sweep it first for plaques, dedications or allusions of any other sort which might destroy his spirits.

'It's like having a minder,' Henry says. 'Will you now check *under* the bench for explosive devices?'

'*You're* the explosive device,' she says. 'I know where the bomb is. My role is to make sure there are no circumstances in which it might go off.'

He likes the idea of that: Henry the Bomb. Even if the only fallout, these days, is tears creaking in his temples.

On the morning of the day they are due to drive back to St John's Wood, they sit looking out to sea, enjoying the sun on their faces. On *his* face, to be precise. Being pale of skin, Moira has to be careful and does not venture out into the sun until she has rubbed sunblock deep into her pores. Henry is amazed at the numbers of tubes and jars of sunblock of varying factors of impermeability she possesses. But by allowing him to apply them for her she forestalls criticism.

'Choose one for me, Henry,' she said, this morning.

He wanted to know on what principle.

So she took him through the science: UVAs, UVBs, fierceness of sun divided by time exposed to it determining desired degree of screening. But already she had lost him.

'This one,' he said, picking the first to hand, a five- or six-year-old at the seaside, confusing the good time he never had with the telling-off he did.

'That's lipsalve,' she told him.

'That you don't need,' he said, bending to her lips and salving them with his own.

Henry loves kissing her full on the lips.

She wants to read the papers before they go. An old holiday indulgence of hers, reading the paper in the sun, in 50 units of SPF.

She has no preference. Whatever takes her fancy. This morning it is *The Times*. Henry is reading *Newsweek*. No reason. He too takes up whatever catches his eye. Whatever doesn't have news in it, preferably. And not too many stories of the sort that might upset him – other men's success, etc. Comes to mind that Berryman poem, 53 in *The Dream Songs* –

> It takes me so long to read the 'paper,
> said to me one day a novelist hot as a firecracker,

because I have to identify myself with everyone in it, including the corpses, pal.

Though Henry's reasons are not so hotly empathetic. More about identifying himself with everyone *not* in it. As for actually *subscribing* to a paper, of knowing what your convictions are, of submitting them to flattery and indulgence every morning – the very idea strikes him as ridiculous. His own ignorance saved him here. Quite old, Henry was, before he could tell the difference, politically, between the *Guardian* and the *Telegraph*. Just hadn't noticed. Never been brought up to notice. His mother always too busy in some other world of affrighted feeling to need newspapers, and his father only ever buying them to cut up. *Guardian, Telegraph* – who cared? When it came to dodging tales of other men's success, there was nothing in the end to choose between them. Moira, too, does not 'have a paper'. It's another reason they get on. They are both random in their belief systems, not knowing on whose side in any argument they'll wake up. Moira reads to pass the time, and Henry to vex himself.

Occasionally she passes on an item of gossip. Henry has his fingers in her belt and isn't listening. It's music between them, that's all.

There are glossy giveaways in *Newsweek* which Henry rolls into balls and throws at the seagulls. In their bullying and persistence, the seagulls remind him of people he has known. Grynszpan and Delahunty.

Moira hits his hand. 'Don't make litter,' she says, still reading.

'Why? Are you frightened the Cleansing Department might catch me.'

'Did you post that card to them?'

'Of course I posted that card to them.'

'You might hear when you get back.'

'And I might not.'

'Do you want to hear?'

'Of course I want to hear. Why wouldn't I want to hear?'

They are still making music only to each other, barely attending to the words.

'I know you,' she says. 'You go off things. You get all worked up, then you think better of it.'

'Well, I'm not going to think better of my mother, am I?'

'No,' she says. She is engrossed suddenly. 'No, I don't suppose you are.'

He has taken to smoothing the side of her skirt, rubbing her flank in the sun. The flesh and bone of her.

'Henry,' she says, lowering the paper, wanting his attention. 'That person you wrote an article about, the one I found on the Internet, the film man . . .'

'What about him?'

'I think he's in the paper.'

'Moira, he's always in the paper.'

'Is he called Osmond Belkin?'

Henry puts up a hand. 'Please don't read anything aloud to me about Osmond Belkin. Not today. It's too nice here.'

She folds the paper on her lap and leans towards him. 'Listen to me, Henry, were you very good friends?'

'Once upon a time.'

She pulls him to her, holding his face. 'Darling, I'm so sorry,' she says.

'What?' Henry fears a knighthood or a Nobel Prize. 'What have they given him?'

Her eyes are like seas, sucking him in. Infinite in their consolation.

'I'm so sorry, darling,' she says. 'He's died. I'm so sorry.'

'Darling' – Marghanita ringing him at his office in the Pennines all those years ago – 'I'm so sorry.'

Daddies turn your face away. Mummies break the news.

So who breaks the news when your mummy and your daddy die? The next mummy.

She is worried about him, sliding her shifty eyes from the road to see how he is taking it.

'Just concentrate on your driving,' he tells her, 'or we'll be next.'

She has changed her car. Not the make – it's still a BMW – but the nature. Now, like everyone else in St John's Wood, she's driving an adventure wagon, the domestic version of the tank. Henry reckons it's the fear of Armageddon that explains this. When they blow up St John's Wood, you'll need a four-wheel drive to negotiate the rubble. The human imagination can only cope with so much disaster, and a rough terrain is as far as anyone has got. Come Judgement Day they'll all be masked and in their Range Rovers, but still shopping in the High Street. That's the advantage of a four-wheel drive – there's plenty of room for babies in the back seat and provisions in the boot, and you get a good high ride so you can spot the parking spaces in good time.

Sweet, expecting parking meters to be standing and operative. And sweeter still, anticipating using them once civil law has broken down, considering that you never took a blind bit of notice of them before.

In the meantime the High Street is getting narrower by the day with armoured vehicles advancing three abreast on either side, at speeds commensurate with reconnoitring the new season's stock in the windows of the women's fashion shops.

'Are you sure you're all right?' she asks.

He is never all right when she is driving. He would say he is most afraid of her driving when they are on a motorway, were it not that Moira made everywhere a motorway.

'I'm fine,' he says. 'Who are you honking?'

Silly question. He knows who she's honking. She's honking humanity.

And how fine is Henry?

A tough question. Never seek to ask for whom the bells tolls – Henry is familiar with all that. Having run through his family, death might claim already to be an intimate of Henry's. In fact that's not the case. They are not yet on speaking terms. Henry doesn't mean to be unkind to his family, but their removal wasn't personal. It was on a different time line. By nabbing 'Hovis', however, death has signalled his intentions. Now it's the turn of your lot, Henry.

One day, though Henry can't nail it down, 'Hovis' threw money at him, coins and notes. Money which Henry had lent 'Hovis' and which he had asked to be returned to him. 'Here, have your shitty money,' 'Hovis' had declared, tossing it into the air and showering Henry with it. Henry can't remember where this happened. Or exactly how old they were at the time. Or why he had lent money to 'Hovis' in the first place, since 'Hovis' was never short. Or why it had been necessary to ask for it back. Or why 'Hovis' had been so angry with him for doing so. All he can remember is the mortification. Having your own money thrown back at you, the refutation of your original generosity, the demonstration, in other words, of your meanness. For it is meaner to sue for the return of a loan than it would have been to refuse it in the first place. What troubles Henry is that he does not recognise himself in this event, but is ashamed of it nonetheless. Is that what remains, after all that time and all those changes – the shame? Is shame the sole immutable entity?

Who wronged whom in that recollection? Suddenly it is important to decide. Why? Henry knows why. It is because 'Hovis' is dead, and the living owe the dead reparation. If Henry wronged 'Hovis', now is the time for Henry to acknowledge it.

This is what he is doing in the front seat of Moira's BMW jeep, when he's not dodging the oncoming traffic. He is going through the list of all the wrongs he ever visited on 'Hovis'. Yes, there is the question of the wrongs 'Hovis' visited on him, but they do not apply now, 'Hovis' having seized the advantage yet again and died first. And would 'Hovis' have been making conscientious mental reparation to Henry, had it been the other way round?

'Sorry, Henry, for calling you a girl. Sorry if that contributed in any measure to your having a shit life. Sorry for having such a good life myself. Tactless of me. Sorry about that.'

Fat chance, Henry thinks. But such certainty is itself a perpetuation of an older wrong. Still at it, Henry, still thinking ill of your best friend? Who, alas, can no longer defend himself.

Am I glad? Henry wonders. Am I, in some small disreputable part of myself, glad that he is dead?

He hears the tears well up for 'Hovis'. Hears them muster, hears their pricking behind his eyes, like the sound of needles going into tracing paper, but they don't fall. Won't fall. Well, Henry is damned if he is going to castigate himself for that. He has cried a lot in Eastbourne. Even the softest-hearted man can run out of tears temporarily. Besides, there is a tight band of pain across his chest. His pulse is not even. There is a dull pain in his head, at the very top, where the skull feels thinnest. And the woman he loves is concerned for him. All these are signs, surely, that although he isn't weeping, he is in genuine distress.

Yes, but is he in distress for 'Hovis'?

Or is he in distress because he isn't?

Moira wants to know if he would care to stop for tea.

'I am all right,' he says. 'I would care to go slower, but otherwise I am all right.'

'Are you sure?' she says, looking sideways at him, taking one hand off the wheel and resting it on his knee.

'I am sure.'

His voice is grave, as befits the gravity of the day. Grave and brave.

Suddenly, he discovers an impulse in himself to laugh. What is he doing being grave and brave?! The effrontery of me, he thinks. Pretending to feelings there is every chance I do not have, because if I had them I would not be questioning their where-abouts. What a fraud!

He turns to look at Moira, squint-eyed at her wagon wheel, driving as always like some vengeful charioteer, fired with vendetta. 'Do you know what?' he says, not at all sure that he can prevent the laughter erupting from his chest. 'Do you know what? . . . I think I might be too all right.'

'That's normal,' she says. 'It'll take time to sink in.'

'No,' he says. 'I mean more than that. I think I might be relieved he's dead.'

'Well, that too is a normal feeling,' she says, rubbing the palm of her hand into his knee, making absent-minded circles of condo-lence, 'if he's been suffering a long time.'

'You're not hearing me,' he says, knowing he can't stop it now, knowing that the laughter must have its way with him. 'What I'm saying – ha! – is that I'm glad, for *me* . . .'

But when the laughter comes it isn't what he thinks it is. It is, after all, an outpouring of grief.

Which gives Moira the opportunity to swerve from the fast lane to the slow lane without acknowledging the middle lane, and bring him skidding on to the hard shoulder, where, on her shoulder, and for the second time in as many days, he sobs like an abandoned baby.

And then there are the obituaries for Henry to contend with. Full-blown obituaries too, big pictures of 'Hovis' at his most loaf-headed, some of the eulogiums three-quarters of a page in length. Call no man happy until he's dead. Well, you can say that again, muses Henry at his little table on St John's Wood High Street, immured in newsprint. Who will ever speak this warmly about a man until he's cold? Osmond's illness bravely borne, his beau-tiful devoted wife, the children in whom he took, etc., etc., and who took in him blah blah, the grandchildren in whom he took still more, his going where others had not dared, his unparalleled contribution to neo-realistic cinema in a country which, before he had the foresight, heigh-ho, an intellectual among entertainers, an entertainer among intellectuals . . .

Yes, yes, Henry thinks, a giant among dwarves, a dwarf among giants, a man among girls, a girl among men – except that that's him, Henry, about whom not a word will be written when his turn comes. So call no man happy until he's dead, and not very men happy even after that.

'This a good idea?' Moira asks him. She is serving him this morning, as in the old days of their courtship, harassed in her maid-of-all-work flatties. Only she has a better understanding today – now that he has divulged all to her – of his unpleasant nature.

Though having coming clean in the car, Henry is in denial on the pavement. 'Is *what* a good idea?'

She flicks his paper. 'That.'

'Why shouldn't it be? He was my friend.'

She leaves him to it.

He has a reason for going through each obituary painstakingly. Spare his blushes, but Henry is looking for some mention of himself. '*As Belkin said in his last recorded interview, the unseen influence on his work was and always had been Henry Nagel, the childhood friend without whom* . . .' That sort of thing. Insane, he knows it. But madder hopes are realised. People win lotteries at however many millions to one. How many millions to one against Belkin expending his dying breath on Henry? Or against an obituary writer who has done his homework coming up with Henry's name – school friend, rival, sometime critic, and so on. Fewer, surely. Easier to be remembered in an elegy to an old mate, at least, than to thread a camel through the eye of a needle.

Whether or not, there is no mention. As he was removed from Osmond's life in life, so Henry is removed from Osmond's life in death.

The which being the case, there is nothing to stop Henry sliding into a broiling ravine of resentment and left-outness.

Doesn't being alive help the smallest bit? The daylight? The soft air? The blue of the sky? The warm populousness of the street? The sounds of voices, footfalls, music, traffic, honking? The fact that he has Viennese coffee and sachertorte on a china plate before him? Moira? Whereas 'Hovis' is deaf and blind now, without touch, without smell, without future, a disgrace?

No, nothing helps. What Henry wants is a mention. Or better than a mention, an obituary of his own. His photograph in the papers, his life told and retold in all its epic heroism, his dates commemorated as though history is not complete without them. *Osmond Belkin – 1943–2003*. There it is. Irrefutable. The span of time arched like a bridge over obscurity. Sure, it's time passed, time done with, but those years have passed for Henry too, and who would bet on his bending history to his will in the years that are left?

Even vanished, 'Hovis' has the beating of him.

Moira comes out again and sits with him. 'Look how lovely the day is,' she says.

'Yes,' he says.

'We could go for a walk after lunch. Do the park.'

'Yes,' he says.

She means well. She is the voice of life to him. But what does life have going for it when the sirens are calling you from the other place?

'Snap out,' she says.

'Yes,' he says. He would like to. But he's in deep trouble. He might not know much about much, as they used to say in the Pennines, but he does know that once you start envying the dead you are in deep trouble.

# FOURTEEN

A letter arrives from Cleansing. They cannot tell him who donated the bench in his mother's name. Data protection. If, however, he can show exceptional circumstances . . .

'We're going round in circles,' he says to Moira.

'Write to them again,' she tells him.

'Saying what?'

'Saying that if they will not make you acquainted with the donor, would they please make the donor acquainted with you. Normal business practice, Henry. You make your address available to the protected party. You can even send them a stamped addressed envelope.'

'And what if the protected party's dead?'

She is losing patience with him. Him and death. 'If he's dead then that's the end of it.'

'What makes you think it's a he?'

'Oh, for fuck's sake, Henry.'

Time was, a bit of horseplay might have followed that. But Henry's gone ghostly on her again.

So she takes him to the salt-beef bar for dinner. When all else fails, salt beef does it for Henry. Red meat, yellow mustard, green sweet-and-sour cucumbers. Primary colours. Make sure everything's bright and keep the appeal simple, she's discovered that.

She has her salt beef lean. 'In which case,' Henry requests, 'can I have your fat?'

See? Already he's cheering up.

Henry doesn't tell her that a dead friend can affect you like that. One minute you're down, the next . . . well, the next you're not.

As it is, today he is half tempted to ask for 'Hovis' Belkin's fat as well.

He is even teaching her a game they used to play in the salt-beef bars in Manchester when they were boys, he and 'Hovis'. Spot the Wej. She's Jewish. She's Jewish. He's Jewish. So's he. That's four points to me. Those two, however, aren't, so that's two points to you!

'Not much of a game in this joint,' she said. 'Everyone's Jewish who comes here. Except me.'

She is continuing to insist she isn't Jewish, isn't from the Danube or the Baltic.

'You're called Aultbach,' he reminds her. 'How can you not be Jewish?'

'I'm only called Aultbach because I married Aultbach.'

'And you're telling me that a man called Aultbach would marry someone who isn't Jewish?'

'Aultbach's barely Jewish himself.'

'When it comes to being Jewish there is no barely,' Henry explains.

'Exactly,' she says, 'and I am not Jewish at all.'

It's funny but he has never asked her maiden name. Maybe he doesn't want to hear it. Moira Smith, Moira Pilkington, Moira Ainsworth – he'd find any of those hard. They wouldn't stop him loving going up and down escalators with her, but they might dissuade him from doing it so often. It isn't the Jewish bit he needs, it's the foreign. He needs her to come from somewhere else.

Here has Henry in it. Somewhere else hasn't. So come from somewhere else, I beg you, Moira.

He wants to play, anyway, whether she does or she doesn't.

'They are!' he shouts. 'That's two more points to me.'

She wants to know how he knows. Still pretending that she needs guidance in Jewish and the opposite-to-Jewish ways.

So he goes along with her subterfuge, and explains. It's to do with the manner in which the sandwich is addressed. True, all people temporarily assume a Jewish air when they enter a salt-beef bar, especially at the moment of examining the contents of their salt-beef sandwich. Indeed, you can almost say, if you are irreligious and given to the joys of stereotyping, that this is precisely wherein being Jewish lies – in choosing to order a salt-beef sandwich and then examining it minutely, either for too much or for too little, or for too fatty or for too lean, or for too dry or for too wet. But look more attentively and you discover that Gentiles also open up their sandwiches to count the pieces of salt beef. The difference being that when the Gentile has finished examining his sandwich he eats it – see him? a point to you! – whereas the Jew invariably calls the waiter.

'I never call the waiter,' she says. 'Doesn't that prove I'm not Jewish.'

'No,' he tells her. 'The only reason you don't call the waiter is that you wait yourself. It's the freemasonry of the profession that stops you. But if you're having trouble with Spot the Wej let's go down market and play Dodge the Draught.'

In fact, you don't so much play Dodge the Draught as watch other people playing it. Why? Because it can help in playing Spot the Wej, the easiest way of spotting Wejs being to notice whether or not they are prepared to sit in a draught. If they huddle together shivering and shouting for the manager, demanding that he find them a table where there is no draught, they are Jews. If, on the other hand, they are perfectly happy sitting in the draught, and what is more haven't noticed any draught, because there *is* no draught – Henry laughs, expounding this – they are Gentile.

'Oughtn't you to have grown out of this by now, Henry?' Moira asks him, folding her arms and looking at him evenly – which isn't easy for her. 'Aren't you a bit old to be finding this amusing?'

He starts as though she has pinched him. 'Aren't you a bit old for this, Henry?' His mother's words, precisely. They were out together, taking tea – where were they? – some hotel, the Midland, yes, the Midland, scene of his father's . . . but he doesn't want to remember that, by the by all that, done and dusted, what he prefers to remember is taking tea, pouring tea, picking cucumber sandwiches from a silver platter, laughing with his mother, agreeing that the dinky oblong of white sandwich with its crusts removed is always the best thing about tea, better than the scones, better than the little cakes, or fancies as they called them in those days, but whether this was before or after she'd become a decorator of cakes herself, that he can't remember, but it must have been after her Nietzsche period because there was something Nietzschean about her attitude, indeed long after, else she would not have been wondering whether he wasn't a bit old for what he was doing, which was playing Spot the Wej.

'It's just a game, Mother.'

Funny, isn't it, what happens to the status of the game between a mother and her son. If Henry, in spite of all his heaviness, liked a game when he could get one, to whom did he owe his love of games but Ekaterina? Ah . . . boo! – who taught him that? Who hid herself behind the chair? Who appeared again from behind another? Who made his dolls talk? Who put him, Henry, at the centre of Schubert's Fifth Symphony? And then, when the boy has mastered play and become a man, who doesn't find any of it funny any more? The greatest difference between the sexes – that men will play and play and play, and that the women who showed them play, won't.

'*Just games* have stolen half my life away, Henry.'

He hung his head. He didn't like being stopped mid-play. It made him feel foolish. No one likes having to choke on their own enthusiasm, the shy – who don't easily show enthusiasm in the first place – least of all. But he was his mother's boy and had read his mother's books. The greatest of all tragedies in Henry's eyes – a woman whose life has been stolen half away.

She was wearing a lovely floaty dress made of flimsy materials, in a print of faded flowers, the flowers you associate with elderly ladies living on their own. The flowers of loneliness. Blow on her, Henry thought, and that was the other half of her life gone.

He wanted to know, though, if she'd have felt the same had he been playing Spot Somebody Else, Spot the Serbo-Croat, for example, or Spot the Irish Catholic.

She thought about it. Probably not.

'So it's the Jew thing.'

'No,' she said. 'It's the self-conscious Jew thing. I think that's childish, Henry. No one's asking you to pretend you're somebody other than you are. If anything, I like it that you're not in flight from any of that. But it's provincial to keep going on about it. And insecure. In my experience people who can't stop making jokes about their identity aren't easy with it. The man of the world accepts who he is and the influences which have made him, and then gets on with living in the world. The big world.'

He was stung. Provincial? Henry! Whose head no sooner hit the pillow every night than it was filled with dances from the Danube.

'Isn't it a Jewish speciality,' he said, 'to enjoy making jokes at our own expense? Hasn't that been the saving of us, our comic self-awareness?'

'Well, if you call that *saving*, Henry . . .'

'You know what I mean. It's our survival strategy.'

'I call it rubbing at an itch. If you leave it, the itch will eventually go away of its own accord. But of course it feels like relief while you're rubbing.'

She had the power, like no other woman, to shame him. Was that all he was doing, rubbing at himself? Was he no better than Warren Shukman who rubbed himself to death?

Was Henry's Jewishness his dick?

Was Henry's dick his Jewishness?

He reddened, having consciousness of dick at the table with his mother. 'You think I'm a footler, I know,' he challenged her, once he'd allowed his high colour to subside. 'You think I'm a footler like Dad.'

Interesting. For a brief moment, although all he was really doing was bringing the conversation back to the point from which it started – capitulating to her, if anything – she flashed fire at him, refusing the alliance. Come the showdown, Henry, it might not be me and you against your father after all. You never know with lovers – and they had been lovers, Ekaterina and Izzi – even those closest to them, even the beloved boy-child, fruit of their union, even Henry never knew the depth of their loyalty to each other at any time.

'At least your father,' she said, 'has never been hung up on Jews.'

'Ma, I'm not hung up.'

She leaned across and patted his hand. Worried about him. But absent too, as though she had left him behind. Which is not meant to be the way of it. In a properly ordered family it is the son who leaves the mother behind.

'Where are you?' Moira asks him, waving her hand in front of his eyes. 'Where have you been?'

'Thinking that you're right. I am a bit old for this silly game. But if I tell you in my own defence that "Hovis" and I used to play it in Manchester in the coffee bars nearly half a century ago, you will understand why it's on my mind.'

'Was he Jewish? I didn't realise that. There was no mention of it in anything I read.'

Is she right? Henry casts his mind back. Maybe she is. No mention of the J word in anything he'd read either. As why would there be? A citizen of the world, Osmond Belkin. A player in that big world which Henry's mother wanted Henry to inhabit.

But Henry, for no reason he would be able to argue success-fully in a court of law, thinks every J should keep the J word somewhere about his person. It's even possible he feels punitive about it. If it's been good enough for me, it's good enough for you! Suffer! This might account for the obduracy with which he persists in interesting Moira – who couldn't be less interested – in continuing their game. 'One point for you,' he shouts, nodding in the direction of the door. 'This one's definitely Gentile. In fact two points for you, he's got a dog with him.'

'How do you know the dog's not Jewish?'

'In general because no dog is Jewish. But in this particular because it's Angus.'

Moira looks up and waves at Lachlan.

Henry wonders whether Lachlan knew he was going to find them here – by them, he means Moira – because he is spruced up, his hair shining and cleanly parted, his moustache bristling, the whole person bathed and dewy, as though newborn. More and more, Henry has been noticing, Lachlan presents himself this way to Moira. Like a gift from God. Henry has been trying it himself, but is no match for Lachlan. He can do clean and eager but he cannot do the elderly male equivalent of Venus rising from the waves. There is some absurdity in it at last, Henry reckons, doing a cherub when at best you're Bacchus; though no such squeamishness appears to inhibit Lachlan.

He is wearing a spotted red handkerchief about his throat, piratical. An identical handkerchief is tied around the throat of Angus.

'Sweet,' Moira says. 'They look like a couple of bounders on the town.'

'If I were a woman faced with those two,' Henry mutters, 'I'd choose Angus.'

'Then we can have a foursome,' Moira says out of the side of her mouth, still waving.

But Angus looks like missing out on his big chance. 'Sorry,' one of the young waiters apologises at the door, making extravagant wipe-out signals with his hands, 'we do not allow dogs in the restaurant.'

Lachlan's face goes from baby pink to ulcer purple in an instant.

'Shame,' Henry says to Moira, 'he'll have to eat somewhere else.'

Moira wonders if she ought to have a word with the manager.

'Don't waste your time,' Henry tells her. 'He knows his customers. Jews who won't eat under a draught are hardly going to eat near a dog. Even the goyim won't eat with dogs, and they sleep with them.'

Lachlan is blowing out his cheeks, threatening to complain to someone higher up. (Who? Henry wonders. Is there an ombudsman for salt-beef bars?) But if it's a battle of attractions between Angus and Moira – Moira in a V-neck violet cardigan as spiky-haired as one of her bags (alpaca, is it?), loose and clingy all at once, the buttons of her nipples visible even from the street – Angus is doomed to be on the losing side. A minute later he is trussed to a parking meter, looking forlornly into the restaurant. Henry shifts his chair. He cannot eat a salt-beef sandwich with a dog envying his every bite, let alone gazing at him with forbidden love.

'Have you ever heard such nonsense?!' Lachlan says, joining them, out of breath.

Moira kicks Henry under the table. She doesn't want him telling Lachlan that his dog is not kosher.

'Poor Angus,' she says. 'Will he be all right?'

'Well, he won't be hungry, if that's what you mean. He's had his.'

'And even if he hadn't, he could always eat shit,' Henry decides not to say, plumping instead for some inanity about loneliness being good for the character.

Moira looks at him. 'Of a dog?'

Lachlan is trying to cool himself down. Hyperhidrotic Henry feels almost sorry for him. As a perspirative man himself he knows how dismaying it is to come out of your house as odoriferous as a daisy and have circumstances flood you back into a tropical rainforest of discomfort. But he had it coming. People with dogs have it coming.

Choosing to make a virtue of his condition, Lachlan unfastens his neckerchief and mops his moustache with it. 'Whew!' he says. 'These petty Hitlers.'

Moira kicks Henry under the table again, lest he is thinking of reminding Lachlan that Hitler's biggest crime wasn't banning dogs from restaurants.

'Anyway,' she says. 'How have you been?'

She is wearing her hair up, the way Henry has noticed that Lachlan particularly likes it, piled to one side, teetering. Henry likes it too, the uncertainty, the imminence of cascade, and of course the asymmetry. Once upon a time Lachlan's liking it would have counted more than his own liking it – the old second opinion routine. But not any more. I am becoming a conventional man, Henry thinks. By the time I'm seventy I will be wanting a woman of my own and wanting her just for myself.

That's if he gets to seventy. 'Hovis' Belkin, he reminds himself, barely got to sixty.

Henry feels his throat tighten. Grief, he hopes. Please God, make it grief.

There was never any serious woman competition with 'Hovis', Henry finds himself remembering, unless you count 'Hovis' having always somehow known the provenance of the women Henry took out. Certainly no borrowing any of Belkin's wives, if only for the simple reason, all else aside, that Henry never got to clap an eye on any of Belkin's wives. Always out of sight, they were, in another country, on another plane, unavailable to the contamination of Henry's curiosity. And there were no problems the other way, either. It was pretty much the done thing, when Henry was at university, to have a crack at the female company your friends were keeping. Lawless times, the sixties, when sex overrode all other considerations. You gave your woman a piece of your mind when you found her in the arms of your several flatmates, but not your flatmates. The latter were exempt from criticism, driven by a natural force over which they had no control.

The woman was different. The woman was meant to be a repository of decency and fidelity. The potential mother of your children, for Christ's sake! But Henry never came home to find his girlfriend of the hour in 'Hovis' Belkin's arms. Not once. Not ever. How strange was that?

Of all the ways there are of betraying your best friend, this, Henry reckons, is the hardest to forgive: not betraying him, sexually, at all.

Henry had his own suspicions as to why 'Hovis' was aloof, and those suspicions did not include 'Hovis' being honourable or gay. 'Hovis' kept his hands off Henry's women because he didn't rate them. Because he wasn't tempted. Because they weren't the business. It was terribly insulting, and Henry for a long time sought alternative explanations, but that was the truth of it: 'Hovis' was only ever Henry's friend, and therefore only ever Henry's rival, for as long as it took him to get away. For 'Hovis', real life was whatever happened afterwards. And in that afterwards everything that pertained to Henry vanished like a dream.

Of course, while they both remained above the ground you couldn't discount the possibility that Henry would one day re-enter Belkin's life, and that Belkin would one day re-enter Henry's. Nothing's over until it's over. Who could say for sure that they wouldn't meet somewhere – by the ancient yew in Totter Down graveyard, say, or outside the paper shop on St John's Wood High Street, 'Hovis' grey-skinned, wasted, hobbling on a stick – and that the sight of healthful Henry with his hand on Moira's clavicle wouldn't force him to re-evaluate the pattern of their history? Would 'Hovis', in those circumstances, have cast a dying man's lascivious eye on Moira, one part defunct desire, three parts envy? Or would he have found a way of communicating to Henry that in his view – for what it's worth, old man – he had bombed again, come up with yet another undesirable, a mere nobody from here instead of one of the glittering somebodies from there?

Now Henry will never know.

It should be a liberation. Now I don't need to wonder. Now I, Henry the Conqueror, sole possessor of the field, can get on with my life, uncriticised, undetracted, uncompared.

But old habits die hard.

And the dead are never vanquished.

About Lachlan, at least, Henry need have no fears. Lachlan's heart belongs to Moira.

Henry watches him with a feeling akin to affection. Whatever else you outgrow, you remain duty-bound to be fond of a person who is fond of those of whom you are fond. Common humanity, Henry thinks, demands that I accept him, as 'Hovis' Belkin never accepted me, as a man made of the same stuff I am. He threw his bowler hat into the Thames and never had a happy day again, I threw myself into the Pennines and have not been able to look at myself in the mirror since. We are the same.

But it isn't easy when the belching starts.


'Love to,' Moira says, when Lachlan asks them back to his apartment for a snifter.

It turns out he has something interesting to show Henry. Some antique he wants me to buy, Henry thinks. Though he notices there is precious little left, Lachlan selling his own inheritance from under him – again. He would like to make an excuse and leave Moira to do the decent thing by the pair of them, but he accepts this isn't wise. It will either look as if he's being rude or being louche. This is the price he pays for having a twisted soul – no one ever takes his motives at their face value.

Not even Angus, who is never more wary of Henry, these days, than when he shows him some attention.

'Do you mind,' Lachlan says, looking at his watch the minute he lets them in, 'if I just nip the telly on to catch the news?'

There are rumours that the police have cracked open a terrorist cell operating in St John's Wood, a small sack of white substance which might easily be ricin has been found, and a map of the

London Underground. Lachlan wouldn't be at all surprised if the cell turns out to have been in this building.

'There are some shady-looking characters around here, I can tell you,' he says, as though Henry and Moira don't live around here themselves.

'Yes, but they're all over eighty,' Henry says. 'Except for us.'

'That's why it's ideal.'

'Yes, ideal for dying in.'

Rude of him, but Lachlan doesn't seem to notice. He is busying himself, now at the drinks cabinet, now in the refrigerator. In between which he doesn't seem able to decide whether to put his red-and-white neckerchief back on or keep it off. Henry catches him checking his reflection in the mirror. Aha, so it's a vanity thing. Henry wonders if Lachlan knows something that he doesn't, that women like a pirate's scarf around an old man's accordion neck almost as much as they like it around a dog's. Sea dog – is that the reference?

'The perfect place for retirement, yes,' Lachlan says, 'and for that very reason the perfect place for terrorists.'

'You've forgotten,' Henry reminds him, 'that we're right opposite a mosque.'

'So?'

'Don't you think that makes us a bit conspicuous?'

Lachlan, back in his red-and-white neckerchief, looks at Moira, as though to wonder how she puts up with him. 'My very point,' he says. 'We're so obvious the police wouldn't dream of looking here.'

'But I thought the whole point of your supposition is that they *have* looked here.'

'Let's just wait and see, eh,' Lachlan says, closing one eye at Henry.

While they've been talking, Moira has been watching television. 'It's a false alarm,' she tells them. 'The cell appears to be a family of Israelis. The ricin was matzo meal.'

Lachlan isn't convinced. 'And the map of the London Underground?'

Henry goes to the window. Checking the skyline. Most days it's still there, but one day it won't be. It's just a question of who goes first – Henry or the city. On balance, Henry would like it to be the city.

When he turns back into the room he sees Lachlan putting what looks like a surgeon's mask on Angus. Because the mask is designed to loop around the ears, Angus can't keep it on.

Something in the material makes the dog sneeze. Would not have made a good surgeon, Angus.

Moira is laughing. 'Poor Angus,' she says. 'His ears are too floppy.'

'I'll have to see what other sort they do,' Lachlan says. 'There's no point me staying alive if Angus pops his.'

'Do you really suppose those are going to be of any help?' Henry asks. A box has appeared suddenly, on a coffee table – one of the last remaining items of furniture belonging to the old lady – containing fifty high-bacterial filtration-efficiency procedure masks. 'Well, obviously you must,' he continues, 'if you're buying them by the boxload.'

'I bought out John Bell & Croyden's entire stock. Do you want a box or two yourself? You're welcome. I've got a few rolls of tape to spare as well.'

'Is that to tape up the terrorists?'

'Doors and windows, old man.'

'They don't look taped to me.'

'They aren't.'

'So when do you tape them, when the crop dusters appear in the sky? Won't that be a bit late?'

Lachlan taps his nose. For a moment Henry takes him to mean that he'll be able to smell the chemicals before they have time to worm their way (if that's what chemicals do – don't ask Henry) into the apartment block. But what he actually means is that there'll be some warning, that we'll all be in the know and able to take precautions, provided we have the masks and the tape, and provided we're at home, and provided we are not asleep, and provided we have the telly or the radio on. And provided, of course, that we have the wit to listen.

'That's a lot of provisos,' Henry says.

Lachlan shrugs. 'Suit yourself. Better to be safe than sorry, we say – don't we, Angus?'

Half masked, half not, Angus gives another sneeze. *Suave, inodoro, no irritante*, it says on the multilingual box. *Doux, sans odeur, non irritant*. But then it doesn't mention anything about dogs. It seems a shame, Henry thinks, that there should be terrorists at this very hour plotting harm to Angus, who, whichever way you cut it, has to be accounted an innocent party.

Moira is sitting girlishly on the floor with her knees drawn up to her chin – showing too much leg, Henry thinks. Not fair to Lachlan, as it would be not fair to Henry were those legs not available to him, at other times, to caress. Just behind the knee he likes, just where the anterior flesh of the thigh begins to swell. Something else Henry loves to do: to weigh the underthigh in his cupped hand, to calculate its sway.

She is looking at some old notebooks Lachlan has dug out for her. His stepmother's diaries. Leather-bound, of course. The best Lachlan's money could buy her.

'I've found quite a few references to you,' Lachlan tells her. 'I've bent the corners of the pages you're mentioned in.'

'Lachlan, you shouldn't have done that,' Moira says, clutching the bundle of diaries to her chest. 'That's sacrilege.'

'Sacrilege? Hardly. The old witch never had a holy thought in her life. Just about the only decent thing she ever said about anybody she said about you.'

'Yes, I see,' Moira says, repairing the ear of each page as she peruses it. '"*Monday, Moira came to see me with strudel. Wednesday, Moira brought strudel. Friday, Moira made tea to go with strudel.*"'

'Vivid by her standards,' Lachlan assures her. 'Most of it's just strudel, tea, television and bed.'

'Age,' Henry puts in. 'Age reduces us all to a few simplicities.'

'Like playing Spot the Wej,' Moira says, *sotto voce*.

'Age nothing,' Lachlan spits. 'It was always strudel, tea, television and bed. The old feller complained of it thirty years ago. Sang and danced to get him, then took to her bed and ate his money. The miracle is that she could remember who you were once she'd scoffed the strudel. I've yet to find myself referred to by name. "He" – that's all I get. "*He* came to see me, long face as usual." "Saturday – *He* was here all afternoon, moping." No bloody wonder I had a long face, considering who was paying for her.'

'Oh, look,' Moira not listening exclaims, 'she calls me a fine gal on this page!'

'Which you are,' Lachlan says.

He is overexcited, like Angus before a w-a-l-k. Only with Lachlan it's before a k-i-s-s. Henry can't believe his eyes but Lachlan has joined Moira on the floor and is actually trying to k-i-s-s her, right in front of Henry's nose. Is the man mad? Moira does the subtle thing, sliding her mouth away and allowing his moustache to find her cheek. 'Mind you,' she laughs – overlaughs, Henry would say – 'she only calls me a fine gal because I brought her over double strudel and *millefeuille* that morning.'

Henry wonders if he's seeing things. Though he has been repulsed, Lachlan has started to whinny. If Henry is not mistaken he is inching his hand to Moira's thigh – the sway of flesh which Henry has taken to thinking of (a novel sensation for him) as his own. From across the room, Angus too is staring at him. Not the usual liquid look of indiscriminate devotion. More consternation, as though he is bewildered by this turn of events as well. And is frightened what might happen next.

Is this my fault? Henry wonders. Have I been insufficiently male-possessive in my signals? Does there still hang about me a whiff of those bad old days when I used to seek confirmation of my choice in the appreciation of other men, indeed when I preferred it that other men had prior claim, so that they could attend to any obsequies necessary – lay out the limbs, comb out the hair, close fast the eyes – not me? Or is it Moira's fault? Has she been leading Lachlan on because I have allowed her to feel that it is all right for her to do so, in which case that is also not her fault but mine. All lines of guilt leading back to Henry.

'I'm thinking,' he says, 'that maybe we ought to be going. It's been a tiring day what with one thing and another.'

'Don't go yet,' Lachlan says, barely flustered, 'I haven't shown you your mention yet.'

Henry squints at him. Is this what loneliness does? Sends you round the bend?

Moira has risen from the floor. Maybe Lachlan is about to lead her into the bedroom. Maybe this time she won't refuse him. But if Henry is not mistaken she is sending him, Henry, messages with her eyes. Don't be cruel messages. Have a heart messages. Put yourself in his place messages. Do this for me messages.

'So what's Henry's mention?' she asks. 'I thought your step-mother never met Henry.'

'She didn't. But here's a coincidence – she met Henry's mother.'

'What?' says Henry.

'What?' says Moira.

'Just a minute, how . . . ?' Henry starts to ask, but cannot see a way to finish the question. His father had a catchphrase to which he resorted whenever he was flummoxed. Not *taugetʒ* – though it had an implication of *taugetʒ* in it. 'How the, who the, what the, why the?' And that's all Henry can think of now. How the, who the, what the, why the? With a when the thrown in.

A wild preparatory, or is the word precautionary, thought has started to run through his brain, wilder than anything running through Lachlan's brain, assuming, after so much loneliness, that Lachlan still has a brain: Lachlan's stepmother, take this slowly, is the person who paid for his mother's bench in Eastbourne. Didn't Lachlan once tell him that his stepmother went through his fortune keeping a suite at a hotel in Eastbourne? No, that was Brighton. Unless it was Torquay. Unless Lachlan was confused. Unless Lachlan was lying. And is that why Lachlan thinks he can kiss Moira in full view, because his stepmother, for some reason, paid for a bench for Henry's mother using Lachlan's money? Is this payback time?

Gibberish, all of it.

'I doubt,' Henry says, while Lachlan is finding the relevant pages, 'that your stepmother could ever have met my mother. They moved in different spheres. My mother lived her whole life in Manchester. As I understand from what you've told me . . .'

'"*Ekaterina*",' Lachlan says, reading from a diary. 'Wasn't that your mother's name? That's what you told me, anyway. "If you would be happy for a week take a wife; if you would be happy for a month kill a pig; but if you would be happy all your life plant a garden" – your mother's favourite saying, too, you said, when I told you it was the old lady's – what chance one of them gave it to the other? Hang on, here we go . . . "*Ran into the Ekaterina woman on the stairs, startled like a rabbit. Something to hide, that one.*"'

'The world is full,' Henry says, 'of Ekaterinas. And the Ekaterina who was my mother had nothing to hide.'

'Ekaterinas who believe happiness comes with planting a garden?'

'Absolutely. It's a common woman's fancy. It sounds to me like something they were all taught to embroider on comforters at school.'

'Actually,' Moira says, 'as it stands it's more a man's fancy. Wouldn't a woman be more likely to say that if you would be happy for only a week, take a husband?'

Henry looks at her with fury.

Lachlan turns another page. 'Here we are. "*Saw the Nagel*

*woman on the High Street, pretending not to see me.*" That's you, isn't it? You're Nagel?'

'Show me that,' Henry says.

He takes the diary to the couch. An Ekaterina on the stairway, a Nagel on the High Street, what does that prove? It would depend, for starters, how many days apart. Nice of Lachlan to bend the tell-tale pages, makes the detective work a damn sight easier. June 9, an Ekaterina on the stairs; June 12, a Nagel on the High Street. Coincidence? An Ekaterina Bates living in the building and a Bertha Nagel in the vicinity, each within three days of the other. What are the chances of that? High? Low? How would Henry know. And even if he found the Christian and the surname linked, what then? Unlikely there were many Ekaterina Nagels, but just as unlikely that his Ekaterina Nagel had breath and being in St John's Wood. If there were another, that could explain the bench. A thought occurs to Henry. The year. If this Ekaterina Nagel – taking her indeed, for the moment, to be one – had turned up in St John's Wood after 1978 then it wasn't his mother. Not unless it were his mother's ghost. So June 9 when? Nineteen seventy-six. Shame. Nice try, Henry. He tries to remember what was happening in 1976. He knew where he was. Where he always was. Rotting like the Count of Monte Cristo in the Pennines. But where was his mother? Icing cakes. Travelling sometimes, yes. Demonstrating her art here, there and everywhere just as Moira had been demonstrating hers in Eastbourne. So it wasn't out of the question, after all, that his mother had been to Eastbourne too, maybe sent him a card from there, nor that she'd called in on St John's Wood, though he couldn't imagine anyone turning up for cake-decoration classes in St John's Wood. Nor was there any explaining, even if she did have pupils hereabouts, what she was doing in this building. Unless – of course! – unless she had tracked Izzi down to this address. That would explain her reluctance to engage Lachlan's stepmother in idle chit-chat. Startled like a rabbit – you bet she was. Pretending not to see anyone –

you can say that again. Desperate not to *be* seen, rather. Cloak-and-dagger stuff, but also shame before the Almighty. To be reduced, at her age, to *this*. And she a Stern Girl! His poor mother. Henry had always taken it for granted that she had caught the coach that killed her in the course of a frustrated attempt – perhaps one of many – to find and bring home her errant husband. In fact, there was no evidence for this. Looked at all round, she was just as likely to have been travelling to an Ideal Home Exhibition in the capital with a bag full of icing tools. But sagas of sinfulness and retribution harmonised more nearly with Henry's nature than work schedules; it seemed in accordance with the pitiless universal laws of marriage and adultery, as Henry understood them, that she should have been sucked into the tangle of his father's deceit and died there, her death triggering his father's. Thus do carnality and its recompense cut us all down indiscriminately, the guilty and the innocent alike. Yet for all the unquestionedness of these assumptions, it never once occurred to Henry to imagine an ongoing drama of the sort that is now emerging, with Henry's lurid help, from Lachlan's stepmother's diaries – his mother locating his father's second home (he had never thought of that), his mother engaged in a tussle with his father's mistress (he had never thought of that), his mother returning to St John's Wood again and again (which alone could explain the suggestion of familiarity and frequency in the diaries), and thus embroiling herself in a hideously protracted battle for his father's devotion. Sad was how he'd envisaged it all until now. Sad, her jealous wonderings. Sad, her lonely expeditions to find the truth. Sad, the failure. And heartbreaking, for both of them, the resolution which resolved nothing. But you can forget the sadness: today, suddenly, what Henry comes face to face with – like Henry James's bad-faced stranger surprised in a thick-carpeted house of quiet on a Sunday afternoon – is raw ugliness. The ugliness of suspicions horribly confirmed. The ugliness of exposure. The ugliness of raised voices, of a brawl and, who knows, maybe the ugliness of violence. Much harder to forgive his father his easeful peccadillos if that were the case, and much harder to forgive himself, come to that, his comfortable accommodation to them. Henry remembers the time he found his father's misdemeanours funny: sorry, Mother, but Dad and Rivka Yoffey, you've got to laugh. Well, not so funny if there were shouted reproaches on St John's Wood High Street, drowning out the honking even, or blood spilled in the lobby of this quiet mansion block. Strange, though, if such things happened, that Lachlan hasn't drawn his attention to them in the diaries, folded down the pages, look, Henry, your mother plunging a dagger into your father's false heart, and his mistress weeping on the stairs, thought you might be interested. *Something to hide, that one.* Stranger still, now Henry comes to think of it, that the old woman makes no mention of Henry's father, unless Lachlan, for malicious reasons of his own, has so far kept that mention back. A distraught wife, startled as a rabbit, comes to seek out and challenge her faithless husband living mistressed like a pasha right next door, and the old woman doesn't have a word to say about it! And something else – how come she knows his mother's name? No, how come she knows his mother's *names?* Distraught wife, startled as a rabbit, with much to hide and much to hide from, comes armed, looking to prise her easily led husband from the pink cushioned arms of his wealthy mistress, comes hammering on the door, comes crying, yelling, threatening, and the old woman comes to be in possession of the Ekaterina and the Nagel. What, she stopped to chat? Hello, here to kill my husband, name's Mrs Nagel, but you can call me Ekaterina, now where is the swine? And Izzi, in all the days or weeks or months or years of his sojourn – how should Henry know how many – had never chatted likewise? Izzi who would address a block of wood if he thought there was any chance of interesting it in his origami or his fire-eating. People had intimate knowledge of Henry's father who had never met him. He was that sort of man. His charm was viral. You felt his influence though you never came within a mile of him. Now here was Lachlan's stepmother, Norma Jean, with an avowed taste for show business, living right next door and not caring to notice his existence. Agreed, there may be more to come, more revelations which Lachlan is savouring and holding back, but surely he'd be there in person, Izzi, on one or other of these folded pages, a reference point whenever Ekaterina creeps by on the stairs. Unless Norma Jean is keeping him a secret to protect herself. She the mistress, then? Norma Jean Henry's father's lover? He and Lachlan as it were cousins in sin? Though it is an evening of shocks, Henry doesn't entertain that shocking possibility for long. He looks over to the other couch where Lachlan is trying one of his anti-toxin masks on Moira. First the dog, now the woman. He doesn't have many variations as a lover, Henry notes with satisfaction. And he isn't scrutinising Henry to pick his perfect moment to tell him the next momentous news, that the old witch his stepmother and Henry's dad, the fire-eater, had made the beast. If he had that information in his pocket he'd have released it by now, Henry is convinced of that. He knows the bounder's logic. 'Your dad and my dad's wife, therefore me and Moira. That's only fair, isn't it?' Besides which, if she'd owned both apartments, Norma Jean, as well as keeping her ducal suite in Torquay or wherever, he'd have heard Lachlan complain of it before now. Nor, had it been hers, would it have come by any means to Henry. Had it been hers, it must even more have been Lachlan's, in which case it would have been on the open market by now, along with its fixtures and its fittings. So no, definitely no, he isn't related by bad blood to Lachlan Louis Stevenson, praise be to God. For which relief much thanks, but that still leaves Henry wondering that the object of his mother's visits, let alone, come to think of it, the object of his father's, are not actors in Norma Jean's little drama, do not have so much as walk-on parts when, as neighbours, however flitting, you would expect them to be principals. Indeed, anyone would think, Henry thinks, still flicking pages –

309

tea, telly, strudel, bed – that the one of them with whom Lachlan's stepmother was on most familiar terms was Ekaterina herself. As though it were she who were resident here, and not Izzi. Ha! Another wild thought, wilder than the last, passes through Henry's head. What if she were – he has lost possession of his verbs – what if she did, what if she had, what if . . . ? What if *what*? What if in her desolation his mother had taken up residence here, women do that, to reoccupy her independent sense of self, to have a room of her own, just to think, sort herself out, clear her head, away from the clattering demands of her husband. A quiet pied à terre where she could, intermittently, attend to her own thoughts again. No noise, no distractions, hence her fleeing Norma Jean on the stairs. How she afforded it he doesn't know, but the Stern Girls could perhaps have lent her money. But why, then, did none of them, after the event, refer to it? And why the mysterious circumstances in which it had been passed on down to him? If the apartment were his mother's to dispose of as she chose, why hadn't it gone to Henry immediately on her death? And why the intercession, so many years later, of Shapira and Mankowicz? Any number of whys. Including why had Henry jumped to other conclusions and landed responsibility for the apartment on his father. How conventional of me, Henry thinks, to lay the blame on poor old Dad, righteously supposing that any irregularity was bound to be his, because he was the boisterous one, because he reached out greedily for his pleasures, because he was the man, because men do that. When all along there was an innocent explanation, if only Henry could lay both his hands on it, involving his mother and her peace of mind. An apartment in St John's Wood, a bench in Eastbourne, God knows what remnants of her elsewhere, all testifying – how much more proof does he need? – to her longing for rest. Sad. He's got the whole thing moving to a sad beat again, the way he likes it. His poor mother, goaded into going away to find a moment's quiet. His poor father, traduced again. Sad. Sad all round. '*How sad she looks*' – an entry of more than usual sensitivity, not to say garrulousness, in the old woman's diary. There you are. Confirmed. '*Spoke briefly to the Nagel woman in the hall, how sad she looks.*' Henry goes on turning pages, gourmandising on tristesse. Give me more sad. He finds a gloomy, which excites him less. '*My gloomy neighbour.*' And a mournful. '*Said good evening in the lift, she unable to raise her mournful eyes. He the same.*' Henry reads that again. *Who* the same? *He* the same. He. He! So who is he? His father? Does his mother have his father over to the apartment – to discuss the marriage, to show him that she is doing well by herself, a day here and a day there, to propose divorce? Has Izzi come looking for her – is that the story? Was it Izzi who needed to get to the bottom of her absences, not the other way round? Now in Leeds – Henry had unexpectedly encountered his mother demonstrating in a Leeds department store – now in Eastbourne, now in St John's Wood? *Why must you have time to yourself? You married me. What is it about me you need relief from? What have I done wrong? How am I supposed to feel, knowing you are gallivanting about the country on your own, and coming back here, for your supper and your sleep, when you should be coming home to me?* His poor father. Mournful in the lift. The two of them mournful in the lift together. Like Dante's wearied souls – *anime affannate* – carnal lovers light as air, as doves called by desire – *Quali colombe, dal disio chiamate* – entwined for ever. Breathless, troubled, ghosts in the hellish storm. Except that Dante's lovers are adulterers, float in an eternity of guilty propinquity, their closeness their desire and their punishment, whereas Izzi and Ekaterina Nagel had nothing to be punished for. They were man and wife, not fornicators. Man and wife with a little marital sorting out to do, but man and wife for all that. Their only possible crime, a touch too much worldly enthusiasm on Izzi's part, and a touch too little on Ekaterina's. And of course Henry, taking Henry to be a sort of crime himself. Henry, the sum of their too much and too little, a dove beckoned by desire if ever there was one, though desire

311

for what he never knew because they never taught him. And still don't. Is that his fault? Is Henry looking for some guidance from his long-dead parents to which he has, and had, no right? Are they imprisoned behind their mournful grille only because he has insisted on their being there? You can come out when you tell me who's to blame. And don't ask who's to blame for what. You know for what. For *me*. A bit old to be doing this, Henry. He accepts that. A bit long in the tooth to be blaming his mum and Dad. But what's this . . . ? On a page not consecrated to the memory of his mother with a fold, and so not considered by Lachlan to be interesting or hurtful to Henry, another name. Yafi. '*Nice man, Mr Yafi, for his persuasion. Helped me find my keys.*' Followed, in the old woman's mothy writing, by '*Food, she calls him. But bills addressed to Fouad. Not so mournful when you get to know him.*' And that's all, in a gust of icy wind, it takes. Room for a hundred misunderstandings and misprisions here, but Henry discounts every one of them. Everything is clear now. He knows what he knows. He knows what he knew already. Marghanita was Effie's child – of course she was. He had always known. And now, a second time, he knows what he had always known. His father was not the guilty party, his mother was! His father did not live here illicitly, his mother did! What was it the weeping bailiff told him at his parents' funeral? You are loved for who you are the son of, Mr Nagel. So what made him leap to the conclusion that the person he was the son of in this particular was his father? Which parent did that demean – either, neither, both? It is like being given a key to a secret chamber of his heart, the heart's equivalent of the mind's unconscious, where the answers to everything are strewn about as familiarly as your own old clothes. A gross deceit uncovered, except that the coverings belonged to Henry in the first place. His mother lived the lie – of course she did. His mother had a lover – of course she had. Fouad Yafi: that's the only detail which is truly a surprise to him. Fouad Yafi – funny the difference knowing the name makes, funny what a name does to your stomach – Fouad Yafi was the last person to take his mother in his arms and Henry is sleeping in the bed where they slept.

Jesus Christ!

For someone who is only discovering what he knew already, Henry has turned a fearful colour. He feels his cheeks – as cold as death (not that he'd know). 'Are you all right?' Moira asks from across the room. Lachlan is showing her how to tape a window against germ warfare. The miracle, so engrossed are they, is that either has even noticed Henry. It must have been the noise his blood made when it left his body. He raises an unsteady hand to her. Of course he's all right. And he is. Or at least he will be. One day.

There is a little Hamleting he needs to get out of his system. Nothing too gross. No imaginings of acts 'that blur the grace and blush of modesty'. No 'shame, where is thy blush'. Always been a matter of pride for Henry that he is not Prince Hamlet nor was meant to be. Not that sort of man, Henry. But he could do with a long soak in a bath. The filial part of any man is vexed, rubbed sore by the idea of father, let alone lover, however sound of mind he is. A good mother lets her son understand that she would have chosen him over her husband had she only met him first, and that should be the end of it. But Henry was a touch closer to his mother than many sons. And it seems reasonable to assume that in this instance, leave the father out of it, she had met the lover some time after she had met the son. Fouad Yafi represented a double betrayal therefore – of his father and of him – and Henry wouldn't be of flesh born if he didn't feel the betrayal, keenly, twice. It is *almost* the same, being jealous of your mother on your own account and on your father's, but not quite: there is more sexual excruciation, at least that you can admit to, when you feel it for your dad. Hence the Hamleting. *Have you eyes? / Could you*

*on this fair mountain leave to feed / And batten on this moor? Ha!*
*Have you eyes?* A wasted pun, Henry has always thought, mountains and moors. The line would have been better employed in
*Othello.* But then, with a name like his, Fouad Yafi must have had
– must still have if he lives – a touch of the Moor about him.
Hence – of course hence! – the Moorish bathroom. Fouad Yafi.
An Arab. *Ha! Have you eyes?* Not the right play suddenly. *Even
now, now, very now, an old black ram / Is tupping your white ewe,*
more like. Except that it goes against the grain with Henry, to
animalise his mother. He will not make a white ewe of her, and
therefore cannot make a black ram of her lover. Look away, Henry.
Look away, as your father taught you. A lesson well taught and
even better learned. What you don't see won't hurt you, nor what
you don't imagine. But he doesn't need his father's blinding hand.
He is quite composed, Henry, for him. No sensuality or body's
greed or other horrors of that sort assail him. The prohibitions
which it would now seem that his mother took it on herself to
flout are of another order. Not ethno-biblical. They came and
went, the Hebrews and the Hittites and the Jebusites and whoever,
in and out of one another's tents, their jewellery clanking. Didn't
Moses himself take first a Midianite, Zipporah, and then an
Ethiopian woman to wife? And what was good enough for Moses,
surely, is good enough for Henry's mother. So no, it isn't an ancient
antipathy that stirs in Henry, if it's an antipathy at all. More a
sense of what is appropriate and seemly in the circumstances. My
mother and an Arab! Of no consequence a couple of thousand
years ago. And maybe of no consequence in a couple of thousand years from now. (Henry would like to be around to judge.)
But his mother and an Arab – an Ekaterina and a Fouad, a Nagel
and a Yafi – with things the way they are! And in sight of a
mosque! Does that mean she'd converted in her heart? he wonders.
Was that what reading Nietzsche was always bound to lead to?
Had his grandmother and the Stern Girls been right? And whether
they'd been right or not, doesn't he owe it to their memory, since

that's all of them that's left, to feel about it as they'd have felt? If that's nationalism, Henry doesn't mind. You have to fly the flag. It doesn't all begin and end with you. You have to allow the dead their say. And he knows what they'd have said. They'd have said go home to your husband, Ekaterina. With all his North Manchester imperfections, at least he's your own. You've made your point, you've stuck your neck out, now go home to your husband. And let this other person – and no, we do not want to hear his name or see his photograph – go home to his wife, or is it wives?

His poor grandmother. Denied, by the mere politics of the times she lived in, the cosmopolitan insouciance which was her birthright. So what chance for Henry, whose birthright was horror and spiders, and who wouldn't have known insouciance had it curled up beside him in his pram? My mother and an Arab! And yet, though it isn't, *wasn't*, in the circumstances seemly, he cannot find the anger – the revulsion, is it? – he is looking for. Or at least he cannot find it in the detail of Fouad Yafi being Fouad Yafi. My mother and an Arab – so what! Too many revelations for one day, maybe. Mothers and Arabs, who cares? They're all family. Rivka Yoffey, Fouad Yafi, where's the difference?

As long as she was happy. He must take it as read that she was happy, whatever face she wore for meeting Norma Jean on the steps or in the High Street. Henry has no idea how long it lasted, but for Yafi or the family of Yafi to have installed Henry in their bower, it must have been of some duration and must have given happiness – palpable happiness – to him as well.

*Gai gezunterheit*, the pair of them.


Everything is changed now, no use pretending otherwise, but in many ways the change is for the better. His mother had not suffered as he thought she had; not in the way he thought she had, anyway, not as a wronged and loveless wife. If it weren't for what that changes for his father, he would be invigorated for her. And even looking at it from his father's point of view, it is a liberation. Henry does not have to go on reprimanding him any longer. He can let him alone, set him free, now he has no major misdemeanour of the heart to reproach him with. Which is queer logic, since if it was all right for the gander . . . But that's not the way you're meant to look at it. The way to look at it, as they tried to teach him at the Pennines enough times, is that you cheer the woman in any wrongdoing and you boo the man. It's not a matter of fairness, it's a matter of evening things out. You take the long view. For sins committed by the patriarchs five thousand years ago, the mini-patriarch of today has to bow his head and take what's owing. It's the woman's turn. And Henry accepts and even welcomes that. It was his mother's turn.

Hers and Fouad Yafi's. Funny how there's always another man in the vicinity, another beneficiary of patriarchy, to benefit a second time. But still, yes, her turn. What goes around comes around.

Which being the case, you would think Henry would sleep soundly that night. But he doesn't. Twice Moira has to wake him, so disturbing to her sleep are his dreams. And when he opens his eyes, he is struck with mortal horror. 'My mother had a lover,' he tells her.

He has already told her that. Told her no sooner than they'd left Lachlan's. 'Well, good for her,' she replied the first time. But she sees that that is not the appropriate response tonight.

'It's all right,' she says, stroking his cheek. 'It isn't for you to judge her.'

'It isn't all right,' he says. 'Everybody is dying and we are sleeping in the bed my mother slept in with her lover.'

'Is that so terrible? You didn't think it was terrible when you thought it was your father's bed.'

'I did, sometimes. Some nights I thought it was a great wrong. But this is different. Whatever they say, it's different.'

'Do you want to come to my bed?'

He looks at her. In the dark he can just make out the grey pinpricks of her eyes. A faint custard glow, like that of street lights, comes yellowing off her hair. This is the first time she has offered them her bed. Though there has been no need of the bed, he has noticed the omission. Henry doesn't have thin skin for nothing. He knows what isn't offered, whether there is need of it or not. What's downright refused, Henry logs under Miscellaneous Insults; what merely isn't offered, he files under Sundry Hurts. That she hasn't offered he has taken to be delicacy on her part. The woman preserves the memory of her bed, the history of its associations and fidelities. Whereas the man behaves like a pig. Jump in. Sure, I did once share this with my wife, but a new day's a new day! And if you really want me to I will launder the sheets. Henry had no wife. Not of his own. So it was his father's memory he besmirched – correction, his mother's. But now Moira has compromised her delicacy to save his. Henry takes the full measure of this. It is like a proposal of marriage. In the dark he gathers her into his arms and kisses her.

But there is no reason to move out. He isn't feeling fastidious. He presses the part of himself where qualms gather and finds no softness. Tries to imagine his mother and Mr Yafi lying here, but no picture will form. Good. Tries to imagine their imagining him, but no picture will form of that either. Good again. Even when he puts on Schubert's Fifth Symphony – 'How lovely you are, how lovely-ey-ey you are' – and tries imagining her singing it to her lover, the Moor, he is unable to locate anguish of the Hamlet kind. A cistern of tears when he thinks of his mother normally, suddenly Henry is dry. What, not even some creaking at the temples? He listens. Nothing. Behind the cheekbones, though, he can make out distant pain. Like needles going in, and a sound like splintering. And that too is good. He wants to be upset.

For what has happened is upsetting – both the fact of it and its coming into his possession – but it is upsetting in the way everything that bears on change and forgetfulness is upsetting . . . and that's the end of it.

So, no, he is all right about where he is. It was all a long time ago.

The distress he feels is centred somewhere else. He searches for it, even as Moira lies folded like one of his father's napkins in his arms, searches for it in the rhythm of her breathing. The association isn't accidental. His father. He can't bear it for his father. This isn't a straight exchange of sorrows: giving to his father the sympathy which had once belonged, unthinkingly, to his mother. It's worse, *was* worse, for his father. His father had no words. You can't breathe out your grief in fire. You can't cut dollies out of paper to express your longing. *Crist, if my love were in my arms* . . . What means did his father possess to body forth yearning of that sort? Why, even when he tried to talk to Henry, Henry looked away in embarrassment. That's what you do with dads; you piss them off. Mums you open your hearts to, dads you turn your back on.

Did the Stern Girls know? Did the secret they were keeping for Ekaterina die, as far as they were concerned, with Marghanita?

'The poor child!'

Henry never asked Marghanita who that poor child was. She was too far gone to tell him, even supposing she knew herself. That was how he explained it, anyway. Never was much of an asker of questions, Henry. Too afraid of the answers. And didn't like to be beholden. Better to lower your eyes and nod your head and pretend to know. What you don't ask doesn't hurt you. And *who* you don't ask doesn't hurt you either.

Also, he had thought it was a composite. The poor child, meaning Marghanita, seen at the eleventh hour as a third party, someone not herself, to be sorrowed over because of the circumstances in which she had come, illegitimately, into the world; and meaning Henry as well. Poor Henry, to be sorrowed over by Marghanita because of the circumstances in which he had failed to conquer the world, when they laid it on a plate for him. Here, Henry, have! Have! Only he wasn't sure how to take it. Poor her, poor him. More recently, since the sighting of the bench in Eastbourne, he has wondered if the poor child could have been his mother too. Poor abandoned Ekaterina, scratching at the earth to find a place of peace.

Now he has another thought.

His father. The father who never grew up.

He remembers that it was Marghanita who told him that his father had been encouraged to think for years that Passover was a party just for him. The poor child. Did Marghanita also know that later he grew frantic for his wife, not understanding why her attention had wandered from him, not grasping that she had bestowed her heart upon another man, only dimly aware – for dim awareness was the best his father ever managed (*taugetz*, Henry) – that though she remained with him most of the time in body, an audience for his fireballs and his origami, in every other respect she was somewhere else, wife to a husband who was not him. An Arab who loved her.

You could do it, presumably, with pages torn from this book, but Henry's father recommended three sheets of newspaper of the sort he never read – *The Times*, *Telegraph*, *Observer*. 'Three full sheets', was the instruction. No half-measures for Izzi. If you're going to go for it, you go for it. A) three full sheets of newspaper, B) a rubber band, C) a pair of scissors.

These for the making of a paper beanstalk, *twice as tall as your-self*. Depends who the self is of course, but Izzi Nagel had in mind an averagely small child, say Henry the size he was when he fucked up with the threepenny bit.

Then what you do is you fold the newspaper in half length-wise and tear along the fold to make six strips. Take one of these strips and roll it into a tube about two inches in diameter, like so:

When you have got six inches from the end, you take a second strip, insert it, and continue rolling.

Now go on doing the same until all the strips are used up . . .

In his mind's eye, perhaps because he was there at the proof stage when his father was preparing his little book of tricks and puzzles for the printer, Henry can still see the triumphant concluding page to this particular example of paper magic, the mounting excitement, the mind-spinning arrows etched with such urgency, as though disaster would surely befall you if your cutting went awry, the exhortation to believe, and the final great flowering beanstalk of newsprint, growing beyond a boy's capacity to imagine.

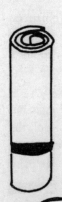

Put the rubber band firmly round one end:

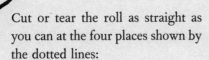

Cut or tear the roll as straight as you can at the four places shown by the dotted lines:

Then fold back the flaps:

Hold the roll with one hand and with the other pull the inside paper gently. Your beanstalk will grow and grow and grow!!

For the same reason, presumably — though he has borne no children to entertain in this way, and hasn't looked at the instructions for half a century — Henry can still remember how to make the paper beanstalk.

So that's what he does, he makes a couple, using unread newspapers containing 'Hovis' Belkin's obituaries, remembering to cut as straight as he can, and to fold back the flaps, and to pull the inside papers gently, and then he stands them on either side of the bed — suitably Middle Eastern they look, too, more like palm trees than beanstalks — from which his father was excluded.

The poor child.

# FIFTEEN

A week or so later a letter arrives for Henry. From Eastbourne Council, Cleansing Department. Permission has been granted to inform Mr Nagel that the bench erected in his mother's name was kindly donated by the family of Mr Fouad Yafi.

So that's that. Ends tied up. Neat as a button. No more to say.

'Would you surmise from that,' he asks Moira, 'that Fouad Yafi himself is dead?'

'I would,' she tells him. She is sitting at Henry's dressing table, that's to say his mother's dressing table – funny how Levantine it suddenly looks with its floral inlays and ornamental mouldings – putting up her hair. Nymphlike.

He has taken to calling her that. 'My nymph.'

'Ha – some nymph!' is her accustomed response.

Henry wonders how he ever managed without a nymph to greet him every morning. All those years, nymphless – because another man's nymph is not your own any more than is a nymph who is merely passing through. All those mornings. Thousands of them. Amazing.

'Me too,' he muses. 'But I wonder when he died. I wonder how close to my mother. It would be touching to think he wasn't able to survive her long. If he did survive her, though, wouldn't *he* have donated the bench? Him personally. A love-offering. Like the Taj Mahal. But if he didn't, and if the bench truly was put up by the family, how come it wasn't dedicated to them both? Do you suppose the family couldn't come at that?'

'Too many imponderables there, Henry,' Moira says. 'And I have a feeling you're searching for a slight.'

'Only a slight slight.'

'If they wanted to slight your mother, Henry, they wouldn't have paid for a bench at all.'

Henry thinks about that. 'True. But there is such a thing as a half-regard. They may have felt well disposed to her, but not disposed enough to see their father's or their uncle's name – whatever their relation to him – entwined with hers. A Jewess, don't forget. Like you.'

'Henry!'

'And then, if Mr Yafi did die all that time ago, how come they have only just got round to offering me this place? His wife could still have been alive, I suppose. But then again –'

'Does this matter, Henry?'

'Only in that I'd like – no, it doesn't matter. It's just that I want it to have been right, through and through, for them. And then, you know . . .'

'I don't know. What?'

'Well, if I can square it for them, I can square it for Dad.'

'Isn't that a bit idealistic? Do you really think it would make a jot of difference to him how it was for them?'

Henry suddenly doesn't like her. Common sense: whenever she tries to send a blast of cold common sense through his cogitations, he doesn't like her. There's a reason, he wants to tell her, why they call common sense common. *Tauget₃*, Henry, his father might well have chosen to say at the very same moment. But his father's *tauget₃* wasn't common. It refused imaginative cooperation right enough, but not in the name of common reason. It had the grace to descend into other-worldly daftness. *Tauget₃, tauget₃, tauget₃.* Let's mess about. If you insist on being oversophisticated you're on your own; I can't join you. Which wasn't quite what Moira was doing. Moira was refusing to see what he saw, because she believed it wasn't there. Make a difference to your dad! How could it make a difference to your dad? But it was obvious to Henry, and should have been obvious to Moira, why it would have made a difference to his dad – because he was a man of

324

immense reserves of decency, sympathetic decency, and would have wanted his wife happy even in her faithlessness, would have wanted her loved by someone kind, treated with consideration, remembered fondly, a credit to them both.

*Taugetz*. Well, maybe. Maybe Henry is imagining a father in the image he would imagine for himself. And maybe he is only annoyed with Moira because she won't indulge his idealism.

He makes an appeal to her. 'Seen all round,' he says, 'and in a long life, though they were cruelly denied that, I grant you, there are errors and brutalities which can be absorbed back into the original edifice – I mean of the relationship if not the marriage – which can be understood to be a part of it anyway, as further interesting contributions if you like, and not just dismissed automatically as fallings off that can never be forgiven. I think it would have made a difference to my father, yes, and added to his own sense of worth, that my mother wasn't being messed about, that she was well regarded, that she hadn't stepped below herself, that she was doing something that made her feel happy and worthwhile even though it broke his heart. Yes, I think that.'

She hears the irritation in his voice. And the disappointment too. It's how she knows that all this is of importance to her as well – the fact that it hurts her to be a disappointment to him.

She has a way of putting her teeth together when she is angry with herself which he likes. There is something of the schoolgirl in it. A sort of resolution, made in the presence of the headmistress, to do better. 'Well, you must forgive my surface cynicism,' she says. 'I have no right to make assumptions about your father. But have a heart, Henry – you are heavy going just at the moment, heavy on yourself particularly, and is it so terrible of me to want to lighten things for you?'

'No,' he says, going over to her and blowing in her hair. 'No, it isn't.'

Bracing, her hair. Like a breeze coming in off the Bay of Riga, if Riga has a bay. Knowing Henry's geography, it could simply be the word rigour he's thinking of. Moira's rigorous good manners to him, her rigorous protection of his feelings, and her rigorous clarity in the matter of her own meanings. Like a breeze coming in off the Bay of Rigour. You can misjudge women, Henry thinks, if you go only on the furry bags they carry.

He considers himself a lucky man. *Have a heart, Henry – you are heavy going just at the moment.* What has heavy-going Henry done – heavy going from the moment his mother went into protracted labour with him – to deserve a woman who tells him that he is heavy going *just at the moment?*

If that isn't tact bred of benevolence bred of love, he doesn't know what it is.

Thank you, God, for finding me such a person. Now organise for me to live for ever with her and You'll be a mensch.


Once upon a time Henry entertained the fancy of meeting his father's mistress. Strange, because when he tries to recapture the fancy it seems to be of ancient origin, like an imagining from childhood, but he cannot understand how this can be since sure knowledge of one mistress in particular, as opposed to mere suspicion of a string of Rivka Yoffeys, with maybe someone special in London thrown in for good measure, came only with the letter from Shapira and Mankowicz. Was the fancy wish-fulfilment, then? Do boys desire their fathers to have mistresses as intensely as they wish their fathers not to have their mothers? All very simple to explain if that's the case. Go to *her*, Dad, go enjoy the rest of your life, and leave Mum to enjoy the blessings of conjugality at my hands.

But why, then, the folderol of imagining actually *meeting* the mistress, Henry is unable say. Unless the mistress is a further mother – alternative and supererogatory – which boys also crave. So was Henry hoping not only to retrieve his first mother from his father's thieving hands, but also to nab the second one into the bargain? Did he want *everything* his father had?

Honesty-box Henry concedes there could be something in this, because the fancy, in so far as he can remember it – and he can, oh yes he can – entailed the mistress being struck by Henry's charms, not flirting with him exactly, but registering wherein he was his father to a T, though with youth and a degree in girls' literature thrown in, and wherein he was another and no less fascinating person altogether.

Whether or not Henry is right that the fancy is of remote unconscious origin, it must, over the years, have been subject to many accretions – like one of Grynszpan and Delahunty's palimpsests of suppressed female creativity – because now the mistress is talking to Henry of his father as a man very much alive, and now she is lamenting him, tears brimming in her black eyes (fathers' mistresses must have black eyes), her ringed hands (ditto) – painted fingers browned in sun and experience, lined with sensuality and grief – seeking Henry's own for comfort. 'Not possible, you will understand, simply out of the question for me to live here any more' – an obvious interpolation, for Henry knew nothing of a 'here', of St John's Wood or its environs, when the fancy first took hold – 'not within a hundred miles of here, nor anywhere that reminds me – I *know* you'll understand this – of Regent's Park, which we so loved.' The face averted. Hand pressed on Henry's. Henry's head big to bursting with the idea that his father loved a park. Did he torch it? he wondered. 'What we would like' – the mistress putting celestial quotation marks around the 'we' – so Henry was not the only one still in communication with his long-abducted father – 'is for you to have it.'

'The park?'

'The apartment.'

Irrelevant now, all of it. The mistress even deader than the father. A ghost of one who never was, let Henry conjure all he will.

But Henry does wonder if he doesn't owe it to all concerned

parties to try to form a comparable image, without the finger-touching, of Fouad Yafi.

Would have been nice, wouldn't it, to have met the man who loved his mother so deeply as to have accommodated her son. Would have been nice to have said thank you. Thank you for what you've done for me, thank you for what you did for Mum. And you will understand if I do not thank you for what you did for Dad. Failing that, taking Mr Yafi to be dead, it would also have been nice to meet the in-laws. The extended family. The *machatonim*, as they're called. Me Nagel, you Yafis. Me Jew, you Arabs. *Shalom*!

Could a lasting peace between Arab and Jew have grown out of this? Why not? You have to start somewhere. And it would have been a scream, would it not, had Henry who knew nothing of the political affairs of the world been an agent in their change. All those years in hiding from event in the Pennines – were they but a preparation, like Christ's days in the wilderness, or Cromwell's in his garden, for this? A peace prize, thereafter, for Henry? The ultimate vindication of his humane ignorance of things. To say nothing of his mother's. For if anyone really deserved the prize, it was her surely, not Henry. Ekaterina Nagel who found peace here between Arab and Jew.

In waves it is borne in on Henry how bold, viewed from every angle, his mother's adultery was. From *Jane Eyre* to a pasha's pavilion in a single bound – all right, to an over-upholstered apartment in St John's Wood – but still, quite a journey. Though then again, wasn't that a version of Jane Eyre's story too? What quiet girls do – they make their way. What Henry has done, no less. From *Jane Eyre* to a pasha's pavilion, pausing only, for most of his waking life, at a poly in the Pennines. And all thanks to his mother.

Could it be that he was always wrong about her? And there-fore wrong about himself? That she hadn't taught him to shrink from life at all, that he had done that by himself? That it wasn't her thin skin he had inherited, but, if anybody's, his father's? Henry would like to be finished with all questions of skin now, thick or thin. Time, at his age, to be done putting your papery wrist to your ear and listening to the unprotected humming of your blood. Time to be getting ready to have no skin. But his father has not let him alone about his skin in more than fifty years. Still doesn't, when Henry invites him along for one of their dusky evening chats – though Henry does less of that now he has Moira to converse with. You would think, listening to him, that there was more skin on the old man dead than there had ever been on Henry alive. *Easy, Henry, easy. Watch that skin now*.

Henry would like to say a few words to his father about this. Not *have* a few words. The son has heard the father out on the question of the son's translucency long enough. Finally, Henry has rumbled him. 'It's not my skin we've been discussing, birthday boy – Passover-birthday boy, get me? – it's yours! That's how you always knew so much about it, why you hated it and mocked it, and why you always happened to be at the right place at the right time, clomping your great paraffin-smelling hand over my fainting eyes. Cut from the same cloth, Dad, extruded from the same sheet of newspaper – was that what you dreaded? Not another Ekaterina on the planet, but another you? Well, you had less to be ashamed of than you think. You were who you were. And I am who I am. Now rest in peace. But before you do, hear this . . .'

Hear what? Henry can't think of anything. That's to say he can think of everything, but neither of them has time for that. It's Moira who tells him what to say. 'Say nothing,' she says. 'Just buy him a bench. I'll ring Cleansing at Eastbourne. Maybe they can find a place for it next to hers.'

In St John's Wood High Street the summer is eking out the last of its *gederem*. *Gederem* meaning bowels, but by implication strength. One of his father's favourite words. In the same way that Izzi loved carveries he loved intestinal Yiddish. *Kishkes* another one. A hard-working man shleps his *kishkes* or his *gederem* out. And Izzi Nagel worked hard. At his upholstery, at his fire-eating, at being married – well, who can say? – and certainly at being Henry's father. Whoever spends time with Henry has to work hard. Should Henry put that on the bench? – IN MEMORY OF IZZI NAGEL WHO WHATEVER ELSE THERE IS TO SAY SHLEPPED HIS KISHKES OUT FOR ME – HIS LOVING SON.

Moira thinks not.

Moira is another one who shleps her *kishkes* out spending time with Henry. And she has already made it clear she doesn't want those words on her bench either.

She is out, delivering. Honk, honk. Henry can hear her all over NW8. He is out, walking, but his nerves are on edge. If you pass between two lovers text-messaging each other from opposite corners of the street, will radiation pass through your body? Will they open you up and find the message burnt into your heart? *Miss you. Hate you. Meet you in an hour. Drop dead.*

If you cross the road at your own pace and a demented motorist honks at you, are you within your rights to pull him (or her) out of his car and beat him to a pulp?

It's not beyond him to do that. He is still just strong enough, provided the motorist doesn't resist.

Better to be sitting. He buys papers, which is always a mistake, and finds a table at Aultbach's. He orders a plunger of coffee for no other reason than that he wants to hear himself say plunge, and allows the papers to swallow him up. Bad news. What other sort is there? You open the page and tumble headlong into it. Today, just Henry's luck, a report of Osmond Belkin's memorial. Held at the British Film Institute. Fear no more the heat of the sun, a recorded extract of *The Blood Donor*, clips from Osmond's best movies, all that. No mention of Henry's article. No ironic reference to that great, resonating misjudgement – 'I am persuaded he does not think as he ought on serious subjects.'

And no reference to the man who made it. No, no Henry. Nor any whisper of Henry. Henry not invited, as he had not been invited to the funeral, though Mel Belkin knew well enough, had he kept the torn-off corner of Henry's *A to Z*, where to find him.

Well, what did he expect? What right to be invited did he have? He had thought ill, written ill, spoken ill of his old friend. He isn't even sure that he is sorry 'Hovis' is dead. How do you tell? Had he been seeing 'Hovis' on a regular basis he would presumably be feeling the lack of him. The clocks stopped, the stars not in their places, the sun blotted out of the heavens, all that. But he's been getting by 'Hovis'-less for half a lifetime. So how to measure the difference? Wordsworth castigated himself for forgetting, in a surprise of joy, that a beloved person was no longer there, turning to share the transport with her when he ought to have remembered, when he ought never *not* to have remembered, not for the least of a division of an hour – Henry loves that 'least division' – that she was gone. There's scrupulousness of conscience for you, since for less particular men there can be no greater love than to imagine the dead among the living, to feel them by you so vividly that it is as though they have never left you. So can it work the other way, that you remember to forget rather than forget to remember? In which case Henry, too, is a marvel of sensibility in that he seems to be remembering to forget 'Hovis' more and more with every hour that passes. Let Henry be surprised by joy and he won't be turning to share its transports with 'Hovis'.

'Hovis'? Who's 'Hovis'?

But Henry knows himself. Or maybe he knows 'Hovis'. His friend will be waiting for him one of these nights, no doubt about it. He will come for Henry in the darkness and bite his heart out. Henry just wishes it would happen soon. The waiting to feel something is killing him.

'Mind if I leave him with you?'

Henry jumps. He has not been in the land of the living. And

331

now here are Lachlan and Angus, man and dog, breathing bad digestive systems into his face, Lachlan's marginally the worse.

As though reading his mind, Angus shows Henry his tongue. Aaaah! Nothing wrong with my insides. Just the smell of curried dog biscuits.

'Depends how long you're going to be,' Henry says.

Lachlan is wearing a suit that seems to Henry to be in about seven pieces, though when he counts he sees it's only trousers, jacket and waistcoat. It's the number of pockets in the waistcoat that does it, and the amount of stuff Lachlan has spilling out of them. Watch chains, handkerchiefs, dog lead, heirlooms. He nods in the direction of the antique shop across the road, man to man, incorrigible, the way some men want you to know that they can't stay out of betting shops or public houses.

'Turns out you were right,' he says, producing from somewhere on his person – Henry's father would have been proud of such legerdemain – the framed photograph of Robert Louis Stevenson's Samoan grave. 'Not his signature. I've had it checked.'

The words bury themselves in his chest, like daggers, making Henry feel it's all his fault.

'Well, it stood to reason,' Henry says. Not exactly an apology, but it's the best he can manage.

Lachlan bangs wind out of his oesophagus. 'Not to mine it didn't,' he says. 'But there's just a chance they won't spot it over there. Be back in a couple of shakes.'

Henry watches him go. Purposeful, but with a weary roll of the shoulders. The air slowly leaking out of him. Is there enough left, Henry wonders – enough air and enough heirloom – to keep him going through his old age? Or will he have to sell the apartment soon, as well, and then be reduced to waiting and gigoloing once more in Eastbourne or Torquay or whatever it was. He has that look. A man forever in the process of drowning, like his hat.

Is that what Angus knows? Is that what he sees as well, and is that what this is all about – the dog aware he has to find a new master quick, quick, while he too still has his looks?

Henry pats him, just for the hell of it. Angus, still roguishly neckerchiefed – does Lachlan make him sleep in that thing, Henry wonders – turns up his eyes in return, not pools of love but lakes of it, oceans of brown devotion.

Cynical bastard, Henry thinks, going on patting.

Then suddenly the dog is wriggling from under him, sniffing the air, wagging his tail frantically, seeing his old master on the other side of the street.

'He only went five minutes ago,' Henry says. 'What's the excitement?'

But who can say how long five minutes feels to a dog. Especially to a dog who's desperate.

He is at the kerb, trying to remember all he's been taught. Looking left, looking left again, nosing piss, smelling shit, confusing smell with traffic.

'Heel!' Lachlan shouts. 'Stay there, boy!'

Henry reaches out to grab his collar or his neckerchief, but Lachlan has done his own looking left and then left again, and is giving the dog the OK. 'Come on, Angus.' Crouching and clapping his hands. 'Come on, boy.'

And Angus is off, ears back, tail going, into a tumult of horns. What happens next Henry doesn't know. What happens next has never been Henry's strong point. Next was what his father always took care of. 'You stupid old fool!' he hears himself say, but the words are no sooner uttered than they seem to belong to another time, another life even. How many cars have slithered into one another – not crashed, it's all too sedate and balletic to be called a crash – that, too, Henry doesn't know. No screeches of brakes, no crunch of metal, for all that the implicated vehicles are four-wheel drives, Armageddon trucks strong enough to take out a buffalo. Behind his eyes Henry sees a wheel spinning in yellow moonlight. Immobile, he watches it, though no car is on its back and the sun is shining. What is more, the car's wheel spins in eerie silence, whereas this is St John's Wood High Street, and with the volume inexplicably turned up – expostulation, recrimination, astonishment (though such things happen every day): voices yelling into mobile phones, the sound of texting, hooting, honking. The madhouse.

'What the fuck is honking going to solve?' Henry wants to shout.

But then what the fuck is Henry shouting going to solve?

Or Henry's doing anything? It's written across his face – I'm better staying put, leaving it to others, those with presence of mind, the quick-witted, the capable, the brave. Those who are living at this moment, and in this place.

How long does it take him to recognise the middle vehicle, the one that slid into the one trying to miss Angus, the one that has rotated gently in the middle of the road as though on a turntable in a showroom window, and is now pointing back to front? Not good at cars, Henry. All look the same to him. Even when they're jeeps. But something rings a bell, number plate maybe, or alpaca cardigan visible from the rear window. Moira! Jesus Christ! Moira's in the middle of all this! He is only a few yards away but in the time it takes him to get to where she is he has given up on her. What if she is cut? Henry cannot help a woman who has cut herself. What if she is badly hurt? What can Henry do for a woman who is badly hurt but feel her pain, howl for her, suffer in the same place she suffers. He is not a nurse, Henry. He is a man who understands the agony of women. He is their spiritual alter ego, which is not much use to them in a car crash. And because he cannot help them he can only give up on them. Their fault for not being immortal. Her fault for being just like other women in the end. Nausea, is it? Disgust? Ashamed of her for bringing the disgrace of death upon them both? Be all right, he says. Please be all right. But even if she is all right this time she can't be all right for ever, can she? Not the way she drives. Postponement is the best he can hope for. Already he can see her as a ghost, fading, leaving him, gone.

In which case isn't it time he was gone as well?

She is all right. Unhurt. Calm even. Certainly calmer than he is, or indeed than the other motorists, parked or otherwise, who want her details. The first thing anybody thinks of here if a matchstick lands upon their bonnet: is the car scratched, who threw the match, and what is the name of their insurance. Anything lying whimpering beneath their wheels can wait.

He runs to take her into his arms but somehow ends up in hers. 'Are you all right?'

Who said that? It should be him speaking, but he is shocked to discover it is her.

He kisses her face. I'm all right because you are, that's what he wants her to understand, whether or not the truth is that she has shown him the shadow of her destructibility and filled him with distaste.

Does he see a man getting quickly out of her passenger seat? Impossible to be sure. There seems to be a man, or to have been a man, dark, Greek-looking, Michael the footballer maybe. But he might have been a passenger in another car, might just as easily have been a passer-by, no more. Would have been mad of her, wouldn't it, to be ferrying a lover up and down the very street where Henry is known to sit out and poison his mind with newspapers. Dare he ask her? Dare he ask her in this mêlée of short tempers and bruised metal, when all he should be concerned about is her safety, whether she is having an affair?

The disgrace of it all. The disgrace of his horror of disgrace, the disgrace of the impermanence of everything that comes contained in flesh. He feels himself giving up on her. Watches her recede into a coldness of his own making.

I don't want this, he tells himself. I don't welcome it. I will it to be gone. I abjure it.

What was it that touched him so deeply the other night? Have a heart, Henry. Have a heart.

Again he kisses her face, her neck, her ear – whatever's warm.

'Tell me that wasn't Angus,' she says.

He sets his mouth. 'I can't, Moira.'

'Ah!' she says. 'Is Lachlan with him? How is he?'

'I don't know,' Henry says. 'I came straight to you.'

She shrugs him off her, irritated that he is standing here, stroking her hair, pulling valedictory faces. 'For God's sake, go and help him, Henry. Don't worry about me. I'm all right.'

He does as he is told. Best this way. Wind Henry up and point him in the right direction.

Go and help whom, though – Lachlan or the dog? Please God let it be Lachlan, Henry prays, because he knows he will not be able to help a whimpering or wounded dog.

No need. Others have already moved Angus on to the pavement. Few spectacles are more interesting to people than that of car owners bickering about paintwork, but poor Angus also commands a little crowd, a semicircle staring down at him and shaking their heads, as though the funeral is over and there is nothing to do now but shovel dirt on him and be gone. Lachlan is on the kerb, a bag of old bones in his seven-piece suit, standing exactly where he was when he'd called Angus out into the traffic. He is opening and closing his fists in a gesture of impotence which Henry recognises at once, though he has never seen it before. Why should a dog, a horse, a rat, have life? – that sort of gesture. Only in this case the dog does not have life.

'I'm good for nothing,' he says, seeing Henry. 'I've been good for nothing all my life. I'm not even fit to own a dog.'

True, Henry thinks. I cannot argue with a word of that. You're a dog-murdering fucking moron. Except that this is not what Moira has sent him over to say. 'For God's sake, go and help him, Henry,' were her instructions. So Henry does what it is not in his nature to do, and puts his arms around Lachlan, exactly as, a moment before, Moira enfolded him in hers. 'It wasn't your fault,' Henry says. 'The car came from nowhere. You couldn't have done other than you did. It was an accident. You mustn't blame yourself. These things happen.'

And though the words sound hollow and without warmth to Henry, miracle of miracles they do not sound that way to Lachlan, who buries himself in Henry's shoulder and lets the accumulated sorrows out of his chest at last, wave after wave of them, as though Henry is a medicine man and the patient's grief the troop of evil spirits Henry has miraculously released.

He is wet, wet from the bone out, and smells of wretchedness and shock. All the more reason, Henry thinks, that I must hold on to him. Don't ask him why, but Henry does something quite unexpected, for him, and very strange. He kisses the top of Lachlan's head, where the hair is thinnest, and breathes him in. God breathed the breath of life into Adam's dust-dry nostrils, Henry thinks, and now I know how Adam must have felt.

Light-headed. And not a little amazed.

And then because he knows Moira would expect no less of him – would want no less of him, put it that way, would hope that he could find such resolution in himself – he bends to scoop up Angus, that thing of piss and shit and undiscriminating love, and carries him half the length of the High Street back to Lachlan's apartment. Henry's first corpse. Done it. Done it at last. Not heavy as he'd expected. Not the cold dead weight he'd always feared. So warm and soft, in fact, that for a moment he believes the dog is not dead at all, that he can feel the bruised heart trying to beat again. But it is only Henry's own pulse, quickening the dog's pelt.

He is dignified in death, Angus. No lolling tongue. No foul exudations or protruding *kishkes* of the sort Henry knows will signal his own demise. Quiet he lies, rather youthful-looking, his scarf tied raffishly at his broken neck – for no one has thought to loosen it – his ears flat like sealed envelopes, his open eyes signalling neither anger nor regret. Not even resignation. Just the uncritical cessation of sight.

Back in Lachlan's apartment, Henry rather reluctant to put him down, they lie him on his tartan rug, tuck it around him, then drink to his memory.

'To Angus,' Henry says.

'The best friend a man ever had,' Lachlan says, closing the curtains. 'The best I ever did, anyway. I can't imagine my life without him.'

Henry muses, looking at the space on Lachlan's wall where the signed photograph of Robert Louis Stevenson's Samoan sepulchre once hung. How much did Lachlan get for it, he wonders.

'I know what you mean,' he says.

He has to sit down to rest his back. It hurts, carrying a dead dog a quarter of a mile, however light the creature makes itself, evacuated of blood and breath and memory and hope.

Lachlan's phone rings. It is Moira for Henry, but wanting first to speak to Lachlan. So sorry, so terribly, terribly sorry. Poor Angus. Poor you, Lachlan. Not such a good medicine man, Henry, for Lachlan still, it seems, has grief he must expel. Henry puts his head between his knees and tries not to listen. Let the poor bastard weep and weep and weep if he must. But whether he wishes to or not he hears Lachlan commend his consideration – his, Henry's, Henry the hitherto uncommendable. 'Yes, carried him all the way. And all the way up the stairs. No, he remembered Angus never liked the lift. But then I always suspected he was fonder of Angus than he made out.'

Was I, Henry wonders. Could they in honesty write that on my stone? – FONDER THAN HE MADE OUT.

When it's his turn on the phone he finds that he too has upset to express. Tears creak behind his cheeks. Must be something in Moira's voice. 'Ah, dear!' he says, gaining control. 'I've been going through hell worrying about you.'

Has he? Well, he has if he says he has.

'Shush,' she tells him.

'Ah, dear!' he says again.

'Look,' she says, 'I'm going to be a little while longer exchanging addresses with these idiots. The police are here as well. It's ridiculous, it's not as though anyone's hurt, or anyone's to blame. Except, I suppose, poor Angus. And they won't be charging him. So I'll be home when I'm home. It shouldn't be too long.'

Home? She has never called it home before.

'I'll come out and help you.'

'No, don't. You stay with Lachlan. Be nice to him.'

'I have.'

'I know.'

'I really have.'

'I know, I know. Don't stop.'

'I miss you,' he says. Not his usual locution. Not a notion he is accustomed to trusting himself with – missing. Start telling people you'll miss them and it's like inviting the earth to crack open its foundations around you. Of course you'll miss them, that's what they're for, for you to miss through eternity.

'Me too,' she says. 'It's all so sad. But listen, when you think you can safely leave Lachlan you could pop across the hall and start to run me a slow hot bath. And you could see if you can dig out some massage oils. I'm half dead. I'll be needing you to revive me.'

'Righto,' he says. He doesn't want to get off the phone. He wants her to go on talking. Put the phone down and she'll be gone. 'And yes, you're right – it has been sad.'

She will die on him, that's what he knows. If he doesn't die on her, she will die on him. Her voice will stop. Impossible to imagine, but he must imagine it. In the meantime . . . well, he will massage her. Keep the blood in circulation. Keep her in circulation.

Lachlan pours him another Scotch. He is beginning to look at Henry the way Angus used to. What you get when you go around

339

kissing people on the head, Henry acknowledges. Or accepting them into your nostrils. God and Adam must have looked at each other this way, too, for a day or more. Until Eve.

'I suppose you'd think I was being morbid,' Lachlan says, 'if I sat here with him on my lap.'

No, Henry doesn't think that's morbid. No. And anyway, what if it were. To be truthful he would like it himself, to linger here a little longer on this elderly St John's Wood afternoon, a Scotch in his hand and the curtains closed, thwarting the encroachment of the cruel light, seeing Lachlan with Angus warm for the last time on his knees, trying to remember what the dog was like, which is becoming difficult already, thinking about running a bath for Moira, waiting for her to come home – *home*, her word – waiting for her to die, oiling her shoulders, reviving her.

It's like a vision of his future. An old fart, a dead dog, and a woman he can't trust not to leave him, one way or another.

Could be hell, Henry thinks.

Then again, could be the making of me.

www.vintage-books.co.uk